BOOKS BY BRENDA S. ANDERSON

WHERE THE HEART IS SERIES

Risking Love
Capturing Beauty
Planting Hope

COMING HOME SERIES

Pieces of Granite
Chain of Mercy
Memory Box Secrets
Hungry for Home

Where the Heart Is, Book 3

Planting Hope

A NOVEL

VIVANT
PRESS

Minneapolis, Minnesota

Vivant Press
Planting Hope
Copyright © 2017
Brenda S. Anderson

ISBN-13: 978-0-9862147-6-9

This novel is a work of fiction. Names, characters, places, and incidents either are the product of the author's imagination or are used fictitiously. Any resemblance to actual events, locales, organizations, or persons living or dead is entirely coincidental and beyond the intent of either the author or the publisher.

Cover Design by Think-Cap Design Studios

Printed in the United States of America

17 18 19 20 21 22 23   7 6 5 4 3 2 1

To Warren and Joan Anderson

I couldn't ask for better in-laws!
Thank you for welcoming me into your family
and for being a living example of what
love and family are all about.

Once you choose hope, anything is possible.

~ Christopher Reeve ~

Prologue

Last Will and Testament
Explanatory Letter
from
Lavina Elizabeth Oakley

Dear Family,

As you can see in my official Last Will and Testament, my earthly belongings are few, but precious. The gifts may seem unequal to you, so I have chosen to write a letter explaining the reason behind the gifts, all given from the heart:

My dearest Lydia,

You have a tenacious aptitude for reaching your goals. Little has come easy for you, but you haven't let that stop you. I am so proud of your give-it-all attitude. You are much like your grandfather in that respect, as well as your father. Hard work is a wonderful ethic to have, and I encourage you to apply that same tenacity to what is most important in your life.

To you I leave the dollhouse your grandfather once crafted for your mother. Remember all those hours you spent playing with your make-believe family in that house? I pray your dear Catherine will experience the same and that your family will create beautiful new memories.

With love,
Gran

My darling Lucas,

We are kindred spirits, are we not? You have such a tender heart and your love for making people happy is so much like my own. I understand that's a common trait for a middle child. Remember when you spent your summers working with me at Superior Sweets? How the customers would light up when you served them? I certainly have missed your help and your companionship these last summers, but I also realize that you play an important role in your father's business. As you delighted in making my customers happy, you also greatly desire to please your father.

One thing I have learned in all my years on this earth is who it's most vital to please. It is my prayer that you learn that lesson well.

So, to you I've left Superior Sweets, along with the land, and everything within the home that was not given to your brother and sister.

I understand that you have your work with Harrison Property Development, and I don't wish to shackle you to my dream, so once you have lived in the little apartment above the store for six months, you may sell the store.

If even six months is too long, I understand, but should that be the case, the store, my home, and the land will instead be given to Roland Bettis. I'm certain you are aware it has long been his desire to own the land, so your not claiming the store will make both you and Roland happy.

With love,
Gran

My precious Timothy,

You seemed to smile from the moment you burst into our world. Life is a joy to you, and I love how you continuously seek new experiences. Oh, how you are like your mother in that respect! Having you around made losing your mother so young a smidgen easier as I could always see her in your reflection.

Like your mother, life seems to come easy to you: riding your bicycle, school, girlfriends, all achieved with seemingly little effort. I pondered what I could leave you that would pose a real challenge.

That would be faith. To you, Timothy, I'm leaving my Bible. No, it's not new anymore. The pages are dog-eared, the words are underlined and highlighted, and nearly every margin is filled with my reflections and questions and praises. It's my prayer that you will embrace reading His Word as a new challenge and that you will seek to find a deeper joy, like I have.

With love,

Gran

Finally, my dear Russell,

When Sherry first brought you home to meet me, I knew you were the right man for her. You loved her with a great passion, and I believed you would treat her as the princess she was. When she died far too young, she left many broken hearts in her wake. Mine. Your children's. Yours. And my heart still breaks for you. Please know that hearts can heal, though not without opening them up to loving again. Yes, picking off that scab is frightening and excruciatingly painful. I had to do that myself after Gerald went to our Father. A mended heart will never be the same as before, but healing can make it stronger.

So, to you, I leave nothing physical, but rather a few simple words: Love them. Period. Love your children, Russell, right where they are. Love who they are without condition.

Love them.

It won't be easy. I know. But the reward for taking the difficult path will be great.

Yes, I sign this with love,

Gran

Chapter One

How could Gran do this to him?

Luke hurled a stone toward the turbulent waters of Lake Minnetonka. No way could he disappoint her. He sat on the sandy shore, not caring about ruining his dress slacks, and removed his shoes and socks. The coolness of beach sand was always a comfort.

"Unca Luke! Unca Luke!"

He turned around and watched his niece run across the expansive lawn toward him, her little hands clutched around some stuffed toy. Her smile and joy was exactly what he needed. "Whatcha got there, Kitty Cat?"

"Look what Daddy gave me!" The towheaded cutie held a stuffed rainbow-colored angel fish in the air. "It's going swimming!"

She ran past him, toward the water.

"Whoa. Slow down there, kiddo." He leapt up, chased her across the sand, and swooped her into his arms just as a wave licked at her toes.

"Put me down." She wriggled.

He responded with a zerbert to her exposed tummy, prompting the giggle he needed to hear. "Fluffy fishies don't like water."

"They don't?" She stopped wiggling.

"Uh-uh." He carried her back to the grass but kept her in his arms. "It makes their fluffiness stick together and they're not as pretty anymore. They like land like your unicorn and panda do."

"Oh." Her wide eyes looked at him as if he were the wisest man in the world. Too bad the rest of his family didn't see him that way, but he

13

hadn't given up proving it.

Which meant letting Gran down.

A door slammed on the massive house behind Luke, telling him his time for reflection was over and business would soon begin. He ran a hand over his face. The coming *discussion* wasn't going to be pretty, but he'd assure his dad that Harrison Property Development came first. That he would finish the North Loop proposal and win over the potential client. His father should be pleased.

"Are you sad, Unca Luke?"

He nodded. "I'm missing your Great Gran, but she's with Jesus now, making the best chocolate He's ever tasted."

"I like chocolate too."

"Me too, Kitty, me too." He hugged her, and she squeezed back. If real love had a physical sensation, this was it.

"There you are, you little squirt." Kitty Cat's dad hustled toward them from the estate house. How was it that a building he'd called *home* nearly his entire life, had never felt like a home? Now Gran's little apartment above the store—that was a home.

"I wanted to go swimming with Fishy, but Unca Luke said Fishy don't like water."

"Your Uncle Luke's very smart." Travis reached out for his daughter, but she clung tighter to Luke. "Come on, kiddo—"

"Kitty." She told her dad with a firm nod.

Travis cleared his throat. "Forgive me, *Kitty*, but your Uncle Luke's got some business to do."

"Like Mommy?"

"Yeah." He didn't cover his disdain. "Just like Mommy." He took Kitty from Luke, set her on the ground, and gripped her hand. "We'll go play until they're done."

Luke would give anything to go with them, but he stayed beachside while the rest of his family strode down the sidewalk cutting through the weed-free grass.

Dad marched forward, a handful of documents clutched in his hand. And Tweedlegrim and Tweedlesnob—rather, Lydia with her ever-serious expression and Tim with that familiar smirk—trailed Dad on the winding concrete path, ready to point their accusing, all-knowing fingers at him.

He hadn't written the will. It wasn't his fault Gran had left him that albatross of a candy store on Lake Superior's North Shore, along with an impossible choice.

Corner office or candy store?

In choosing one, he'd be letting Gran down; choosing the other would let Dad down. Neither was palatable.

Should he be defiant and make them come to him? Or compliant and go to them? Dad would approve of compliance.

Or so Luke hoped.

Leaving his shoes and socks by the beach, he squared his shoulders and strode to meet the judge and jury, deliberately taking a shortcut across the manicured lawn. What good was lush grass if you couldn't run your feet through it?

Dad's scowl deepened as the physical distance between them shrunk. Why couldn't the man lighten up for one little moment? Sheesh. Gran had barely been gone a month.

And just like that, his throat clogged with missing her.

He blinked and steadied his breathing as Dad gestured with his head toward the pergola-covered table and chairs. They sat without saying a word. Lydia slapped her certified letter on the table. Tim smacked his against his open hand. Dad set the papers on the table, aligning the edges perfectly, with the certified letter on top.

Were they planning to contest the will?

His father folded his hands over the paperwork. "Your siblings and I have had a discussion."

And surprise, surprise, they didn't include me. Well, he'd have to channel that hidden assertive self and take charge. "Before you go on, I want you to know that Harrison is my priority, and I plan on completing the North Loop project." There. No room for discussion. That should make his dad happy.

Instead, Dad grimaced, dug through the papers, and pulled out a stapled stack. "Have you looked into what Gran's land value is?"

Luke blinked. "Uh, no."

"Or any of the land on that stretch of road?" Dad's irises became mini black bullets firing at Luke.

He couldn't help but flinch to avoid getting hit.

"I didn't think so." Dad cleared his throat. "We've decided—"

"We?" Luke's gaze flitted from the 'good' older sister to the 'good' younger brother. A mere four years separated Lydia from Tim with Luke squeezed in the middle and often forgotten.

It hadn't always been that way.

He shook off the memories that should have been buried with his mom and raised his chin. "According to the will, *we* don't have a choice. That store was left to me to claim or deny, and I plan to deny it."

Tim grabbed the paper stack from his father and waved it at Luke. "Then you're making the wrong decision. As usual." He stabbed a chart in the middle of the front page. "Gran's few acres may not mean much to our company, but if Harrison Properties acquired the adjacent land? The potential for profit is huge."

What happened here? Luke rubbed his temples, warding off a headache. "There's no way I can live at Gran's and work on the North Loop project." If he did, there'd go any promise of promotion in the company, something his siblings had attained years ago.

Dad planted his elbows on the table, crossed his hands, and leaned toward Luke. "Effective today, you're off the North Loop."

His heart took a nosedive. "But what about—"

Dad sliced a hand in front of his throat. "You go live at Gran's, fulfill her wishes, and in the meantime, purchase the land from the neighbors on both sides. After that, we'll talk promotion."

"That's all I have to do?"

"That's all?" Lydia laughed, but her face never lost that dour expression. "Roland Bettis was a thorn in Gran's side for thirty years. You think you can go up there, flash one of your smiles, and convince him? Good luck. And the family next door to Gran? That land has been in their family for as many generations as Gran's has been in ours.

They're not going to be swayed easily."

He resisted rolling his eyes. Maybe he didn't have the innate business sense his brother and sister had, but he wasn't a complete idiot either. He glared at his older sister. "I can do it."

Before she could argue, he turned to his father. "What's my budget?"

His dad gave a number far too low to be a real enticement for stubborn sellers.

Luke groaned. "Seriously?"

"Dead serious." Dad took the papers from Tim and gathered them into a neat bundle. "You want to become someone in this company? It's time you learn to do the impossible."

GETTING ALL THE PLANTERS filled before her parents arrived home tomorrow would be next to impossible, but she would do it. An evening shadow crept over Jess Beaumont as she tucked dirt around the red geraniums, her mother's favorite flower. Once satisfied with the arrangement, she stood and stepped backward toward the street to get a full view of the completed planter. The red blooms were the perfect complement to the home's stucco siding.

Her mouth crooking to the side, she eyed the tall ceramic planter by the foot of the driveway. It would take a while to fill, but once completed, the container garden would make a beautiful *Welcome Home* for her parents.

They could certainly use day brighteners.

A forceful breeze pushed against her, drawing her attention westward, up the hill. Wind swooped down and thrashed branches on the big oak beside the house, a sign that a storm was rushing in. She checked the weather app on her phone. Apparently, it was rolling in faster than the forecasters first anticipated. Storms seemed to creep up on those living on the east side of the hill. She loved the storms, but only when she was inside burrowed under a blanket and cuddled up next to her dad.

Once upon a time, he'd been her hero, but then a stroke stole more than his mobility.

She pulled the wagon filled with annuals, compost, and black dirt to the end of the driveway. The plants were all ordinary, but when arranged together they created an eye-catching *Welcome Home*. She combed her fingers through the dirt in the planter from the previous year, and added fresh Miracle Grow and compost. On top of that she set the spike, four geraniums, white verbena, and a Vinca vine, and then played with the arrangement.

One of the geraniums looked off somehow. Its flower wasn't as full, or colorful as the rest. It was imperfect. Like her. And her family. But, despite their imperfections, they loved each other and would weather whatever storm life blew their direction. In a way, her dad's stroke had brought them closer together. It certainly had changed Jess's perspective on life. That, combined with the sudden end of her modeling career, had launched her faith journey.

And made her a new, unique creation, someone who was working on becoming firmly rooted in Christ. Even her agnostic mother had commented on the change in Jess's attitude and lifestyle.

She pinched off a dying bloom from the geranium. It had once been full and pretty, but now would steal energy away from growing and living flowers, impeding their health and growth. Jess had a whole bunch of growing to do yet, too. At least her energy was focused on the right things, for the first time in years.

Thunder grumbled in the distance as she stepped back for a wider perspective of the planter. The flowers danced and waved with the wind like an unchoreographed ballet. Simple but elegant. Her dad—maybe even her mom—would love it. He'd always lauded her green thumb.

Now to bed the plants in the mini-garden before the rain came.

A car pulled up the driveway as she shook the spike from its plastic container. Callie and Haven? Back from their date already? She checked the time on her phone. Seven on a Saturday evening was way early for Callie to be home. Those two lovebirds took advantage of every minute they had alone. Not that she blamed them. They were adorable together, and were so good for each other, and Jess loved seeing her older sister so happy.

Or were they home because they'd broken up? Would their romance be another casualty of her parents' struggles?

More thunder bowled overhead as she mulled over that thought. A breakup would fracture Callie's heart. And their dad's. He loved Haven like the son he'd never had.

If only Jess could find someone worth bringing home to show off to her parents.

Someday that would happen. She had to believe it.

She continued tucking the plants into the dirt and heard Callie call out behind her. "Hey, Jess."

Jess put down her trowel as Callie ran toward her, pulling Haven behind. Her sister's face glowed. Definitely not a breakup. Could it be?

With Haven in tow, Callie bounded up onto the front porch and motioned for Jess to join them.

"One second." She yelled out while bedding the final plant into the dirt. With excitement dancing in her heart, she patted the dirt from her hands and wiped it off on her shirt and jeans while jogging to the house. The starry-eyed couple had taken a seat on the glider bench. Jess sat in the wicker chair opposite them and homed in on Callie's left hand, but it was entwined with Haven's, covering her ring finger. "Well?" Her gaze flitted between the lovebirds' faces.

Haven nodded to Callie. "Go ahead."

Her cheeks blooming the same shade as the geraniums, Callie tugged her hand from Haven, but kept her ring finger covered with her right hand. "Promise you won't say a word to Mom and Dad."

It would be hard not to blurt it out when their folks arrived home tomorrow, but she could do it. "I promise." With her hand, she made a cross over her heart.

Biting into her lower lip, Callie unveiled her hand.

Jess gasped and jumped up from her chair. "Oh. My. Goodness!" She grasped Callie's hand and gaped at the enormous rock. "It's

19

gorgeous!" She quirked a brow and looked to Haven. "Did you rob your bank, or what?"

He laughed and retook Callie's hand. "The diamond came from a necklace Dad had given Mom before she passed. Dad gave it to me for Callie. Said repurposing the diamond is what Mom would've wanted."

Jess fluttered her hands in front of her face. "It's about time. I'm so happy for you two!" She hugged them both. "Tell me about the proposal." Knowing Haven, she was certain the proposal wasn't average.

"We're saving that story until Mom and Dad get home."

Jess retreated to her chair. "Haven, at least you can tell me Callie's response."

Haven laughed. "It is rather memorable."

"And he'll be reminding me of it forever." Callie rolled her eyes.

He ran a finger over the ring and grinned at Callie. "Oh, puppy dogs and carrots," he said in a high-pitched voice.

"That's carats spelled c-a-r-a-t-s." Callie elbowed her fiancé.

"I distinctly heard c-a-r-r-o-t-s."

"Which is exactly what you're going to be wearing for your wedding ring, mister."

"If that's what it takes to be your husband, I'm all for it."

"You two are nauseating." And adorable. She couldn't be happier for them. "The important question now is, when's the wedding?"

The couple exchanged a glance, and Callie grimaced. "October."

"October?" Jess fell back in her chair. "As in five months from now?"

Callie and Haven nodded.

"Oh boy, oh boy." Jess grinned. "You realize Mom's gonna freak, don't you? That's not nearly enough time for her to pull off a grand wedding."

"Exactly." Callie gave a single nod. "I . . . *we* don't want a Mom-styled wedding, but a simple, exchanging of the vows at the cabin, by the lake at sunrise. Can you imagine the colors the first part of October? We won't need decorations because God will provide them for us. Mom can update the cabin and refresh the gardens instead. She's wanted to for years. A wedding will give her a reason to get it done now rather than putting it off again."

Jess shook her head. "Good luck telling Mom."

Callie and Haven laughed together, their voices blending in a joyful harmony. "Thanks." Callie grinned. "We're definitely going to need it."

"Yeah, you will." Their mom was not going to be happy that she couldn't plan an extravagant gala and invite Duluth's elite crowd. Now if Jess ever married . . .

Thunder clapped overhead and the storm's first drops hit the S-shaped red brick walkway leading from the porch to the city sidewalk. Shoot. In all the excitement over the engagement, Jess had completely forgotten the planters, and now all her supplies were getting wet. "I gotta get my stuff."

"I'll do it." Haven was off the porch before she had a chance to stand. He grabbed the wagon, tossed in her tools, and pulled it up the driveway while rain pelted down. She didn't have to watch him to know he'd secure it in the garden shed in the backyard. Yeah, the man was a catch, all right.

A minute later he rejoined the sisters on the porch, soaked from dark blond hair to boat shoe, and still wearing that lovesick grin. He cuddled up to Callie, who promptly pushed him away with an "Ewww!"

But then she took his hand and focused on Jess. "Sorry we interrupted your planting. I know you wanted to complete it today."

"It is what it is." She waved her hand so they wouldn't worry, even if she did. "I've got tomorrow yet, right?" A day she'd planned to spend opening up the cabin. Time spent at the cabin always salved family wounds.

A silver sedan pulled up the driveway leading to the garage behind the house. In spite of the pep talk to herself, worry knotted in her throat. What were her parents doing home today?

"Uh-oh," was all Callie said.

Tension sizzled hotter than the lightening flashing around them as the three entered the Tudor house owned by Jess and Callie's parents. The sisters shared the second-floor apartment while their folks resided on the first floor.

Inside, Callie and Haven communicated in whispers, and Haven detoured to Dad's den while Jess and Callie took seats in the living room.

"You don't suppose . . . " Jess watched the back entryway, muscles tightening in her shoulders.

"Bad weather brought them home, that's all." Callie stared at her feet, drawing figures on the floor.

So, Pollyanna wasn't optimistic either.

The grandfather clock noisily ticked off the seconds before the back door finally opened. Their father came in alone, leaning heavily on a walker he hadn't used prior to the vacation, and looking far older than his fifty-five years. Moments later, the silver sedan whooshed past the living room window, down the driveway, and onto the street.

The knots in her shoulders tightened as both she and Callie raced to help their dad to his recliner.

He said nothing, just sat there, staring at the window that the family car had zoomed past.

"Daddy, what's wrong?" Callie took his right hand, the one affected by the stroke, and Jess pulled a footstool in front of him and sat so she could look up at his face.

A single tear trickled down his cheek.

Jess touched his left knee to draw his attention, but his gaze remained on the carless driveway. "Daddy, where did Mom go?"

He sighed, and his shoulders heaved. "Your mother...and I...filed for s...separation." His speech slurred nearly as bad as when he'd first had the stroke.

Both Jess and Callie gasped.

"No." Jess whispered and blinked away her own tear.

"Tired of d...dealing with...invalid."

Callie caressed his arm. "You're not—"

He raised his trembling right hand. "Yes. I am."

"But that'll get better with therapy." Jess took his hand. "You were doing so well. This is a little setback."

He jerked his hand away. "She wanted me...to tell you, she's looking for old people's h...home. For m...me. Now help me to...g...guestroom."

Silenced by his pronouncement, Jess and Callie escorted their dad to the guestroom. Then Callie went to talk to Haven alone, and Jess sat numbly on her parents' couch.

Separation wasn't permanent, right? It only meant their parents had to work things out. If their dad was struggling, wouldn't a care center be best for him right now? Or was she making excuses for their parents' bad behavior?

Ugh!

She blinked back tears. Finishing the planter arrangements could wait. She needed to get out of this house and go to the cabin. Her place of healing.

Maybe that was the answer for her parents too.

If she fixed up the cabin and restored the gardens to their luster of years ago, maybe that would provide the healing balm for their marriage.

Operation: Planting Hope would begin tomorrow, and by the time Callie and Haven got married, her parents would be renewing their vows.

Chapter Two

'll be back tomorrow to manage the office." Jess opened the Jeep hatch and Haven loaded several large plastic containers. One day wasn't a lot of time to open the cabin for the summer, especially when working by herself, but it could be done. After today she'd have the rest of the summer to work on the gardens. Besides, working alone would give her plenty of time to have a one-on-one with God.

She'd only been a Christian a few months, but already she cherished the conversations. For the first time in her life, someone listened to her, understood her. She didn't have to show off to get His attention, she could be who God created her to be, so she craved their quiet moments together.

"I wish I could help." Haven closed the hatch. "But Dad and I have planned this event for months."

"And I'm sticking around to keep an eye on Dad." With furrowed brows, Callie looked to the house then back at Jess. "I wish Mom would call. I'm worried about her."

"Huh. I'm not." Jess tucked the vehicle keys into her pocket. They did know that Mom was staying with her sister, Aunt Tib, but that was all they'd gotten out of Dad. "I'm more concerned about Dad. Why the setback? It's like he stopped trying to get better, but before they left on vacation, he was all gung-ho."

"I know." Callie reached for Haven's hand, but he stretched an arm around her shoulders instead. She looked up at him, her brows nearly meeting. "Do we put off the wedding?"

"No." Jess and Haven said at the same time.

"Then we should elope. Tonight."

"Don't tempt me." He kissed her forehead. "But I want to do this right. Your dad's already given permission—"

"He has?" Callie's brows rose.

"Well, of course I asked his permission. Before they left for vacation. He asked me what took so long."

"So they know." Callie's shoulders slumped.

They knew of the engagement, but hadn't bothered to say *Congratulations*? Talk about selfish. Something Jess was far too familiar with. But God had shown her she was a work in progress, and He loved her as she was.

"They know I planned to ask, but didn't know when I was doing the asking."

"I still like the idea of eloping."

Haven tipped up Callie's chin and kissed her. "Five months. It'll fly by faster than I can say *supercalifragilisticexpialidocious*."

"If you say so." Callie gave him a push. "You better get going before I try to convince you otherwise. Your dad's waiting."

"Love you, Super Cal—"

"Please." She rolled her eyes.

"—and tell your dad I'm praying for him."

The lovebirds kissed again before Haven strode off. Oh, to have that kind of love. The kind her parents once shared.

And would again. They just had to be reminded of why they fell in love.

Jess dug the keys from her jeans pocket. "You gonna be okay with Dad?"

"We'll be fine."

"I'll check in periodically." They didn't have cell phone service at the cabin, and the landline wouldn't be hooked up until later this week, so she'd have to drive to that little candy store next door to the cabin to get service.

The candy store . . .

Where her parents first met thirty-plus years ago. Another important piece of Operation: Planting Hope. When you combined flowers and chocolate, romance was certain to bloom.

Jess gave Callie a hug then got in the Jeep and took off. Stress slipped away as she drove the scenic route along Minnesota's North Shore bordering Lake Superior. Now that she knew the Artist who'd created this Minnesota masterpiece, she marveled even more at the ocean-sized body of water, the massive boulders tossed shore side, and the ever-changing trees and skies reflected in the water.

Not to mention the diverse wildlife: deer, bald eagles, black bear, wolves, loons, and so much more. She loved it all.

And once she got the cabin fixed up, her parents would make this drive and fall in love with each other again.

In under an hour she neared the cute little candy store where her parents first met, and slowed down. No vehicles waited in the tiny lot and a *Closed* sign hung in the front window. Why was it closed at the beginning of tourist season? She hoped it wasn't a permanent closure. Getting chocolate from Superior Sweets was an important part of Operation: Planting Hope.

A vehicle behind her honked, and she resisted giving them a one-finger salute like she once would have done. Rather, she pulled over to let the impatient driver—make that drivers—pass. Apparently, she was holding up a slew of travelers heading north. After they passed, she pulled back onto the highway and drove another few hundred feet or so to the next driveway on the right, leading down to the cabin.

She turned on her blinker and slowed, then slammed on her brakes, stopping in time to avoid hitting a fallen tree blocking the driveway entrance.

"No . . . " she moaned and banged her forehead on the steering wheel. The tree was young, but still too large and bulky for her to move on her own. That meant she'd be spending the afternoon with a chainsaw and wheelbarrow rather than opening the cabin.

For once, couldn't things go right for her?

THERE WAS NOTHING LIKE a Sunday drive up the North Shore. Too much time had passed since Luke had been up here, and that showed in the rapid loosening of muscles as he took in God's sculpting. Wow, could He create a shoreline! How had Luke allowed work to take precedence over visiting God's art gallery?

How had he let work stop him from visiting Gran? He'd missed so much . . .

He pounded the steering wheel. Letting work dominate his life would not happen again. He'd come up here, make the land purchases Dad wanted, live in Gran's apartment for six months, then he'd get the promotion to Vice President that Dad had been promising for years. Luke would finally be his own boss and have more freedom over his schedule. Trips to the North Shore would no longer be relegated to when-I-get-this-next-proposal-done.

And maybe he'd make Gran proud again too. She'd see him from Heaven, wouldn't she?

A line of vehicles in front of him slowed, and he tapped on the brakes of his Chevy Colorado pickup as he entered the almost-there town of Spoon Creek, population 138. In the summer that population grew times one hundred when the tourists flocked in.

Which was why Dad had his eyes set on the lake property. For what exact purpose, Luke didn't know. Another resort maybe. Perhaps executive living. Or a split-share building. Any would be a hit.

He crept along behind the traffic until he passed the city limits. Roland Bettis' property was on the right. The man had thirty acres, many fronting the lakeshore, but none of the views could compare to those at Superior Sweets. For as long as Luke could remember, Bettis had tried to cajole Gran into selling.

And now Luke had to turn the tables? Dad was expecting a miracle. With Luke's meager budget, how was he going to convince Bettis to sell to Harrison Properties?

He'd have to get to know the man, find out what he valued, and go from there. He could—he would do it, and make his dad proud of him again.

Luke pulled onto the gravel curb, got out of his truck, and breathed in the smog-free air. He trespassed on Bettis' land to get to the shore where boulders the size of a wrecking ball hemmed in the stone-strewn shoreline. What would happen to the pristine air, the rocky beaches, if Dad developed the land? Sure, he'd create gorgeous landscapes around the buildings, all with breath-stealing views of Superior, but manmade landscapes could never compare to God's handiwork.

That aspect of Harrison Property Development never sat well with Luke. Redeveloping a city block? No problem. But cutting up God's creation always gave him pause.

He dug through the lake-smoothed stones, found a semi-flat one, and flung it out on the water. Plunk. Not a single skip. By the end of his six months, he'd be a pro again.

Luke returned to his pickup and took his time driving past Bettis' property, undeveloped but for a monster log home that hid among the trees. Around the next curve would be Gran's store.

His stomach roiled at the thought of seeing Superior Sweets again. It had been what? Five? No, six years. Six years! Since he'd visited Gran. If not for her trips to the Twin Cities during winter, he wouldn't have seen her at all. Unbidden tears stung his eyes as the quaint shop came into view. White with red trim. A white-picket porch inviting guests up, encouraging them to sit on the slatted swing.

A *Closed* sign in the front window.

He pulled into the lot and let the tears come. Tears he'd held back in front of his family. Why did it take Gran dying for him to realize how much he missed her? Needed her?

She'd tell him, "Leave the past where it belongs: behind you." And that was exactly what he intended to do.

He wiped his eyes and blew his nose, then got out of his Chevy and walked across the five-car lot filled with more potholes than Mars had craters. That would have to be completely torn up and repaved. The store's exterior paint was cracked and peeling. And that railing on the porch looked like a whisper would blow it over.

Dad would probably tell Luke the store wasn't worth saving, but Dad didn't understand value beyond monetary. This home was Luke's and he planned to use every penny of his savings to make it the grand store it had been when Luke was a child.

Wait . . .

Luke blinked as the truth hit him. If Dad wanted both the Bettis and Beaumont properties, he'd also need Luke to sell Gran's place. He'd tear this building down faster than Luke could say Gooseberry Falls. So, fixing up this place would be a complete waste of money and time.

That thought made him want to cry all over again. Gran would weep with him.

Instead he got into his pickup and traveled north, surveying the Beaumont land. It really was a prime piece of property that had been in their family for three generations. How could he convince the family to sell an heirloom?

A cabin sat on the property, hidden from the road. He remembered that from the couple of times the Beaumonts had invited Gran to a weenie roast. The Beaumonts also had a couple of annoying little girls. Well, not so little anymore. He did the math in his head. They'd be in their twenties now. Were they still around?

Up ahead, right after the Beaumont driveway, a Jeep sat on the side of the road, and a young, blonde-haired woman was heading from the driveway toward the Jeep. He slowed and pulled off onto the curb. And sighed.

A fallen aspen covered the entire width of the driveway to the Beaumont cabin. Not an old tree or a large one, but still it would be difficult for a single person to move.

He got out of his pickup and jogged toward the Jeep. The woman must have seen him approach, as she got out and walked toward him.

"Need some help?" He nodded toward the tree.

"Would you?" Her face lit up into a pretty smile. Real pretty, actually, with blue eyes shining like a sunlit sky. She sashayed toward him. "I was going to head to the cabin and grab the chainsaw."

He couldn't contain a grin. He'd love to see this woman—one of the Beaumont girls maybe?—wield a chainsaw, but they shouldn't need it right now. Getting the tree moved off to the side should be their priority. With all this traffic, someone was likely to plow into his truck or her Jeep. "I think you and I can handle it." Or maybe he shouldn't have assumed she'd pitch in.

"Wonderful." She crossed the driveway and offered her hand along with a bright smile, then quickly drew both back and stepped away. "Wait. You could be Jack the Ripper for all I know. Just to warn you, I have taken self-defense classes." She kept backing toward the Jeep, her gaze riveted on him.

Luke stayed still, hoping to gain her trust. "I can promise you I'm not Jack the Ripper, but you wouldn't know that." He gestured to the busy roadway, with trails of cars zooming past them. "And I have plenty of witnesses." He began to pull a business card out of his wallet, but tucked it back in. If this was one of the Beaumont daughters, he wanted to establish a relationship with her before she knew what his job was with Harrison Property Development. Revealing that would put an immediate halt on the land sale.

He'd try another angle, and bank on her remembering him. "Are you one of the Beaumont daughters?"

She said nothing, but kept creeping back to her Jeep, her gaze never leaving him.

"I'm Luke Harrison. My gran owned Superior Sweets and I used to make s'mores at the cabin." He nodded down the driveway.

"Owned?" She stopped backing away. "Did Gran sell?"

He blinked and looked to the cloudless sky. "She passed away a few weeks back."

Her hand flew to her heart. "Oh no! I'm so sorry." The woman closed the gap between them. "Gran was amazing. So nice all the time. I didn't know about her passing. Mom and Dad . . . " She closed her eyes and heaved a sigh. "Mom and Dad will be sad. They met at Superior Sweets. So her passing . . . that's why the store's closed."

"Until early next week anyway."

"Does the store have new owners?"

"You're looking at him." He spread out his arms.

"Seriously?"

"Serious as chocolate."

She giggled. "Now *that* is serious. You don't plan to close down?"

"Not if I can help it." At least for six months. "I've talked with all Gran's employees and they're looking forward to coming back. But I have to relearn the ropes. It's been years since I helped out."

"Well you're certainly the best-looking candy store owner I've ever seen."

Heat flooded his cheeks.

"Oh, snickerdoodles, forgive me. I tend to run at the mouth, but I'm not taking back what I said."

"I wouldn't want you to. Now, I'm sorry, but I don't remember your name. It's been a while."

She stuck out her hand and didn't pull away. "Jess Beaumont. I'll have to tell Callie I ran into you."

That was right. Jess and Callie. He jotted their names in his memory under the Beaumont sale file. "For now, let me give you a hand with this tree."

"Thank you so much. I have one day to get the cabin clean, and, surprise! I ran into this."

"Not a problem." Not at all. Actually, if he stayed and helped her clean, that would be a good way to build a relationship and find out what would motivate her parents to sell.

Besides, working alongside a good-looking woman would certainly not be a hardship.

WITH HIS HELP MOVING the tree, Jess should be able to get the cabin cleaned yet today. She hurried back to her Jeep and grabbed a couple pairs of work gloves.

What had she been thinking when Luke first got out of the pickup? She bonked the side of her head. A gorgeous guy, dressed in black slacks and teal dress shirt, steps out of a shiny black pickup, and her first reaction was to flirt with him? Sheesh, she had a long way to go. Sure she'd had her share of boyfriends over the years, but every one of those relationships, if that was what you would call them, had been shallow and about taking one thing from her.

Something she'd been more than eager to give.

She shivered. She was no longer that woman who'd starved for love and attention. She hurried back to Luke with her dad's gloves. It was amazing how in the short time she'd known Jesus, He'd transformed her. But she still had a lot of learning to do.

And that started with treating guys with respect, and seeing them as human beings not another conquest. Just how she wanted to be treated.

She handed Luke the gloves and grimaced. "You look like you've come from church. Are you sure you're okay with helping?"

He looked down and laughed. Such an easy-on-the-ears laugh, too. "Hadn't even thought of that. Yes, I did just come from church. But assisting a not-at-all-helpless damsel is far more important than keeping neat and clean."

"Well, my knight-to-the-rescue, or shall I call you Sir Luke? I'm very grateful for your help."

"Any time, milady." He bowed, and gestured to the fallen tree. "Shall we slay the beast?"

"We shall." She giggled.

He headed for the tree, with her close behind. He stopped abruptly and she slammed into him, knocking him headfirst to the down-sloping ground. He did an awkward somersault before landing on his behind.

"Oh my goodness, I'm so sorry. Are you all right?" She offered her hand.

"And now the damsel comes to my rescue." He stood, then took her hand.

"Only after said-damsel pushed you off the cliff." She giggled.

"There is that." Grinning, he stretched his limbs out. "Nothing broken." He brushed dirt and dead leaves from his backside, and from his hair, but missed a tiny leaf above his right ear.

Oh my, was that tempting to brush away, so she stuck her hands in her pockets.

"As I was going to say before you tried to off me . . . " He winked and pointed to the tree. "You wouldn't happen to have a handsaw in your Jeep? It'll be a lot easier to move if we can trim some of those branches first."

"Actually, I do." She jogged back to the Jeep. Damsel? Sir Luke? Really? Turning off the flirt in her was not easy. She dug through the cabin supplies and pulled out a handsaw and a pair of pruning shears. With both of them working, the tree would be moved much more easily. And if she was working, the flirt would hopefully stay hidden.

She loped back to Luke and handed him the saw. In only a few minutes, they had the branches cut and piled alongside the gravel driveway. Once the wood dried out, it would make good kindling for the fire pit. Luke trimmed the rough edges off the root system, making it easier for him to grasp.

"Ready to give it a try?" He laced his fingers and stretched his arms out in front of him.

"Let's do it." She headed for the branch-free top.

And he stood at the base. "I'll walk it backwards a few feet, then you swing the top around."

"Sounds good." A few feet from the top of the tree, she bent and secured her hands around the trunk.

He squatted and wrapped his arms around the base. "Lift on three. One . . . two . . . three."

She grunted and, pushing up with her knees, lifted the tree from the ground.

"Now walk it toward me."

She took baby steps toward him, her muscles protesting with each step. Dang, this tree was heavier than it looked! The tree slipped from her fingers and landed on her right foot. "Yow!" She squealed and pushed the trunk off her foot.

Tears filled her eyes as she dropped onto the ground.

"You okay?" Luke rushed over and knelt beside her.

"I'm not sure. It hurts like the dickens." She bent over to take off her tennis shoe. Why hadn't she worn something sturdier?

"Let me help." He untied and loosened the laces, then gently tugged off the shoe. He began taking off the sock.

That wasn't happening. "I've got this." She rolled her sock off and studied her throbbing foot. The skin wasn't broken, and her toes all moved, but a lump was already forming on the top.

"You should see a doctor."

"But I can't." She looked down the curving, wood-lined driveway toward the cabin. Smaller branches littered the gravel, and the shuttered log home looked forlorn, as if begging to be opened up so it could breathe. "I need to get the cabin cleaned today." Her parents' marriage depended upon it. She tried standing, and pain shot from her foot up her leg.

He helped her sit back down.

How was she ever going to bring her parents back together if she was an invalid?

Chapter Three

Luke tried helping Jess stand, but she grimaced with the attempt to put weight on her foot. She slumped to the ground and covered her face with her hands. She wasn't crying, was she? He had no clue what to do about that.

What he should do was pick her up, carry her to his truck, and drive her to urgent care and have that foot looked at. But she seemed adamant about getting the cabin cleaned today. Helping her open it— rather, having her tell him what to do—would certainly be one way to establish a friendly relationship. Certainly, after he let her boss him around all afternoon, she'd trust him. And, he'd hopefully get some insights into what he could offer for the cabin and land.

He knelt beside her and said in his best British accent, which wasn't good at all, "Tell you what, Sir Luke will carry you to your abode and will allow you to instruct him in how to properly prepare your cabin."

Sobs leaked through her fingers. Wait, no, that was laughter. Okay then.

"You haven't changed a bit." She uncovered her face and smiled up at him. "I remember being out by the fire pit, and you finding a way to make us smile."

"I live to serve." He bowed, and she laughed again. "But in all seriousness, I'd be glad to help you—let you boss me around—and get your cabin in tip-top shape, in exchange for you going to see the doctor afterwards." Which meant he'd have to put off getting settled in his temporary home as planned, but developing trust with Jess was more important.

Besides, she certainly wasn't difficult to spend time with.

"And I don't want you walking on that foot in case something's broken, so I'll have to carry you."

Her eyes grew wide and she vehemently shook her head. "No way are you picking me up. Then we'd both be in need of a doctor."

"I seriously doubt that. I'll have you know, I worked out once this year." He flexed his muscles which weren't too bad, if he said so himself. It was true that he'd worked out once. Usually once a day, but who was he to brag?

"Not happening. But." She pointed toward a shed near the cabin. "We keep a wheelbarrow in the shed. You could give me a ride."

"Now you're talking." He studied the fallen tree. They'd moved it far enough that it wouldn't be difficult for him to roll it to the side of the driveway. "Or I could move the tree and drive you in my pickup."

"By yourself? And dressed like that?"

He shrugged. So what if his church clothes were now relegated for work? "Shouldn't be a problem." He proceeded to clear the driveway. The trunk wasn't nearly as heavy as it looked. "I'll get my truck, give you a ride to the cabin." He aimed for his pickup.

"But what's the fun in that?"

There was that teasing lilt again. Sounded awfully nice. He looked back at her with raised brows. "Oh yeah?"

"I haven't had a wheelbarrow ride in years. Remember when you used to haul Callie and me around?"

Yeah, he did, and he'd hated it, but like he'd done all his life, he'd pasted on a smile, and did what was expected of him. Hauling around Jess now, though? His smile would be genuine.

She dug into a pocket and pulled out a key ring. "That's for the cabin. The key to the shed is taped to the underside of the bottom drawer in the bathroom."

"Aha!" He dangled the ring and grinned. "Now I know your secret hiding place."

"And I know where you work."

He snapped his fingers. "You got me there." He nodded toward the cabin. "Be right back with your carriage."

Was that a blush? It sure was pretty. He jogged down the driveway. And why was he flirting with her? Sure, she was nice looking—better than nice—but women had been off his radar for years. They always took his focus off business. He wasn't like Tim, who could handle both simultaneously. The fresh air must be making him loopy.

Making him genuinely happy once again.

He opened the cabin and immediately pinched his nose while gagging. The place reeked. The smell wasn't musty, but more of a stale stench brought on by lack of airflow. The hardwood floor was littered with evidence that mice had found shelter in the home this winter. Yuk.

Well, he'd volunteered for this job, so he'd do it without complaining. He found the bathroom, pulled out the bottom cabinet drawer, and there was a key, just as she'd said. Quite an ingenious place to keep one, actually. At least it had been. He hurried to the shed, unlocked it and found the wheelbarrow tipped up against a wall. He tested the tire. A little bit flat, but it would easily hold Jess.

He wheeled the barrow up the hill to Jess and she attempted to stand before he got there.

"No you don't." He gestured to the ground. "Our agreement said I would do the work, and you would boss me around. Got it?"

"Yes sir." She saluted him. "But I do have to get in it."

"Yes, you do." And before she had the chance to object, he swooped her into his arms. She let out a yelp before he gently lowered her into the metal tray.

She batted his arm as he released her. "I said no lifting." But there was a tease in her voice.

"And I said no standing." He teased right back. Oh boy. He was having way too much fun, and the day had just begun. And now he was rhyming in his head! "Hang on." He grasped the handles and wheeled her downhill. She held out her arms like that chick on the Titanic with Leonardo DiCaprio. Yeah, this was fun.

He carted her down the driveway, taking care to avoid the bigger bumps and potholes, and drove her right up to the cabin's deck. He rested the wheelbarrow and came around the side.

She attempted to push out. "You are not going to lift—Ahhh." She screeched as he scooped her up. Her arms flung around his neck as he carried her up three steps, onto a deck, and over the cabin's threshold.

The symbolism of that was a bit too much for him, so he looked for a place to set her where she could elevate her foot. The couch would do, and it was placed so that she'd have full view of almost the entire cabin. He whipped off the sheet covering the sofa and dust whirled through the air. He held in a sneeze while setting Jess down, then let loose three body-wracking sneezes.

"Bless you." Jess pointed to a tissue box on a kitchen counter.

"Thanks." He grabbed a tissue and sneezed a couple more times.

"Are you all right?" She started to get up.

"Stay put." He pointed at her, the sneezing finally done. "I'll get you a pillow." He grabbed a throw pillow off a nearby chair and took it outside where he held it away from his face while slapping the dust from it. Only then did he bring it to Jess. For a second he considered putting it beneath her foot, but this knight-in-slacks-clad armor had pretty much worn out the intimate gestures for now.

After tucking the pillow beneath her foot, she held out the key for her vehicle. "The cabin supplies are in my Jeep, if you wouldn't mind driving it down here."

"'Tis my job to serve." He bowed, accepting the key chain, and was rewarded with a giggle. He'd take that kind of payment any day. "Be right back."

It took him about ten minutes to bring both vehicles down to the cabin, then he carried in several plastic containers plus a cooler full of ice, beverages, and sandwiches. "Where can I find towels?"

She nodded to one of the containers, all of which were labeled. "In there."

"Perfect." He removed the cover from the plastic box and dug through the linens until he found what he wanted. From the cooler, he took a couple handfuls of ice and wrapped it in the towel. "For your foot." He carried it over to her and gestured toward the injury. "Do you mind?"

"I'd be very grateful. Thank you."

"You won't be saying 'Thank you' when this cold wrap touches your foot."

He gently raised her foot and carefully arranged the wrap so the cold would stay on the swollen area. He didn't know much about nursing, but in his energetic youth he'd had a bruised or sprained limb or two . . . make that three.

Then he rubbed his hands together. "Time for me to get to work. Tell me what to do, and I'll do it with little complaint."

"I noticed you didn't say 'no' complaint." She grinned.

"My father raised me to tell the truth." He returned her grin.

"Must be a wise man."

Luke snorted. Maybe once upon a time. He shoved that from his thoughts. "What shall I do first?"

"Unshutter the windows from outside." She gestured toward the windows. "We need some fresh air in here."

He pinched his nose. "Yeah, I noticed."

"Sounds like a complaint to me."

"Nope. Just an observation." He whistled while opening the shutters around the house. After that, he raised the windows to let fragrant spring air flow through the screens. Ahhh, much better. "Next task."

"The utility room is next to the bathroom. Turn everything on in there, and we'll have power and water."

He did as he was told and voilà! they had electricity and running water. Then he turned on the refrigerator. Later, he'd fill it with food and drink from the cooler. The beauty of modern-day luxuries.

He brought a semi-cool bottle of water to Jess. "Next?"

"You're gonna hate me for this."

"Uh-oh."

"You'll find some latex gloves in that container." She pointed to the box on the far right.

That did sound like an uh-oh. He took off the lid and found gloves right on top. Whoever packed the box planned well. "And now?"

She nodded toward the sink. "You'll find an ice cream bucket and plastic liners beneath the sink."

"So you're going to tease me with an empty ice cream bucket. I'm thinking that after our trip the doctor, you owe me a sundae."

"Oh yeah, especially after this next task. My dad called it 'retaking the throne.'"

He wrinkled his nose and slapped on the gloves. "I can guess where I'm headed, and if I'm correct, you're going to treat me to a triple-scoop sundae."

"Sorry." She shrugged and grinned.

Ha! She wasn't one bit sorry. "Methinks you hurt your foot just to get out of retaking-the-throne duty."

She rubbed her hands together. "You've discovered my evil plan."

With a laugh, he raised his chin and marched to the bathroom, bucket in hand. He lifted the lid on the toilet seat and gagged at the sight of an entire mouse family who'd died attempting to swim in the antifreeze. Too bad for them.

Holding his breath, he ladled the skeletal creatures into the plastic-lined bucket and carried it to the living room. "Would you like to say farewell to the family?"

"You're nuts. Has anyone ever told you that?"

Only his dad and siblings. "Moi?" He suspended the bucket. "Where do we bury the dead? And would you like me to erect little markers for them?"

She stared at him as if he were crazy, which he probably was. Then she burst into laughter, a loud, happy laugh he'd love to hear again. "Tie off the bag and wrap it with another one, throw it in the trash. And, yes, I expect a stone marker for each member of that family. Though they will not be missed."

"As you wish." He hurried outside. The banter with Jess almost made this job worthwhile. He double-bagged the remains and tossed it into the trash bin, along with the gloves. He re-entered the cabin and stood in the living room, his arms stiff at his side, legs locked, and chin jutted out. "The Beaumont clan has once again dethroned the evil mouse family, and we have taken back the castle."

"Huzzah!" She clapped. "And you shall be rewarded with a triple scoop sundae of your choice, Sir Luke."

"Thank you." He bowed and clicked his heels together. "What shall I do next?"

"Now you get to clean up the mess that family made. Cleaning supplies are beneath the sink."

Yippee. "It shall be done." He clicked his heels again. Boy, if Ivy, Dad's cleaning lady for thirty-plus years, could see him now, she'd wonder what happened to the boy who refused to clean his room.

After squirting on and rubbing in hand sanitizer three times, he stretched on a new pair of gloves. He squeezed toilet cleaner into the bowl, and sprayed the entire room with lemon-scented Lysol. In case that didn't kill enough germs, he scrubbed down the room with a bleach-and-water mixture. As an added touch, he plugged in a wax warmer with a lemon-scented cube. That seemed like a scent Jess would like. In no time, the stale stench of an unlived-in home would disappear.

It took him a few hours to do the remainder of the cabin. He removed dryer sheets from cupboards and drawers. They'd done their job in keeping away more of the unwelcome mouse family. He swept away cobwebs and vacuumed up anything their creators had left behind. Then he swept, dusted, and/or washed every surface in the kitchen and family room area, including the windows. After ridding more spider webs from the loft and master bedroom, and removing plastic mattress protectors, also filled with dryer sheets, the cabin was finally ready for its finishing touches.

He made the beds with fresh linens, and hung out clean towels. Candle warmers were plugged in in the master bedroom and in the loft, eating up more of that stale air.

He was rather enjoying watching the little home's transformation from abandoned shack to lived- and loved-in home. It would be a shame if Dad tore down this place.

Dad . . .

Luke plopped down on the newly-made bed in the master bedroom. He was supposed to be getting to know Jess so she'd sell this place. Instead he'd turned the day into a time of make-believe and flirting. If she hadn't flirted back, it wouldn't have been a problem, but she made flirting easy.

Yes, his job was to get to know Jess, but become attracted to her? And, oh yeah, he was definitely attracted. But that was an absolute no-no, because if—when—he purchased the cabin, this newly-found friendship would be destroyed. That thought alone hurt his heart.

Becoming distracted had always been his problem. 'Keep the main thing, the main thing,' a quote from Stephen Covey's book on time management, *First Things First*, had been Dad's mantra for much of Luke's teen years.

And, apparently, his adulthood too. He and Jess could be acquaintances, yes, friends, maybe, but never more than that. So his attitude had to change.

Now that the indoor cleaning was complete, he'd carry Jess to his pickup, drive her to urgent care, and her family could take care of her from there. He'd even forgo the triple-scoop sundae—which was truly a sacrifice.

With that resolve, he returned to the living room where she lay curled up on the couch, eyes closed, looking way-too-adorable. But it was time to leave. He gave her shoulder a gentle shake. "Hey Jess, time to get going."

Her eyes blinked open, and she stretched into a yawn. "I can't believe I fell asleep."

"Must have been all that hard work you were doing."

"Yeah, bossing you around was really difficult."

And there she got him smiling again. That had to stop. "It's time to get that foot taken care of." He squatted next to the couch and took off the wet towel. "How does it feel?"

She wiggled her toes. "Still sore, but not as bad. I can try walking."

"Nope. Not on my watch. You get the carry treatment."

"To the wheelbarrow?"

He smirked. "Thirteen miles is an awfully long way to push a wheelbarrow."

She laughed that fun laugh again. "No, to the lake. I can't leave the cabin without going to the overlook."

"Ahh, gotcha. And then we head to urgent care."

"I promise."

He carried her outside and set her in the wheelbarrow once again. He pushed it down the tree root-rutted path surrounded by weed-filled gardens, to the clearing overlooking Lake Superior. Little had changed since the days when he'd come here with Gran and they roasted marshmallows and hot dogs and told funny stories around the fire pit. This would be gone too, if—when—Dad took over.

Jess must have sensed his solemnity, as she too sat silent. Then she sighed. "This was Dad's favorite place when we were little. He'd wake up me and Callie and bring us out to watch the sunrise. His easel and paints would be all ready to go. Callie would bring her paper and crayons. I'd pose for Dad, always trying to get his attention."

She took in a deep breath and wiped below her eye. "He can't even make it out here anymore."

Luke sat on a metal bench. "Why not?"

She sat up straight as she could in the tray. "He had a stroke last summer, and he'd been doing so well, but now . . . " She wiped her eyes again. "He and Mom have split up and he's worse than ever." She spread out her arms. "This place is the key. He needs to come here to be healed. He needs to come here to find hope again. They need to come here to restore their marriage. It's where they fell in love. But"—she pointed to the rutted path leading back to the cabin—"with Dad using a walker, I can't imagine him making it out here."

The Beaumonts were breaking up? But they'd always seemed so perfect together. "I'm so sorry, Jess." He rested his hand on her shoulder as a gesture of support, not attraction. "Is there anything I can do to help?"

She stared out at the water, the breeze rustling her blonde locks, then turned to him. "I know we've just become reacquainted, but I need someone's help fixing up this place, sprucing up the cabin for Mom, rejuvenating the gardens, making the cabin and path handicap-accessible for Dad. Would you help me?"

"Of course, I would." The words hurried from Luke's mouth before he had time to think. If she wanted this place fixed up, no way would she ever sell. Dad was not going to be happy.

"Thank you, thank you! I could kiss you." She blew him a kiss instead, and he pretended to catch it and patted it to his cheek.

Keep the main thing the main thing. Dad's voice intruded.

"And if we get this fixed up, if I can freshen the gardens, they'll fall in love all over again."

And by helping Jess, Luke would ruin any chance he had of getting that promotion.

"SEE YOU SHORTLY." JESS ended her phone call to Callie as Luke pulled his pickup next to the hospital's emergency room entrance. "When Callie's fiancé gets home, she'll come stay with me, so you don't have to stick around." As much as she'd enjoyed this day with Luke, she hated hospitals. She just wanted to get in, get fixed, and go home.

Luke put his truck into park. "And that would be how long?"

"Not sure." Jess shrugged. "Today."

"And leave you here by yourself? That doesn't sound very knight-like. Besides, I'm looking forward to my ice cream reward." He opened his door. "You wait here while I retrieve your chariot."

She giggled. "You're not going to carry me?"

His eyebrows rose, and he smirked. "If that's what you want . . . "

She gave him a shove. "Go get my chariot, Sir Luke. I shall await you here."

"As you wish." He winked and hurried into the hospital. A few minutes later, he returned with a wheelchair. He opened her door and assisted her into the chair. "A warning, milady, these chariots have been known to pop a wheelie on occasion. You should prepare yourself, just in case."

The pain and throbbing had faded, and she could probably put some weight on her foot now, but Jess wasn't going to admit that to Luke. Besides, she had to hold up her end of the bargain. See a doctor, then treat Luke to a three-scoop sundae. Whoever would have figured a downed tree and a bruised foot would lead to such a fun day?

Hopefully, not the only day spent with Luke. He had promised to help her fix up the cabin, but what was he supposed to say at that moment she'd asked him for help? She'd unfairly cornered him.

"By the way, I—" She squealed as he popped a wheelie going through the automatic doors. Maybe hospitals weren't so bad after all.

"You were saying?" He lowered the chair after others in the room sent disapproving glares his way.

She giggled. "Is life always an adventure with you?"

"Ha!" He snorted while steering the wheelchair between rows of filled chairs. The wait to see a doctor was going to be forever. "My life is dreadfully mundane. You have infused this day with color. It's not every day I get to hold funeral services for a family of invading mice."

"You've certainly done more than your share, and I wish to release you of your promise to help with the cabin, Sir Luke. You have served me well."

"A gentleman never reneges on his promises." He wheeled her to a check-in window. "I'll be over there." He gestured to an empty seat by a children's play area. "Signal me when you're ready."

He walked away.

And she sighed. Was it possible to fall in love in one afternoon? She couldn't recall ever being made to feel so special, and with no reciprocation required. In her former life as a model, every favor had a quid pro quo attached.

She filled out forms and the person at check-in informed her that the wait to see a doctor could be up to two hours. Yippee. She motioned for Luke to come get her.

He parked her beside his chair.

"You don't have to wait, you know. I'm fine here." She dug her phone out of her purse and brought up her Kindle app. "I always have a book to keep me occupied."

He crossed his arms and shook his head. Then covered a yawn.

Which she echoed as she leaned back in the chair. Only then did she really take a look at the man beside her, a stranger, but a true gentleman who hadn't thought twice about messing up his church clothes, whose droopy eyes and yawning mouth indicated it had been a long day for him, and yet, here he was.

Besides Haven, had Jess ever known a man who would make such a sacrifice? Unfortunately, not even her dad would have done the same. He loved her and Callie, yet many of his actions were selfish, probably stemming from a career alongside Mom in front of the TV camera where life was about them only. Was ego the root cause of her parents' break-up? If so, how could their self-centeredness be broken without irreparably damaging their relationship?

It all came back to the cabin and flowers and chocolate and breathing new life into their romance.

A familiar Skillet tune played on Luke's phone. So, they even enjoyed the same type of music.

He looked at his phone and scowled. "Sorry. Gotta take this." He raised the phone to his ear and said without warmth and devoid of emotion, "Dad." And with that, the funny, easy-going gentleman morphed into an uptight businessman. Shoulders squared, chin raised, cheeks taut, eyes focused on the wall opposite them. "Give me a second."

Luke stood and looked down at Jess, no smile, no hint of the knight-in-dress-pants. "Be right back."

She closed the Kindle app and checked her messages. Nothing yet from Callie. Nothing from her mom either. She wiggled her toes and tried putting a little weight on her foot. A tingling of pain, but not the fall-on-the-ground type of pain she'd had earlier. Maybe she should leave. Not waste the doctor's, or Luke's, time. But what if her foot was broken? Sprained? What if she needed surgery? Or crutches? How would she ever get any work done at the cabin? Argh!

Callie would tell her, give it up to God. Being a newbie Christian, Jess still hadn't learned how to do that. She liked to grip all her problems tightly and solve them herself. Like that had ever done her any good.

She reopened her Kindle app and continued reading a book she'd recently downloaded. After several minutes, Luke returned, but he wasn't the same affable man she'd spent time with today. Rather, he focused on his phone, scrolling through messages, thumbing out return messages. She didn't know him well enough to ask what was wrong, did she?

Didn't matter. She laid her hand on his as it ferociously typed out a message. "Can I ask what's wrong?"

He startled, dropped the phone on the carpet, and let loose a curse word. "Sorry," he mumbled and picked up his phone. "Just work."

"Work? Besides the candy store?"

"Ha. I wish." He jabbed at the phone, put it to sleep, and pocketed it. He rolled his shoulders. "Nothing I want to burden you with."

"Okay . . . " But after all he'd done for her, she'd gladly listen to him. Still, the knight who'd spent the day with her had vanished.

Two hours later, after seeing the doctor and getting X-rays, she was diagnosed with a bruised foot and prescribed R.I.C.E. Rest, Ice, Compression, and Elevation, exactly what Luke had done for her. Even though his easy-going charm had been stolen by that phone call, he was still here with her.

"Jess?"

She startled and looked to her right. Callie and Haven hurried toward her. She glanced between them both. "Isn't someone with Dad?"

Callie sighed and dropped down in an empty chair across from Jess, her normally smiling eyes downturned. "Mom is. And she has more news for us."

News that clearly wasn't happy. Suddenly, going home sounded a lot worse than staying at the hospital.

Chapter Four

He was a Class-A jerk. Luke pounded his steering wheel as he squealed away from the hospital parking lot without collecting his promised sundae. Would that still happen? He sure hoped he hadn't blown it.

But for now, he couldn't wait to get to Gran's store and collapse on the bed in his closet of a bedroom. That room—Gran's home—had always been a place of respite for him, where expectations were high, but served with love, and smiles were frequent and genuine.

But he couldn't possibly force a smile after his dad called asking for an update. Luke had six months to go at Gran's, and his dad wanted an update on a Sunday on Luke's first day in the area? He hadn't even had a moment to move his stuff into Gran's apartment yet, much less contact Bettis about selling his property.

Boy, that commandment about honoring your father and mother had to be the most difficult commandment to keep. What in the world did it mean anyway? That he blindly follow everything his dad said? Probably not, but still, Luke had caved and spilled all about his afternoon connection with Jess Beaumont as if he had helped her out merely as a means to purchase the property easier and cheaper.

Jerk!

And after all that, did his dad say, "Thank you," or did he offer any encouragement or offer a pat on the back for a job well done? Luke snorted. When would he stop expecting the impossible?

To help unknot his tension-strained back, he turned on the local

Christian station and sang along with the artist. God didn't care that Luke couldn't sing on key, He heard what was in Luke's heart. Wasn't that how loving fathers were supposed to feel? God should send Luke's dad a text. Maybe then the man would listen.

He rotated his shoulders and relegated thoughts of his dad and his Harrison Property assignment to tomorrow's agenda. Or maybe even Tuesday's. Give him a little time to get settled in before going to work.

He belted out praise songs for the next twenty minutes, until he arrived at the store. Evening shadows had settled on the front entrance, making it look forlorn as if disappointed that little kids hadn't come to visit. This place hungered for life.

And Luke fully intended to bring it back to life. Gran would want that. No, running the store hadn't been part of the will's stipulation, but he couldn't imagine living here without opening the store again, even if it ate up every cent of his savings.

He climbed onto the white-spindled porch and put his hand on one of the railings. It moved, and he jerked his hand away. That was a lawsuit waiting to happen. Job number one would be to replace it with a new railing. He eyeballed the chipping white paint. That needed a good sanding and a fresh paint job. Then there was the potholed parking lot. His savings were definitely going to take a hit, and that was just from the building's exterior. He dreaded what he'd find inside.

His heart ramped into overdrive as he put the key into the store door. It had been years since he'd been here, and he didn't have a good reason why. Only that he'd been "busy" with Harrison Property Development, doing peon work for his dad.

Gran must have been so disappointed in him.

And now he'd never be able to tell her how much he loved her, how much he needed her in his life. He wiped at his nose. God must have needed a master chocolatier in Heaven.

He took a breath, opened the door, and a stale scent rushed past him, not unlike the stench at the cabin. Like people, buildings didn't like to be closed up and unused. Still, he shut the door and locked it because the second a traveler saw the door open, they'd stop in to make a purchase.

But nothing was left. Not even a stale piece of chocolate. Gran had passed away during tourist offseason, which meant the store had been closed when she died. The shelves and glass display were bare but for a month's worth of dust. A plastic cover was draped over the candy scale. Looked like a fairly new one too. Would be a shame not to use it.

This place needed to see families and preschool groups and couples seeking romance. Even if it lasted only six months. With the help of Gran's long-time friend and employee, Luke would make that happen.

Tomorrow he'd give Mary Obermiller a call and find out what needed to be done to get the store up and running again, beyond the necessary changes to the building.

He went behind the glass display. Tucked beneath the counter were empty candy boxes waiting to be filled, plus a stack of Granisms, wisdom his gran had voiced over the years that another wise person had decided to write down and share with the customers. One Granism had gone into every box of Gran's Goodies, a one-pound box of mixed chocolates, and the customers had loved it.

They would again.

He shuffled through the stack of calligraphied cardstock. "Nobody's perfect, but Jesus loves you just as you are." Very true. Luke was loved. He just forgot it at times. Ah, here was one that fit Jess Beaumont to a T: "A strong woman can handle problems on her own; a wise woman knows to accept offered help." How many women had he met in business who were insulted by his offerings of help? Far too many, his older sister included. Maybe that Granism had been voiced specifically for Lydia.

But Jess? She definitely wasn't a wimp, yet she'd graciously accepted his help. And he'd abandoned her the second Callie and her fiancé walked into the waiting room. Okay, maybe he hadn't exactly abandoned her. He had been with her all day, but the way he'd departed seemed too abrupt. Tomorrow he'd give her a call to check up on her foot, remind her that she owed him a triple-scoop sundae.

That returned his smile quicker than his dad had stolen it.

He set down the Granism cards and walked through the back of the shop. The huge copper kettle was there waiting to have more chocolate stirred. The metal shelves begged to hold trays of goodies.

But the hardwood floors needed sanding and polishing, the walls a paint job, the ceiling a good scraping and a new layer of paint. All cosmetic. All something he could handle on his own. Maybe he'd bring in a cleaning company to scrub every inch of the place so the health department would have no complaints.

The costs kept adding up.

What would Dad say about Luke pouring money into the old place? Foolishness. And a complete waste of money.

Made Luke even more eager to breathe life into this place.

He checked the little office beneath the stairs. Gran had fit perfectly, but she'd been five-foot-nothing. At six feet, Luke would be eating his knees if he attempted to squeeze into the room. His niece would love it. Maybe he'd make it into a playroom for her. He'd find a different space for the office.

All in all, though, getting this place up and running shouldn't be difficult, and he could do much of the work on his own, having spent several summers doing construction.

Thunder rattled the windows, and he peeked out the back door. Sure enough, dark, fast-moving clouds were sweeping toward the lake. Sweet! He thought he'd missed out when storms hit the area last night.

But first he had to get his stuff into the apartment. Thunder clapped again, telling Luke to hurry.

He hustled outside, drove his pickup around the back, and parked near the apartment entrance. As a kid, he'd thought Gran living above a candy store was the coolest thing ever. Okay, maybe he still felt the same way.

Light raindrops came down as he unloaded his pickup and piled his belongings into the stairway leading up to Gran's—his—apartment. Before carrying everything up the stairs, he surveyed what would be his home for the next six months.

Size-wise, it compared to his now-sublet condo in Minneapolis, but that was where the comparisons ended. His condo was barely two years old, this place over a century. His condo was decorated with black leather, and Gran's with floral furnishings. No way was he keeping that, no matter how much it reminded him of her. Her furniture would go into storage for six months. After that he'd sell it—rather, give it away. People wouldn't pay good money for those old pieces, would they?

The appliances and dishes, pots, and pans would suffice for the little cooking he did. So what if the fridge and stove were a putrid shade of green?

Like downstairs, the place could use a good paint job. Something other than its current sunbeam yellow. The color had made Gran happy, but would drive Luke to the funny farm.

Lightning flashed outside the window. Thunder followed several seconds later, telling Luke the storm was miles away yet. Still, he wanted to be settled in his room before the rain and winds pounded the lake. Just a quick tour through the small apartment, then he'd get cozy in what would be his bedroom for the next six months, until mid-November at least.

Against the north wall of the living room sat the dollhouse Lydia had inherited. Two floors, each large enough for a Barbie doll to stand. Six wallpapered rooms that still housed Gramps' homemade doll furniture. The entire piece was a treasure. Lydia should be grateful for the gift. Her daughter certainly would be. Kitty Cat loved playing make-believe with her uncle. And, yeah, Luke would enjoy playing make-believe too. He loved that little squirt.

He checked Gran's bedroom with the white wrought-iron bed and the frilly bedspread. The bedspread would go—Lydia might like it—but he wouldn't get rid of the bed. He doubted he'd ever be able to sleep there though.

On the round end table, covered with a top-to-floor embroidered tablecloth, was Gran's Bible. Sighing, he picked it up and sniffed it. Still smelled like Gran. He flipped through its highlighted and underlined pages and read Gran's thoughts in the margins, then clutched it to his heart. This was the true treasure, and it torqued him off that Tim was gifted with this heirloom. Luke's younger brother had never made time for church or Bible reading, which was probably why Gran had given it to him. The question was, would Tim keep it or throw it away? If Luke even hinted at how important this book was to him, Tim would toss it. No doubt about that.

The best way to give Tim the Bible would be to not show how much it meant to him.

Rain now pattered on the roof, so Luke hurried from Gran's room, scanned the tiny bathroom with its shower built for munchkins—that would be a trial these next months—and checked out his bedroom, if you could call it that. A double bed took up nearly the entire room. Lydia would complain that it was too small for a closet. For all her girl stuff, that was probably true. But for him, all he needed was a bed, a pillow, and a blanket, and he'd sleep sound as a baby on a car ride. With rain coming down, nothing was more relaxing. As Gran had always told him, a man is blessed if he has food in his belly and a roof over his head.

This was the perfect prescription to his Dad-induced stress.

But first he had to bring all his boxes upstairs. Tomorrow, he'd unpack and figure out what else he needed. A peal of thunder coincided with his stomach growl. Groceries topped the necessity list. After carting his belongings upstairs, he found a can of Campbell's noodle soup in the cupboard, nuked it, and downed it in less than a minute, leaving him still hungry. That ice cream sundae sure sounded good right now.

Instead he grabbed a bottled water from his cooler. That would have to hold him for tonight.

He brought the water to his bedroom and reached across the bed to the dormer in which he'd spent so much of his childhood reading or watching storms like this one. Stress slid off him as he crossed his legs in the dormer and watched rain beat the lake. But Superior fought back with waves that crazy area surfers loved. He took a drink of his water and wiped at a drip on his knee.

Wait. On his knee?

There was another one.

His gaze slid from his knee upward to where the dormer edge met the slanting roof line. Right where a stream of water coursed its way downward.

Enjoy a stress-free evening? Ha! Was that too much to ask? Massaging the back of his neck, he hurried to the kitchen to find buckets and towels.

He mentally added another costly line item to his repair budget. He could hear his dad warning him to not throw his money away, so tonight he'd pray that it would be an inexpensive fix.

But his gut told him this was a budget-busting repair.

He'd find out the truth tomorrow.

WHO KNEW CRUTCHING UP steps would be so difficult? Jess grunted and hopped up the second step toward her home's back foyer. Her heart pumped with exertion. Just three steps into the house, and she was this exhausted? This put her dad's struggles into a whole new perspective.

"You doing okay?" She felt Haven's hand on her back, steadying her.

"I'm good." If her dad could manage with his stroke-paralyzed half, she could certainly climb the stairs with mostly-healthy limbs. And she'd do it without complaining. Another change from her before-Jesus attitude. She steadied herself and, using a crutch and the stair railing for support, she hopped up the final step. She would no longer take healthy limbs for granted.

Nor would she take a happy and healthy family for granted anymore. With both her mom and dad here, that would give them an opportunity to begin the mending process.

She made her way into the dining room where her parents awaited, both seated in their usual chairs opposite each other. But both were silent, and Dad didn't even look up as she, Callie, and Haven entered. Typically, he'd greet them with a smile and shake Haven's hand, but he acted as if he didn't know he had company. Mom's lips pinched while staring at Jess's crutches. It wasn't like Jess wanted to drop a tree on her foot. Sheesh. This was a few-day setback. Not a big deal.

Jess met her mom's gaze and flinched. Red-veined eyes stared back at Jess. Had her never-show-emotions mother been crying?

The separation clearly hurt her, a sign that getting back together with Dad wasn't impossible.

Hope stirred in Jess's gut as Haven pulled out Jess's chair beside Mom. He helped Jess sit, then did the same for Callie, across from Jess. Before his stroke, Dad had always done the same for Mom.

Mom's eyebrows raised above her bloodshot eyes when Haven also took a seat. Family meetings were not to include friends or boyfriends, which probably meant Callie was going to break their good news. Yay! She'd removed her ring before walking into the room, and Jess had wondered if they were putting off the announcement until tensions eased a bit. But maybe an engagement announcement would be the beginning of drawing their parents back together.

"Now that you're all here." Mom flipped over a stack of papers. "Your father—"

Callie loudly cleared her throat. "I have something to say, first."

"Callista, that was rude." Mom's lips pinched even tighter.

"No." Callie crossed her arms. "Rude was dropping off Dad without a comment and letting him bear the brunt of your decision alone."

Whoa, Callie. Where had Miss Assertive come from?

"Haven and I have some news too." Callie took Haven's arm. "We debated whether to make the announcement at this time, but figured we weren't going to let your decision influence our future." She raised her hand above the table and held it in Mom's direction while Haven put his arm around Callie's shoulders. The diamond created an array of rainbow sparkles throughout the room. "With Dad's blessing, Haven and I are getting married."

Mom blinked and then smiled. Dad looked up and his eyes had a glint to them, rather than the dull fog that had covered them these past hours. Yes! Their engagement was going to be the seed putting

Operation: Planting Hope into motion!

"Con...gratula...tions." Dad stumbled through, but finished showing the first smile she'd seen from him all weekend. "I'm proud to c...call you s...son."

"Thank you, sir, that means a lot." Haven reached in front of Callie, and Dad did his best to extend his right hand.

Mom sighed. Were those tears in her eyes? "This is very good news." Mom nodded, still smiling. "Very good news indeed." She looked between the couple. "Have you set a date?" She got up and retrieved her smart phone. "There's so much I need to do."

"October eighth," Callie squeaked out.

"Oh, that's perfect. A full seventeen months to prepare." Mom typed into her phone.

"No, not next year, Mom, this year. This fall."

The phone fell from Mom's hand and clattered onto the floor. The grandfather clock ticked off otherwise silent seconds. "This. Fall," Mom muttered and fired her gaze at Callie. "Even with my influence, getting the best venues at that time will be an impossibility. You need to wait."

Jess snorted then slapped a hand over her mouth.

Even Callie let out a muffled chuckle. "You don't have to worry about the church or the reception hall. We've got it taken care of."

"You do?" Mom's eyes brightened. "But what about caterer and orchestra. Flowers. Photog—"

"Whoa." Callie held up her hands, and nibbled on her lower lip. "I know this isn't what you'd plan, but we want a small ceremony at the cabin. At sunrise."

More silent seconds ticked off. Mom's face reddened with each second, and Dad seemed to draw into himself even more, with his chin tucked, shoulders drooped, and eyes downcast. Couldn't they be happy for Callie? Jess wanted to scream out, "What's wrong with them having a small wedding?" but as the don't-make-waves daughter, she remained silent.

"Well." Her mom's pinched lips returned, and she drummed her fingernails on the table. "I'm afraid that won't work. Your wedding could be the talk of the city, so it will not take place at the cabin. Besides, by October the cabin should be sold, along with this house."

"Wait . . . what?" Jess finally found her voice. "You're selling the house and cabin?"

"If Callista hadn't interrupted, you would know that by now."

Jess leaned toward her mom, anger fueling the fire in her gut. "Well, maybe not everything is about you."

"Since when do you disrespect me, Jessica Rose?"

Haven cleared his throat. "Mrs. and Mr. Beaumont, may I say something?"

Mom gave an exaggerated roll of her eyes, but nodded. And Dad, he just sat there, unmoving as if he knew nothing he said would matter. But it did matter, to her and to Callie and Haven. And even Mom, though right now the stubborn woman wouldn't admit it.

"As a disclaimer, I'm obviously going to take Callie's side." Haven folded his hands on the table, his voice a soothing balm. The man could have been a diplomat. No wonder he excelled as a collection agent, the full-time job he used to supplement his income until his photography business took off. "I realize this is a difficult and stressful time for all of you. As I know from my own broken relationship with my son's mother, everyone has an opinion, a perspective, that's important to be heard. I'd be glad to mediate your discussion, if you'll allow me." He looked directly at Mom.

Who nodded. "If that will help our discourse, we'll accept your offer."

"Mr. Beaumont?"

Dad raised his head, but his glazed eyes showed disinterest. Or was it defeat?

Haven took Callie's hand. "Your input, Mr. Beaumont, is valuable to us. None of us can imagine what you're going through, so forgive us for overlooking your concerns."

And with that, Dad seemed to sit taller, and his eyes became brighter. "Thank...you, son."

"Let's begin with Mrs. Beaumont." Haven gestured to her. "Tell us about the home and cabin sales, and the reasoning behind it."

Even Mom seemed to sit taller and appeared less fatigued. "It doesn't take a genius to realize that with Kenneth's disability, caring for our house and for the cabin is no longer feasible. As much as I love this house, and the history behind the cabin, the upkeep simply adds more stress to an already impossible situation. As for this house, with Callie's upcoming marriage, and Jessica's previously-expressed desire to move out on her own, I see no need to keep this monster of a home any longer."

"But what about—"

Haven raised a hand, cutting Jess off. "I promise, you'll have your say."

"Okay." She'd have to trust Haven to be fair.

"Please continue, Mrs. Beaumont."

Please. Mom may as well have stuck out her tongue and said, "Na na na na na na."

"Thank you, Haven." Mom's gaze softened as she looked at Dad out of the corner of her eye. "I've located a senior care center for Kenneth that will help with rehabilitation. And I've begun searching for a condo on the water for myself. In the meantime, I'll stay with your Aunt Tib. Now about the wedding—"

Again, Haven held up his hand. "Before we talk wedding, does anyone want to respond to the house sale?"

"Yes." Dad gripped his cane. "M...Mackenzie is right. C...caring for m...me...house...cabin is too m...much."

What? Jess looked between her parents, willing them to fight. She gave an exaggerated sigh, but pursed her lips in quiet.

"Mr. Beaumont, you're fine with going to a care center?"

"No. I'm t...too young." The words struggled from his mouth. "B...but I can't m...make it on m...my own right now."

Maybe not, but just because Mom wouldn't be around to care for him, didn't mean the rest of the family had to give up. Jess raised her hand. "May I say something?"

"Go ahead." Haven nodded to her.

Jess reached across the table and took her dad's wilted hand, though her natural reaction was to reach for his healthy hand. She really wanted to smother him with a hug, let him know he was loved. "Dad, maybe there's another option. Instead of staying at a rehab center, could I bring you to Superior Suites with me every day? Since Callie's now working at Gooseberry full time, Superior could really use you. And your physical therapy office isn't too far from there either. I'd be glad to drive you there every day, and if I can't for some reason, I'll find someone to take you."

"Great idea, Jess." Callie nodded to her sister. "On weekends, I'll give Jess a break and you and I can hang out."

"B...but—"

"Nope." Jess interrupted. "You'd tell us, 'No buts.' We want to do this for you." Besides, having Dad help out at the office meant she could spend more time at the cabin. "Mom, I don't know much about care centers, but aren't they expensive? We'd save a lot of money if he stayed at home."

Mom drummed her nails on the table. "True, but what will you girls do when the house sells?"

Good question. Jess understood selling this house, but it did leave her with a housing problem. "I guess we'll figure that out." For Callie, moving in with Haven before they were married wasn't an option.

"If I may offer a solution," Haven said. "Callie and I have been looking at houses. Our original plan had been for me to move in alone prior to our marriage, but instead I can remain at Dad's, and Callie can move into whatever we purchase."

Callie took Haven's hand. "Our home will be open to Jess and Dad, too."

"Not happening." Jess shook her head. "Living with a newlywed couple? No way. Like Mom said earlier, maybe it's time I found my own place." On her wages at Superior Suites, though, she'd be lucky to find a studio apartment. That would hardly have room for her clothes.

Their mom's fingernails clicked an erratic rhythm on the table. "I guess we have everything figured out. Now all I have to do is put the house and cabin on the market."

"Just the house." Jess blurted out then winced. Her shoulders hunched, she glanced at Haven. "Sorry, is it my turn?"

He laughed. "I think we're safe to move on to the cabin."

"Okay." Jess cleared her throat. "I understand the cabin needs a lot of work, and it takes a lot of time and money to keep it up, but it's been in the Beaumont family for three generations. It belongs in our family."

Mom's lips pinched again. "Kenneth, would you care to respond?"

Selling was Dad's idea? He loved the cabin too.

"Too much w...work," he said, his focus on the table.

"I can handle it."

"Really, now?" Her mom nodded to the crutches leaning against Jess's chair. "And how did that work out for you?"

"The work all got done." Thanks to a handsome candy man. But if not for the bruised foot, she could have handled it on her own.

"We'll help too." Callie exchanged a glance with Haven, who nodded.

"No." Mother waved her hand. "With everything else, I don't want to deal with it. It's got to go, and you'll have to find a different locale for your wedding."

"Fine," Callie said with far more snark than Jess had ever heard from her sister. "Haven and I will elope and you won't have to worry about a thing."

"You would be that selfish?" Mom stopped clicking her nails.

"When it comes to my wedding, yes, I would be."

Haven put his arm around Callie's wilting shoulders. "I've got to stand with Callie. If having the wedding at the cabin is too much trouble, we'd rather elope. For us, it's not about the wedding ceremony, but the marriage. I don't care where we exchange our vows, just that we do."

Exactly. It was all about the marriage. Jess's parents' marriage. Which was why the cabin needed to remain in the family. Without it, Operation: Planting Hope would be a failure before she planted one seed.

Jess splayed her hands on the table as if laying out all her cards. "Give me five months. Until after the wedding. I'll whip the cabin into shape and plant new gardens." She concentrated on her dad, hoping to appeal to his emotional attachment to the cabin. "If you still want to sell it, go ahead, but give me a chance to show you I can handle the work."

Her mom's fingernails began their drumbeat again. "Until the wedding."

"Yes, until the wedding."

"You have five months, and not a day more."

Yes! Jess pumped her fist beneath the table. Five months would be more than enough time to whip the cabin and gardens into shape, and if she planted her seeds right, her parents' marriage would grow stronger than ever.

She'd begin tomorrow after work, with a trip to the candy store, the place her parents first met.

Hopefully, she'd run into Luke too.

Chapter Five

Luke aligned the final baluster of his new porch railing, and screwed it tight to the top and bottom rails. He stepped back and eyeballed the railing then gave it a tug. Not a wiggle. He'd like to see his dad do that. Ha! Next up was the paint job, beginning with a good pressure wash. If he could get that done today, along with some sanding and scraping, he'd be happy. And it would keep his mind off his desk job and the stress that went along with it. He had six months to purchase the land Dad wanted, so it didn't need to be done today. No matter what his dad would say.

There was something liberating about working with your hands, creating something from scratch. Thanks to Gran for encouraging him to learn beyond the four walls of his office. When he'd stayed the summers here, when he'd complained about the menial jobs like washing dishes, mopping the floor, pounding the occasional nail or two, she'd often repeated, "The best employers are those who've walked in their employee's shoes." Back then those words hadn't meant anything to him.

Finally, as an adult, he got it. He'd turned down his dad's offer to pay for college, only if he attended St. Thomas, Dad's alma mater. Instead, he went to the University of Minnesota, paying his way through by doing construction. That certainly hadn't helped his relationship with his father, but subcontractors hired for Harrison Property Development respected him because he understood their job from ground level. His siblings couldn't say the same.

He rewarded himself with a swig of lemonade.

"Hope you got something stronger than lemonade in that drink." The roofer handed Luke a paper with a budget-smashing figure on it. Couple that with the quote he'd received earlier in the morning for parking lot repair—not replace—and his savings account would soon be emptier than a dry well.

"You sure know how to hurt a guy." Luke slapped the quote in his hand. "This is for a full tear-off and re-shingle. What's wrong with doing a repair for now, doing the whole roof later?" Once he actually had some money coming in. Or, assuming Gran's store would eventually be torn down—the thought alone made his heart hurt—a full repair would be a complete waste of money.

"No can do." The roofer crossed his arms. "That'd be like putting a Band-Aid on a broken leg. I patch that part of the roof, and tomorrow you'd have another part leaking. I won't do a halfway job."

Luke puffed out a long breath of air. His dad would tell him not to throw away money, and to tear down this place. Sure, financially that would make sense, but bringing Gran's store back to life was about more than financial health. Besides, what else was Luke going to do with all his savings? He already had everything he needed, all except for the leak-free roof over his head. "When can you get to it?"

"Tomorrow. You caught me in between jobs."

Thank God for small blessings. He dug his credit card from his wallet for the down payment. The roof job meant putting off exterior painting for a couple of days, so he'd spend his time making the interior sparkle instead.

First, though, he had to advertise to potential customers that the store was currently closed, but would soon be opening. The little closed sign in the window wouldn't suffice. In the garage, he found a four-foot by two-foot scrap piece of plywood, plus leftover red and white paint. Perfect. He laid the plywood on the workbench and coated it with white paint. Waiting for that to dry, he went inside the store, found his Spotify playlist on his phone, and broadcast it through small but powerful speakers. Gran always said, "Music makes everything better." She'd say the same about chocolate and flowers. Who was he to argue with that wisdom?

He opened every window in the store to air it out, then set about cleaning. First the customer area, followed by the back-of-the-store candy-making area. The walls and ceiling could use a fresh coat of paint, and the floors a good sanding and re-staining, but the floors could wait until after Christmas when the shop closed for the season.

Assuming the store didn't belong to his dad by Christmas.

Just like that, tension zinged up his spine. *Stop it, Luke. No Dad-talking, remember?*

He hurried back to the garage and tested the paint on the sign. Dry enough for his purpose. Using a two-by-four as a guide, he painted on the words: Opening Soon! Simple, but effective. He rigged up a stand for the sign and set it up at the top of the porch steps, blocking the deck entrance. Now he could leave the front door open, so lake breezes would cross through the back door and out through the front.

With that taken care of, he could begin sanding.

Humming along to the music, he climbed a stepladder and scraped loose paint from the ceiling in the customer area of the store. A knock sounded behind him, and he startled. He grabbed window molding to keep from falling, then looked back to see who had circumvented his Opening Soon sign.

A John Deere-capped man dressed in jeans and a flannel shirt, probably his dad's age, stood in the open doorway. The man looked familiar, but Luke wasn't certain from where.

"Can I help you?" Luke climbed down the ladder, but didn't offer his hand. Instead, he clutched the scraper, just in case.

"You Gran's kid?" The man hooked his thumbs in his belt loops.

"Grandson. And you?"

"You the one who inherited this place?"

Luke stood still, hoping his body language didn't give away any information. The man offered his hand. "Name's Roland Bettis. I'm a neighbor of your gran's."

Okay, that was why he looked familiar. Luke shook Roland's hand.

"Welcome, neighbor."

"I see you're fixing the place up. The store needed a lot of TLC Gran wasn't able to give it."

Sure, play the guilt card right off the bat. "Is there something I could help you with?" He raised his scraper. "I'm a bit busy right now."

"Perhaps I'll save you a bit of work, son. I stopped by to make an offer on this land, one you won't be able to refuse."

Luke laughed. So, Bettis was jumping right in, no small talk before negotiations began. Well, Luke would do the same. "Like Gran told you, the answer's *no*. Matter of fact." Luke crossed his arms. "I plan on purchasing your land from you."

"That's how you're gonna play this."

"Yep." Luke nodded to the door. "If you wouldn't mind, I'm getting Superior Sweets in tiptop shape. Sales are going to be hopping this summer."

Bettis tipped his hat. "We'll see about that. Have a good day." And the man walked out of the store, knocked over the Opening Soon sign, got in his mid-life crisis convertible, and zoomed off.

Have a good day. Huh! The man had stolen all the goodness from it. Luke needed to get this store open and selling chocolate by next week and start paying back his investment. That wouldn't entice Bettis to sell, but success would sure compel Luke to keep the store. After all, if he couldn't get Bettis to sell, this store was going to be Luke's career. Didn't matter what happened with the Beaumont land.

He reset the sign, and shut the door this time, hoping to discourage more uninvited guests. Finally, he climbed back up on the ladder and continued scraping peeling paint.

Again, someone knocked on the door, and it opened. Why hadn't he locked it too? "What now?" he growled as he turned around, then wished he could swallow his words.

Miss Jess Beaumont was certainly a day brightener, even with the wrapped foot and crutches.

He climbed down the ladder once again, lowered the volume on his music, and bowed. "Welcome to my humble abode, milady."

And she giggled the entrancing giggle. Yep, definitely a day brightener.

"What brings you to my chocolateless home?"

She pouted. "Not even a sucker?"

"Not even a chocolate chip. Probably nothing until next week. But"—He wiped his hands on his pants—"I do recall a certain damsel promising me a triple-scoop ice cream sundae, and I plan on collecting."

"Hmmm." She tapped her chin. "I've come with a request, but requests are always better over ice cream, wouldn't you say?"

"Every time. Let me lock up, and I'll chauffeur you to town." He'd told her he didn't have any suckers. Well, that was a lie, because he was a sucker for whatever request she had for him. Whatever the question, the answer would undoubtedly be 'Whatever you wish.'

JESS GAVE LUKE HER hand, and he assisted her out of the pickup onto the ice cream shop's parking lot. Did he have an angle behind his gentlemanly behavior? Did he want something from her? That had certainly been her experience with men in the past.

He handed her the crutches and walked beside her into the shop.

Yet, she didn't feel that user vibe from him, unlike every other guy she'd dated. Not that she and Luke were dating or anything, but Jess hoped Luke was different. Being attracted to a non-user likely meant she'd changed too.

"After you." He opened the door and gestured toward the inside. Sugary, chocolate sweetness swept past her nostrils and made her mouth water. It was over-indulging at places like this that had cost her her modeling career. Funny thing was, she didn't miss it. Too many demands with very little satisfaction. She had never pleased anyone, especially her agent, and she was much happier now that she'd said good riddance to that career. Surprisingly, she found maintaining her preferred weight was easier now than when she'd fretted over every calorie.

Still, she planned to not go overboard here. She aimed for the order counter with three lines all five-people deep, and felt a hand on her shoulder.

"I'll get your order." He nodded toward the dining area. "You go sit."

"Gladly." She dug into her purse and pulled out a twenty.

He gently pushed away her hand. "Now how chivalrous would I be if I allowed you to pay for my ice cream?"

She shoved the money back. "That was part of our deal. You free the throne from the dastardly mouse family, and I treat you to ice cream. And I won't say no."

"Hmph." He was frowning, but took the money anyway. "I wonder what Gran would say about this."

"She'd say that a good young man always keeps his promises."

"Right before she'd say, 'A gallant knight always pays for ice cream.'"

"I guess you have a conundrum."

"Yes, yes I do." He grinned. "Especially since I don't even know what you want."

"Oh . . . " Guess that would help. She studied the menu on the wall and swore she felt drool dribbling down her chin. They might have to make coming here a weekly occurrence so she could sample everything on the menu. For now, she'd go with her can't-go-wrong favorite. "I'll have a chocolate-chip cookie-dough hot-fudge sundae. One scoop."

"Two." He held up two fingers. "One is barely a taste."

"And *two* will end up on my hips. Actually, *one* will end up on my hips, but I've got to live a little bit."

"One it is, but you're missing out."

She flung the back of her hand against her forehead. "Ah, the sacrifices we women make to keep our girlish figures."

He coughed. "Darlin', the last word I'd use to describe your figure is girlish." His face suddenly went rose red. He scratched the back of his neck and cleared his throat. "Um, I'm . . . "

"Adorable?" Oh, yeah. That fit. She nodded to the worker waiting at the counter. "I think she's ready to take your order." Hiding a smile,

Jess aimed for the dining area. Technically, this wasn't a date, but it sure felt like one, and she would not object to him using that term. She sat at a table and elevated her bruised foot on another chair.

Luke wasn't a user, of that she was certain.

But what about her?

Wasn't she taking advantage of his goodness? As much as she needed his help at the cabin, she didn't want him to feel obligated, especially when he had a store to get up and running. Though he'd said moments ago that he didn't go back on promises, she'd graciously let him out of this one.

A few minutes later, Luke arrived carrying two sundaes, and neither of them had just one scoop. She gave Luke the stink eye. "I said *one* scoop."

He raised his hands. "And that's what I asked for. Honest. But the ice cream artist oopsed and gave you two instead."

"Well, then you'll be eating four scoops of ice cream."

"You say that like it's a hardship." Eyes twinkling, he scooped an overflowing spoonful of hot fudge, walnuts, caramel, a cherry, and probably some ice cream, into his mouth. "Mmm, mmm. That is just what I needed after a hard day's work."

She took a much smaller bite, but her eyes rolled back from the flavor explosion. She spooned a second, larger scoop. "Um, what I said about having leftovers . . . "

"Uh, uh. No going back on your word. That extra scoop is mine." He aimed his spoon toward her sundae.

She knocked his spoon with hers. "Not if I eat it first."

He leaned back in his chair, the sundae in his hand, a lazy smile on his face. "Thank you."

"I'll remind you, I paid for the ice cream." Which was going down way too easy. Suddenly two scoops hardly seemed enough.

"Yes, but . . . " He set his half-empty bowl on the table. "When I came up north, I was completely stressed. Two days with you, and I feel like I can breathe again, so yes, thank you."

She waved hands in front of her eyes. That had to be the nicest thing any guy had ever said to her. "I'm the one who should be thanking you. You not only rescued me yesterday, but you cleaned my entire cabin. Including that invading mouse family. And then I have the nerve to ask for more help. I'm sorry about that, and I will not hold you to it. That was unfair."

"Uh, uh, uh." He wagged his finger in the air. "I made a promise—"

"Under unfair circumstances." She sat up straight in her chair and air-wrote a message as she spoke it. "I hereby release you of all promises made to pretty up the cabin." She signed *Jessica Rose Beaumont* with a flourish beneath it.

"Let me have that pen." He grabbed the invisible pen and began writing. "And I hereby declare that I, your gallant knight, shall never break a promise to her royal highness." He dotted the air emphatically.

"You are impossible, Sir Luke."

"I aim to please." He bowed and took another scoop of his sundae. "Now that I've double-promised my help, I'm curious as to how fixing up your cabin will bring your parents back together. Sounds like there's a story behind it."

Jess sighed. "They had such an amazing romance. Dad would tell it all the time, and Mom, who's about as stoic as can be, would even get dreamy-eyed. Now, instead, she fires laser eyes at him, and he's given up."

"I'm sorry to hear that. Sounds a lot like my mom and dad's romance. When she died, she took his heart with her. Before that, he and I were best buddies." He dipped his spoon into his sundae, but only swirled the ice cream. "I'd give anything to have that relationship back."

"I'm sorry." She put her hand on his.

"Yeah. Me too." He cleared his throat. "But we're not here to talk doom and gloom. I want to hear this amazing romance story that'll bring your parents together for a second time."

"Well . . . " She spooned ice cream into her mouth while formulating thoughts. "Did you know your gran set up my parents?"

"Really?"

"Yep. Dad stayed at the family cabin—now our family cabin—during the summer, and one week, a bunch of his college buddies were there with him. On one of their daily trips to your gran's shop, Mom was coming out the door as the guys were going in. Apparently, it was love at first sight for dad, who declared to your gran, 'That's the woman I'm going to marry.' Didn't matter that Mom hadn't paid one bit of attention to him."

"Confident, wasn't he?"

"Oh, he was. But he also was a planner. From Gran he found out that Mom was staying in the area with friends for the summer. That gave him three months to learn about her. Dad started hanging around the store, doing odd jobs for Gran, just so he'd get a chance to talk with Mom. He'd ask your gran what Mom's favorite chocolates were, her favorite flowers, her dream vacation, where she lived, went to college, what her major was. At first Mom ignored him, but she couldn't ignore his free offerings of her favorite chocolate. She couldn't ignore him when he was planting her favorite flowers in Gran's planters. And she certainly couldn't ignore him when he invited her for a bonfire at the cabin and led her on the flower-lined path toward the lake. And then he did the gutsiest thing: he changed his major. Went from a painting major to a broadcast journalism major, like Mom."

"He's an artist?"

"An amazing artist. And that's how he caught Mom. He brought out his easel and paints at the cabin and painted her portrait, and she fell for him." Jess searched her phone for snapshots of paintings he had for sale in various Duluth locations. "Here's one of me and Callie at the cabin." Her favorite, actually. She handed over the phone. Dad had perfectly captured the two sisters as toddlers. Callie with a crayon and notebook in hand, and Jess twirling around, seeking attention. They hadn't changed.

"Wow, it's beautiful, Jess." He handed back the phone. "And he gave up his art for your mom?"

"Oh no, he never gave up painting, at least not until the stroke, but he figured a journalism career was a smarter choice. As it was, it really worked out for both of them. He and mom anchored the local news together for over twenty-five years. They became a fixture in many locals' homes."

"And now it's just your mom on the news."

Jess nodded and played with her ice cream. "It's not the same. His stroke ended his career and his ability to paint, but the stroke also was the catalyst turning me toward faith. I couldn't deny any longer that I really needed God in my life."

"God often uses tragedies for good. Gran would say, 'The best way to learn about hope is to walk through tragedy.'"

"That sounds depressing."

He shrugged. "But it's true. Unfortunately, some people, like my dad, they stop walking and get stuck in the middle of grief."

"So, my parents need to keep moving and they'll get through this?"

"They will, and with you nudging them in the right direction, it can't hurt."

Jess sighed and swirled her spoon around in her ice cream, but didn't eat any.

"Take a bite." He nudged the bowl with his fingers. "It'll make you feel better."

She brought the filled spoon to her lips, and swirled the ice cream around in her mouth, savoring the flavor. Yes, it did make her feel better, but she better stop eating before guilt ate at her. "You want the rest?"

He glanced down at his near-empty bowl and back up at her, grinning. "How'd you guess?" He finished the remainder of his treat before starting on hers.

"Where do you put all of that? I'd be sick all night if I ate that much."

He patted his stomach that didn't look like it had an ounce of fat. So not fair. "Gran would ask that all the time too. When I was little, I told her I had a second stomach especially for treats. I must have had a super metabolism."

"If you help me at the cabin, even your first stomach will have a super metabolism."

"Not *if. When* I help you. Which begs the question, when do we start?"

"I have to work during the week. I keep an eye on Dad and get him to his PT appointments, which he grumbled about all the way there today, but I made him go anyway. On top of that, I'm the office manager at Superior Suites—"

He blinked. "Where?"

"Oh, that's another part of Mom and Dad's romance. Because they met at Gran's Superior Sweets, they wanted to pay homage to her store. So, when they opened the offices in Canal Park, they called it Superior Office Suites, spelled S-U-I-T-E-S instead of S-W-E-E-T-S. Technically *Office* is in the middle of the name, but we all shorten it in conversation."

Luke finished off Jess's sundae. "If ever a couple needed to get back together, it's your folks. And since Gran played a part in their early romance, I'm perfect for the job of bringing them back together."

"So you'll conspire with me in Operation: Planting Hope?"

"Hmm, I like that. We'll walk with them through their tragedy and plant hope along the way." He pushed away the empty bowls that looked as if they'd been licked clean. "When do we begin?"

"This Saturday?"

"I'll be there. But this time, I'll bring my work clothes."

Jess couldn't wait. Not only to whip the cabin into shape, but to spend more time with Luke. What could be more fun than rekindling her parents' romance while sparking her own?

Chapter Six

Luke pounded up the stairs to his apartment. What was it with Jess Beaumont that made him lose all sense? After driving her back to the store, and seeing her off, he caught himself smiling a super-goofy grin as if he'd never shared ice cream with a beautiful woman before. Truth was, he probably hadn't. Most women he knew from work wouldn't have touched their lips to ice cream, much less attempt to move an entire tree trunk.

Yeah, Jess was something special.

And he was going to break her heart. And her parents' hearts. Which made him the lowest of low creatures, probably some sea slug. No offense to the slugs.

He kicked at Gran's floral sofa and yelped. *Idiot.*

How could he make everyone happy? Gran said people-pleasing was his special gift, only that gift had never worked on his immediate family.

The other option was letting his dad down again, and proving to Dad that he didn't have the chops to make it in business. Speaking of which . . . He pulled out his cell phone and checked for messages. No surprise, Dad had tried reaching him several times, but Luke had the phone muted. He scrolled through the messages, all wondering what Luke was doing and what kind of progress he was making. *Sure, Dad, I've got both the Beaumonts and Bettis begging to sell. See you in six months.* What he'd give to hurl his phone against the wall and be free from his helicoptering dad.

Maybe Luke was an oddity for this generation, but he didn't like being at everyone's immediate beck and call. He wasn't a doctor, for Pete's sake, he was a peon in his dad's multi-million-dollar company.

So, should he message his dad right away? Luke surveyed Gran's very floral apartment and decided his dad could wait. Not that he didn't like flowers, but this was overload, and he'd be committed to a mental institution if this room didn't change. Storing Gran's furniture and buying his own was job number one. That he could work on tonight and tomorrow.

He'd call Lydia and tell her if she wanted her dollhouse, she'd have to come up here to get it. Maybe Luke would get a visit from his favorite niece. Catherine—his little Kitty Cat—would love that dollhouse. Chances of Tim making the trek north for his inheritance were slim to none, so Luke would bring the Bible to the cities next time he visited home. In the meantime, he would make use of the time he had with it.

Job number two would be to finish cleaning and painting downstairs. He could do that while the roofers worked. Oh, and also, he needed to get in touch with his chocolatier, Mary Obermiller, to find out what else needed to be done to open up shop. Maybe she didn't want to come back.

Then, on top of work for the store, he'd promised to help Jess with her cabin. Foolish, maybe, but being around her brought sunshine into his life, and he wasn't about to pull the shade on that relationship, whatever it was, wherever it was going.

Nowhere in this next week's schedule did he have time for Harrison Property Development. Now to let his dad know. He typed 'Dad' into the contacts and his thumb hovered above phone call. Nope. He was going to take the coward's way out and message his dad. Getting yelled at wasn't on Luke's to-do list for today. He wasn't even going to mention the conversation with Bettis or spending another day with Jess. When Luke had actual progress to report, he would. He typed out:

Got all your messages. FYI – this week I'm cleaning up Gran's place and will not be working on the HPD project. It will get done, just not this week, and I ask you to respect that as one businessman to another.

Was that taking it too far?

Nope. Dad needed to respect Luke, and that meant Luke had to stand up for himself. Obviously, no one else was going to do it for him.

When I do have progress to report, I will let you know ASAP.

He reread the message. Short and to the point. Dad should appreciate that, even if he didn't like the message. Luke hit send, then made sure the phone was muted.

Now to find a storage unit for Gran's things and new furnishings for himself. He got out his laptop and sat at the kitchen table. Thank goodness Gran had listened to him years ago when he'd encouraged her to add Wi-Fi. Otherwise he'd have to head into town for this simple task.

He found a portable storage company out of Duluth and signed up to have a container delivered tomorrow. As for getting the larger furniture down the stairs, there must be a neighborhood teen looking to make a quick couple of bucks.

Then he looked up furniture rental. There was a place not too far from Canal Park in Duluth where Jess worked. He leaned back in his chair and drummed fingers on his thighs. What would she think if he dropped in to say hi, maybe took her out to lunch?

There was only one way to find out. Early tomorrow he'd call his candy maker to see if she could do him a small favor, one that should bring a light to Jess's day.

Yep, tomorrow was going to be a good day.

COULD TODAY GET ANY worse? Jess resisted slamming the door to her dad's office. All she wanted to do was go to her office, shut off the phone, and nap for the rest of the week. Life had become one big pity-party for Dad. Maybe if he tried a little harder, he'd get better, and Mom wouldn't have walked out on him, and . . .

And she was being a brat. Dad needed her love, not her judgment.

Just this morning she'd read that more than a third of stroke survivors were affected by depression, and that depression affected how well the stroke survivor recovered. So that meant Dad not only needed physical rehab, but mental as well.

She arrived in her office, closed the door, and slumped down in her chair. Speaking of pity parties ... She was leaving hers behind and getting back to work on Operation: Planting Hope, which now included finding a therapist to deal with her dad's depression, if that was what his problem was.

Convincing him he needed to see a counselor was an entirely different matter.

But she'd do it.

Putting aside her Superior Suites work, she researched therapists in the Duluth area, and found a few that used art therapy. He'd like that, wouldn't he? She sent the links to Callie. Between the two of them they should be able to find someone who would help Dad gain victory over his stroke. Only then would he and Mom have a chance of getting back together.

Now to tackle her office work, which meant contacting renters and asking them to pay up. That had always been Mom's job, but with her busy schedule, and with Callie working full-time now as a naturalist, that left the collection job to Jess. She was good at it, but that didn't make the rotten task any easier.

Once done with that chore, she handled calls for toilets overflowing and Wi-Fi not working and a child getting sick all over the first-floor retail area. Next she hurried to get coffee for her dad, and then clean up that coffee which he immediately spilled across his desk. At least he didn't burn himself.

What she'd give to be up at the cabin, working on the gardens. Not only would that be good for her parents' marriage, but also for her own mental health. That would have to wait until Saturday, when she could hand the Dad-sitting job over to Callie.

Two forever-hours later, she was begging for time to go faster. She wouldn't close the office for another hour and a half. After that she'd go home and continue packing up her belongings to prepare for putting the house on the market. Mom gave Callie and her until Friday, wanting to have the house ready to show this weekend.

Her office phone buzzed, signaling a call from the Suites' receptionist. Jess prayed it wasn't another building problem. The tenants were never too friendly about that. Regardless, Jess donned her happy face and answered. "This is Jess."

"There's a gentleman here to see you. Says he has a delivery for you."

"Tell him to leave it with you. I'll be up soon."

"He says it needs to be made in person."

Seriously? "What kind of delivery?"

"He won't say."

"Fine. I'm on my way." It better be important, that was all she had to say.

She saved her work on the computer then crutched her way to the front office area at Superior Office Suites.

She braked to a stop. And grinned. She had a delivery all right, a candy-box-shaped wrapped gift from a very handsome man. This was exactly what she needed for today.

"Got a minute?" Luke held the box toward her.

"For you? Any time." She nodded toward the hallway. "Come back to my office."

Only a few months ago, inviting a good-looking man to her office was always accompanied with flirting. Nothing ever happened in her office, but an invite out for a drink wasn't uncommon.

Flirting with Luke, though, was entirely different.

She showed him into her office and he immediately went to the picture window framing in Lake Superior.

"Wow." A typical reaction, one she echoed. "If you have to work inside, this is the place to do it."

"I agree." Yet she often took the view for granted. Maybe that was why God gave them hardships, so they would treasure His everyday gifts. "This is really my mom's office, but she's putting more time in at the news station, and I've temporarily taken over management."

"You manage this office?"

"Actually, Mom and Dad own this entire building." She gestured to a guest chair. "Have a seat. You are just the medicine I needed for today."

"Rough one, huh?" He sat and crossed an ankle over his knee.

She sat in her chair and wheeled it around the desk. "Mostly family stuff. I'm trying to remind myself of my blessings. Up until a few minutes ago, I was failing at that."

An easy grin slid to his face. "Oh? And what happened a few minutes ago?"

"A handsome knight came bearing gifts."

"Not gifts, milady, but bribery."

"Bribery?"

He nodded. "I'm in town looking at rental furniture for my apartment, but I'm in desperate need of a female opinion." He pulled folded pages from inside his jacket and handed them to Jess. "My go-to is the black leather. What do you think?"

She wrinkled her nose. "It's fine if you're looking at having guys over for poker night."

"Not a bad idea, but"—he looked her directly in the eye—"there's always the possibility of having someone of the female persuasion over."

"For poker?"

He laughed. "Also not a bad idea, but I was thinking more along the lines of dinner, maybe a movie."

"Is that an invitation?"

"Do you want it to be?"

Oh yeah, she did. But rather than respond, she studied the sheets of paper with different living room sets. "Comfort is important?"

"Priority number one."

"What color are the walls?"

He snorted. "Right now, they're bright yellow with a rose border circling the room at about hip height. Tomorrow, I'm banishing the border and will be painting the living room pale grey."

"You prefer a modern look?"

"I guess. Like you said, comfort's the most important."

She handed him a sheet with a grayish sofa and loveseat. "How about this? Not as harsh as black, but still masculine. Says the upholstery is super soft."

"That's not too much grey?"

"That leads me to my next suggestion. Since you're painting, why don't you paint one wall an accent color, maybe a sapphire or cornflower."

"Wait, what? Cornflower? I want to get away from yellow."

Jess giggled. "Cornflower is a shade of blue."

"Blue?" He scratched his head.

"Like the flower."

"I'll take your word for it."

"Let me show you." On her phone, she brought up images of the cornflower and showed Luke. "What do you think? That grey sofa would look great against a wall that color."

"Whatever you say." He shook his head.

"I say so." She set her phone on her desk. "Now for bribery payment." She reached for the box of candy.

"Maybe I've changed my mind." He pulled the box tight to his chest.

She grabbed it away. "A smart man never offers gifts then reneges. As a knight, you should know that."

"Haven't taken that course yet." He grinned and nodded at the box. "Open it."

She tore the wrapping paper and found what she expected. A box labeled Gran's Goodies. "You found some?"

"Not exactly. I went to the source, Mary Obermiller. She's our master candy maker, and she was more than happy to whip up a few batches of chocolate special for you."

Jess took off the cover and the scent of chocolate drifted into the air. She breathed in and sighed. "I think I've gone to heaven."

"And you haven't taken a bite yet."

"Oh, I'll take a bite, but I have to read the Granism first." She picked up the square slip of paper and read, "Blessings are often disguised as storms."

"Thought you'd like that one."

She closed her eyes and raised her face toward heaven. How could Luke know her so well after a few short days? "Thank you," she whispered. A thought struck her, and she grabbed her crutches. "Come with me. There's someone who'd love to meet you."

Leaving her crutches behind, she led him around the corner to her dad's office. No surprise, the door was closed. Before the stroke, he'd never allowed it to be closed, preaching an open-door policy. He wanted the tenants to know they could approach him at any time. Now, even his daughters needed permission to enter.

With nerves tingling in her hands, she knocked on his door. Reintroducing her dad to Luke had to be a positive step toward Dad's recovery. Add the box of chocolate to that, and Dad would practically beg to get back together with Mom.

She didn't hear a response, so she tried the door. It was unlocked. She slowly pushed it open. Dad sat in the guest chair, his gaze on a book in his lap. She laid a hand on his shoulder. "Dad?"

He jerked and looked up at her. "Jess. Sorry. D...didn't hear you." His gaze slid to Luke. "And your young m...man?"

"Remember when Callie and I were little, and Gran would come over for weenie roasts and sometimes she had her grandson with?"

"I remember." His stroke-affected hand slowly reached out. "And y...you're the grandson."

"Yes sir." Luke took her dad's hand. "Luke Harrison. I've been helping your daughter with the cabin."

"Please. Sit." Her dad gestured to the other guest chair, which Luke sat in. She took the desk chair. "Thank you...for helping."

"It's my pleasure, Mr. Beaumont."

"Ken, please."

"Ken it is."

Jess was practically doing handstands. This was by far the most animated she'd seen her dad, and the least stuttering, since coming back from his vacation, and one of the rare times he'd donned a smile since the split. Before she knew it, her parents would be planning another honeymoon.

"Luke brought us a gift." She set the box of candies on her dad's lap.

Her dad's smile evaporated, and he swatted the box onto the floor, scattering the chocolates around his office and under the desk. "Did M...Mackenzie put you up t...to this?" His eyes burned toward her.

She choked back a sob, and her chin quivered. "No. I thought that this would remind you—"

"I n...need no r...reminders."

"Dad. She loves you."

"Pick up c...candy. Time to go home." He reached for his walker. "And I don't...want...see those...those candies again."

Chapter Seven

L uke pulled into the tree-shaded driveway leading down to the Beaumont cabin. Jess had explained to him that today was a big step in planting hope for her father and mother. He couldn't wait to get started. His heart still ached over the way Jess's dad had treated her earlier in the week, when all she'd wanted to do was brighten his day. But sometimes, when people are stuck in storms of their own choosing, they don't want to see light.

Grief changes a man. As a ten-year-old, he'd witnessed the change close-up in his own father when Mom died. His dad still chose not to look for the light. Mr. Beaumont hadn't lost his spouse to death, but wasn't the death of a marriage the same thing? And what about the loss of his former way of life? How does a formerly active man accept that his limbs and his speech will never function the same way again? His grief was different from that of Luke's dad, but it was grief none the less.

The question now was, would Mr. Beaumont choose to keep walking through this storm, or, like Luke's father, would Mr. Beaumont make forever-friends with hopelessness?

If Jess had anything to say about it, her dad would keep walking. It might be a stumbling, jagged walk with a lot of missteps and potholes, but if he kept walking, he would eventually leave this storm behind.

Luke pulled beside the Jeep parked by the cabin. He found Jess inside the log structure, bent over the kitchen table, drawing on a sheet of paper that covered much of the tabletop. Her crutches lay on a chair beside her.

"What's this?" He studied the crude drawing.

"I know it's not much to look at, but these are my plans for the gardens." She drew her finger down a curvy line. "This is the path leading to the lake." She pointed to the daisy-like squiggles framing in the path. "And these are the gardens. When Dad first courted Mom, he found out her favorite flowers—anything red—then he surrounded the path with pink and red perennials. He had coneflowers, roses, peonies, phlox, but it wasn't easy to maintain. The busier Mom and Dad got, the more the gardens were neglected and weeds took over. My plan is to create a more manageable garden, give the plants room to breathe, make use of mulch, add in hostas for easy-to-maintain greenery so that the red pops rather than being a blanket of red. Does that make sense?"

"Perfect sense. I love the idea."

"Are you sure you're willing to help me implement that idea? This is your last chance to back out. I know running a store is more than a full-time job."

He laughed. "So true, and it hasn't even begun yet. On top of that, there's my job in the family biz."

"That's right. I never even thought about that. You obviously worked somewhere before the candy shop."

Shoot. Why had he brought that up? Well, better now than later, though he wasn't about to divulge his dad's mandate. "I did—actually, I still do. My dad owns Harrison Property Development out of Minneapolis, and I work there as a property acquisitions associate. Been there since I was fifteen. I worked the candy store some during my teens, and construction during college, but otherwise I've been at Harrison."

She wrinkled her adorable nose. "Sounds dreadfully boring."

He snorted. "And the actual job is worse than it sounds. When posting for hiring, 'dreadfully boring' should be part of the job description."

"Why do you do it?"

Good question, one he'd asked himself several times over the years, and it always came down to one thing: getting an *attaboy* from his dad. "I guess I'm doing what's always been expected of me. You don't know how freeing it's been living up here. Both jobs leave me exhausted at the end of the day, but in the HPD job, I dread the next day. Whereas up here, I look forward to the coming day. Yeah, getting the store in shape is eating up my savings account, but I'm seeing something worthwhile—something I have a personal attachment to—come alive, so every penny spent, every minute worked fills me with joy."

"Do you plan to leave Harrison?"

Don't I wish! "Believe me, I've thought about it, but Dad would probably disown me."

"Or maybe it would get his attention. You haven't talked much of your family, but I don't get the impression that you're all lovey-dovey."

"Ha. Since Mom passed, the word *love* hasn't even been spoken in our household."

"I'm so sorry." She gave Luke a hug. "My family is obviously far from perfect. My mom can be stiff, and to outsiders she comes off as unfeeling, but she feels things deeply and doesn't show it. My dad's the complete opposite. He's a very touchy-feely type person, and right now he's going through the doldrums. But up until last week, it was always clear that Mom and Dad loved each other and they loved their girls. I won't let them throw away thirty years of marriage because of this setback."

"You're a good daughter, Jess Beaumont."

"I'm a work in progress."

"Aren't we all?" He nodded to the door. "How about we go outside, talk more, show me your plans, get our hands dirty."

"Good idea." She grabbed a couple of water bottles from the fridge and gave one to Luke. They walked out onto the front porch that spanned the front of the cabin. Her crutches apparently banished, along with the limp.

"Your foot's obviously feeling better."

"Much better, thanks to you. I religiously followed the R.I.C.E. method this week so I could work this weekend. But, out of curiosity, I did attempt to crutch my way down the path toward the lake. No way would Dad make it. The ground is too rough, and there are too many obstacles for someone who isn't determined. My plan is to make it as easy as possible for Dad to get around the area."

She gestured to the three steps leading from the deck down to the grass. "I've hired a carpenter to install a ramp. I'd love to see Dad walk without the walker, and I know he can do it. He was just using the cane before he and Mom went on their trip. But if he's going to be using the walker, he needs to access the house easily."

"Good plan."

She led him down the rutted, twisting and turning path toward the lake, pushing branches away from her face as they walked. "If Dad tried to walk this, he'd get so discouraged. I want to create a path that's wider—more than thirty-six inches—and is easier to walk on than this uneven dirt. I'll probably use a crushed stone instead of concrete." She ducked under a branch. "And I'll get rid of obstacles." She gestured to the side of the path. "I want plants lining both sides of the walkway. The one thing we have in our favor is that the path doesn't follow a steep slope."

The path spilled out into a wide opening that showcased magnificent lake views. Jess stopped a few feet away from the edge of a high cliff that jutted sharply down toward the water. Looking down to his right, Luke saw a stone beach tucked between this cliff and one other.

"Still have the ladder leading down to the beach?" Back when he worked with Gran, a rickety metal ladder connected the upper land to the beach, and climbing down it had been a grand adventure.

"That ladder died several years ago, but Dad had it replaced with a much sturdier one a few years back. It's still the best place to find quiet. Callie loves it because it's the best place to look for agates."

A place a tourist would love. What would happen to the quiet place if Dad developed the land?

Luke shook off the depressing thought and took in the clearing. A metal bench and a couple of wood Adirondack chairs sat around a weed-filled fire pit that didn't look like it had been used for a couple of years. What a shame. That would change this summer. Maybe even tonight.

This property, though, was breathtaking, hand-carved by God himself. What would happen to it if Dad acquired the land? And the cabin? That rustic building that had to be decades old. If Harrison Property Development purchased this land, that cabin would likely become a casualty. Could Luke convince his father that preserving a piece of history would add to the appeal of a new resort or condos or whatever Dad had in mind for this place? Could he convince his dad that whatever was built here shouldn't take away from the natural grandeur? He had to try.

Or maybe he should tell his dad to leave well enough alone. Oh, he wished he could!

Jess pointed to the sharp drop-off past the fire pit, breaking through his reverie. "I think we should put up a wood fence. I have images of Dad in a wheelchair rolling right over the cliff." She turned to him. "What do you think?"

"I think it sounds amazing. Have you ever given thought to doing landscape design?" She certainly had the vision.

She looked out toward the water. "Not until recently. Up until a few months back, I'd hoped to expand my modeling career—"

"You were a model?" That shouldn't be a surprise. She sure had the looks for it.

She shrugged. "I was, until I couldn't live with the unhealthy demands and the insecurity. My agent told me about this amazing position, one that would have given me international exposure, but she wanted me to drop twenty pounds. And that was for a plus-size gig. I couldn't do it anymore. As long as I modeled, I never felt I was pretty enough, skinny enough, but Callie helped me see that God loves me just the way I am. It's my job to take care of the body God gave me. I try to eat right and exercise, but that was never good enough for my agent, so I quit. But there's a huge part of me that feels like a failure for not continuing in a profession I'd given so much time to."

Luke grabbed Jess's shoulders and turned her toward him. "You are not a failure, Jessica Beaumont. It's only been a week since we reconnected, but when I think of you, when I look at you, I see a gifted woman who loves deeply, who's got amazing vision and a fun sense of humor, and one who fills me with joy. I love your new, innocent, unjaded faith. When I'm with you, I feel like I can be myself, and that's a miracle. I haven't felt like that since the summers I worked with Gran. That tree toppling on your driveway was definitely a blessing in disguise."

A tear trickled down Jess's cheek, and he thumbed it away as a longing to be loved stirred in his gut. "I don't know where this . . . this relationship between you and me is going, but I'm very excited about the journey."

She looked up to the sky. "I come with baggage, Luke. I've done things I'm not proud of, things I'm ashamed of."

"And I haven't?" Kowtowing to his family topping the list. "None of us is perfect, Jess. When I'd make a mistake, my gran would tell me, 'You can't change the past, but you can impact the future.' So, no looking back. Yes, your past is a part of you. It helped shape the beautiful woman I see today, but it doesn't define you unless you let it." Words he spoke as much for his own benefit as he did for Jess's. What did he see in his future? A career at Harrison? The idea alone soured in his gut. So did the thought of disappointing his dad.

But that wasn't a decision that needed to be made today. "For now, let's get to know each other, enjoy our time together, and we'll see where it goes. And that begins with grabbing a shovel and getting dirty. What do you say?"

She laughed, such a beautiful sing-song laugh. "I say it's time to get to work."

"Let's do it." Because if they didn't grab a shovel soon, he was all too-tempted to kiss her.

"But first I want to thank you." She turned toward the lake, stretched out her arms, breathed in, then slowly let it out. "This cabin and land has become my place of healing, and I can't imagine my folks selling it, so—"

Her words were a punch to his gut. "They're selling?"

"Can you believe it?" She shook her head. "This is where they fell in love, and it's been in Dad's family for decades. They've promised to wait until after Callie's wedding, but then they plan to put it on the market. If only I had the means to buy it from them . . . Hopefully, once they see what we're going to do to this place, they'll change their minds. About the cabin and their marriage. So, you helping me out . . . I can't thank you enough."

No, she couldn't. And definitely shouldn't. The Beaumonts wanting to sell made his job for Harrison a whole lot easier. His dad would praise him for gaining this insider info. Or would he? Chances were, Dad would ask why Luke hadn't already approached the Beaumonts with an offer. But Luke couldn't do that to Jess.

When—if—he purchased this cabin, this place of healing and hope for Jess, she'd likely never forgive him. That shouldn't matter. He didn't even know her. Not really.

The problem was, he wanted to know her more.

With the job he had to do for his dad, a relationship with Jess could only end one way. With two broken hearts.

Chapter Eight

O h. My. Goodness! For a second there, Jess thought for sure Luke was going to kiss her. No doubt, she would have responded with glee. Was that a remnant of the woman she used to be, or did she really care for Luke?

Just hearing him follow behind her made her grin, and she felt like skipping down the path toward the garden shed. In her young life, she'd had plenty of empty relationships. Not one felt like this. None had made her smile from the inside out. Not one of those guys had cared for her. But Luke? Everything about him was genuine. And he liked her.

Working with him would make this weekend go by way too fast. Maybe they could cap it off with another trip to the ice cream shop.

She reached the shed, dug out a couple of garden hoses, and handed one to Luke. She found a tape measure in Dad's workbench and pocketed it.

"Vut is yer plan?" Luke said in an exaggerated Scandinavian accent.

Jess cocked her head to the side and squinted at Luke. "Excuse me?"

"Dese hoses, vut do you vant to do vith dem?"

She stared at him. "Why are you going all Sven and Ole on me? Where's Sir Luke?"

Luke tugged on his plaid shirt then gestured to jeans worn thin at the knees. "Knights von't vear flannel, don'tcha know, so Sir Luke sent me to verk for him."

She poked him in the chest. "Well you tell Sir Luke that the queen has given him permission to don flannel and holey jeans, got it?"

Luke slapped a hand over his heart. "Methinks I should be offended that you don't like my Scandihoovian accent."

"You betcha, I don't." She giggled. "I want my knight back."

"As you wish." Luke stood up straight, his shoulders squared, and his chin high. "Sir Luke at your service, milady." He bowed, keeping the hose in his arms. "What is your plan for today?"

"First thing I want to do is figure out the layout of the path. You run your hose parallel to mine, a minimum of thirty-six inches apart. That should give plenty of room for a wheelchair." Hopefully her dad would recover and not need a wheelchair, but she had to plan for the worst, and not give him any room for excuses.

Together they arranged the hoses alongside the proposed path, then measured to make certain it was wide enough. Once satisfied, Jess took a can of line-marking spray paint and drew in the path borders. That was the easy part. Now they got to dig.

From the garden shed, she brought out two spades purchased specifically for this project, and handed one to Luke.

"We need to go down four inches all the way across, and try to keep it even. Let me get you a tape measure." She dug around in her dad's workbench and didn't find another tape measure, but she did find a ruler. That would work.

"I'll start out by the fire pit. You dig here." She pointed to the beginning of the path. "And we'll meet in the middle. How does that sound?"

"You really have this all planned out."

"Well, Superior Suites has a landscape designer who gave me some tips. I would have loved to hire him, but Mom gave me a set budget for the renovations, and a designer isn't in that budget."

"Looks to me like you'll do fine without a paid designer. I like your vision for the place."

"You really think it's good?" That had been a concern. Sure, she had a flair for creating container gardens, but this kind of project was a completely different mindset. Honestly, though, she had enjoyed creating the design.

"I've only seen what you have on paper, but now that we've got the path laid out, I can visualize your design. This alone will raise the market value for the cabin."

Her face went white and she dropped the spade. "Maybe I shouldn't do it. Maybe if I leave things as they are, no one will want to buy the place, and Mom and Dad won't sell."

"Whoa." He raised his hands. "Sorry. Hazard of my city job, I'm always thinking market and bottom line. More importantly, I don't know how your folks could come out here together, once the garden's completed, and not fall in love again. And think about the setting you're creating for Callie and her fiancé. It'll be the most beautiful wedding ever."

"You really think so?"

"Why do you doubt yourself?"

She shuffled her foot in the dirt and shrugged. "I always seem to be an A- person. While I do things well, nothing's ever good enough to reach the A level, and I'm scared that this is going to be another failure." And she couldn't fail this time. Losing her modeling career was one thing, but having her parents permanently split? That she couldn't abide. The project had to be better than good.

"Jess." He tipped her chin up then took her hands. "When I was afraid of not being good enough, Gran would always ask me if I'd talked to God. She said, maybe I'm not good enough on my own, but that's where He comes in to help."

"Your gran was a wise woman."

"Yes, she was. Can I pray for you?"

A lump clotted Jess's throat, and she blinked back tears. She'd prayed with Callie and Haven before, but to have Luke make the offer overwhelmed her. All she could do was nod.

He held her hands tight and closed his eyes. "Lord, you know better than we do what's going on with Jess's parents. You know their struggles and their heartbreaks. You know their desires. You have knit them together as one, and I lift them up to you that your bonds will weather this storm they're going through. And I also lift up Jess to you.

She has such an amazing heart, Lord, and a gift not only for wanting to keep her family together, but also for working with Your creation. Work alongside her, Lord. Give her wisdom in making the path, and breathe life and beauty into the flowers she plants. I pray that hope will grow with each flower, and that you will fill Jess with unquestionable hope, that she might know deep inside that she is a beloved child of God. Also, Lord, I pray that I may be a good companion for her, that in working alongside her, you'll be lifted up. May the work of our hands be for your Glory. In your precious name, Amen."

He squeezed her hands and looked into her flooded eyes.

"That was beautiful, and the most thoughtful thing any man has ever done for me." She dragged the words from a tight throat.

"Just trying to treat you as the priceless gem God created you to be." He bowed. "And that means we need to get to work. No more wasting time. If we get this dug out today, tonight I'll treat you to roasted hot dogs and s'mores."

She laugh-snorted, grateful for his lighter tone. "Not wine and caviar?"

"Is that what you want?"

"Nope. Hot dogs and s'mores sounds perfect."

"Then off you go with your spade." With a flair, he gestured down the path. "We shall meet again soon."

"We shall." She curtsied and floated between the painted lines of the path. Was this what love felt like? True love? Or was this too early in the relationship to wonder. What she did know was that she was falling fast and falling hard for one Lucas Harrison, and if she was correct, he was falling for her too.

She reached the fire pit area and looked down the pathway—probably fifty feet or more—toward Luke, and her stomach turned topsy-turvy. She wasn't opposed to exploring that relationship further. Today, with the promise of a bonfire beneath the stars, with Lake Superior clapping below, would be a perfect time to dig into that possibility. She laughed at her little pun as she pushed the spade into the ground still softened by rain earlier in the week.

Several hours, and a long, hot shower later, Jess slumped exhausted on the bench overlooking the lake. Every muscle in her body screamed 'ouch,' but only half the path was dug out. If her muscles hurt this badly today, would she even be able to lift a shovel tomorrow? She massaged the foot she'd bruised last weekend. It hadn't hurt at the beginning of the day, but right now, it was protesting. Loudly.

Luke handed her a glass filled with ice water, then dragged over a chair. He propped her foot on the chair and wrapped that foot in a towel-ice bandage.

"Ahhh." She sighed and looked up at him in wonder. "Thank you." No guy had ever treated her with this kind of selfless care. Not even her father—not for many years anyway, since he and Mom had become big stars on the local news scene. Since then he'd become as self-centered as the guys she'd dated. The stroke had only enhanced his inward focus. Though, before the stroke, his actions had pointed out how great he was. Now, they were all about what an awful break he'd had.

Hopefully, with this place getting fixed up, he'd be able to look beyond himself again, like Luke had. Luke was chivalry personified.

He slumped beside her on the bench and groaned. "I used muscles today I didn't know I had."

"Tell me about it." She sipped her water and caught a glance of her once perfectly-manicured fingernails that would probably never come clean again. Her agent would have had a fit. Surprisingly, the dirt and the jagged, unpolished nails made Jess smile. They showed she'd put a lot of elbow grease into something worthwhile, something that wasn't all about getting the younger generation to purchase more clothes or makeup or hair products, but about drawing a family back together.

So, yeah, her muscles screamed out at her, but it was a good feeling.

Beside her, Luke sat unshowered, with rank, dirt-covered clothes. It shouldn't feel romantic. Still . . .

To know that a guy, a virtual stranger, had spent an entire day with her, throwing dirt for a project that didn't benefit him at all, was very attractive, and if he tried to kiss her tonight, mud-covered face and all, she wouldn't fight him.

Luke slapped his thighs and stood. "You hungry?"

"Very." On cue, her stomach growled. Besides a few snack bars, some watermelon, and several bottles of water, they hadn't had anything to eat since breakfast. That likely contributed to her fatigue right now. Tomorrow they'd have to be more intentional about eating if they wanted to have the strength to complete digging out the path.

While Luke started the fire, Jess found a couple of roasting forks in the shed. She washed them then filled a serving tray with hot dogs, buns, s'more fixings, and watermelon. That should hold them over for the evening. For tomorrow, though, she wanted to come up with something a bit more special. With all the work Luke had put in, he deserved more than mystery meat.

They held their hot dogs over the fire while a light breeze toyed with the leaves and licked at the lake below. She could stay out here forever. How could her parents think of selling this place?

No. She wasn't going to think about the *what ifs* tonight, only *what is*. And that was Sir Luke Harrison.

"How did your week go?" She rotated the fork, warming the dog on all sides as the manly scent of Luke wafted toward her on the breeze. "Get the roof done?"

"All done. No more leaky dormers."

"The parking lot looked good."

"Not perfect, but we won't lose any more Mini Coopers in the potholes."

She giggled. "And your furniture?"

He flexed the muscles on his open arm. "My place now looks manly." He made the guttural sound like Tim Allen on the '90s sitcom, *Home Improvement*.

Jess laughed. "So, no more flower borders?"

"Completely eradicated, and the blue accent wall—"

"You mean cornflower?"

"I mean blue, and you were right. It does add the right touch to the room."

"Of course, I'm right. About the cornflower color too."

"Tenacious, aren't you?"

Jess grinned.

"Your hot dog's on fire!" Luke yanked Jess's roasting stick away from her and blew on the wiener, dousing the flame.

"My hero." She fluttered a hand in front of her chest and took the stick back from Luke.

"Please." He rolled his eyes, but there was a definite smile in his voice.

She slid the dog onto a bun. Black bubbles had erupted on the meat, but it still looked edible. She squiggled ketchup and mustard on the dog and bit into it. Not bad at all. "Is yours okay?"

He smothered his hot dog with mustard only. "Good enough." He bit into it and frowned. "Conversation's better."

She took another bite of hers. "Agreed, but this isn't too bad." She swallowed and took a drink of water. "Did I tell you that Dad agreed to see a counselor?"

"No. That's great." He spoke with his mouth full. So the man wasn't perfect.

"He starts next week. He wasn't happy about it, but Callie and I wouldn't take *no* for an answer. We honestly felt like we were the parents and he was the child. Mom thought it was a good idea too. At least she's rooting for him to get better."

Luke covered her hand with his, and butterflies took flight in her stomach. "I'm sorry you're going through this, Jess. Know that I'm praying for all of you."

A few months back, prayer wouldn't have meant anything, but now she coveted it. "Thank you" was all she could think to say.

They both finished their hot dogs. Luke had a second and third one plus a couple of s'mores. Jess stuck to one s'more, though she could have easily downed more.

What she hungered for most was for this evening to never end. Should she try snuggling up next to him? Or would that be too forward?

Instead, she kept the conversation going, hoping he'd be the one to make a move. "How are your plans coming for opening the store again?

I'm eager to get more chocolate for my parents." Dad may have rejected that first box, but he wouldn't have reacted so badly if it didn't matter to him. Maybe what he needed to do was get mad. At least then he'd be feeling something. Otherwise, he acted like he was numb. "And, before you even offer, I don't want you making special trips over to your candy maker."

"You couldn't stop me." He elbowed her. "You'll be happy to know that as of this coming Tuesday, Superior Sweets will be open for business once again. I've got the employees coming in on Monday to get ready and start making candy. Tuesday we're opening the doors. I'd like to update the website, get on social media, and put out some ads. I'm uncomfortable telling people, 'look at me, see how great I am,' but as Gramps would have told me, 'If you don't toot your own horn, your horn will remain in a state of untootedness.'"

Jess giggled. "That sounds like something Callie would say." She snapped her fingers. "Speaking of Callie, before she took her naturalist job, she was a full-time graphic artist and web designer. She's a wiz at making businesses look good. Also, her fiancé is a semi-pro photographer, so we could ask them if they'd be willing to set up a plan for you."

"Sounds great, but after fixing up the store, my budget has pretty much been eaten up."

"Seriously? You think we'd charge you after all you've done to get the cabin ready? Uh-uh." She poked him in the shoulder. "You won't owe us one penny."

"Oh, I'll bet your sister will love to have you volunteering her services." His tone was sarcastic. "If I volunteered my siblings for anything, they'd have my head."

"Callie would be upset if I didn't volunteer her."

"You sure about that?"

"Absolutely. But, I'll talk to her first, just to satisfy you."

He was silent for a moment, staring off at the darkening horizon. Then he slowly put his arm around her shoulders and pulled her into a side hug and whispered, "You more than satisfy me, Jessica Beaumont."

Have mercy! Her heart took off at a shooting star's pace as she rested her head on his shoulder and snuggled in. Yep, no doubt she was falling for him.

Lights flashed behind them, and they both turned. A vehicle was coming down the cabin driveway.

"Expecting someone?" Luke asked.

"No one." A chill slunk down her spine.

"I'll check it out." He headed down the path.

"Right behind you." No way was she staying at the fire pit alone.

A figure got out of the vehicle—a medium-sized sedan—and headed for the cabin's front door. The automatic light by the front door flashed on, illuminating an unfamiliar man.

Luke stretched his arm out in back of him. "Stay here."

This time, she didn't argue. Tension zinged down her arms and through her hands as Luke neared the cabin. Cell phones didn't work here, so calling for help wasn't a possibility, not unless they could somehow get into the cabin.

"Can I help you?" Luke, standing rigid with his shoulders back, feet set apart, and fists clenched, called out from the end of the path.

The man turned, and Luke relaxed. "Dale, is that you?"

"Luke?"

They knew each other? Jess caught up to Luke, but stayed behind him.

"Hey man, I've been trying to reach you."

Luke pulled out his phone as he walked toward Dale. "No service up here."

"Well that explains it." Dale held out his hand. "How ya doing? Grandma Mary says you're taking over."

"Looks that way." Luke turned toward Jess and waved her forward. "Dale Obermiller, this is Jess Beaumont, a new . . . friend."

"Obermiller?" Jess offered her hand. "You're related to candy-maker Mary?"

He laughed. "That's my grandma."

"Dale and I worked a lot of summers together at Superior Sweets."

Luke put his arm back around Jess's shoulders as if it were the most natural thing for him to do. "And I met Jess during those summers. What brings you here?"

"Oh yeah." Dale dug into his pocket and pulled out a piece of paper. "Message from your family. When they couldn't reach you, they contacted Grandma."

Luke retracted his arm and read the message. His hands fisted against the paper, crumpling it. "When did this come in?"

"I guess they've been trying for four or five hours."

"Thanks for finding me." He stuffed the paper into his pocket and offered his hand to Dale. "We'll be in touch when I get back."

"Sure thing." Dale nodded to Jess. "Nice to meet you."

"You too," she said as Dale headed to his car. Although she wasn't so certain she was happy to meet him. His arrival had interrupted a very romantic evening. Now, tension sizzled from Luke, transforming him into the stiff man she'd seen in the hospital.

The sedan turned around and disappeared up the driveway, and Luke had yet to say anything.

She touched his arm. "What's wrong?"

"I've got to go." He sighed and dug into his jeans pocket. "And I don't think I'll be back for tomorrow. I'm sorry." Without looking at her, he pulled out his keys and spun away.

Her heart sank as he strode to his pickup, got in, and peeled up the driveway.

Imperfection number two noted, and this was a biggie. The man was moodier than her dad. That alone could end this budding romance before it even broke the dirt's surface.

Chapter Nine

Luke pounded his steering wheel as he turned onto the state highway. "Seriously, dude, you up and leave her without a goodbye?" No doubt she'd write him off now, and after such an amazing day, too. Once he figured out what was going on, he'd call her, apologize. If he had her number, that would help, but had he thought to ask for it?

Idiot!

He reached into his pocket and pulled out the note. A message from his big sister. "Family emergency. I need you ASAP." And that was it. Was Kitty okay? Travis? Tim? Dad? He pulled into the driveway leading to the back of the candy store, parked in the now-empty garage, and hurried up to his apartment.

He tried his cell, but had no bars. Sometimes it did, but not having a constant connection was perfectly fine with Luke. Though it likely rankled his family, so much so that his dad would try to fix it. He'd probably work with a phone company to erect a tower and manage to make money off the deal too. A metal tower would completely mar the landscape, but if they could disguise the tower as a lighthouse . . .

An idea to pass on to his dad?

Not something to worry about right now, not when Lydia needed him. He picked up the landline, a harvest-gold corded phone that had to be forty years old. Luke loved it. He dialed his sister and waited through three rings before she answered in typical Lydia fashion.

"Where have you been?"

"Working." She didn't need to know he'd been helping Jess. Lydia would no doubt take that as conspiring with the enemy. Perhaps he was, but he didn't regret a minute of it. His only regret was how he'd left Jess with no explanation.

"Don't you check your cell?"

"Sure." He rolled his eyes. "Every fifteen minutes I drive to a hot spot just in case someone's trying to contact me."

"You don't have to be nasty about it."

"Isn't that the pot calling—" He clamped his mouth shut. Here she was facing a family emergency, and he was being a jerk. "Sorry about that, Lydia. What's wrong? Is Kitty all right?"

"I don't know," Lydia whispered.

Uh-oh. "What happened?" Catherine was the best thing that had happened to their family since Mom's death. She'd been the only thing to break through his dad's frozen heart. If something happened to her . . . Luke started to drop down on his couch, but remembered he was filthy from working all day. Instead he walked to the kitchen peninsula, stretching the phone cord to its full six feet, and sat on one of the metal stools.

"Travis took her," Lydia said between sniffles.

"He took her? Where?" Travis was the next best thing that had happened to the Harrison family, especially to Lydia. And to Luke. It was Travis who'd reignited Luke's faith in the past couple years, and the two had become close friends, far closer than Luke's relationship with his own brother.

"He left me, Luke. He packed all his clothes and Catherine's things, and told me not to call."

Luke sighed, his body slumping as air expelled from his lungs. His first reaction was to ask, "What did you do?" but that would shut down Lydia rather than getting her to open up. Instead he calmly said, "I'm sorry. What can I do?"

"You and Travis get along. Can you talk to him? Get him to see reason?"

Talk to him, yes. Get him to see reason? Well, chances were Travis wasn't the one who needed his eyes opened. "I'll give him a call."

"No. That won't work. He's in no-man's-land like you."

"His family's lake home?"

"That's not too far from you. You'll go see him, won't you? Please?"

If you could call two-hours' driving distance not far. "Yeah, sure. I'll head over after church tomorrow." Which meant abandoning Jess. And with that bruised foot of hers, she'd struggle to get anything done tomorrow. She'd braved through it today, hadn't complained at all, but he'd seen that limp before she sat. What she needed was a day to put her foot up while someone waited on her.

But family came first. Gran had always stressed that.

"You have to go to church? You can't skip it one time?"

"No. Especially at a time like this. Spending time in worship is even more important."

"You're just like Travis. And look where his self-righteous faith got him. Isn't there something in the Bible about not getting divorced?"

"Divorce? He's filed?" A separation was one thing, but Luke couldn't imagine Travis filing for divorce.

"No. But that's the next step, isn't it?"

"Not for Travis, it isn't."

A sob came over the phone. Never had Luke heard his big, tough sister cry. He drew in a deep breath. "I will talk to him, but tomorrow after church is soon enough. And I'm not making any promises about the results. I'll call you tomorrow night." If not sooner, but he didn't want her to expect a call earlier.

"Thank you," came out in a whisper followed by the beep-beep-beep of a dead line.

"You're welcome." He stared at the phone. His world was completely upside down. He was pouring thousands of dollars into a store that wouldn't last past six months. He was falling for a woman whose beloved cabin he was supposed to take from her. And now his steadfast friend had up and left his sister.

If ever he needed to spend time in worship, it was now. He rubbed a hand down his face, then looked down at the hand, nearly black from all the digging he'd done today. Multiple washings barely helped. His jeans were filthy as an uncleaned pigsty. His shirt too. To top it off, his deodorant had likely worn off hours ago. To think he'd hugged Jess like this. Oh, man, he was an idiot.

Her last impression of him would be a stinky jerk who left her without any explanation. He stared at the receiver still in his hand. He didn't know the cabin's number or Jess's cell number, for that matter. And if he drove back to the cabin at this time of night, it could freak her out. He drew his dirty hand through filthier hair.

He'd have to get in touch with her on Monday, and apologize over the phone, as much as he hated that idea. In person was always better, but with the store opening on Tuesday, that demanded his attention.

"Lord, help," was all he could think to pray while heading for the shower. If only his life could be cleaned up as easily as a shower washed away dirt.

JESS LOOKED TO THE star-bedazzled sky and spread out her arms. "Help me, Lord." Without Luke's help, she'd never get this path completed. She mentally paged through her contacts list and found no one who'd be willing to sacrifice their day for her. The problem with leading a selfish life was that you eventually ended up alone. Haven, Callie's fiancé, would be glad to help, but he'd promised his son a trip to the cities to see a professional baseball game.

So that left Jess and a foot that was hurting more than she'd shown Luke. With her working during the week, this path would never get done, and her parents would never get back together.

"No!" she fisted her hands. Giving into negativity was the old Jess's way, the self-centered Jess's way. She was a new creation, and that meant she always had an ally.

She hobbled down the half-dug path toward the cabin.

Tonight, she'd get some sleep. Tomorrow after church, she'd tackle that path with God by her side.

LUKE PULLED INTO THE country church's gravel lot and parked beside a pickup that had more rust than paint. He imagined his truck boasting about its high-gloss paint job. Gramps would have told him that pride will slap you on the back, right before it knocks you on your behind. That man had had a way with words. And he'd always built Luke up, even after Luke had made ridiculous mistakes.

Luke wanted to be like Gramps, a man whom Kitty could come to for wise, loving advice, a man who loved unconditionally, a man unafraid to speak the truth in love, whatever that meant.

He followed a young family into the white, clapboard church with the traditional cross-topped steeple and stained-glass windows. Unlike his contemporary church home in the cities that looked like all the other warehouse buildings in the area, there was no disguising the purpose of this building. Back when this church was built, it didn't have to pretend to be something it wasn't in order to draw in worshippers. Luke appreciated the honesty of that.

And he appreciated the welcoming smiles and handshakes from strangers when he walked through the double wood doors leading into the narthex. These people didn't know him, yet they welcomed him.

He stopped at the back of the sanctuary. Ten wooden pews sat on each side of the red-carpeted aisle that led to the altar, and a stained-glass cross lit the sanctuary with the morning sun. Wow! Easter sunrise service had to be spectacular! Maybe next year.

He scanned the pews filled mostly with grey-haired worshippers, and his gaze landed on the left side, third pew from the front. Exactly who he was looking for. She caught his eye as he strode forward, and he lifted a finger to his lips hoping to silence her.

"Unca Luke!" Kitty's precious voice echoed around the sanctuary, and more than one person chuckled.

"Hey, Kitty Cat." Ignoring the deep-freeze glare from his brother-in-law, Luke slid into the pew beside his niece and opened his arms.

She flew right into them and hugged life into his bones. "How's my favorite girl?"

"I a good girl. Daddy's gonna take me to 'Donald's."

"You certainly have been a good girl." He tucked her onto his lap and wrapped his arms around her before finally meeting Travis's glowering gaze. "Can I come to McDonald's with you?" He said to Kitty as much as he did to Travis.

"Yes! I love it!" She squeezed him in another hug.

Travis crossed his arms and looked forward.

Oh boy. Luke rotated the stress from his neck. Somehow, he was the bad guy here. Not that he should be surprised. He tended to be the scapegoat for any problems within the Harrison regime. Usually, that didn't include Travis.

Following the service, he and Travis would talk, and if McDonald's had one of those playlands, that would be the perfect location to hash out their problems. The bell from the steeple chimed, signaling that service was about to begin, and just in time. He really needed this worship and prayer time before talking sense back into his friend.

After a short greeting and opening prayer from the pastor who didn't look old enough to have graduated from high school much less seminary, the organ chimed out the melody to the opening hymn, "Guide Me, Oh Thou Great Jehovah." A perfect song to ground him, to take the focus off himself and open his heart to worship.

An hour later, he sat across from the still-glowering Travis at McDonald's while Kitty zoomed to the play area, oblivious to the tension between the two men. At least, Luke hoped she was oblivious. She didn't deserve to be burdened with the problems that childish parents create.

His gaze on his daughter, Travis broke the silence. "Did Lydia send you?"

Luke snorted. "Of course."

"Of course." Travis took a bite of his burger. "And did she tell you what happened?"

"Just that you left her and took Kitty with you."

Travis laughed, but he wasn't smiling. "So she said nothing about her not seeing Catherine one day this past week, nothing about her promise to Catherine that they'd spend yesterday together at the American Girl store at the Mall of America, and then, without an apology, said she had to go to work instead."

Lydia . . . Luke shook his head. "She told me none of that."

"What were you thinking passing the North Loop job off on her?" The Antarctic glare returned.

Luke couldn't help but lean back. "Say what?"

"Her work's been doubled now, taking on your duties so you can go play candy man, leaving Catherine without a mother, me without a wife."

"Whoa." Anger bubbled inside, stealing his appetite, so he shoved aside his burger. "Apparently, she didn't tell you that the edict came from Dad. It was my choice to stay in the cities and complete the job. Dad took that contract from me and told me to head north to fulfill Gran's will."

Travis seemed to deflate. "I knew it," he said barely above a whisper. "I knew your dad was at the heart of this, but didn't want to see it."

"He sees an opportunity on the North Shore for development. Wants me to acquire some land."

"Of course he does." Travis watched his daughter slide through a tube to the ground, then she rushed back to the beginning of the vertical maze.

"I didn't know he dumped the entire project on Lydia." Luke nibbled on a fry.

"Who, like the rest of you Harrisons, doesn't have the guts to tell the man *no*."

Luke winced from being struck with the truth. Well, Tim didn't have problems speaking up. He seemed to get away with everything, which was a different problem altogether and not Luke's concern for today. He needed to focus on getting his sister and brother-in-law back together.

"Tell me what happened." His appetite overriding his emotions,

Luke picked up his cheeseburger and bit into it.

"I couldn't take it anymore." Travis shook his head. "She's never home. Never sees Catherine. Heck, Catherine doesn't even miss her when she's gone. And yesterday, when Lydia broke her promise, and Catherine spent all morning on meltdown, I couldn't take it anymore. I had to leave. Coming up north where she can't reach my cell was my best solution."

"She said you packed everything."

Travis sighed. "I was upset, and I wanted to make her angry. I wanted her to feel what I feel, and I wanted her to be scared. That was yesterday. Today I . . . I don't know if I want to go back." His Adams apple bobbed as he turned toward the play area.

"You can't mean that."

Travis shook his head. "I've basically been a single parent for over a year now. Why not make it official?"

"That's why." Luke pointed to the playland, at Kitty crawling through the tunnels. "She needs both you and Lydia. Lydia's going through a stage right now. She's always striving to please Dad, which is an impossible task."

"She's not the only one." Travis looked Luke in the eye.

"I don't have to—"

Travis's raised brows and cocked head stopped Luke midsentence.

"You really think I won't stand up to Dad?"

"You believe you will?" Travis crossed his arms on the table and leaned toward Luke. "Why aren't you in the cities yet? What do you hope to accomplish at the store? A business that even your gran knew wasn't a profitable venture."

"I . . . " Luke stared off at the playland, adjusting his thoughts. "A promotion at Harrison hinges on my success up north. A promotion I've been denied for too many years."

"A promotion that'll fill your schedule more than it already is. You think that'll make you happy? For Lydia, all it's done is made her more stressed."

"I'm not Lydia."

"That's for sure. She was made for the business world, but you? You're a completely different person away from it. A much happier person."

"Wait a second." Luke held up his hands. "I'm here to persuade you to come to your senses about leaving Lydia. This isn't about me."

"No, it's not, but it is about you understanding from my perspective. Your dad is an imposing figure that no one dares cross, and I can't compete with him. Not even with Lydia. If I could pull her away from the business, or even get her to stand up to your father, we'd get back on track, but as long as her life goal is to make him happy, family will never be a priority to her, and I can't live like that. Catherine needs her mother."

Travis took a sip of his drink. "Tell me, since you've been up here, how has your stress level been?"

"Stress? The only stress I've felt is when family calls, and that's because it's always business."

"Exactly. And Lydia says that she can't even reach you by cell most of the time—"

"Good thing, or I'd never get anything done."

"Harrison business."

"Is there anything else?"

"Yeah, it's called life. You need to get one."

Luke shook his head. "Why didn't you go into psychology?"

A smile flashed across Travis's face, but quickly disappeared. "Seeing a psychologist wouldn't be a bad idea for you. Work out those Mom and Dad issues."

Luke stared out the window at traffic zooming past. If only they could go back to the days before Mom's rebellion took her life and stole Dad's joy, leaving three kids behind in a loveless home. Travis' suggestion was something Luke had considered in the past. Maybe it was time to take a serious look into it. But first . . .

"I'll think about it, soon as you and Lydia make an appointment."

Travis snorted. "Lydia said she doesn't have time."

"You go without her."

"Maybe . . . " Travis stared over at the playland, his face a grim mask. "I love Lydia. Honestly I do. Part of me wants to make it work, and another says 'it's not worth it.' And don't quote the Bible at me. No one knows better than I do that God is very disappointed in me right now. I just can't do what He wants. Today. Maybe tomorrow I'll feel differently—I'm a messed-up work in progress right now—but today, this is where I need to be. And since I teach online, my job goes anywhere."

"There's nothing I can say to convince you otherwise?"

"Nope." Travis wiped at his nose.

Luke sighed. His friend was putting up a brave front, but Luke saw past it into a broken heart. He hated seeing his friend in pain, and he wanted to shake Lydia to her senses, but when had she ever listened to him? "How can I help?"

"You're doing it. You're here. You're praying. That's the most important thing."

But it still didn't feel like enough. Gran would tell him, "People don't fix people. God does." Still, he had a tough time leaving the fixing up to God.

"Daddy, Unca Luke!" Kitty ran over to the table and grabbed a fry from Luke's carton. "Did you see me slide fast?"

Travis scooped her onto his lap and pressed a kiss to her cheek. "We sure did, Kitty Cat. Let's see how fast you can go through the tunnels."

"I fast!" She took off for the play area.

"She doesn't seem to be bothered." Luke nodded toward Catherine.

"Why would she be? She's used to not having her mother around." He took a long sip from his drink. "But I'm done talking about us. I need to know what you've been up to. You've got yourself quite a tan already, and as we talked about, stress isn't radiating off you like it usually does. I'd say getting away from Harrison headquarters has been healthy for you."

An image of Jess popped into Luke's thoughts, and he couldn't help but smile. "Yeah, it's been good."

"More than the candy store? I know you like the place, but my gut tells me something else is going on."

Luke leaned back and rubbed his hands on his khakis. "I don't know. It's only been a week, but, there's this girl—"

"Ha! I knew it."

"—woman, I mean." He scratched his head. How did he put his . . . friendship with Jess into words? "I knew her years ago. When I worked at Gran's during the summer, we'd visit the neighbors when they'd have bonfires. They had two annoying little girls."

"Ahh, and one of those girls has grown into a woman."

Luke puffed out a breath. That was one way to put it. "Yeah, she's seriously hot, used to be a model—"

"Dude!"

"—but there's more to her. She's not afraid to get her hands dirty. Can wield a shovel better than I can. And she's got a gift with landscaping that I don't think she fully realizes yet."

"And you want to help her."

A sideways grin snuck out. "Yeah. I do."

"What's the problem? It's about time a woman catches your eye. I was beginning to wonder about you."

"Aren't you funny." Luke deadpanned and stuffed his mouth with fries, giving him time to respond. Travis was right. Luke had hardly taken a second glance at a woman since college. Even then, he'd been a monk, focusing on his studies while working part time at Harrison. He'd gone on five, six dates at the most, and never with the same woman twice. And now, the woman he was attracted to was the very woman he was going to hurt.

"There is a problem. Big problem. Dad wants me to buy the land on both sides of Gran's."

"And one of the lots belongs to . . . ?"

"Jess. Well, her folks own it. They want to sell—"

"That makes your life easy."

"Not really. Jess is attached to the property and is fixing it up to keep her parents together. They've split up too."

Travis snorted. "Seems to be a rash of that going on. Are you trying to fix them too?"

"Uh, well, no." Luke shrugged. "But I have been helping Jess out. Was supposed to be there today too, but Lydia called, and here I am."

"Man, you've got a hot woman interested in you and you're here doing the bidding of your sister?"

Luke nodded to the playland. "No, I'm thinking of Kitty. And you."

"The only love life you should worry about is your own." Travis checked his watch. "It's only noon. Two hours back gives you plenty of time to lend a hand, right?"

"I guess."

"What are you still doing sitting here?" He gestured toward the door with his head. "Get your heinie in gear and get back there. Catherine and I'll be fine. And I promise not to make any rash legal decisions, okay?"

Luke stood and looked down at his friend, throwing a mock glare. "You hurt my sister . . . "

"Yeah, yeah, I know, you'll hurt me. I'm scared." He faked a shiver and nodded toward the door. "Get going."

Luke aimed for the door, then spun around and headed for the playland. "Hey Kitty Cat, come give your favorite uncle a hug."

"*Oldest* uncle," Travis said behind him.

"Favorite." Luke caught Kitty when she slid out of the tunnel and squeezed her in a hug. "You be a good girl for your daddy, okay?"

"Uh-huh. I always good."

"Love you, Kitty Cat." He kissed her cheek and put her down, then made his way to his pickup. Travis was right. The only love life Luke needed to worry about was his own. He'd lift Lydia and Travis and Jess's folks in prayer and let God take care of them. As for Jess? Well, maybe it was time to think past putting the path together and taking her on a real date.

Tonight. After he'd helped her finish the path, he'd get up the nerve and ask.

Chapter Ten

Using the shovel as a crutch, Jess hobbled down the path. She'd overdone it big time yesterday, and shouldn't be out here today, but her parents' marriage was at stake. The sooner this garden path was completed, the sooner they'd be reunited. Today, she'd be ecstatic to finish the shoveling so she could layer in the gravel next weekend. Hopefully by then her foot would be healed and she'd be able to work on her own.

If only Luke were here.

She didn't even know where he was, what the emergency was, or even how to contact him if she did want to get in touch.

Did she want to get in touch?

The wings tickling her insides said she did, but what did they know? He wasn't here, and that was what mattered. She could do this on her own.

Lifting her foot to keep the pressure off it, she thrust the shovel into the dirt. She pushed, squinting her eyes and gritting her teeth, and managed to sling up half a shovelful. Seriously? This was going to take her until midnight to clear a few feet, much less the entire path. Using both feet was necessary. She stood on her wrapped foot and flinched, but that didn't stop her from stabbing the dirt with the spade. Wincing, she lifted the shovel and heaved another half-a-shovelful to the side.

And she went down with it.

She wiped her nose with blackened hands, not caring that she drew a dirty mustache beneath her nose. Gritting her teeth, she flung down the shovel. This was impossible. She lay back on the ground and shielded her eyes from the sun winking through waving leaves. *God, for once can't something go right?* Was it okay to complain to God? That was a question for Callie or Haven.

She pushed herself into a sitting position and her eyes widened as a vehicle rumbled down the cabin driveway. A very familiar vehicle. What was he doing here? She reached back and grabbed the shovel. Using it for leverage, she stood and hobbled toward the cabin.

Haven got out of the red crossover, followed by his son who wore shorts, showing off a prosthetic leg that looked like he'd borrowed it from Iron Man. Cool!

"Hey, Reese." She waved, and the boy ran toward her. "Awesome new leg, dude. Did Iron Man say you could keep it?"

Reese grinned. "Yep. Forever. And it does make me faster."

"I believe it does." Haven caught up to Reese and ruffled the towhead's hair. "I've got to really push myself to beat him in a foot race."

"Wanna race me, Aunt Jess?"

"Not on your life, kiddo. But I would like to know what you guys are doing here. What about the Twins game?"

"Rained out." Reese pouted, but his smile returned faster than he could run. "Dad said we could help you instead. Said I might find some cool bugs."

Jess wrinkled her nose. "You will find bugs, maybe even a snake, but I don't think they're so cool."

"Aunt Callie does."

"Well, your Aunt Callie has always been a little weird." Jess circled a finger by the side of her head, making the 'crazy' sign.

"Guess that's why she chose me, huh?" Haven still wore that goofy-in-love grin whenever he talked about his fiancée. He rubbed his hands together. "Lead the way, boss. What do you want us to do?"

"You guys are lifesavers."

"It's the least we could do. After all, this is where we plan to be married. We should take some ownership in it too. Besides, we want your folks back together as much as you do. If we have to use a little elbow grease to—"

"What's elbow grease?" Reese butted in.

"It helps you work harder." Haven nodded toward the shed. "See if you can find any in there."

Reese sprinted off.

And Jess laughed. "Sounds like something Callie would say. She's rubbing off on you."

"I couldn't ask for a better influence."

"True. But seriously, thank you for coming. Luke was called away, and my foot is killing me."

"And you're still trying to dig?" He nodded toward the spade. "We're relegating you to supervisory duties."

"But I—"

"No buts. So, sit on yours—butt, that is. Your foot won't get better if you don't stay off it."

"Aye-aye, Captain." She saluted and looked toward the shed for signs of Reese. "How long do you think he'll look?"

"The kid's tenacious. He'd be in there all afternoon, if I let him." He gestured toward the cabin. "Let's get you seated, we can talk more there."

Though she felt guilty for getting out of digging duty, she was grateful for the opportunity to sit. Haven was right, if she kept aggravating the foot, it would never get better, and then she'd never finish the path. It might even be fun bossing the guys around.

She limped onto the porch, dropped into one of the Adirondack chairs, and raised her throbbing foot onto the accompanying footrest.

"Be right back." Haven went into the cabin and came out seconds later with icepack, towel, and pillow and handed them all to her before going back into the cabin.

She elevated her foot on the pillow and wrapped the cold compress around it. Now, if Luke was here, he'd have taken care of this nursing step on his own, a gesture she found hummingbird-sprouting intimate. *I wonder what he's doing* . . . Should she even care? Maybe not, but she did. A man had never treated her with such tenderness before.

Haven came out and handed her a glass filled with iced lemonade and a blanket. "In case you get cold."

"Thank you." And without the physical exertion, she likely would get chilled. Not much sunlight made its way through the tree growth, and the air temps were always cooler near the lake.

"You're welcome." He sat in the other Adirondack chair, and rubbed his drink glass between his hands. "Callie wanted me to tell you that the For Sale sign is now up by your house."

Jess sighed. So, it was really happening. Everything in her life was being ripped away. She couldn't let the cabin go too. And now, in her spare time—ha!—she'd have to start looking for a new place to live.

He touched her arm. "You okay?"

"I guess." She shrugged. "I've wanted to move out on my own for a while. Funny how that doesn't sound as appealing anymore."

"Until you do, you have a home with Callie and me."

Living with newlyweds? Not happening. "Uh-uh. The last thing you and Callie will want in your little love nest is your sister-in-law." She nodded to the shed. "It'll be adjustment enough to have him living with you part-time."

Haven laughed. "True. What I meant to say is that *until* Callie and I get married, I'll bunk with a friend and you're welcome to stay in our home. We found one, by the way."

"So quickly?"

"Actually, we hadn't begun looking. We planned to talk to a realtor tomorrow, but Dad informed me that he's moving into a senior apartment complex. He's tired of the upkeep at the house."

"And you're buying his home? Callie's okay with that?"

"Yep. It was her idea. She loves Park Point and the old house and can't wait to add a feminine touch, which, since Dad and I have been baching it for years, will keep her busy for a long time."

"You're fine with her changing your home?"

"I'm all for her making it *our* home. Dad's moving a week from tomorrow, so she can begin the de-male-ization project."

"Let me guess, that was Callie's word."

Haven chuckled. "How'd you guess?"

"But what happens when Mom and Dad's place sells? Callie moves into your house, you bunk with a friend, what about Reese and your puppy?"

"I helped save a friend's house a while back, so he's more than glad to share it with me and my family." He jutted his thumb toward the shed. "Guess I better rescue Reese and start shoveling if we want to make progress while it's light out."

"You two are awesome."

"We are, aren't we?" Haven polished his knuckles on his chest, then blew on them.

Jess shook her head, but grinned. "Callie is totally wearing off on you." She enjoyed seeing the slightly-goofy side of the often-too-serious Haven.

Nature called, and Jess attempted to stand.

"Let me help you." Haven rushed back and took her hand. She managed to stand, and put a little weight on her sore foot, but lost her balance and fell into Haven as a pickup came around the cabin.

Luke?

With butterfly wings tickling her stomach, she pushed away from Haven as Luke parked beside Haven's red crossover.

"You know him?" Haven nodded toward the truck.

"That's Luke."

"Ahh, the candy man. The guy we met at the hospital, who's been helping you."

"Yep." She held on to Haven's arms for balance while Luke got out of his pickup.

Luke's gaze zeroed in on Jess's arm, so she pulled away. He walked stiffly toward the porch, his mouth a straight line. Could he be jealous? Naw, they weren't even going out. Not that she would mind dating him. Still, he didn't look pleased to see Haven standing so close to her. Or was she being self-centered? More likely, he was disappointed about whatever took him away yesterday.

"I'll get Reese." Haven helped her sit back down then hurried past Luke with a quick, "Good to see you again," on his way to the shed.

Luke walked up the steps and stuffed his hands in his pockets. "Jess."

"Hey, Luke. Everything okay?"

He sat on the edge of the chair Haven had vacated and stared off into the woods. "Not really. My best friend took my niece and left my sister."

Jess's hand flew to her heart. Talk about pain on multiple levels. "Oh, I'm so sorry."

"The thing is, I totally get why he left her. Lydia's a pain in the tush, but Travis has always been a solid rock, for me and everyone else. He's the last person I expected to skip out on his vows. I'm still trying to reconcile the whole mess."

"Do you think it's permanent?"

He shrugged. "I don't think so, but I didn't think it would go this far either. I'd be grateful for prayer for them."

"Absolutely." She reached over and touched his arm. "Thank you for coming back."

He looked over his shoulder at Haven and Reese walking back from the shed, then turned to Jess and said with no expression. "Looks like I had good timing."

He *was* jealous! That thought freed the butterflies again. They had to get tired pretty soon. "There are some important people I'd like you to meet." She waved Haven and Reese onto the deck and watched Luke's expression as she introduced them. "Luke Harrison, remember meeting my brother-in-law to-be, Haven Carlysle? And this is his son, Reese."

"That's right." Luke leapt from the chair to shake Haven's hand. "We met briefly at the hospital. Good to see you again." He bowed to Reese and turned on his English accent. "And pleased to meet you, Sir Reese."

Reese wrinkled his nose. "What?"

Luke made a motion like unsheathing a sword from his back. He aimed his empty hand toward Haven. "I feared I would be challenging

Sir Haven to a duel for milady's affections, but you have saved him from a painful death."

A single brow shot up on Haven's face. Reese snickered.

And Jess giggled. "Too bad. I've always wanted to watch a duel."

"No human battle today." Luke pretended to resheath his sword. "Only the battle to clear your path." He bowed to Jess. "At your service."

"Thank you, Sir Luke. And you will be grateful that you did not slay Sir Haven since he has promised to help promote your store."

Luke blinked and turned to Haven. "You're the photographer."

Haven nodded. "And you're the candy store owner. Callie and I are looking forward to helping."

"Candy store?" Reese butted in. "Can we go, Dad, please?"

Haven put a hand on Reese's shoulder. "I'm afraid it's not open yet."

"Not until Tuesday, but . . . " Luke held up a finger. "I'll be right back." He hustled to his pickup and returned with a candy box. "I came bearing gifts of apology for Lady Jess. I am certain she will be most happy to share."

"Apology?" She accepted the box from Luke.

His gaze focused on her, and he took her hands. "For leaving so rudely last night. I would have called, but I don't have the cabin's phone number."

"Hey, I understand." She winked. "We'll have to exchange numbers later, but for now." With her never-to-be-clean-again fingernail, she slit the tape securing the lid on the candy box. "I think we need a little chocolate energy before you gentlemen get to work."

Each guy took a couple pieces of candy, while she resisted temptation and selected one. She gestured to her foot. "Sir Haven has requested that I allow you men to take over shoveling duties for the day. How could I refuse?"

"Sir Haven is a worthy knight." Luke clicked his heels together and gestured toward the path. "Shall we begin?"

"Let's do it." Haven grabbed the spade off the deck while Luke hurried to the shed for the second one. He also found a bow rake for Reese to spread the dirt on the sides of the path.

She obediently watched them work and served them lemonade and even promised grilled steak when they finished today. Luke seemed to get along with Haven and Reese as easily as he did her. The man was a chameleon, changing his personality depending upon who he talked with, and always in a way that would leave everyone smiling.

Unless it involved his family. Like last weekend when Luke's dad stole his joy. And last night when the note from his sister snatched him away from her.

Otherwise, he did whatever seemed to make people happy.

So, did that mean he wasn't attracted to her, but knew how to make her smile?

Arghh! There went that negative Nelly again, whispering in Jess's ear that she wasn't good enough. She banished Nelly from her thoughts. If only she'd stay away.

Several hours, three huge steaks, and one smaller steak later, she was seated alone on the porch with the guys. They were filthy and rancid-smelling, but the path was completely shoveled out. Three grimy guys never looked more handsome.

Until they started a conversation about passing gas. Men! No, make that, Boys!

Jess groaned. "Seriously, Haven, does Callie know this side of you? Because if she doesn't, you need to tell her. It's not wise to keep secrets from your fiancée."

He grinned. "What do you think, Reese, does Callie know this side of me?"

"Oh yeah, she does." Reese giggled. "And she pretends to be all upset about it, especially when Dad and I have contests."

Jess moaned. "I didn't need to know that." With the guys laughing, she got up and gathered the plates. "Time to remove myself from this conversation."

"Let me help you." Luke started to get up.

"Nope." She gave him a slight push in his chest—a solid chest at that—and he sat back down. "You boys have done your work for the day. Now it's time for me to do mine." She brought the dishes into the cabin, washed them, then returned outside.

In that short span of time, Reese had fallen asleep on the wooden deck, and the other guys looked like they could follow suit any moment.

Haven yawned with a stretch. "Guess it's time I get my buddy home to his mother. My weekends with him go way too fast."

But at least he now had shared custody of his son. Just over a year ago, he didn't even have visitation rights. Haven shook Reese's shoulder. "Time to go, buddy." The kid didn't move, so with a groan, Haven picked him up and hefted him over his shoulder. "The kid's getting too big for this."

"When he wakes up, tell him thank you. I'm sure this wasn't as much fun as a baseball game."

"I don't know." Haven shrugged. "He enjoyed the work. And . . . " He nodded to Luke. "And the pretend time. Especially when you saved Jess from the dragon."

Luke laughed and stood. "That snake was at least a foot long." He offered his hand to Haven. "I enjoyed meeting you. Glad we didn't have to duel. My sword-fighting skills are pretty rusty."

"Although, your determination would be hard to beat." Haven patted the phone in his back pocket. "Callie and I will see you Thursday night. She'll get your social media buzzing."

"That means a lot to me." Luke fell back into the chair as Haven took off with Reese. "Man, my arms feel like jelly. I swear you could spread them out on a peanut butter sandwich."

"Good thing you've got a week to recover before we begin Phase Two."

"Which would be?"

"Adding gravel. It should be delivered on Friday."

"You remember that I can't help until Sunday? Once the store's open, that's going to be my day off. No candy-making on Sunday, only sales, so a couple of teenage girls will man the store."

"Some day off. You get to come shovel rock."

"But I get to shovel with a beautiful woman. Sounds like a win to me."

Jess felt the blush flame on her cheeks. Sure, she'd been called beautiful before. Quite often, even, but never had it sounded or felt as genuine as when Luke said it.

"Which brings me to another topic." Luke turned his chair to face hers, and he took her hand. "I don't know that I want to wait until Sunday to see you. And I don't want to spend all my time with you working. Would you happen to be free Saturday night?"

He was asking her out? "Like, to go on a date?"

"I guess that's what it's called." He grinned.

Oh, there went those butterflies again. She tamped them down long enough to answer, "I'd love to."

LUKE RANG UP THE candy order for two preteen boys. Just two baseball-shaped chocolate suckers, but those boys were already drooling. Nothing felt better than watching the joy on customers' faces when they purchased chocolate. Even going back to his days working here as a teen, he couldn't ever recall someone being angry after their purchase. Maybe beforehand, but chocolate brightened everyone's day.

The boys ran from the store, their purchases already in their mouths, leaving the customer space empty for the first time today. He checked the wall clock. Seven already? Where had the time gone? How nice to be so busy that he hadn't had a moment to check the clock. His receipts for today were going to take a bite out of that roof bill. Okay, maybe a nibble, but a nibble was better than a lick.

So, nothing could spoil this opening day of the store. Not the rain that had been coming down in sheets since six this morning. Chocolate fans wouldn't let that stop them. Not the newfangled cash register that decided not to connect to the internet during the first sale. No problem. Instead, they dug out Gran's vintage machine with its five columns of numbers that you pressed in before hitting the Total button. It even made that fun *ka-ching* sound with each addition. That thing was a beast and would work forever. So what if his high-school-aged employees had to figure change the old-fashioned way? It was good for them to learn how to calculate without a machine.

And that new, useless machine? It was going back to where it came from, and he'd get a nice little refund, so its break-down was a double-win for the store.

Not even the ruined batch of candy could get him down because he'd learned something: never tell jokes around Mary Obermiller when she was mixing chocolate. Although, it was rather funny watching her false choppers land in the center of the chocolate-filled copper kettle. He hadn't had a gut-aching laugh like that since . . . he couldn't remember when.

So, as Gran once said, "When life hands you lemons, coat them with chocolate." He did enjoy a chocolate-covered lemon now and again.

The bell chimed above the door signaling the arrival of a new customer. A very pretty customer.

His good day was getting even better. "Hey, Jess."

"Hey yourself." She sauntered toward the glass display counter and looked around the customer-less store and frowned. "I hope it's been busier than this all day."

"Haven't had a break until this moment." He motioned toward the end of the counter. "Come on back. Let me give you a tour and introduce you to the brains behind this business." He unlocked the hinged counter and lifted it so she could pass through, then locked it back in place.

He brought her into the back room where Mary was finishing up a batch of dark-chocolate-covered cherries. "Mary, I'd like to introduce you to someone special."

Mary looked up and grinned. "No introduction is needed." She slid off her vinyl gloves and wrapped Jess in a hug. "It's so very good to see you again. It's been too long." She stepped back, keeping her hands on Jess's shoulders. "Looks like life has been treating you well. Such a healthy glow to your cheeks."

"Thank you." Jess elbowed Luke. "He's had a little something to do with it."

"Has he now?" Mary peered at Luke out of the corners of her eyes. "Are you what's been keeping our Lucas whistling all day long?"

"Maybe." Jess looked down, but that didn't hide the gorgeous shade of pink flaming on her cheeks.

"Definitely." Luke put an arm around Jess's shoulders. "She's even agreed to a date with me this Saturday. Mighty charitable of her, don't you think?"

Mary tut-tutted and returned to her candy-making. "You make sure you treat her like a queen, Lucas Harrison, or I'll report you to her parents. By the way, Jessica, how are your folks doing? I know your father had a stroke last summer, and I watch your mother every night on the news, but word of his recovery has been slim since then."

"Not so good, actually."

Luke side-hugged Jess even tighter.

"It's been tough on both of them and ... " She sniffled. "They've since separated."

"Oh, lands, no. Not Mr. and Mrs. Beaumont." She held a cherry mid-air. "I remember back when they were dating. Your father was smitten. Oh my! And your mother? She was just as smitten but played hard to get. Loved watching that romance blossom." Mary shook her head. "I'll be sure to add them to my prayer list. And you too, Jessica. I know this is hard."

"Thank you, Mrs. Obermiller."

"Mary. Just call me Mary like Lucas here, and we'll get along fine."

"Mary it is. And I'm very thankful for your prayers. We certainly need them."

"God can perform miracles in people's hearts. Just you watch."

"I will." She checked her fitness tracker and sighed. "It's time I head home, but I couldn't miss opening day."

"One moment, young lady." Mary plucked a finished candy off a tray. "No leaving until you try one of my chocolate-covered cherries. They are truly scrumptious!"

"If I have to." Jess grinned and accepted the chocolate. She bit into it and sighed. "That is downright sinful. I could eat the whole tray."

Luke gave Mary a one-armed hug. "This lady's a magician with chocolate, and I'm grateful she works for me."

"And you are a pleasure to work with." She shrugged away from his arm. "Now, I need to return to work."

Jess licked chocolate from her fingers. "And I have to head home before I sample more of your concoctions. Nice to see you again, Mary."

"You too. Don't be a stranger now."

"I'll walk you out." Luke followed Jess to the front of the store and helped her pass through the counter opening. Thoughts of leading her outside and giving her a goodbye kiss dashed through his mind, but now wasn't the right time. Maybe on Saturday . . . ? His heart sprinted at the idea. Instead, he reached up and tucked a strand of hair behind her ear. That almost felt too intimate for this setting. "Thanks for coming in. You topped my very good day with homemade whipped cream and a maraschino cherry."

She giggled. Such a beautiful sound. "See you Thursday night to talk marketing?"

Marketing? All he needed to do was put Jess's picture on the front of the website and he'd have every red-blooded male in the north country stopping in. "Yep. See you Thursday." His hand slid down to the small of her back as she made her way out the door.

Yep, this was a good day all right. Whistling "Toot Sweets" from the *Chitty, Chitty, Bang, Bang* musical, he returned to the back of the counter.

"I hear you, Lucas Harrison." Mary's motherly voice came from the back room. "Sounds like someone else I know is smitten."

No doubt about it, he was definitely smitten. Still whistling, he began straightening the candy display when the door chimes alerted him to a new customer. "Welcome to Superior Sweets." With a smile he looked up.

And his smile evaporated. No, this didn't ruin the day, but it sure added a sour taste. "What are you doing here, Tim?"

Chapter Eleven

Luke remained still as Tim swaggered up to the counter and whistled.

"Hoo-ee. Who was that woman who just left the store? I'm thinking I need to get her number."

Anger zinged through Luke's body like lightening striking an antenna. "No one who'd be interested in you."

A sideways grin grew on Tim's face. "You got a thing for her, don't you? Huh. Setting your sights higher than you used to."

Luke crossed his arms. "What do you want?"

"Looks like you found yourself a home, big brother." Tim smirked and picked up a pink bunny sucker. "Dad would be proud." He returned the sucker to its cup.

"I'm sure he'd be ecstatic," Luke said without emotion. "Are you up here checking on me? Dad can't take my being out of touch?"

"You really think you're that important?" Tim pressed his palms flat against the display glass.

Luke clenched his fists. Oh, he wanted to tell his brother to get his blankety-blank hands off the glass, but that was exactly what Tim wanted. Besides, he could hear Gran whispering in his ear, *If you can't say something nice, what are you going to do to change?* So, Luke took a breath and returned to straightening the display. "Can I get you something?" he said in the nicest tone he could muster, which still wasn't very nice.

"Is that the tone you use with all your customers? With that chick who—"

"She's not a chick. She's a woman who's miles above your pay grade."

"So, you do have a thing for her." Tim walked around the small customer display area and picked up a wrapped piece of fudge. "Gran's recipe?"

"Of course."

Tim unwrapped the candy, dropped the wrapper on the floor, and popped the chocolate into his mouth. His eyes rolled back. "Oh, man, as good as I remembered." He looked at his Rolex. "What time do you close?"

"Half an hour," Luke said through gritted teeth. "And pick up your wrapper."

"Yes, Mom." Tim picked it up, scrunched it together, and stuffed it in his pocket. The bell jingled behind him and a group of four—two adults and a couple of preteens, likely a family—came in, saving Luke from spewing something he'd regret.

Why was it his family brought out the ogre in him?

Tim nodded upward. "I'll wait for you in your apartment. Got a key?"

Luke eyeballed the family while they browsed through the products. "You still didn't tell me what you're doing up here."

"I thought that was obvious." Tim grabbed another piece of fudge and unwrapped it. "I came to pick up my inheritance." He opened his hand as if to drop the wrapper, but instead closed his hand around the wax wrap and tossed the candy into his mouth.

Luke balled his fist into a wad that tightened his muscles all the way to his shoulder. *God, give me strength, because I really, really want to belt him.* Tim didn't deserve that Bible. He wouldn't treat it with the love and respect Gran had shown it over the years. But keeping it for himself wasn't Luke's decision. At least he'd had a week-plus to take in Gran's wisdom. If only Tim would treat it in the same manner, maybe he'd finally grow up.

"Your key? Or do you keep your place unlocked in Hicksville?"

"Ask Mary." Luke grumbled. He opened the counter to let his brother pass through. "Don't touch anything."

"Ha!" was Tim's only reaction as he ambled into the back room.

Luke squeezed and loosened his fists several times while observing the family in the store front. They deserved his best. Unfortunately, his best right now was only a notch above grumpy. Still, he took a deep breath and summoned up a smile. "Welcome to Superior Sweets. How can I help you?"

"What do you recommend?" The woman's gaze flitted over the display.

"A box of Gran's Goodies is always a hit. That's a one-pound box filled with about thirty pieces of chocolate-coated candy. Some with nuts. Some creams. Some fruit. And it always comes with a piece of wisdom from Gran for the customer."

The adults conferred among themselves while the boy picked up a football-shaped sucker. "Can I?"

The girl found a sucker with a soccer-ball design. "Me too?"

"Sure. Why not?" The man got a stern look from the woman, which he ignored.

The woman shook her head, but smiled. "We'll take a box of Gran's goodies and the two suckers."

"Yay!" the kids shouted together.

Luke taped up a box of Gran's Goodies and rung up the sale. The woman handed him cash, which he laid on the flat surface right above the cash drawer. He punched in a button on the register and it *ka-chinged* as the cash drawer popped open. Ah, he loved that sound. Yep, going with the antique machine had been a good idea. He counted back the change.

"Would you like a bag?"

"Not necessary." The woman shook her head. "Have a good evening."

"You too." And just like that, he was in a good mood again.

People always smiled when they bought chocolate. Maybe that was why Tim was grumpy. He took his chocolate without any sacrifice, but rewards tasted much better when there was some sacrifice involved. Had Gran said that? Probably.

For the next hour, a steady stream of customers came through the door. Didn't matter that the store officially closed a half hour ago and Mary had already gone home. Luke wasn't going to miss one sale. A single sale today could easily ripple into many more sales over the summer. Word of mouth was the best advertising. Well, that and creating a quality product, which Mary and her crew did.

Finally, the last customer left the store. Luke locked the door and put up the Closed sign. He wrapped today's proceeds in the sales tape and bagged it up. For now, he locked it into the safe below the stairs along with the cash they'd already pulled from the drawer. Once he sent Tim on his way, he'd count out today's receipts, and that could take some time. With the exception of the surprise visit from his brother, today's opening had been exceptional. He wouldn't let Tim ruin it.

Whistling, he made his way up into his apartment.

No one was there. He checked his bedroom. Gran's bedroom. The bathroom. No sign of Tim.

He checked the dormer in his room where he kept Gran's Bible for nightly reading.

It was gone, and in its place was a manila envelope, large enough to fit unfolded eight-and-a-half-by-eleven paper.

Oh boy.

His shoulders tense as a sailor during a storm, Luke slit open the sealed envelope and pulled out a sheaf of papers with a Post-It note on top that read, *I won't let Dad know I told you.*

Say, what?

Luke rifled through the papers. An official county map of Bettis' land, and an amount in arrears on property taxes.

Bettis was going to be foreclosed on for tax evasion! Luke slapped his forehead. A few minutes of research would have given Luke this same public information.

No wonder Dad was so teed off about Luke not being in touch. No wonder Dad gave him such a measly amount for purchasing the properties. Dad already knew this information and was testing Luke to see if he could find it too. A test he'd received a big fat F on. Sure, Luke still had to approach Bettis with an offer. Sell to Harrison Land Development and make some money, or lose everything to a county sale. It was a no-brainer for Bettis and for Harrison. And would gain Luke zero brownie-points with his dad.

Luke flung the papers onto his bed and let loose a curse. Now the only way to appease his dad would be to purchase the Beaumont property.

The next day, he called Roland Bettis and took him to lunch, dangling the deal-you-can't-pass-up carrot, and he blindsided Bettis with his information. No surprise, Bettis settled for a super-low price that would allow Harrison Property Development to pay off the taxes and still leave a nice amount for the Beaumont property.

After Bettis huffed away from the restaurant, Luke remained at the table, the meal sitting like rotten eggs in his gut. Gran would probably come back to haunt him tonight.

But what haunted him worse was the meeting with Jess and her family on Thursday when he'd have to call off the date. He'd keep his promise and help her get the cabin in shape, and then he'd make her parents an offer they couldn't refuse.

Jess would hate him for life.

She wasn't the only one. He'd hate himself too.

"I'LL TAKE CARE OF your planters." Jess's gift wasn't marketing, but she had to add something to this conversation. Most of the evening, she'd spent listening to Callie, Haven, and Luke brainstorm ideas to increase Superior Sweets' public exposure.

"Great idea, Jess." Callie wrote *Jess flowers* on a whiteboard she'd brought to record all the ideas. "Your floral creations are always eye-catching." She nibbled on her lower lip and read off what they'd already written down:

Talk up selling points such as:
- Locally owned
- Recipes passed down through three generations
- Candy still made old-fashioned way, stirred in a copper kettle
- Use only high-quality ingredients
- Local ingredients used when possible

Then they talked about ways add to the customer base:
- Add healthy products to appeal to a more health-minded generation
- Draw in customers during the winter season, between holidays
- Make Superior Sweets a destination, rather than a quick stop
- Update the website
- Establish a bigger social media presence
- Get professional shots of candy and the store
- Jess could even model for them

Blah, blah, blah. None of that mattered right now, because Luke had hardly looked her in the eye all evening, though he'd been friendly enough to all of them. With their first date in two days, she'd anticipated a little flirting, not friendly. What was wrong with him? Could it be his family again?

"You okay, Jess?" Callie rested her hand on Jess's arm, waking her from her musing nap.

"Fine, I guess." Her gaze slid to Luke, who looked away.

"Haven and I are taking off, then. See you at home?" Callie picked up the whiteboard and markers, her voice hinted at worry.

"Yep. Soon."

"We'll talk when you get home." She squeezed Jess's shoulder. "And Luke, thank you again for all the work you've done on the cabin. I can't wait for the big reveal."

"Glad to do it, especially with you prettifying the store's image."

Jess couldn't hold back a chuckle. "Prettify? Sounds like something Callie would say."

"Hey, I resemble that comment!" Callie planted her hands on her hips.

And Haven kissed her cheek. "Yes, Super Cal, you definitely do." He shook Luke's hand. "See you Sunday?"

"I'll be there."

Silence overtook Luke's little apartment as Callie and Haven walked downstairs. Jess didn't want to say anything until she heard the outside door shut, but then she'd find out what was wrong with Mr. Moody, who'd gotten up to bring dishware to the kitchen.

Finally, the downstairs door opened and closed, and the rumble of a motor started outside. That was her cue.

"It's your family, isn't it?"

His head shot up and his gaze met hers.

"That citified man arriving at the store on Tuesday when I left, got into some expensive car. He's related to you, isn't he? And he's what's made you so grumpy."

Luke shook his head. "Are you clairvoyant, or what?"

"It's simple math. Whenever your family's involved, you're cranky. Otherwise, you're fun to be around."

He scratched his head. "That pretty much sums it up." He returned to the cozy living room and sat kitty-corner to her in an arm chair. "And, yes, that was Tim, my younger brother. And, yes, he has this uncanny ability to turn my mood upside down."

"Only if you let him."

"I don't . . . " He groaned and flung his head against the chair back. "Gran always asked me why I gave my family so much power. I still don't have an answer."

"Well, on Saturday night and Sunday, or whenever you're with me, you're not allowed to let them spoil your time."

"That's just it, Jess, about Saturday." He sat forward, his elbows on his knees, and hands folded, his eyes finally focused on her. But instead of her heart skipping, goosebumps sprouted on her arms. He scratched his forehead. "I . . . "

"You what?" They couldn't break up. They weren't even a couple yet.

He took a deep breath, and smiled at her. Boy, was she confused.

"I'm sorry, Jess. I haven't had a lot of time for dating, and honestly, going out Saturday night's got me tied in knots." He nodded to the open space next to her on the couch. "May I?"

She nodded.

He sat beside her and once again looked her in the eye. "I'm scared to death I'm going to blow it with you. You make me smile, Jess. You make me laugh, and I really want to get to know you better, but there's a huge part of me telling me I don't deserve you, and that voice doesn't like to shut up."

"Deserve me? Ha! If you knew what I've done, you'd probably run away quicker than a kid can eat a sucker. Callie tells me I'm forgiven. I know it here." She pointed at her head. "But struggle to believe it here." She placed her hand on her heart.

"I guess we're a matched pair." He bowed at the waist. "Will you do me the honor of accompanying me on a date Saturday evening, Lady Beaumont? I shall pick you up at seven and promise to leave my family behind."

"Sir Luke, I would love to join you, but I do have one important question."

"Anything."

She chuckled. "Do I dress up for the occasion? Or is it a jeans event?"

"Hmm." He tapped a finger on his whiskered chin, drawing her attention to lips she really wanted to kiss. Not too long ago, she would have acted on that urge without hesitation, and it likely wouldn't have stopped with a kiss. Callie hadn't warned her that being a Christian would be so hard. "Casual, with walking shoes."

"You have me intrigued." She swallowed. It was time to remove herself from temptation. "And now I need to get my beauty sleep, so I'm at my best come Saturday." She got up, and he followed suit.

"Allow me to escort you to your carriage, milady."

"I would be honored."

He followed her down the stairs, took her arm the rest of the way to her car, and even opened the door for her. "Until Saturday." He blew her a kiss and gently closed her door.

Oh boy, was she a goner.

But could she be serious with someone who let his family dictate his moods?

That wasn't a decision to be made today, but it was definitely a test for the future.

JESS RUSHED UP THE steps to her apartment and banged open the door. She'd never be ready in time for her date tonight! She shouldn't have gone to the cabin today, but the work had called to her this morning. Shoveling rock certainly wasn't glamorous, but it had given her one-on-one time with God, something she was only now beginning to appreciate, and she'd completely lost track of time. Luke would understand, wouldn't he?

She grabbed clean undergarments and a robe from her bedroom and hurried to the bathroom. The door was closed, and she prayed that Callie wasn't planning to use the shower too. Or that she hadn't recently gotten out of the shower and used all the hot water. She knocked. "Callie?"

"Out in a sec."

"Thanks."

Jess tapped her foot against the hardwood until Callie stepped out, all primped and ready for an evening with Haven, even though it would be an evening spent with their father and Reese too.

"Running late today?" Callie pushed past Jess.

"Very." Jess closed the door and took the fastest shower of her life. When done, she put on her robe and bundled her hair into a towel and sped to her walk-in closet that had more clothes and shoes than she could wear in a year, and a purse to match any outfit.

What was it Luke had said about tonight? Dress casually, with walking shoes.

Seriously? Walking shoes? What did he have planned? Most of the previous dates she'd been on had been dress-up events where she got to wear high heels and spangled dresses. Scrunching her nose, she scanned her rows of shoes. She'd mucked up one pair of tennis shoes today, and her other pair of tennies would not go with anything but work-out clothes.

She drummed her fingers against her thigh. What would Callie wear? She was an expert at casual. Jess stepped out of her closet and called out, "Callie, can I have some help?"

This was quite the turnaround for the sisters. Usually, Callie was the one asking for dressing advice.

"Be right there." Callie called back. In another minute, Callie joined Jess in the closet. "What do you need?"

Jess sighed. "I have nothing to wear."

Callie chuckled, then slapped a hand over her mouth and talked through it. "Sorry, but it looks to me like you have too many choices."

"But I don't have the right shoes. Luke said, 'shoes for walking.' I always thought the purpose of shoes was to make your legs look longer and slimmer." She laughed to convey a joke, but if she honestly thought about it, that had been the purpose of the majority of her previous shoe purchases. Anything to draw attention to herself.

"Okay . . . you going hiking? Walking?"

"No clue. He just said 'dress casually and wear walking shoes.' I didn't realize until this moment how hard that would be."

Callie tapped her chin for a bit, then raised a finger. "I've got it." She hurried from the room and returned with a pair of burgundy Converse low tops. The sisters couldn't share clothes, but they did wear the same size shoes. In the past, that hadn't mattered because Callie's taste was a lot more rugged than Jess's. "How about these with . . . " Callie rummaged through Jess's dresses. "With this?" She pulled an Aztec-like patterned dress from the rod. The red in the scoop-necked dress with the full, twirly skirt, matched the shoes perfectly.

"Yes!" Jess took the dress. "And I could wear this"—she selected a waist-length jean jacket—"over the top in case I get cold." She held the dress in front of her and frowned at the mirror. She did love the dress, but it tended to emphasize her chest, which wasn't small, and it did end above her knees. "Do you think it's too short for the night?"

"Too short?"

"Yeah, you know, I don't want to be, um, well, too sexy."

"Oh, you're too funny, Jess. There's nothing you could dress in, including that dirty outfit you wore home today, that would make you unsexy. Sorry, sis."

"But . . . " Jess worried her lower lip. "Luke is different, Callie. I want him to see *me*." She splayed a hand over her heart.

"From what I saw on Thursday night, he does see you."

"No, no, no, you don't get it." Jess draped the dress over her arm and gestured toward her bed. Sitting beside Callie, Jess ran her fingers along the dress's soft fabric. "When you create a website for clients, you're going for a specific audience, right? You're looking to send a specific message."

"Yeah."

"Well, is how we dress any different? Whenever I've dated in the past, I dressed to send a certain message, one that said, 'Look at me. I'm sexy.' I dressed to get attention, and not just from my date. That's not the message I want to send to Luke. You said when I believed Jesus died for me, I became a new creation. I believe that, and I want to show it."

"Oh, Jess." Callie embraced her sister. "You do show it, not only in how you dress, but in how you behave. You have the biggest heart, and Luke sees that. This outfit." Callie touched the dress. "It says you feel good about who God made you to be. It's fun and flirty and, yes, on you it'll be a little sexy, but that's okay. That's part of who you are."

"You're sure?"

"Yes. Now, hurry and get dressed." Callie glanced at the wall clock and gave Jess a little shove. "You have twenty minutes."

"Twenty?" Jess felt her toweled hair and groaned. "My hair'll take longer than that, and I haven't done my makeup, and I want to talk to

Dad before Luke gets here."

"Don't worry about Dad, he's doing fine today. Reese even got him to play Connect Four this afternoon. Tonight, Haven's challenged him to a game of checkers. Both are supposed to be good stroke therapy. If we don't tell Dad the games are therapy, we're fine."

"That's not why I want to talk to him." Jess took her hair out of the towel and shook it. "Remember when Haven picked you up for that non-date-that-turned-into-a-date, and Dad came out to meet him before calling you, and gave him the you-better-not-hurt-my-girl speech?"

Callie giggled. "That was so cute."

"I know." Jess took a minute to put the dress and jean jacket on and formulate her thoughts. She didn't want to come across as whiny and jealous, but didn't know how to phrase it otherwise. "Dad's never done that for me. He's never met my dates. Never gave them that stern-Dad look." Which really wasn't that stern, but still, Jess coveted the loving action from her father.

"I'm sorry, Jess. Yes, you need to let him know. But first . . . " Callie fingered the tips of Jess's very wet hair. "You need to take care of this."

"Tell me about it. Thanks for the talk, Cal."

"Any time." Callie gave her a hug and got up. "I need to get ready for my guy, too." And with that swoony look in her eyes, Callie drifted out of the room.

Okay. Time to stop feeling sorry for herself, and get ready. She looked in her full-length mirror and twirled around, making the skirt swirl with her. Not bad. Not bad at all. Well, except for the hair. Ugh! Maybe if she dried it and braided it loosely off to the side, that would certainly fit the fun, flirty, and casual look, and wouldn't take nearly as long as straightening or curling her hair.

But first, she needed to have a talk with her father.

She hustled downstairs and found him in his recliner/lift chair which he seldom left anymore, watching a game show channel. The show couldn't be all bad for him, could it? Some of the game shows did force you to think. "Hi Daddy." She approached him and gave him a kiss on his cheek, and knelt by his chair. "How are you feeling today?"

He stared at the television screen. "Same as always."

And same answer as always. Maybe her request would encourage him to try. "I wanted to let you know I'm going on a date tonight."

"Good. Good." He patted her hand. "You need...to get out and...have f...fun."

"Um, this is a new guy I'm seeing, and . . . " She shrugged. "I really like him, Daddy."

"Good f...for you." He patted her hand again, not taking his gaze away from the TV. He wasn't getting her hint.

"Could you?" She cleared her throat. "Would you like to meet him? He should be here in . . . " she checked her fitness tracker. "About five minutes." And she still had very wet hair.

"Sure. Bring him...to m...me." His stuttering was getting worse not better. Was her request flustering him?

Didn't matter. Her dad wasn't going to get better if they molly-coddled him. "Luke'll be here before I'm ready, though. So, could you let him in, please? You met him briefly at the office."

His gaze turned steely, but he still didn't meet her eyes. "The candy m...man?"

Jess swallowed. "Yes. I really like him, Daddy."

"Hmph." With his good hand, he changed the channel to a University of Minnesota Duluth baseball game.

And apparently, that was the end of the conversation. She got up and patted her dad on the shoulder, letting him know she loved him, but she couldn't say the words right now. Not with tears so close to the surface. So what if Dad wouldn't get up to answer the door? He was fully capable, but that would take effort he wasn't willing to give. That didn't mean he didn't love her. She hurried back to her apartment and dried her hair. Mid braid, she heard the doorbell for her apartment.

"I'll get it." Callie called out and hustled down the stairs.

"Thank you." Praying Luke would forgive her for being late, Jess finished her braid, and touched up her make-up, keeping it casual to match the outfit. Someday, maybe, she and Luke would have a date where she could go all out. Unlike Callie, Jess loved dressing like a princess, and she'd love to see Luke's reaction when he saw her.

But that was for another time.

Hopefully, he'd want another date after tonight.

She attached the gold strap to her burgundy clutch and draped it around her head and over her shoulder, adding a touch of bling to the casual. She slid on Callie's shoes, inhaled a deep breath, and made her way down the steps to the landing that led to both the upstairs apartment where she and Callie lived and the downstairs apartment occupied now only by their dad. She opened the door, and there he stood. Hair combed and beard trimmed to the sexy five-o'clock-shadow look, and a smile that slowly grew into a grin, making his eyes shine. His slim-fit jeans, a light blue button-down shirt, and a tan linen blazer fit him perfectly. Casual looked super-sweet on him.

Luke took her hands and looked her in the eye. "You look amazing, Jess."

She felt a blush rise to her cheeks and she looked down at the hardwood and shrugged. "Thank you." Summoning courage, her gaze met his. "You're not so bad yourself."

His grin grew wider. "I did okay without my sister's help?"

"Oh, yeah, very good. I, on the other hand, needed my sister's help."

"Well, she did—you both did a very, very excellent job."

Sheesh, could she blush any more? Why even bother wearing makeup?

He held out his arm. "The chariot awaits."

She gave one last look to her parents' apartment before taking his arm. "Let us be off." She flung her free arm into the air.

Luke opened the outside door for her, and she began to step through when the door to her parents' apartment swung open.

There stood her dad, his eyes stern, cane in hand. "Wh...where do you th...think you two are g...going?"

Chapter Twelve

"... UH ... " LUKE STAMMERED and swallowed the cotton-candy-like knot sticking in his throat. He straightened to full height, like a good knight should, and met Mr. Beaumont's gaze. "Sir, I plan to escort your daughter on—"

Mr. Beaumont drew a hand across his throat, silencing Luke, and grinned. "H...had you going there, didn't I?"

"Daddy!" Jess shook her head, but she was smiling.

And, dang, was it a pretty smile. Made his insides act like jumped-up jelly beans, and made him really want to kiss those full, silky lips.

Mr. Beaumont raised his cane and pointed it at Luke's midsection. "I see that l...look, young m...man, and I'll have y...you know I expect you to...to treat my Jessica Rose with r...respect."

"Yes, sir." Luke gulped.

"And I expect her b...back home at a decent hour." He tapped his watch. "I'll be w...waiting up." He winked at Jess. "Did I do g...good?"

"Perfect." She raised on her toes and kissed her father's check. "Love you, Daddy."

"Now you have f...fun tonight." Mr. Beaumont said to Jess then turned to Luke and the father-glare returned. "Not too much fun."

"No sir." And with that, Luke whisked Jess outside, not certain how to take her father's command. It seemed half serious, half fun. Regardless, Jess's pretty smile showed she relished the attention.

A smile he wanted to see all night tonight, and with what he had planned, that shouldn't be a problem. He didn't know her very well yet, tonight should remedy some of that, but he knew enough to know she'd enjoy the evening. And if she enjoyed it, he would too. Nothing felt better than making someone happy.

He drove to Fitger's, the brewery built in the 1850s, now restored as a hotel and retail complex along with the brewhouse. He found an open spot in the nearly-filled parking ramp, and pulled in. They walked from the ramp and through Fitger's winding, old brick building, past independently-owned retail stores and restaurants. Then he led her outside, down a long flight of steps to the Lakewalk. On another date, they'd dine at one of the fancy restaurants inside.

Assuming they had another date.

A swift breeze whooshed off the lapping waters of Lake Superior, and he shuddered. Beside him, Jess hugged herself, and he could see her shivering. Wasn't the wind blowing the other way earlier? All Duluthians knew that when the wind came down the hill, it was much warmer than when it blew off the lake.

Well, he'd make the most of this opportunity. As any gallant knight would, he switched sides with Jess so he was closer to the lake and taking the brunt of the cold breeze, and he curved an arm around her shoulders. "Do you mind?"

Her snuggle gave him the answer he desired. *Ha! Take that, cold wind!* On the way back, though, they would take the sidewalk up on Superior Street instead.

"Where are we going?" she asked, her head tucked against his shoulder.

"You'll see." And when she did see where he was taking her, her eyes would light up with joy. He couldn't wait. Until then, they shared small talk while others whizzed past them on the asphalt walkway. Bikers, in-line skaters, joggers, families peddling together on surrey bicycles. That would be fun for another time. There was no end to the entertainment along Lake Superior. He breathed in the fresh lake air and listened to the seagulls laughing around him. Even they were joy-filled.

Maybe he was meant to live up here.

Maybe that was what Gran was trying to tell him with her gift.

Could he live here and still work at Harrison? If he did the job his dad wanted, that would open this area for the business. But did Luke really want to see the kind of development Harrison specialized in, up here, marring the North Shore?

Or, there was one other option. Did he really want to work at Harrison anymore? Wasn't he happier without the stresses Harrison Property Development laid on him?

"Dollar for your thoughts." Jess gave his waist a squeeze.

"What?" He shook his head. "Oh. Just thinking how much I love it up here, debating if I'll go back to the cities."

She stopped, shook out of his hug, and stared at him, her eyes narrowed. "That's an option? What about the candy store?"

"Well, you see, uh . . . " He scratched the back of his neck. How did he tell her about his promotion without revealing what was required of him to achieve it? "I love the candy store. I love the employees, the customers, seeing everyone skip out of the store as if the day's burdens aren't so heavy anymore, but there's no way I can make a living at it. Gran could barely feed herself, much less keep the store open. The repairs I've had to do, that were neglected over the years, have nearly exhausted my savings." His most accessible, liquid savings anyway.

"I'm sorry, I don't get it. If you're not planning to stay, why put any money into it at all?"

"On your left." A jogger shouted behind them.

Luke pulled Jess off to the side, to a bench facing the water and the gray-boulder filled beach.

Why was he putting money into a store that his dad would tear down the second Luke's six months were up? "I've been asking myself that since I came up here. Why throw my money away? Dad's not too happy about that either, but he has no say. All I know is that I've felt compelled to get the store going again. God's been nudging me, and I'm going where He nudges."

"Hmmm." She leaned against his shoulder.

"Hmmm?"

"I'm new at this God-thing, but it seems to me that maybe God's nudges are telling you it's time to make a change."

Exactly what he was afraid of.

"That's what happened to me." Jess tugged her skirt so it covered her knees. "I'd modeled for over ten years, and that's where my identity was, but deep down I wasn't ever happy with that because my identity was whatever my agent or clients wanted to make it. Before I met Christ, I never knew that there was a unique person in here." She pressed a hand to her chest. "And I still struggle believing that, but ending my modeling career was a new beginning for this new creation, a healthy beginning, and I've never regretted it, even though I still fight the desire to be in the spotlight." She looked directly at him. "Does that make any sense?"

He nodded and bent down to search the rocks for a flat, skipping stone. Jess made too much sense, actually. And it hit too close to home. What was his identity? Who was he anyway? A lackey for his dad? Did Luke really enjoy working at Harrison, or was he there only to gain approval?

"Tell me about your job at Harrison. What do you do? Do you like it?"

He snorted at her last question. "Like? That's a relative term. I like working with the people in the company, and I'm involved somewhat in contract negotiations. Mostly I spend my days looking at spreadsheets and researching."

Jess yawned and covered her mouth. "Sounds dreadful."

He laughed. "It really does, doesn't it?"

"So why stay? If you're miserable, get out."

"It's not that easy. Harrison Property Development has been in the Harrison family for over a hundred years. That's a hundred years of sons—and daughters—keeping the company alive."

"But there's more to it than that, isn't there?"

Dang, she was intuitive. Talk about putting a damper on the evening. Not anymore. He nodded to the walkway. "How about we save shop talk for another time? I will talk about it, I promise. But today, I want to enjoy being with you." He stood, held out his hand, and bowed.

"Shall we continue, milady?"

As always, the term brought out the radiant smile that lit his mood. "Lead the way, Sir Luke."

He tucked her hand into the crook of his elbow and they continued on the Lakewalk. Soon he'd see her smile grow even brighter. He couldn't wait! He guided her off the Lakewalk onto a path that climbed upward and over a pedestrian bridge. Taking a cobblestone pathway, they passed a statue of Leif Erikson with an inscription that claimed Erikson discovered America in 1000 A.D. Then they sat on a grassy hillside and listened to a women's trio sing from a stone stage that had turrets on both ends and fronted Lake Superior. If he'd been thinking, he'd have brought a picnic along for the evening. Another day.

When the trio left the stage, he helped Jess up and his heart accelerated with anticipation. This was going to make her day!

His heart slowed, though, when they neared the garden, and his shoulders drooped.

The roses were growing, but weren't in bloom yet. Strike two for his perfectly planned evening.

But Jess squealed and ran ahead. Like Maria at the beginning of *The Sound of Music*, she spread her arms and twirled around in the center of the massive gardens, her skirt flowing out beneath her like a rose in bloom. He could watch her all day.

Hands tucked in his back pockets, he slowly walked toward her.

She ran back to him and planted a kiss on his cheek. "How did you know this is my favorite place?"

"Flowers?" Feeling his cheek burn where her lips had been, he spread his hands. "Your face lights up whenever you talk about the gardens you're planting for your parents. Simple math. One plus one equals . . . "

She breathed in and closed her eyes. "I could spend forever here. We'll have to come back when they bloom. You wouldn't believe the scent."

"When exactly do they bloom? I researched gardens in Duluth, found this one, and knew this was where I wanted to take you. Didn't give a thought to their not being in season."

She knelt beside a bush with a bud just appearing on the end of a stem. "But don't you see, each stage is beautiful. Inside this little bud is a bloom waiting to break out. I find that fascinating."

He knelt beside her and pushed her braid away from her face. "I find you fascinating, Jessica Rose. The name fits you perfectly." And he loved that deep shade of pink glowing on her cheeks.

"Callie's and my names were Dad's idea. The flowers at the cabin couldn't grow year 'round, so he and Mom named their daughters for flowers so they would always have blossoming flowers around."

"Callie's named for a flower?"

"Callista Lillian, like Calla Lilly. No surprise, that's her favorite flower."

"Your dad sounds like a wise man."

She looked down and fingered a thorn-covered stem. "He used to be anyway."

Luke lifted her chin and their eyes met. "He still is. That man who lectured me this evening loves you dearly, and when he sees what you're doing for him, that will give him the motivation he needs. It'll be the reminder your parents need to see that their marriage may be going through a prickly time, but there's beauty at the end."

"You think so?"

"How can they not be drawn together by what you're doing?" He stood and offered his hand and nodded to a white gazebo reminiscent of the one in *The Sound of Music*. He grinned imagining Jess leaping from bench to bench singing like Liesl. "Do you sing?"

She stopped. "What?"

"Sing, you know, tra la la?" His voice squeaked through notes he knew hurt her ears.

"Not like that, I hope." And her smile was back again. "Other than in the shower, the only singing I do is in church, and I hope the people around me don't go cross-eyed listening to me."

He grinned. "We shall make a beautiful duet."

"God hears our hearts, right?"

"I certainly hope so, or He has massive sound-blocking headphones."

Her laugh sent those jelly beans pinging around his heart again.

Man, was he moonstruck or what? So far tonight, he'd swung at two strikes, yet she somehow turned that around. But for this final part of the date, he really wanted it to be perfect. His stomach rumbled, and she laughed at that too. "Guess it's time to eat." He checked the time. Fifteen minutes until their reservation.

"Wonderful. I'm starving." She patted her stomach. "Working at the cabin today, I forgot to eat, I was having so much fun."

"I thought you weren't going to the cabin until tomorrow."

She shrugged. "I hadn't planned on it, but it called to me and I went. That's why I was late meeting you tonight."

He pretended to pull out a sword. "We shall slay the hunger."

That prompted the giggle he'd hoped for. He held out his arm, and she linked hers around it.

They followed the path out of the garden onto a sidewalk lining Superior Street. It teemed with people enjoying the beautiful spring night. A few minutes later, he and Jess arrived at *Per Vivere*, an independent Italian restaurant in an old brick building overlooking the lake. He gave his name to the maître d', who led them to the outdoor patio and a little round table for two.

The breeze was still blowing cold from the lake, so he removed his blazer and draped it over her already-jacketed shoulders. "Is that okay? Or would you prefer to go inside?"

"When we have this view?" She looked him in the eye. "A few goosebumps are worth it."

Was she talking about him or the lake? *Shake it off, Harrison. Not everything's about you.*

The server came by, brought them water, informed them about today's specials which included Zuppa de Pesce, and that made Luke laugh out loud.

The server frowned and left.

"Zuppa de Pesce is funny?" Jess took a sip of water and set it in front of her.

"The Zuppa isn't, but . . . " He hovered his hand about three feet off the ground. "When I was little, I remember Dad taking me and Tim and Lydia out to an Italian restaurant that didn't impress me at all. White tablecloths. Candles. Cloth napkins. Dining out meant burgers and fries, not Italian. That was for grownups. Anyway, I ordered spaghetti, because you can't muck up spaghetti, and Dad ordered the Zuppa. Something in it reeked to me." He plugged his nose. "So, I reacted by pushing it away . . . "

He stretched his hand out mimicking the motion and bumped Jess's water glass. "Oh no." He reached for the glass, but was too slow, and water gushed toward Jess's lap.

"Oh, snickerdoodles!" She shrieked and jumped up, her chair falling and clanking behind her, but was too late. Her lap was soaked!

"I am so sorry." He grabbed his napkin and rounded the table. Realizing he wasn't about to dry her dress, he handed her the napkin and went to find a server or busser. This was strike three for the night. Of course, she'd want to go home now; their beautiful evening was ruined. All his research to plan the perfect evening, and he struck out at every level. Seemed he wasn't any more successful in his love life than in his business life.

Heart plummeting, he found a server who gave him several napkins. He hurried back to the table, the server right behind him.

Jess was . . . laughing?

Luke jerked to a stop, and the server bashed into him, knocking Luke into the table, spilling his glass of water across the table. Klutz!

She laughed harder as she wiped the cloth napkin over her dress. "You should have seen your face." She handed wet napkins to the server then wiped down her chair while the server dried the table. "Talk about a look of terror."

He stood there mute, trying to reconcile what he was seeing and hearing, and finally eeked out, "Well, yeah, I just spilled all over you."

"Water, Luke." She sat and folded her hands on the now tablecloth-free table. "You spilled water. It's harmless. My dress is fine. Damp, but fine."

He plopped down into his chair and the server scurried away. "Cold water, and the air is cold, and now you're—"

"Having the most fun on a date I've ever had."

"Say what?" He rocked back in his chair, catching himself before toppling backwards. That would have been par for the night.

Yet, Jess was having fun. He had to be caught in the *Twilight Zone* or something.

"You are so cute and real and none of this evening is about seducing me."

He blinked. "You mean guys have . . . " He couldn't imagine treating a woman so horribly, be it first, second, or twentieth date. Now, ending this date with a kiss? That was a different matter altogether.

"All the time, and I used to encourage it." She looked to the lake and swallowed hard, then turned back and faced Luke. "There's you who gave me an evening walk and the jacket off your back. You didn't just give me a bouquet of flowers, but an entire rose garden. Now you're giving me a sunset dinner. Do you know how sweet that is?"

Heaven help him, he felt his cheeks blush. "You deserve to be treated like a princess, Jess."

The server came up behind Luke and spread a new cloth over the table. With eyes dancing over smile-free lips, she handed both Luke and Jess plastic cups with a lid and straw. "Can I get you anything else?"

Luke snort-laughed and Jess covered her mouth, trying to hold her chuckle in, but failed.

They accepted the cups and clinked them together.

"To memorable first dates." Luke sipped through the bendy straw. "I knew I liked this place."

"My new favorite." Jess grinned and his heart did an end-over-end flip.

Luke was falling, and he was falling hard.

Maybe he should listen to what his heart was telling him, and about the direction God was nudging him in. Because the more time he spent with the lovely Jessica Rose, the more he wanted to be with her, which meant he needed to make a decision.

If he were to pursue a relationship with Jess, that meant turning his back on his promotion and the family business. Jess was making that easier than he imagined because going through life with her sounded like a lot more fun than spending time with family.

They placed their order then chatted about life and family and flowers. The food came and they talked about work and family and candy. Before they realized it, the sun had set and stars now squinted through the sky's blackness. In that little bit of time, he'd made his decision. He wanted to pursue a relationship with Jess, unfettered to the family business, and the thought alone was freeing.

The bad part was telling his dad and hoping Dad would someday forgive him. His phone buzzed as the thought flitted through. Whoever it was, they could wait.

Jess laid her napkin on the table. "Go ahead and answer, I need to take a break." She sashayed past him.

And he groaned. She had no clue what she was telling him to do. Answering the phone could ruin their evening, but he tugged it out anyway. By the time he got it out, though, whoever had called had hung up. Luke looked at the caller I.D. and fought the urge to hurl his phone into the lake. For once, could his sister not interrupt his time with Jess?

But she rarely called unless it was important, so he called her back. If she wanted to talk business, he'd be firm about not doing any work for Harrison until tomorrow. Tonight was for Jess alone.

She answered at the second ring. "Luke?"

"What do you need?" He practically barked, then realized how rude he sounded. "Sorry about that. I'm in the middle of something."

"Where are you?" Her voice crackled over the line. "I'm in your apartment above the store."

"You're where?" His head dipped back on his shoulders and he stared upward. "I'm on a date, Lydia."

"Well you need to end that date now because I'm here and Travis is on his way with Catherine. We need you to moderate between us."

We *need* you. Not will you or could you, but we need you. He squeezed his shoulders, trying to loosen tensing muscles. How could

Luke tell them no if they really wanted to get back together?

"Fine," he said through a sigh. Doing what was right was more important than doing what pleased himself. "I'm about forty-five minutes away, but I'll be there." After he talked the two into getting back together, he'd wring both of their necks for spoiling his imperfect-perfect date.

Chapter Thirteen

Jess practically floated back to the table. She couldn't remember ever having such a fun evening. She couldn't remember laughing so hard, or so much, that her gut ached. So what if her dress got a little wet, she now had memories that would always prompt a smile. And she had a great souvenir cup to help her remember the evening.

It would make a great little vase.

She reached the table, and her happiness evaporated like water in a desert. Laughing-Luke had been replaced with somber-faced Luke, and it didn't take a cardiac surgeon to figure out who stole his joy.

"Your dad called?" She sat across from him and took his hands. At least, that provoked a glimmer of a smile.

"No. My sister. She's at—no, she's *in* my apartment."

"In? And you didn't know she was coming?"

"No clue. She probably figured I'd tell her to stay home, so she invited herself in, and now she's begging me to mediate between her and Travis, who'll be there soon." He squeezed Jess's hands. "I couldn't say no."

"Of course not. I know how important it is to hold marriages together, especially when children are involved." Even adult children.

"You're not mad?"

"I'm disappointed that our date has to end, but if it ends with a family being restored? I can't think of anything better."

Luke shook his head. "You're the best. I don't deserve you."

She grinned. "The feeling's mutual." She grabbed her clutch. "Let's go save a family."

He stood and grabbed both water cups. "Can't forget these." He bowed at the waist and gestured toward the door. "After you."

She led him out of the restaurant, where he took her hand. His strong, callused hand in hers felt so right and natural as if God had created their hands to fit together. Was this what real love felt like? Or was it too early for that? What she did know was that she was crushing on Luke in a major way. She loved his sense of humor and desire to make others smile. She adored his gallantry, and even his devotion to an obviously broken family. He set the example for her to never give up and made her even more eager to complete the cabin path that offered hope for her own broken family.

They walked side by side down the block, past a couple more renovated buildings, and back to the darkened parking ramp at Fitger's to his pickup. He'd been quiet since the call, but she'd come to know that was how he processed information and feelings. He drove out of the ramp and took a left onto Superior, heading south rather than north toward the store.

"Need something before you head to the store?"

"What?" His brows furrowed, he shot a quick glance her way and refocused on the busy road.

"I thought you needed to hurry to the store. Heading north on Superior is the fastest way."

"Yeah, but you live this way." He nodded to the road ahead.

Oh. Duh. A little communication on her end would help. "I don't want you to take me home. You need me with you."

"Uh-uh, not happening. It's gonna get ugly tonight, and I don't want you to see that."

"And your niece shouldn't see it either. Who's going to watch her while you adults have it out?"

"Oh . . . " He tapped a finger on the steering wheel, and pulled over on the side of the road in downtown Duluth. "What about clothes?"

"Clothes?"

"For working at the cabin tomorrow. I don't anticipate coming back to Duluth tonight."

"I have work clothes at the cabin."

His finger continued its tapping. "What about getting home? Your vehicle's at your home."

She shrugged. "I have a neighbor I'll call. He owns a cute candy store next door to the cabin."

"Oh. Yeah." He chuckled nervously, but his finger slowed its dance.

"Do you think with a little flirting, he might give me a ride?"

"Flirting, huh?" The corner of his mouth lifted. "He might be convinced, that is, if you agreed to a second date with him."

"Hmmm. That's a big price to pay, but I think I could swing it. He is rather cute."

"You think so?" His brows flitted up and down several times.

"I do. But don't tell him. I don't want him to get a big head."

"Mum's the word." He made a zipper motion across his smiling lips. His finger began its steering wheel dance again. "You'd really watch Kitty Cat for us?"

"No. I'd do it for . . . Kitty Cat? That's your niece's name?"

He laughed, the love for his niece breaking through his anxiety. "Yep. Catherine is such an adult name for a little girl. I couldn't call her that, but Kitty Cat or Kitty fits her."

"And it goes with your store."

"There's that, too. I guess you're coming with me." He grinned and whipped the pickup around to head north. "How is that you have this way of lifting me up when I'm feeling cranky?"

"It goes both ways."

"Speaking of cranky, I don't want to face your dad's wrath, so you should call him."

"Oh, right." He'd likely be sleeping by now, so she called Callie instead, who informed her that a couple had gone through the house tonight, apparently their second walk through. The realtor felt positive about this couple.

If selling the house would ease their dad's frustrations, she was all for selling it. Still, it was going to be difficult saying goodbye to the only home she knew. That made keeping the cabin even more important. Once her parents saw what she and Luke were doing, they'd have to change their minds.

She closed her eyes, breathed in, and lifted a quiet prayer of thanks for Luke. In a time when her parents' separation should leave her stressed out, his presence gave her a surprising calm. Callie was right, God would provide exactly what was needed. Why had she been so blind to that all these years?

As Luke drove, she rested, knowing it could be a long night. And tomorrow would definitely be a longer day of hauling rock. At least Luke would be there to help.

Or would he? With this new family problem, did that mean he'd have to back out again?

Nope. Not going to worry about it. Today had enough worries of its own. Wasn't that a Bible verse? She'd have to look it up when she got to the cabin.

Until then, she'd rest.

It seemed she'd barely closed her eyes when Luke gave her shoulder a little shake. "We're here, Jess." His voice came out flat, as if he was trying to mask his anxiety.

She yawned and stretched. "You ready?"

"I'm ready to keep going down the road and hang out at your cabin for the night. I could pitch a tent by the lake and sleep like a hibernating bear."

"Or get woken up by a very hungry, just-out-of-hibernation bear."

"Let's see." He held up one hand, palm upward. "Cranky bear." He held up the other. "Cranky sister. Looks like the bear wins."

Jess sat up straight and motioned like a TV model toward Luke's apartment. "Sir Luke, you are required to mediate a conflict between two warring factions of my kingdom. I trust you will have success in bringing peace to the realm once again."

He shook his head, heaved a sigh, then sat up, squaring his shoulders. "I shall do as Lady Beaumont wishes, and I shall bring peace to your kingdom, as well as mine." He pushed out of the pickup and came around to Jess's door and offered his hand. "A warning, milady, it could be a bloody battle, and I wish that neither you nor Princess Kitty Cat witness the skirmish. We will draw our swords elsewhere."

She curtsied, accompanied with a giggle. "For that I am very grateful."

He offered his arm, and escorted her to the stairway entrance. He opened the door, heard yelling on the inside, and blocked her from going in. "I will lead the way, and will take any darts or arrows intended for the enemy."

"Your chivalry is much appreciated."

She climbed the stairs behind him, each creaky step announcing their arrival, quieting the verbal battle waging above. That poor little girl, hearing every cutting word flung by parents. At least Jess's parents hadn't ever fought in front of her and Callie.

No. They just didn't speak to each other at all. Wasn't that equally bad?

Luke reached the top of the stairs and stepped aside for Jess. She stayed beside him, her gaze darting from Lydia to Travis, who held a clinging toddler in his arms. The tension filling this room was thicker than chocolate fudge. She reached for Luke's hand and he grasped hers tightly.

His jaw was stiff as he introduced the couple. "Lydia, my not-so-wise sister, and Travis, my best friend and usually-wise mentor, this is my . . . " He stood tall. "My girlfriend, Jess Beaumont."

At his 'girlfriend' declaration, she beamed inside and that flowed to her mouth, curving it into a smile she didn't want to show right now.

Lydia, her mouth agape and brows arched high above her eyes, glanced between Luke and Jess and then at their hands. "Girlfriend? Jess Beaumont, as in the people-next-door Beaumonts?"

"One and the same." Luke stretched his arm around Jess's shoulders. "She's come to watch Kitty while the three of us hash it out downstairs."

Lydia looked at Jess with a sly smile that made Jess shiver. "Interesting."

But Travis stepped toward Jess, relief relaxing his features, and offered his hand. "I'm grateful for your help."

Jess reached for the scared child, taking note of the two-story dollhouse nestled in the corner of the living room. Dolls didn't inhabit the space, rather, a trio of stuffed animals sat on the Barbie doll-sized furniture. Did Luke keep that around for his niece? Wouldn't surprise Jess if he did. "Hey, sweetie." She made a circular motion on the child's back. "How about you and I play with the dollhouse?"

The girl raised her head and peeked over at Jess while clinging to her father. "You play house?"

"I love playing house." And that was the truth. She'd spent hours as a child playing with her Barbie dolls, mostly having them on stage singing or modeling, but this couldn't be too much different.

The girl looked up at her dad, who nodded and smiled. Worrying her lower lip, she slowly reached over to Jess, who enveloped her in her arms. "And you can call me Auntie Jess, okay?"

Kitty nodded.

Out of the corner of her eye, Jess watched the three adults head downstairs. Once she heard the door close, she let the girl down.

"I'm hungry." Kitty ran straight to the refrigerator.

Jess followed slowly, nibbling on her lower lip. Should she give the girl something without asking first? But asking meant interrupting, and she wasn't about to do that. She opened the fridge and stared at its near emptiness. Water bottles. Milk. Pop. She looked through his cupboards and found canned soups, peanut butter, and soda crackers. Crackers were safe, weren't they?

"Would you like a cracker?"

"I love crackers!" Kitty rubbed her stomach.

"Me too." Jess mimicked Kitty's tummy rub. "Let's sit you up on a chair, and I'll give you a cracker and water snack, okay?"

"Okay!" Kitty ran around the mini-peninsula and attempted to climb up on the barstool. Before the toddler could pull the chair over on herself, Jess scooped her up and set her on the stool.

"Stay put and I'll get your snack."

"I be good."

Jess certainly hoped so. She set a few crackers on a paper towel, poured a small glass of water, then sat beside Kitty. Jess nibbled on her cracker while Kitty downed three.

"I done!" Kitty started to get down, and the chair tipped.

Jess grabbed Kitty and the chair before either could tumble over. Whew. A crash certainly would have brought all three adults running upstairs.

"Play now?" Kitty squirmed out of Jess's arms.

"Good idea, sweetie."

"I not Sweetie, I Kitty." The precocious child clamped pudgy hands on her hips.

Jess didn't have to wonder where Kitty'd seen that action before. Jess didn't know Lydia at all, but from the way Luke described her, Jess could easily envision Lydia taking that same stance and having the same attitude.

"I'm so sorry, Kitty."

"Okay." And just like that all was forgiven. If only adults forgave as easily. Kitty toddled over to the house, sat on the floor, and hugged a panda Beanie Baby against her chest. "This my Dada."

Jess sat cross-legged beside her. "Your daddy is very nice."

"Mmm-hmm." She picked up a pink unicorn with a purple horn, mane, and tail. "This is Kit Cat."

Jess stroked the unicorn's mane, while listening to the door to the apartment open and close, followed by footfalls heading up. It was best to keep the child occupied so she wouldn't want to go to the familiar adult. "Kit Cat is so soft and pretty."

Kitty grinned up at Jess. "Like me."

"Yes, just like you." Jess bopped Kitty's nose with the panda, then picked up the rainbow-colored inchworm, while keeping a peripheral eye on Lydia staring into the mostly-empty refrigerator. "This must be Mommy?"

"No, siwwy, that's Nana." Still holding the panda, she got up and walked to what looked like a bedroom. A second later she came out with a tie-dyed dragon. "This my mommy. She live at work, not home."

Lydia gasped behind Jess, drawing Kitty's attention, but only briefly. Instead of bringing the dragon to the playhouse, she dropped it on the floor by the bedroom door and toddled back to the Jess.

Listening to Lydia rush down the stairs, sniffling, Jess's heart sank. How Lydia must be hurting!

But, maybe her heart breaking was exactly what was needed for the young family to begin mending.

LUKE LEANED BACK IN the unforgiving folding chair and yawned. This conflict would likely go all night, and tomorrow he'd be exhausted. But he'd promised to help Jess tomorrow, letting his teen employees man the store. He'd be at the cabin regardless of whether he got sleep or not. Most importantly, if he could get these two talking tonight, they'd be on the road to reconciliation. The road would be filled with potholes, but life's journey was often broken up with potholes.

Footsteps shuffled into the storefront, and Luke looked up, puzzled. Lydia plodded into the room, sniffling, and her eyes red as licorice. Quite the change from the in-control attitude she'd had prior to heading to his fridge.

He peered over at Travis, who sat sideways and unmoving on a window seat, his arms crossed over his chest, his eyes observing his wife. Luke wanted to shove him, tell him to go comfort his wife, but Luke also didn't know how often this type of scene had repeated, numbing Travis to Lydia's histrionics.

So, he kept quiet, as he'd done the entire time with the two, just watching, listening to two people he loved put each other down, and it broke his heart. Yeah, Lydia could be pigheaded, and she did work too much, but she did love her daughter and Travis.

Then there was conflict-avoiding Travis, who didn't make a move until things got out of control. Luke wanted to smash their two heads together, but they were doing a good enough job of that on their own.

Finally, Travis sighed and uncrossed his arms, though he didn't move from his seat.

Through glassy eyes, Lydia stared at her husband, her shoulders hunched as if weighted down by Superior-sized boulders. "She doesn't need me." The words blew from Lydia like a frigid lake breeze.

"What do you mean?" Travis leaned forward, but didn't get up from the seat.

Lydia wiped at her eyes, and glared at Luke. "It's your fault, you know."

"Whoa." He held up his hands. "I never talk bad about you to Kitty."

"No, but it's your fault Dad gave me this extra assignment. Your fault I sleep at work half the time. I'm too exhausted to go home and be mom to Catherine." Her gaze slid toward her husband. "Wife to Travis."

"Uh-uh. Not taking the blame." He thrust his pointer finger southward. "This was totally Dad's idea. I said I'd stay on at Harrison."

"You didn't put up much of an argument. You caved to him faster than I could say 'wait.'"

"And you haven't caved?"

"I have a family to support."

"Gee, thanks, Lydia." Sarcasm dripped from Travis. "Sorry my teaching salary doesn't afford the lifestyle you want."

"Okay, guys, that's enough." Luke held out his hands like a crosswalk cop motioning people to stop. He gestured to the folding chair he'd brought in for Lydia, and a bang sounded above them, followed by a quick stamping of feet.

"No, Luke, I'm not done." Lydia came over and got in his face, obviously oblivious to what was going on upstairs with her daughter. "I'm done with you bowing to Dad, leaving Tim and me to do all the work. You get this sweet assignment up here where you get to play candy man all day and even find time to court the enemy's daughter. Or . . ." A wicked smile drew across her face. "Or maybe, Lucas Albright Harrison, you're using that smooth-talking gift to sweet-talk her."

He leapt up and went nose-to-nose with his sister. "Don't you dare bring Jess into this."

"Hmmm." She turned around and walked a few feet away, then turned back as crying now echoed from the back room, coming closer.

Jess appeared in the doorway, hugging a sobbing toddler and talking faster than a child ate chocolate. "I'm sorry to interrupt. She's okay, just scared. She knocked a pile of books on the floor and ... " Apparently realizing the tense moment she stepped into, she quieted, and her gaze flicked from Luke to Lydia,

"I never knew you had it in you, Luke." Lydia's haughty gaze flicked to Jess.

"Quiet, Lydia." Luke growled.

Jess's eyes widened, and she slowly began backing out of the room.

"Toying with a woman's affections so you can make the deal for Dad? Get the Beaumont cabin at a lowball price?" Lydia stepped closer to him, a wicked smile on her face. "That's more Tim's turf, isn't it? Maybe there is a bit of bad boy in you after all."

Chapter Fourteen

hat?" Her body suddenly numb, Jess let Kitty slide to the ground. The child ran to her dad, her crying turned to sniffling. Jess stared at Luke. "You've been using me?"

"Let me explain." He opened his hands.

And she balled hers into fists. Let him explain. Ha! That was code for 'I have a really lame excuse for my bad behavior.'

"No," she said, her voice shaking, along with her body. She fled from the front of the store and ran through the candy-making room to the back door. She flung open the door and it slammed against the side of the building while she stepped onto the small deck overlooking Lake Superior. Yes, she'd been used before, but not like this, not by someone she'd grown to care about. Had tonight been an act? She hugged herself, trying to ward off the shivers.

She looked to the north toward the family cabin. It wasn't far, but to get there, she'd have to go through a thick copse of trees that hid any number of hungry, wild animals. Bats. Bears. Wolves. And she had no car up here either, so she was stuck. Well, she'd go grab her clutch and get Lydia or Travis to take her to the cabin. She went around the side of the building and tried the door to Luke's apartment, but it didn't budge. Couldn't one thing go right for her?

Refusing to cry, she returned to the deck and sank down in a cushioned chair. Luke wanted to buy the cabin? Why? Had he been helping her all this time only to get on her good side? The man could win an Oscar for his acting performance, because earlier this evening, she'd felt cherished.

That was what she got for letting her emotions rule. This meant she was on her own again, but she could do it. When she'd begun the cabin's improvements, she'd planned to do it on her own. With Luke's help, she was ahead of schedule—for that she was grateful. So what if he'd used her, she'd actually benefited from his deceit, and now that she knew his plans, she could tell him adios.

Why did it hurt her heart so much to think that?

The door to the store creaked open behind her, so Jess closed her eyes and slowed her breathing, hoping whoever it was, probably Luke coming to beg for forgiveness, would think she was sleeping and leave.

"I'm sorry, Jess."

Lydia?

Jess's eyes snapped open and she watched Lydia sit in the other deck chair, her legs off to the side so she could face Jess.

"What I did in there . . . " Lydia wiped at her cheek. "It was vindictive and very wrong."

You think? Jess had no kind words to answer with, so she nodded in agreement.

Lydia looked down at her hands, folded tightly together. "When I overheard Catherine say 'Mommy lives at work,' I lost it because I knew she was right. And there I see you playing with her, connecting with my daughter in a way I never have, and I became jealous. And mad. Not at you, but at myself for becoming a clone of my father. For doing to Catherine and Travis what Dad did with the three of us kids after Mom's stupid stunt. I know shutting out the family is Dad's way of dealing with a broken heart, but I don't want it to be mine."

Jess turned to Lydia, but wasn't ready to forgive yet. Didn't the Bible say something about guarding your heart? While Jess appreciated the words Lydia said, part of her told her this was a trick. Another big city way of duping the seller into selling cheap. Jess wouldn't be so easily fooled again, so she clamped her mouth shut and let Lydia ramble on.

"I was jealous of Luke for escaping Harrison, leaving me behind. And seeing that joy on his face when he looked at you? How could I let him be happy, when I'm miserable?"

Jess's heart softened more, but she wasn't quite ready to forgive. "Was what you said true? Is it Luke's intention to buy the cabin?" Because that was what really mattered. His intentions would show his heart.

"I can't speak for Luke. Will you talk to him again?"

"I don't know." Jess stared off at the black waters and an owl hooted.

"Then let me tell you this. I know he cares for you, and in more than a casual friend way. Don't let me be the reason you two break up."

The thought of breaking up before they'd barely begun dating left a bitter taste in her mouth, but if Luke planned to buy the cabin, how could she continue to date him?

Wind rustled the trees around her, its voice singing through the leaves, almost sounding like they were whispering, "Listen."

Fine. But that was all she'd do. She breathed in the fresh air, and nodded. "I'll talk to him."

"Thank you." Lydia steepled her hands by her chin and nodded, then got up and went into the store. Seconds later, the door creaked again.

Luke claimed the deck chair and anger zinged through her veins.

"I'm sorry." Remorse imbued his voice, but he'd already proven to be a great actor. Or had he?

"Is it true?" She didn't dare look at him, knowing she'd fall for the wounded expression that was likely covering his face.

"About me planning to buy the cabin?"

She nodded.

"It had been."

"As in past tense?"

"As in . . . " He sighed. "Here are the facts. When Gran died, she left me this place in her will, but to inherit it, I had to live here six months following her death, or the store and land would go to our other neighbor." He nodded sideways, directing Jess's attention south. "I wanted to turn it down, let Bettis take it, and work at Harrison, but Dad said go. He said if I fulfilled my end of the deal and bought both Bettis' land and your land, I'd finally get the promotion I've been wanting for years."

"But why? What does your dad want with our land?"

Luke shrugged. "I don't know his exact plans, but it would be some kind of development."

Jess clenched her teeth together. "And ruin the shoreline?"

"I don't know. There are ways to develop land to blend in with nature, not steal from it, and that's what I would have pushed for, but I don't have the final say."

"Do you still plan to buy the land?"

"No, Jess, I don't. When I moved here, buying your land had been my intention, but then I met you, and reconnected with all the people who'd worked for Gran, and fell in love with working with customers again. It makes no fiscal sense to stay here, to pour money into this store, but for the first time in years I've felt alive again. With you, I've felt joy again."

Her heart softened some more, but she wasn't ready to give in, not when her parents' marriage was at stake. She crossed her arms and raised her chin, but didn't feel the confidence, especially with her parents planning to sell. "Well, you'll never get our land." She didn't have the means to buy it herself, but maybe her parents would give her a deal. Anything to save the cabin.

"I hope that's true."

"Just hope? You either buy it or you don't. Sounds easy to me."

"Not really, because I'm not the only acquisitions associate for Harrison. If I don't get the job done, someone else will. I don't know that I can prevent that from happening, and I'm sorry, but if it makes any difference at all, I promise you that I will not be the one making the purchase."

Jess stared northward, toward the cabin. She was helpless, unless she could convince her parents not to sell, which meant getting that path done quickly so her parents would fall in love with each other again.

Luke's hand touched hers, drawing her attention back to him.

"I want you to know, you can still count on me. If you'll have me, I'll be at your place every Sunday until the work is done."

"That's not a ruse to blindside me again?"

He sighed. "That has never been my intention."

"Well, that's what happened."

He grasped her hand. "Jessica Rose, I know it's only been a couple weeks, but I think you and I have something good together, and I'm excited to keep exploring that, if you'll allow me back in."

Shatter! There went all her heart's defenses, crumbling to the floor, except for a big one: could she trust him? "I don't know . . . "

"I promise you that, not only will I do everything in my power to prevent Harrison Property Development from purchasing your land, but I will also do everything I can to help bring your family back together. And that means tomorrow following church, and every Sunday from here on, I will be at your cabin ready to shovel, throw rock, cut trees, plant flowers, whatever you need me to do. No strings attached."

And there went her final defense. Inside, she was smiling, but she held it back. "What if I have a string?"

"I'll abide by it."

"That you promise not to give up on us either."

"I promise."

Chapter Fifteen

No, Jess would not give up on them yet, but the weed of mistrust had been planted last night. She wished she could yank it out, but it was stubborn and strong. Unless that weed was choked out with truth, in action and word, it could choke out the healthy relationship she desired.

She flung a shovelful of gravel onto the path that she and Luke had carved out. Would he show up today? And what about the cabin sale? What would he do when the cabin went on the market? Would he choose family over her? Shouldn't family come first? If she had to choose between family and Luke, family would win. No contest.

Ugh! She dipped her shovel into the wheelbarrow and scooped up another load of gravel. He'd made a promise to her that he'd do what he could to help her keep this land, but would that be enough? Did his promises mean anything?

She heaved that shovelful onto the path, her muscles already aching from exertion. Her mom and dad had promised each other that they'd be together in sickness and in health, but the first sign of sickness had ripped them apart.

What good was a promise anyway?

She wiped the perspiration from her forehead and checked her fitness tracker for the hundredth time, or so it seemed. Almost noon, and still no sign of Luke. The last couple of weeks, he'd arrived much earlier.

Seriously, Jess? Get over it! She tamped down the layer of rock already placed, then measured the depth. Only one inch? Leaning on the shovel handle, she looked up the pathway. Only half of it was coated with a thin layer of stone. This was going to take forever.

But it wouldn't get done at all if she stood around and moped.

She stretched out her arms and rotated her head before digging into the wheelbarrow. She threw gravel onto the path, and a motor rumbled behind her. She turned, and seeing Luke's pickup, followed by two other vehicles, she dropped the shovel and literally jumped for joy. "Thank you, Jesus!" she yelled out and jogged toward the line of vehicles.

"You came!" She hollered out when Luke opened his pickup door.

His brows puckered. "You doubted?"

"Well . . . " She grimaced and drew in the dirt driveway with her foot while the other two vehicles parked alongside Luke's pickup. "We did sort of have a disagreement last night, and I sometimes have this nasty little voice whispering lies in my ear."

"A pox on that voice!" He gestured to the other vehicles from which stepped Travis and Lydia. "I have recruited additional workers for you."

"Recruited?" Lydia joined Luke and Jess, along with Travis. "Ha! More like, blackmailed." She punched Luke's upper arm. "He told me nothing brings a couple together like a little manual labor, and if we wanted his help, we had to help you."

"But we are glad to be here." Travis offered his hand to Jess. "At your service. Luke tells me we're laying stone for Lady Beaumont."

Jess chuckled. "Yes, Sir Luke has been assisting me, but alas"—she dramatically pressed the back of her hand to her forehead—"we have much yet to do." She led the small group toward the path before realizing they were missing someone. "Where's Kitty?"

"Mary O is watching her today." Luke walked alongside Jess. "Since all her grandbabies live down in the cities, she's thrilled to get to babysit."

"Well, thank you, and thank Mary O." She stopped by the nearly full wheelbarrow. "I filled it too full and can't dump it. Your manly muscles will come in very useful."

"Huh. I feel used." Luke flexed his arms. "You only like me for my Captain America-like biceps?"

"That weenie?" Travis rolled up his sleeve. "Thor's jealous of these guns."

Jess snorted.

Lydia rolled her eyes. "Way too much testosterone here." With hands on hips, she looked down the pathway. "What's your plan for today?"

"To spread gravel on the path, maybe get it tamped down too."

Lydia shook her head. "No, that's your goal. What's your plan? How do you want to achieve your goal?"

"Come on, Lydia." Travis picked up the scoop shovel and jammed the bottom edge into the dirt. "Can't you leave work behind for a minute?"

"Is it too much to ask to know how we're going to proceed?"

Travis glared at his wife. "We'll do what Jess tells us to. Period."

Yikes. Maybe having these two working together wasn't such a good idea after all, but they were here, and she'd make the most of it. "Actually, having a plan isn't a bad idea, especially with so many of us working. If you guys could scoop the gravel onto the path—I'll grab another shovel from the shed—Lydia can level it out, and I can hose it down then tamp it."

"Or we could dump the wheelbarrow load onto the path." Luke did just that. "Travis and I can both fill, and take turns dumping."

"Sounds like a plan." Jess clapped her hands then looked to Lydia for confirmation.

"Works for me."

For the next several hours, the four shoveled and evened and tamped the gravel until two inches were spread out evenly on the pathway. Lydia made certain it was even the entire way. When they'd completed the work for the day, Lydia retrieved Kitty while Jess grilled steak and veggie kabobs. They sat around the glass table on the deck, devouring the meat faster than Jess could grill.

"These are amazing." Lydia grabbed a second kabob. "Don't let me leave without getting the recipe."

"Good idea." Travis snatched his third. Or was it his fourth? He glanced warily across the table at his wife. "Maybe I could grill them for us sometime?"

"Does that mean you're coming home?" Longing flickered in Lydia's eyes.

"It means I want to work on it. Find a counselor first, and see what she recommends. But yes, the ultimate goal is to come back home."

Lydia blinked rapidly and looked upward. "Whatever it takes. If that means I meet you up here every Sunday until the path is done, so be it. I don't want to be a cranky single like Dad."

"It's a date." Travis winked at Lydia then looked at Jess. "What is your plan for the upcoming weeks?"

"You really mean you're coming to help?" Their kindness almost made her want to cry.

Travis reached across the table, took Lydia's hand, and looked her square in the eye. "I'm pro-restoring marriages. Your parents' and ours, and if that means we have to sweat out our differences, I'm all for it."

Now Jess really wanted to cry. "I'll clean up." She gathered the dirty plates together.

"Let me help." Luke collected the remaining dishes and followed Jess into the cabin. She set the dirty dishes in the sink then fluttered her hands by her eyes. Seconds later, Luke's arms wrapped around her.

"I didn't think it would work." He spoke into her hair, sending shivers down her spine.

"Me neither, especially with how they were barking at each other at first, but . . . " She turned around in his arms and rested her forehead against his chest. "God performed a miracle out there. He's bringing them back together, like He brought Mom and Dad together thirty-some years ago, like He's bringing us . . . " Was that too forward?

"Bringing us together?" He tipped her chin up and his milk-chocolate-colored eyes met hers.

Heaven help her, she was past falling for him. She'd already fallen, heart first. Butterflies awoke in her gut, and her lips tingled with longing she'd never felt in all her empty relationships.

He lowered his lips to hers and feathered across them. His masculine blend of steak and sweat only made her thirst for more.

Her arms circled his waist and she rose up on her toes to kiss him again.

With a groan, his lips parted hers, sending electric currents through her body, igniting the desire to draw him closer yet. She hugged him tighter, and he didn't resist.

"Unca Luke, I gotta go potty."

His lips and arms flung away from Jess and he spun toward his niece. "Uh, Kitty Cat, I didn't . . . um, the bathroom's this way." He started down the short hall to the bathroom, but Jess grabbed his shirt.

"Don't get lost."

He grinned and touched a finger to her nose and drew it down to her lips. "Not a chance." His voice was husky and oh-so sexy.

Oh man, oh man, she was a goner. As Callie would say, she'd fallen heels over head for Mr. Luke Harrison.

But was it right?

With longing for him still stirring in her gut, she sat at the kitchen table, looked upward, and breathed one word. "Help."

In all her past relationships, a longing like this drew her not only into the man's arms, but into bed. That wasn't what Luke wanted, because if he did, she certainly didn't have the strength to resist. Which meant she had to leave this place right now. Go be with others and remove the temptation.

She hurried outside and looked for Travis and Lydia. And her jaw dropped. The two were locked in an embrace tighter than she had been with Luke. Awesome for them. Not so much for her. Hoping not to interrupt the couple, she tiptoed off the deck and hurried down the path to the lake where God's voice was always clear. Where her focus would shift upward rather than inward.

She sat on the bench and stared out over the calm waters until peace enveloped her. Why had she been so blind—immune to God's peace during her growing up years? "Thank you," she whispered.

Seconds later, she felt a touch on her shoulder and she looked up at Luke.

"Mind if I have a seat?"

She pointed to a chair. "Over there. Far, far away from me."

He cocked a crooked smile and sat. "Guess we did get a little carried away."

"A little?"

He sighed, and his smile faded. "I'm sorry, Jess." He looked down at wringing hands. "I . . . I've never felt like that before, and I liked it far too much."

"Never?"

He laughed but there was no smile on his face. "Um, yeah, this is embarrassing, but . . . " He scratched the back of his neck and his face bloomed a sunburn red. "I'm a . . . "

No. Couldn't be. Not in these hook-up-with-a-stranger times. "You're a virgin?"

He laughed uncomfortably. "Hard to believe, huh?"

"Well yeah, not that any other girl wouldn't find you attractive enough . . . "

His brows flew up. "Hey, I've dated."

"I mean, nowadays casual sex is the norm. It's . . . when I started dating, the only thing my parents warned me against was getting knocked up. It's like they expected me to be promiscuous, and I've learned that people usually live down to their expectations."

"Sounds like something Gran would tell me. People live down to their expectations, so set your goals high. Something like that, anyway." He took out his phone and typed in something then returned it to his pocket. "There. Now a Granism will be credited to you. Or should we call it a Jess-ism?"

"You're too cute."

He shook a finger at her. "No more flirting."

"That's where you two disappeared to." Travis came up the walkway, Kitty's hand in his, followed by Lydia. She stopped at his side. They didn't hold hands, but they also didn't keep an intentional distance either.

"Well, the two of you were, um." Jess cleared her throat. "Doing some catching up when I came out, so I left you alone."

Travis grinned and Lydia's face pinked, and then Travis did take her hand. "If you'll have us, we'll be back next week."

Jess stood, and Luke followed suit.

"I'm grateful for all your help." She gave her three visitors a hug and said goodbye. Luke walked them back to their cars. Something had to be in the air on this land that made people fall in love. Which meant she had to get her parents up here, but not until everything was completed. That would increase the odds for them getting back together. As Luke had said, set her goals high. In the end, she did expect her parents to reunite.

Once again, she sat on the bench, staring out at the water, and shot up a Thank you for Travis, Lydia, Kitty, Luke. For a day that had begun with fear and distrust, it had ended with surprising grace.

"Time to get you home?" Luke came up behind her and massaged her shoulders.

She practically melted at his touch, reigniting that desire. "I'm thinking it's probably a good idea not to be alone here with you. You don't suppose God planned it to have Travis and Lydia here to act as chaperones?"

"Planned?" He sat on the chair kitty-corner to her. "Don't know about that, but He certainly used it."

"So we should be grateful that we'll have help in the future too."

He grinned. "Most definitely."

Chapter Sixteen

Hair still damp from her post-work shower, and every muscle protesting, Jess climbed down the ladder-like steps from the clearing to the private bay below the cabin's cliff.

Luke had showered first and beat her to the beach where he lay face up, eyes closed, on a blanket. A cute little snore whistled from his nose. Shoot, he was adorable.

She sat down beside him and let out a slow sigh.

The path was done! Hallelujah!

She could never have completed it without the hunk of man snoozing beside her. What would it be like to go to bed beside him every night? Wake beside him in the morning? Good thing he was asleep, because the man oozed brawn and chivalry and goodness, and she didn't know if she could resist him much longer.

Knowing that if she rested beside him, she'd fall asleep, so she got up and walked to the shore. She dipped her toes into Lake Superior and shivered. Even in August, the lake temps remained frigid, though the lapping waters soothed feet that could no longer appear in an ad for sandals. That was all right. She'd earned every callus on those feet.

Like Luke had certainly earned a nap for his work these past months. To think they were almost done with the cabin restoration! She couldn't have done it without the help of Luke, his family, Callie, Haven, and Reese. All that was left to do was create the gardens bordering the path.

These past couple of months had been crazy busy. In between June and July storms, they'd laid the landscape fabric over the path, then installed the edging. No surprise, Lydia had made certain the path was the same width the entire way. They'd finished it off with crushed stone, compacting it tightly and smoothly so that Dad wouldn't have any problems walking. By the edge of the cliff, they'd added a rustic wood fence similar to those seen in old farm pictures, with three rails suspended between posts. It added a safety element without blocking the view.

Now all she had to do was frame the sides of the path with flowers.

The bathroom in the cabin had been made handicap-accessible, and a pocket door had been installed. The kitchen had been freshened up with refaced cabinets and new countertops, and the wood floors were sanded and stained a dark walnut. Outside, a ramp had been added to the deck.

Now her dad had no excuse for not coming to the lake. Once her parents came up here together, all thoughts of their separation and selling the cabin would be gone, and they'd be acting like lovebirds again.

It had certainly worked for Travis and Lydia.

And Jess and Luke.

She turned and watched Luke's T-shirted chest rise and fall. Oh, she could get used to this. No, to be honest, she was already used to him being here with her, working side by side. Sharing the occasional, okay, frequent toe-curling kiss that made her hungry for more. Was it too early to think marriage?

She knelt and dug through the stones, looking for agates Callie could polish, turning an ordinary-looking stone into something of beauty.

God had certainly been polishing her rough edges. Her parents' house had sold quickly, so Jess had moved into Haven's home with Callie. Their dad had moved into an assisted living facility, and was now walking without the walker, with only occasional use of the cane. And Mom still lived with her sister, Aunt Tib. The fact that she hadn't purchased something new meant that she hadn't given up on her marriage either.

Once Callie and Haven got married, Jess would be on her own.

But would she?

She found a flat stone and underhanded it toward the water, creating little ripples in each skip.

Life had changed for Luke too. Lydia and Travis were back together and acting like newlyweds. Superior Sweets had almost doubled its business, thanks to all the marketing help from Callie and Haven. The low-fat, frozen slushie-on-a-stick didn't hurt, and no sane person could resist cookie-dough ice cream sandwiched between two chocolate chip cookies. That had been Callie's idea.

Now they were all brainstorming ideas for a fall specialty. Luke's store couldn't close. And if it did, what would he do?

"What are you thinking about?"

Jess spun toward Luke, who sat up with a yawn. She grinned and joined him on the blanket. "I'm thinking I feel like an old married couple sitting here." She wrapped her arms around her knees.

"Doesn't sound like a bad idea."

Was he hinting? If he asked her to marry him, she'd say, "Tomorrow." Well, not really. She still wanted that princess wedding her mom longed to throw, but even that wasn't as important as it had been a few months ago. Funny how faith and real love had changed her priorities.

He sat up beside her. "I don't ever want to leave."

"Me either." With a few minor updates to the cabin, she could live up here full time. And waking up beside Luke Harrison every day? The thought alone made her heart zing.

But work tomorrow at Superior Suites called to her.

She checked her fitness tracker. Like every other day this summer, she'd far exceeded her step goal for the day, and it showed in her physique. All those pounds she'd fought to keep off for years had melted into bronzed muscle, and her hair had been gilded by the sun rather than a bottle. She looked good, even if she said so herself.

Combine that with a white wedding dress?

Slow down, Jess. For now, it was time to head back to Duluth. Maybe, someday, that would change.

"Come here." He motioned to his lap.

"Uh-uh." She got up, intending to hurry for the steep metal stairs leading up to the cabin, but Luke caught her waist from behind and pulled her back down onto his lap.

"I think we need to do a little path-completion celebration." He aimed for her lips.

But she planted her hands on his chest and pushed away. "It's not done yet."

"Yes, it is. You said so yourself before Travis and Lydia left."

"Okay, maybe the path is complete, but the framing isn't." She pressed a finger to his lips. "No celebrating until the flowers are planted."

"Pre-celebration?" He kissed her finger.

"That's a thing?" She wrapped her arms around his neck and folded her hands together.

"Oh, definitely." He kissed her nose. "And I happen to excel at pre-celebration." He kissed her cheek then traced her jaw line with more kisses, igniting a fire in her she didn't want to snuff out, but needed to.

She tried pushing away, but he held her tight and drew a circle of kisses around her mouth, before connecting his lips with hers.

She moaned and returned the kiss with fervor, and when his fingers traced the skin beneath her shirt's hem, more than anything she burned for him to explore further. Heaven help her, if she didn't get up right now, they'd both be sorry come morning. Summoning every ounce of strength within her, she pushed off Luke's lap and fell bottom first onto the rocks.

"Ow."

Luke stared down at her, his mouth agape.

She waggled a finger at him, doing her best to douse the fire he'd ignited, but it still flamed hot. "You, Lucas Harrison, do not play fair."

With a sideways grin, he offered his hand to help her up.

"Uh-uh. I'm not going there again." She stood and wiped sand from her backside.

"I was going to stop." He reached for her again. "Eventually."

But she leaped back before she dove into his arms again. "Seriously? Are you in high school?"

His grin grew, but then the cockiness slowly faded from his face, pulling his lips into a frown. He folded his hands behind his head, drew it downward, and groaned. "Oh, Jess, I'm sorry." He looked up at her and heaved a sigh. "But you . . . you drive me crazy. I've never been . . . " He shook his head. "Now I get it."

"Get what?" she crossed her arms, keeping herself a good yard away from him.

"With Tim, and even with Christian friends who used the excuse that they couldn't stop, I'd judge them. It had never been a problem for me before, but I get it now, darling, because I wanted to treat you like anything but a lady, and I am so, so sorry."

She walked to the water's edge and looked outward, watching water leap up as if trying to touch the sky. "What do we do?" She whispered then spun around. "What are Christians supposed to do? Do we always have to have people around because we can't trust ourselves? That doesn't seem right."

"No, it doesn't." He sighed and ran both hands through his hair. "I think one thing we've been missing is prayer. Before we spend time together, we need to spend time in prayer, ask Him to help us keep our relationship pure."

"But I'm not pure, Luke." She hugged herself. She hadn't been pure since the age of sixteen when she'd eagerly given away her virginity. Until recently, that hadn't bothered her.

"Yes, you are, Jess. You've said yourself, that with Christ you are a new creation. That means all of you." He shook his head. "And if I steal that from you, the woman I love . . . "

Her jaw dropped, and she stared at Luke. Did he say love?

"Yes, Jessica Rose." He narrowed the gap between them, with Lake Superior licking at their toes, and cradled her cheeks in his hands. "I love you. I love your smile, your enthusiasm, how you're unafraid of hard work and digging in the dirt, your love for you family, your eagerness to learn about God." He pressed a gentle kiss to her lips, then leaned back. "I love how you brought joy back to my life. I cherish you, Jess, and I love you."

Her heart raced like the waves rushing toward shore. He cherished *her*. Loved *her*. A broken, impure failure, and he loved her. Words she'd heard before from men who wanted one thing from her. Yet Luke saw beyond her façade into her heart and treated her like a princess. How could she not love him back? She opened her mouth to share her heart, but he pressed a finger to her lips.

"I don't want you to say it because I did." Then he pressed a hand to her heart. "I want it to come from here."

"But—"

His finger on her lips stopped her again, and his lips tipped into a sexy grin. "What do you say to an evening out? Friday maybe? Fancy dinner. Some dancing. Me in a tux, you dolled up like the princess you are?" His brows rose.

Now he was talking her language. "I'd love it!" It had been ages since she'd gone all out, probably since her last photo shoot. The mere thought made her giddy with excitement. Besides—she stared at her ring finger—she had a feeling that Luke had other plans for the evening.

"It's a date." He crooked his elbow. "Shall I escort you to your chariot?"

"Not yet." She ignored his arm and took his hands instead. She leaned in and whispered a kiss across his lips, sending her heart into an erratic rhythm. Then she pulled back from his tightening grip so she could read his milk chocolate eyes. "First you need to know that I love you too."

DRIVING HOME, JESS SANG out loud along with the radio. It didn't take a Stephen Hawking brilliance to know Luke planned to propose on Friday. Her knight dressed up in a tux while she donned spangles and lace? She did a little jig right there in her seat. She couldn't wait to talk to Callie tonight.

Her true feelings for Luke were no longer in doubt, hadn't been for a while. This was no crush, and she was no longer falling in love. She'd fallen and landed with her heart completely safe in his callused yet gentle hands. And since they'd both given voice to their feelings, nothing could get in the way. Not his dad's company. Not her parents' separation. That had to be what God wanted. Didn't He?

Now, she needed to go shopping to find the perfect dress for Friday night. Something that would wow Luke without being too flirty, but not too conservative either.

Maybe she could talk her mom into going with her. Mom would see how wonderful it was to be in love, and she'd try harder with Dad. The prep alone for this date would be fun. Getting a hair appointment with less than a week's notice wouldn't be easy, but Mom could pull a few strings. The business community would do anything for the regal Mackenzie Beaumont.

Jess crossed Duluth's famous lift bridge and drove down Park Point toward her temporary home with Callie. In a few months, her big sister would be saying her vows up by the lake while the sun rose. Wouldn't it be amazing if her parents renewed their vows the very same day? And wouldn't it be even cooler if a diamond engagement ring circled Jess's finger that day?

And yes, while other women her age wanted something less traditional than a diamond, that wasn't a trend she desired to follow. Nope, give her a big, shiny diamond that would make passersby gasp.

She turned on the blinker to take a left into her driveway, already occupied by her mom's Lincoln, so Jess parked in the street. What was her mom doing here? Wedding plans with Callie, maybe? But ten at night was a bit late for that. She walked up to the front door, which opened right before she reached the steps.

Haven came out, his golden retriever pup on a leash, and closed the door behind him, his face a mask of stoicism.

That couldn't be good.

"What's going on?" She looked past him to the window in the living room, but the drapes were closed.

"Callie said I should give you a little warning."

Oh no. The blood seemed to drain from Jess's body. "Is it Dad? Is he okay?"

He swallowed. "Your dad's fine. He's here too."

With Mom? That was good news, right? Haven was keeping a straight face to fool her. They were announcing they were getting back together. That had to be it. Still, the churning in her gut foretold otherwise.

"O . . . kay? What's going on?"

He sighed. "Your parents have some . . . news, and it's not mine to tell. Callie thought you should be prepared.

That churning in her stomach threatened to inch up her throat. She pushed past Haven and went inside. Her dad sat in the recliner, his hands white-knuckling on the cane in his lap.

"It's about time you got home, Jessica." Her mom made a show of looking at her diamond-studded watch.

Jess sat beside Callie on the sofa and curled her legs beneath her. In an effort to add a smile to the somber faces around her, she brought up today's accomplishment. "We finished the path today, that's what took so long. Now all I have to do is line it with flowers." So that come Callie and Haven's wedding in less than two months, the path would be blooming with greenery. She'd add in a few annuals for color, and God would paint the leaves with autumn reds and golds.

"Well, that m...makes our plans easier, w...wouldn't you say, Mackenzie?" Her father bounced the cane on his lap.

"I agree." Her mom sat straight-backed in her chair, crossed a slender leg over the other, and folded her hands. Not a hint of emotion showed on her face. "Your father and I . . . " Her gaze flicked upward for a millisecond, but Jess caught the glassy look and blinking eyes. Mom cleared her throat and her lips pinched. "Now that the house is sold, your father and I have decided this is the perfect time to place the cabin on the market, so—"

Jess leaped up. "You promised you'd give us until after Callie's wedding, you promised—"

Her mom held up her hand.

And Jess clamped her mouth shut. They couldn't do this to her. After all her hard work.

"Dear, we are just putting it on the market with a closing date no earlier than after the wedding. Buyers will be eager to take over the cabin in the fall." Her mom picked at imaginary dust on her dress pants.

"But . . . what about if I buy it?" Her parents would give her a deal, right? After all, she did stand to inherit the cabin someday, her and Callie.

"Nonsense." Her mom shook her head. "You couldn't afford the annual property taxes, much less the mortgage payment, dear. Besides, we've already spoken with our real estate agent and the listing will go live tomorrow morning. It's best that we bring closure to this as soon as possible."

"Closure?" Jess looked from one parent to the other, worry clawing at her throat. No surprise, her dad's focus was on his lap. Why didn't he stand up and demand they keep the Beaumont family heirloom? "Dad, is this what you want?"

"Yes," he said without looking up, and without a hint of stutter. "Once the divorce goes through, that's one less thing we'll have to worry about."

"Divorce?" Jess squeaked out. No. They couldn't. She didn't even try to stop the onset of tears.

"Yes, dear." Her mom raised her chin, but the action didn't disguise her chin's tremble. And her puffy, bloodshot eyes belied Mom not caring. "The separation isn't working, and your father and I have agreed to make it permanent. We are getting a divorce."

Chapter Seventeen

ut ... but you can't!" Jess accepted a tissue Callie offered and wiped her cheeks and eyes. The delicious meal she'd shared earlier with Luke now gurgled in her stomach, threatening to erupt.

She looked to her dad, who'd always been the more rational of the two, but the firm set of his jaw said his mind was made up too. How could they do this to each other? To her and Callie?

She couldn't deal with them right now, couldn't abide by their decision, so she ran through the living room, kitchen, and outside into the moonless night. Parents were supposed to set the example. They were supposed to be together until 'death do us part.' What part of those vows didn't they understand? She hurried down the paver stone pathway to the shipping pallet walkway that led to the sand dune beach.

Seagulls squawked overhead as if they too were upset. Jess slumped onto a bench Callie and Haven had crafted from more wood pallets. She pinched her eyes shut, and reopened them, hoping she was in the middle of a nightmare, but nothing had changed. The moon still hid behind the clouds. Superior's waves still rolled toward her, the wind whipped cold off the waters. To the west, lights from Duluth glowed like pinpoints unaware that her family's life was being snuffed out.

"You okay?" Callie touched Jess's shoulder before sitting beside her and pulling her into a side hug.

"What do you think?"

"Yeah ... " Callie breathed in then slowly puffed it out. "Stupid question."

"What is Mom thinking?"

"Mom?"

"You know she's behind this, right? Since his stroke, Dad's not the same man, and she's not happy about it."

"I don't know. It does take two." Callie stared outward. "Did you know Mom's been going to church with Aunt Tib?"

"Mom at church?"

"My reaction exactly when Aunt Tib told me."

"Then a divorce makes even less sense."

"I know. This whole thing makes no sense." Callie rested her head on Jess's shoulder. "When they told me and Haven, I came here too, and shouted a whole bunch of creative phrases to the lake, some God wouldn't approve of. And poor Haven, he listened and held me while I went off the deep end. I desperately tried to convince him to elope tonight, and he said that sounded very appealing, but he knew I'd regret it."

"I don't know." Jess hugged herself as much from disappointment as from the cold breeze. "I think it sounds like a great idea. Maybe Luke and I'll join you."

"Wait . . . What . . . ? Seriously?" Callie turned Jess toward her, her eyes big as chocolate truffles. "Are you engaged?"

"No." Jess stared at the ring finger on her left hand, imagining a diamond sparkling from there. "But we love each other, and Luke's thinking about it, I'm certain. He promised to treat me to a princess night out this Friday, and I have a feeling he's planning to propose. I was so excited to come home and tell you and ask Mom to help find a dress . . . " She wiped her nose.

"You should go. You need to go. Take your mind off things. Do something special for you rather than trying to be everything for everyone else."

Jess shook her head. "Uh-uh. I'd be a Debbie-downer that night. How could I think about beginning a life with someone when my parents are breaking up? When Luke treats me to a princess night, I don't want any distractions. I want to enjoy it."

"I understand, I guess." Callie shrugged. "You going to call him? He'd want to know about Mom and Dad."

"Not tonight. We had such a good day, I don't want to spoil it for him. Besides, he's driving down to Minneapolis tonight for business. I'll let him bask in today's glow and call him tomorrow morning. One of us should be happy anyway."

"So, what do we do?" Callie kicked at the ground, spraying sand particles toward the lake.

A couple walked past, holding hands, oblivious to Callie and Jess only feet away. That was how Jess imagined her parents' rekindled romance. It could still happen. Who was she to give up on her plan?

This was one setback. Wasn't their parents' future worth fighting for? She slapped her thighs and sat up straight. "Operation: Planting Hope is still on, Cal, but we need to speed up the process." Which meant she had to have a conversation with her parents. "Are they still up at the house?"

"Probably. They're worried about you."

"Let's go stop their worrying." Jess strode to the house, mimicking her mother's raised chin. She breezed through the kitchen, where her mother stood doing dishes. "We need to talk," she said without slowing until reaching the living room. Haven sat on the piano bench, chatting with her dad, whose weary shoulders were slumped. She'd let him know it wasn't time to raise the white flag yet.

Her mother followed into the living room, a dishtowel in her hands. "We've said all we're going to."

"That's fine." Jess jabbed a finger toward the couch. "Now it's my turn to say something."

Haven ran a hand over his mouth, but Jess caught the smirk.

Callie stopped in the doorway between the kitchen and living room. "Do you want me here too?"

"Absolutely." Jess nodded. The more witnesses, the better.

Callie joined Haven on the piano bench.

Jess crossed her arms, her gaze flitting from one parent to the other.

"Since both of you are acting like children, I'm going—"

"Careful, Jessica." Her mom held up a finger, but Jess talked through it.

"—to treat you like children. Yeah, you two have hit a rough patch, but that doesn't mean it's time to give up. This isn't about just the two of you. It's about Callie and Haven and Reese and me and Luke and everyone else who's stood beside you. Did you know that over the last couple of months, I've had a half dozen friends helping spruce up the cabin? For you?"

"That was never our idea." Mom pinched her lips together.

"Well, maybe, some of us love you too much to see you do something stupid."

"Jessica Rose . . . " Her father tried to sound stern, but his voice lacked energy. Would this cause another physical setback for him?

"Let me have my say, then you two can speak. Like at our family meetings." Her legs felt like jelly, but she remained standing.

"Fair enough." Dad slumped further into the chair.

Jess inhaled a breath and lifted a silent plea for strength and the guts to say what her parents needed to hear. "Since the two of you are making a decision that will impact more than *your* lives, I'm asking that you hold off on deciding anything permanent for one week. After next Sunday, if you really feel this is what's best for all involved, I won't stand in your way."

"And what, pray tell, do you plan to do in one week?" Mom folded her manicured hands on her lap, but Jess could see them tremble.

"Next Sunday, after church, I want all of you, including Callie, Haven, and Reese, to meet me up at the cabin."

Mom vented an obvious sigh. "For what purpose?"

"I guess you'll have to come up and see, won't you?"

"We'll be there." Dad's response wasn't enthusiastic, but at least it was the answer she desired.

"Good." Jess's voice cracked a bit, emotion pleading to come out, but she reined it in. "One more thing. I won't be at work this week. The office manager can handle Superior Suites."

"And where will you be?" Her mom's lips pinched tighter, but Jess didn't care. This was for the survival of her family.

"I plan to do whatever it takes to save my family." With that, Jess walked from the living room and up the stairs to her room, where her wobbly legs finally gave out. She'd done it. Given her parents an ultimatum and didn't back down.

The question now was, would her plan work? Tomorrow, she'd call Luke and enlist his help again. He might not like having their date cancelled, but once her parents were reunited, Jess would be up for a celebration.

LUKE COULDN'T WAIT FOR Friday night! Now to sneak into Dad's safe without anyone noticing. He didn't want to answer a lot of questions about Jess or his North Shore assignment.

Luke used the keypad to the back door to let himself into his dad's estate. The mudroom was spotless. His dad would accept nothing less. But what good was a mudroom if it couldn't get dirty? Never did make sense to Luke.

He took off his shoes, tiptoed out of the room into the kitchen, and listened. Not a creak, not even a television, but at nearly midnight, his dad was probably asleep. Soundlessly, Luke made his way through the kitchen to the living room and to the staircase reminiscent of the one in the *Gone With the Wind* movie. It made for great first impressions when Dad needed to influence someone, which was quite often.

At one time, apparently Mom had been impressed by those stairs.

Until living in this estate and raising three rambunctious kids had her yearning for freedom.

He shook the thought away. Mom's abandoning her family would not ruin his plans. Jess was nothing like her.

Taking each step slowly, he climbed the stairs and followed the carpeted hallway to the end and took a left into his dad's office with its walls of books. He searched the bookcase on his left for the *Alice in*

Wonderland hardback and pulled it out. Once upon a time, Dad had had a sense of humor, placing the hidden room latch behind the whimsical story.

Luke pushed the button on the bottom side of the shelf above and heard a whoosh as the secret door released. He swung out the shelves and entered the closet where Dad stored his mementoes of Mom. Her favorite chair. Her old stereo system complete with massive speakers, a cassette player and turntable. Some of her favorite outfits.

The room always felt a little creepy to Luke as if his dad were trying to keep her alive.

He picked up a picture of the once-happy couple. Dad grinning, wearing his double-breasted suit, sure resembled Tim. Mom, her lips painted a bright red, and eyes heavily-shadowed in colors that should never be on skin, gave her sideways, gum-smacking smile to the camera. Luke's smile. Back then, Mom had been a Madonna wanna-be, had even styled her hair like Madonna's character in that old movie, *Desperately Seeking Susan*, complete with the wide headband and sloppy bow. Her paint-splatter-look T-shirt hung off the shoulder and was tucked into high-waisted, white-washed jeans.

Talk about two opposites. The free spirit and the restrained. Yet they'd been in love, and they'd been good together. Mostly. If only Mom could have restrained herself a bit more . . .

Don't go there, Harrison.

He'd wasted enough of his life pondering her choices.

He returned the photo to the shelf and unlatched a second secret panel, this behind a shelf filled with Mom's favorite record albums. Duran Duran, AC/DC, Queen, Bon Jovi, Journey, and so many more. On days when he was feeling nostalgic, he'd put on a record, get cozy in her chair and sing along.

But today wasn't about reminiscing, it was about moving forward.

He punched the combination into the keypad, but the pad beeped at him, and the door didn't budge. He tried it again with the same result. *Really, Dad, you had to go change the combo?* He fisted his hands, but held back from punching anything. Who knew what would set off the alarms? Dad was plain paranoid.

Now what? Heaving a sigh, he plopped down in Mom's chair. When he'd been younger, he'd sit there just to soak up her lingering scent, some perfume Dad had loved to buy her. But that had long since evaporated.

He could always ask Dad for the combo. It wasn't like Luke was trying to hide anything, but he didn't want anyone to get excited yet.

He'd give the combination one more try. Dad had always used a number associated with Mom. The last one had been her birthdate. Luke punched in the numbers for his parents' anniversary, and it still beeped failure.

"Having problems?"

Tim . . .

Luke spun around and faced his younger brother. Tim might look like their dad, but everything else about him screamed Mom. Crazy-smart and free-spirited, too handsome for his own good. He'd been named for Timothy from the Bible, who'd accompanied Paul on many mission trips. The name meant honoring God. The only person Tim honored was himself. At times, Luke worried Tim was heading down that same road Mom had taken.

The road to heartbreak and grief.

Luke pointed his thumb at the door behind him. "Dad changed the combo."

Tim snorted. "About the second you left. What do you need?"

"None of your business."

"Fine." Tim turned on his heel and headed out of the room.

"Come on, give me a break."

Tim stopped and slowly turned his head, cocking it to the side as he stared at Luke. "Lydia tells me you and your girlfriend played matchmaker."

"Is that all she told you?"

Tim shrugged. "Pretty much, except for the fact that you and the Beaumont chick are pretty hot and heavy."

Luke shook his head. No matter what he said, Tim would twist the answer into something else. He held out his hand, and gestured toward the locked door. "Please?"

"As long as you said the magic word." Tim punched in a slew of numbers and the pocket door swooshed into the wall.

"My birthday . . . "

Tim gave a cockeyed grin. "Dad knew you'd never try that."

"What's he so paranoid about?" Luke stepped into the room and headed for the shelf he'd hid the item on. He shifted a couple boxes of tax forms to the side, and found nothing but an empty shelf. "Where is it?" he mumbled under his breath.

"Where is what?"

Luke scratched his head while continuing to move around boxes. *Don't tell me Dad took it.* His blood began to boil. Changing the safe lock combination was one thing, but taking this? Gran had specifically given it to Luke years ago. He shoved around a few more boxes and grunted in failure.

"Looking for this?"

Luke turned toward his brother. In his hand was an oval, cream-colored celluloid box with an intricate floral design on top. The box housing Gran's wedding ring set.

"How'd you know?"

"Asks the guy who can't beat a toddler at poker." Tim grinned.

"Hey, Kitty Cat's a smart kid."

Still grinning, Tim underhanded the box to Luke. "You're really going to do it?"

"This Friday night."

"Huh. And here I thought, with your lack of love life, you might be batting for the other team, but I guess that blonde beauty could make any guy straight."

"Watch it." Luke growled.

Tim held up his hands. "No offense. That was a compliment. Or it was meant to be anyway. I'm happy for you, bro."

A compliment from Tim? They came so rarely, he latched onto it. "Thanks."

"But I do see that you have a problem."

"I know." Luke's jaw shifted from side to side. He hoped to remedy that problem during this trip home. First thing in the morning he planned to call his financial advisor.

Tim leaned against the doorway leading into the safe. "What do you plan to tell Dad?"

"Good question." Luke opened the jewelry box and studied the unique wedding ring set. The engagement ring was rose gold shaped into flowing vines that surrounded a circular diamond. The wedding band had roses, also fashioned from rose gold. It was as if Gran knew he'd be giving this to Jessica Rose Beaumont. Gran had called it an art deco ring, if he remembered correctly. By giving this ring to Jess, would he be ending his career with Harrison? "Dad fell in love once. I hope he understands."

"Good luck with that." Tim checked his watch. "See you in the morning for breakfast?"

"Wouldn't pass it up." Not with Shirley cooking. The thought of her bacon and eggs made his stomach grumble, but it soured quickly. Staying for breakfast in the morning also meant dining with his father, and Luke wasn't delusional enough to believe that Dad would place romance above business. That very act had burned his dad before.

Chapter Eighteen

Luke awoke in his childhood room, disoriented, and it took seconds to clear the fog from his brain. Dad hadn't touched the room since Luke had moved out. Of course, Dad hadn't been too pleased with Luke for buying a condo, not when this house had so many rooms to fill. But being under his dad's thumb at work was all he could take.

And now he had to tell Dad that he was going against his wishes once again. Just like Mom had.

Would it break his dad's heart again?

After showering, he dressed and followed his nose down the back stairs to the kitchen where Shirley, Dad's cook since before Mom died, was whipping up the perfect comfort-food breakfast—crisp bacon, sunny-side-up eggs, and Johnny cake—while humming a familiar and favorite tune, "In Christ Alone."

He snuck up behind Shirley who, with her slender figure and up-to-date hairstyle, looked more like she should be out water skiing than a grandma of twenty slaving over a stove. How she kept her figure and youth while cooking mouthwatering meals was beyond him. He cuffed his hands on her shoulders, and landed a kiss on her cheek. "How's my favorite girl?"

"Slim and sassy." She laughed and pushed him away. "Go sit so I can fatten you up a bit."

"Yes, ma'am." He checked inside the formal dining room that overlooked Lake Minnetonka. For all Luke knew, his dad still preferred being served here, even if he was alone. Sounded incredibly lonely. But the room was empty, so he joined Shirley in the kitchen. Luke had always preferred to eat at the kitchen dinette where he could give Shirley grief, but she could sass back even better. "Dad come down yet?" He eyed the bacon-filled plate on the counter, and his mouth watered.

"Down and gone already."

"Already?" He checked the clock above the sink. Seven AM, the exact time Dad usually ate breakfast, and Dad rarely deviated from that.

"Said he had some pressing meeting in St. Paul, and not to worry about supper."

The greasy scent of bacon wafted to his nose, and he could no longer resist. He grabbed a slice.

And Shirley swatted his hand, making him drop it. "Patience."

"But it smells so good."

"Go. Sit. Down." She gestured with a spatula toward the dinette.

"Bossy, aren't you?"

"I'm just getting started, young man."

Grinning, he grabbed salt and pepper shakers, plus a butter dish, and brought them to the table.

A minute later, Shirley set an overflowing plate in front of him. "Eat up, and maybe you'll get seconds."

Seconds? He'd be lucky if he could complete this massive amount of food, but he'd sure be happy trying. After saying a quick prayer of thanks, he bit into a slice of bacon. Oh. My. Goodness! The flavor exploded in his mouth like Fourth of July fireworks. How was it Shirley could fry bacon better than anyone else?

"Good?" She placed a glass with orange juice in front of him.

He nodded, too busy enjoying the food to talk. Besides, if he did try to talk, she'd sass him for talking with his mouth full. He buttered the Johnny cake with a thick layer of butter, and sampled it. Oh, man. Good thing he didn't live here anymore. He'd be bigger than a Smart car. He downed the cake in a few bites, and his taste buds pleaded for more.

"That was amazing, Shirley. Could I have another one?" He dipped his toast into an egg yolk which, no surprise, was cooked perfectly for dipping.

Shirley stood at the stove, cocked a hand on her hip, her chin down and eyes narrowed. "Are you forgetting something?"

He ran over his question. Oh, yeah. "*Please*, may I have another slice of Johnny cake?"

"That's better." She delivered the corn bread. "This living on your own has stolen your manners from you."

"Which is why I need you." He patted the seat beside him. "Join me."

"Don't mind if I do. I need to catch up on what's going on in your life."

He fingered the ring box in his pocket. "A lot of good."

Shirley filled her plate with a third of what she'd given him and sat across from him. "Word has it, Cupid's been toying with you."

He couldn't keep his grin down. "That's one way of putting it." He cut off a piece of egg white. "Tim tell you?"

"Said you were looking for Gran's rings last night."

"And I found them." He took out the ornate box and opened it. He couldn't wait to watch Jess's expression when she saw the engagement ring.

"Mm, mmm, that's a fine ring set. Must be a pretty special young woman to finally take your mind off the office."

"Yes, she is." And that was exactly what she'd done. Luke gave a SparkNotes version of the romance, ending with the dilemma of whether or not to buy the cabin for Harrison Property Development. "What should I do? My heart's telling me one thing, but my head goes in the opposite direction."

Shirley finished off her cake. "That is a problem, isn't it?" She pushed her plate aside and looked Luke in the eye. "My mama told me it's always best when the heart and head work together. Letting either take charge is a formula for trouble."

Which he well knew. He stared out the window at the lake. His mom's actions had been all heart-led, which, in the end, left a trail of broken hearts. And since his mom's accident, Dad's actions were completely head-influenced, leaving frozen hearts in his wake.

Shirley's hand on his drew him back to the present. "You, Lucas, much more than Timothy or Lydia, are the perfect blend of both your parents. If anyone can figure this out, you can. You helped Lydia and Travis."

"Nothing gets by you, does it?"

"That's my job." She gathered the dirty dishes and brought them to the sink. "You'll be sure to keep me informed now? I'd rather hear about your love life first hand."

"I promise." He downed his orange juice and began to get up, when Tim sauntered into the kitchen, a tablet in hand.

"You see this?" Tim set the tablet in front of Luke, a very familiar log cabin on the screen. A log cabin for sale.

Apprehension seized his newly-filled stomach and threatened to back up. Jess had told him her parents were going to wait to list it.

"How'd you know about this?"

"Seriously? You think Dad wouldn't have a second pair of eyes on those properties?" Tim joined Luke at the table.

Right.

Luke scrolled through the listing and focused on the price. "You've got to be kidding." He frowned at Tim. "They're giving it away."

"My thoughts exactly."

Shirley set a filled plate in front of Tim.

And he winked at her. "Thanks, dear. Will you marry me?"

"Only if you get permission from my husband first."

"He keeps saying no."

She chuckled and busied herself with clean-up.

Luke continued to ponder the low asking price for the Beaumont cabin and land. Not nearly low enough, though, for him to buy it. Paying the annual taxes would be bad enough, but he'd never qualify for that large of a mortgage, especially if his dad canned him, which would likely happen if Luke let this business opportunity slide by.

Although, he still planned on meeting with his financial planner this afternoon. "Do you suppose they priced it low to create a bidding war?"

"You know the family better than I do." Tim took a bite of the Johnny cake and sighed. "Are you certain you can't marry me, Shirley?"

"Ha! You wouldn't be able to keep up with me."

Tim laughed. "True that! But you won't blame me if I keep trying." He gestured to the ring box on the table. "And now that Luke here is out of the race, my competition has been cut in half."

"That's if Jess says 'yes.'" Luke pocketed the ring and continued to read through the cabin listing. What had happened between the time he'd left Jess and this morning? Did she know about this? He had to call her right away. "Does Dad know?"

"That I'm going to marry Shirley?" Tim spoke with his mouth full of egg.

"I'm serious." Luke shoved the tablet in front of Luke. "Does Dad know about the cabin listing?"

Tim drained his orange juice glass. "Right now, probably not. He trusts me to keep watch and keep him informed."

Which also meant their dad didn't trust Luke. "So, you're going to tell him."

"If I want to keep my job."

Luke sighed and drummed his fingers on the table. There had to be a solution, one that would keep the land in the Beaumont hands without Luke taking the blame for slacking off on his assignment. "Can you give me a week?"

"Don't know." Tim smirked and leaned back, holding his head in locked fingers. "What's in it for me?"

Luke wanted to punch the smirk from his brother's face, but he kept his hands balled in his lap. "How about the satisfaction of doing a good deed for your brother."

"Fine. But it'll cost you a box of Gran's Goodies."

"Done." Luke was surprised that was all Tim wanted. Had he been reading Gran's Bible? Or was he planning something else? Luke never could understand how his brother's mind worked.

Tim sat up straight and crooked a wicked smile. "Remember, there's no guarantee that Dad won't discover the listing on his own, then it's your butt on the line."

"If it happens, it happens." He prayed it wouldn't, but his dad could nose out a deal quicker than a kid could gobble up a sucker. Besides, whatever it cost him would be worth it when Jess said 'Yes' on Friday.

JESS LOADED THE JEEP with supplies to make it through the week at the cabin, then headed down to the beach by the home she temporarily shared with Callie. Talking to Luke, she wanted quiet and privacy. She hated that she was going to disappoint him. She was upset enough about having to postpone their Friday date, but she had no choice.

She sat on the bench she'd shared with Callie the previous night and called Luke's cell. He answered on the first ring as if he'd been waiting.

"Hey there, pretty lady, I was about to call you."

"Hey yourself." She fingered the hem of her T-shirt, winding it between fingers. "How are the cities?"

"Busy. Haven't seen Dad. Fought with Tim. Had an amazing breakfast. Picked up what I needed for Friday night."

Her heart sank lower than she imagined possible. "About Friday night, I'm going to have to take a rain check."

"What? Why?" His disappointment rang through clearly.

She sighed and tears threatened. How could she possibly have more to shed after last night?

"What's wrong, milady?"

She managed to whisper, "They're getting a divorce."

"Jess, no. I'm so sorry."

"And they've already put the cabin on the market."

Silence answered from Luke's end, then he finally said, "I know. Tim told me."

"They don't see any reason to wait any longer." But she'd give them one this weekend. They wouldn't be able to resist falling in love again. She sat up straight. "I haven't given up, though. I'm heading up to the cabin today, will be there all week planting flowers, and Mom and Dad promised not to do anything—won't file divorce papers, won't sell the cabin—until after next Sunday. They're coming up to see it, and it's gotta be perfect, Luke."

"It will be. I won't be able to help every day, but I will when I can. And we'll still do something Friday night. We'll have to save our princess outing for another evening, but I'll make Friday special."

A smile slowly lifted her heart and found its way to her lips. "Every day with you is special."

"I'll see you later today, spade in hand."

And he was there Monday evening. After praying over the path, he helped her spread newspaper to smother the weeds and grass in the spots marked out for garden. They watered the newspaper as they went along, and sprinkled dirt on it, so it wouldn't blow away.

He was there Tuesday evening also. Even though rain prevented them from working outside, he helped her shine up the cabin. The bathroom remodel had spewed dust in every nook and cupboard and drawer. He also helped her hang one of her dad's paintings from years before, one of her and Callie as pre-teens playing in the rocks below the cabin. If only he'd pick up the paintbrush again, his recovery would get back on track.

On Wednesday night, Luke showed up with a sample of a new truffle his candy maker was fiddling with. The gluten-free, sugar-free chocolate truffle was a good concept, but it tasted like sawdust. After washing away the taste with a Superior Sweets ice cream bar, they prayed over the path, and he helped her shovel mulch bark over the newspaper.

On Thursday, candy store issues kept him away all day. Jess couldn't believe how much she missed him, how well they worked together, laughed together. Prayed together. How was it that only a few months ago, she'd mocked the idea of prayer. Now she thrived on it, gathered strength from it. And hope.

With each plant, every hosta, iris, daylily, and bleeding heart she nestled into the dirt, she whispered a blessing over it. By the end of the day, she'd only completed about a quarter of the path, but she had two days remaining before the big reveal. Come Sunday, when her parents arrived, the flowers would be nowhere near fullness, but infant flowers were still beautiful.

On Friday, after completing another quarter of the path, she collapsed on the bench near the top of the cliff. Every muscle in her body made itself known, and not in a nice way. Dirt was permanently embedded beneath her fingernails, what was left of them anyway. And the hands that had once modeled were cut, bruised, and callused. How was she going to survive two more days of this? What she'd give to have that Jacuzzi back in her parents' former home. And Luke? He'd take one look at her grubby face, baggy eyes, and scraggly hair and run screaming back to the cities.

Yawning, she rubbed a grimy fist over her eyes. Maybe she should tell Luke to stay home. Right now, she needed a long shower and a good night's rest.

She looked back at the path and sighed. Not only did she need to complete the garden path, but she wanted to add container gardens around the cabin and here by the fire pit. To accomplish everything by Sunday, she needed an extra twenty-four hours and a half-dozen additional helping hands. How was she ever going to get it all done by Sunday?

If only Luke could be here tomorrow, but Saturday was one of the store's busiest days, and he couldn't take it off. She understood, but she still wished he could be here.

Speaking of Luke . . .

She checked the time. Ugh, he'd be here in another hour, and she had a body to scrub. With a groan, she pushed off the bench and forced her legs to move one after the other, slowly picking up speed with the realization that Luke would be here. Soon. And she looked like a *Walking Dead* extra. Tonight might not be the princess date he'd first promised, but he did say it would be special, and for that she needed to put in a little extra effort.

She showered quickly, although she wanted to stay in much longer. When they'd installed the new bathroom, along with safety rails, an adjustable hand-held shower, and a bench seat, they'd added a few extra shower heads. Jess had reasoned to her mom that the extra heads would provide helpful massage for Dad's limbs.

They weren't too bad for Jess's limbs today either.

Her fingernails were mostly clean when she stepped out. Some bright red polish would hide what dirt remained. After drying her hair, she put on a bare covering of makeup, enough to even her skin tone, and she highlighted her lips in a bold pink, perfect to draw Luke's attention. Not that he'd needed too much encouragement to share a kiss or two following a day's work.

Blushing at the thought, she pulled on distressed jeans, a tomato-red satin T that matched her nails, and a new pair of white Converse tennis shoes. She dressed up the outfit with a silver chain. For a final touch, she pulled back her hair into a messy bun, and posed in front of the mirror as if posing for a camera. *Not bad, Jess, not bad at all.* Luke would most certainly admire her effort.

Reenergized, she hurried out to the porch, a glass of lemonade in hand and waited.

And waited.

The house's shadow grew longer and filtered through the trees, with no sign or phone call from Luke.

She went inside and checked the time. He was nearly a half hour late, which was highly unusual. Yes, he was running a store on a very busy stretch of highway. Chances were, the store had been swamped with customers, and he refused to close the door on anyone who needed their chocolate fix.

Still, he usually called if he was going to be late. She tried his cell. No answer. Then the store phone. Got voice mail.

That meant he was on his way, right? She returned to the porch and lit several citronella candles to keep the mosquitoes at bay.

She slapped a mosquito on her arm and more buzzed around head.

Clearly the candles weren't working as their labels promised.

Her stomach growled, reminding her that she hadn't eaten since around three, and then only a sandwich and salad, hardly what she needed with all the physical work she was doing. She went inside again. Now he was forty-five minutes late.

Where are you, Luke?

Through the screen windows, she heard gravel popping beneath tires, and Luke's pickup finally appeared around the cabin. Unable to contain her smile, she ran outside to greet him.

And screeched to a stop when he stepped out of the truck, his smile absent. He slammed the door.

What had his family done now?

He came around the pickup, scratching the back of his neck. His gaze connected with hers and, finally, there was the smile she couldn't resist.

"Hey there." She jogged up to him and gave him a quick kiss. "Bad day?"

"Huh." He took her hand and led her up to the front deck. "Good day. Bad evening." He plopped down in one of the cushioned chairs, leaned back, and closed his eyes.

"Family?" She sat beside him and took his hand.

"Gee, how'd you guess?" He ran both hands through his short hair.

Foreboding awoke a volcano in her stomach.

"As I was about to head over here, I got a call from Dad."

"Uh-oh."

"Exactly. I need to warn you, Jess. My dad knows that this land is up for sale, and he's teed off at me for not making a move."

"And you're not going to, right?"

"That's just it, Jess, as an employee of Harrison Property Development, purchasing this land is part of my job, and if I don't do it I not only will lose my job, but Dad . . . " He squeezed her hand and let go, then rubbed his hands down his face. "He said that if I don't do my job, don't bother coming home again."

Chapter Nineteen

Jess couldn't do anything but stare at Luke, trying to absorb what he was saying, because there was no way he'd be taking this land from her now, not when so much was at stake.

"You understand what I'm saying, don't you, Jess?"

Shaking her head, she stalked away from him to the far end of the deck and stared out at the shadow-filled woods. During the day, those trees were beautiful, inviting, and friendly, but now? She shivered and spun back around, leveling Luke with a glare. "No. I don't understand. What I'm hearing is that not only is Harrison Property Development planning to buy my cabin, but that you're the agent making the offer, and you promised—you promised!—you wouldn't do that to me."

Shoulders hunched, he stuffed his hands in his jeans pockets and said so low she could barely hear him above the wind rustling through the leaves. "I don't have a choice." He cleared his throat and stood tall. "But, I can prolong it until Monday, until after your folks see this place. Then it'll be a dead point because how can they help but fall in love again?"

And if they didn't? No, she couldn't give in to doubt. She had to believe that her parents' romance would be rekindled this weekend. She sat on one of the deck chairs and stared at the wood boards below her feet.

The soft creak of footsteps neared, and Luke was in front of her, kneeling, lifting her chin, searching her eyes. "This doesn't change how I feel."

How could it not change the way she felt? She yanked her head away, looking up at a sky darkened with clouds, and whispered, "Please go." All along she'd been romancing the enemy, and it was time she faced that truth.

Luke stayed in front of her, his breaths deep and long, for an interminable number of seconds before he finally stood. "I'll be back tomorrow after store closing. I'm not giving up on your parents." He bent down and kissed her forehead. "Or on us." And with that he hurried off to his pickup.

Don't leave! The thought struck her the second he opened the truck door. She leapt up and yelled at the same time the door slammed. She ran toward the truck, waving, but it zoomed up the driveway and out of sight.

Even with all that was against their relationship, he wasn't giving up and that filled her with hope, not only for them, but for her parents too.

She wasn't going to give up either.

SUNLIGHT PIERCING THROUGH THE windows reached to the loft and awoke Jess. Waking to a sunny day was far better than any mechanical alarm. It rang out hope, as if God was personally telling her He had this. If He could cause the sun to come up every morning, He could certainly be the author of romance.

But that meant she had to get up now and get those flowers planted. With no help until Luke got off work, it was going to be a long, exhausting day.

She stretched out the kinks in her neck and shoulders, and her muscles reminded her that they'd already done their fair share for the week. Come tomorrow night, to celebrate the success of Operation: Planting Hope, she'd treat herself to a hotel stay and soak her worn muscles for a couple hours in a whirlpool tub.

She got out of bed and did a few more stretches before heading downstairs. She blended strawberries, a banana, and almonds together with water, ice cubes, and protein powder to make a smoothie that would give her plenty of energy for the beginning of the day. She hoped.

No, she knew.

Armed with an ice-water-filled thermos, she tromped outside and packed the garden wagon with perennials she'd purchased from a local nursery. She tugged the wagon up the path, and her shoulders sagged as she took in the amount of work yet to be done. Not even a Master Gardener could complete the work in one day.

What would it take to become a Master Gardener? On Monday, assuming these gardens turned out the way she'd planned, she'd look into it.

She pulled the wagon one-quarter of the way up the path to where her last hosta had been cradled into the dirt. For the parts of the path winding through the darkest part of the woods, she'd stick with hostas, which preferred shade. They came in a wide enough variety to make the garden interesting.

The diverse assortment of just one type of plant amazed and overwhelmed her. How was it she'd never seen God's hand in creation before?

She looked over her selection and chose a Lakeside Paisley Print that had white feather-like printing in the middle of the green leaves. Next summer, lavender flowers would shoot up. She couldn't wait!

She dug a hole through the mulch and dirt, and freed the plant from its plastic container. No two plants were ever alike. Amazing. She bedded the plant into the dirt then laid her hand gently on the leaves and whispered a prayer that it would grow hardy and healthy and that those walking the path would be blessed by its beauty and reminded of the Creator of that beauty.

Every plant had the same words spoken over it. She could bed the plants and water them. God would cause them to grow.

But planting with this much care was taking way too long. The sun was already midway up the sky. Getting all this work done today was going to be impossible.

Still, she wasn't going to give up. She tucked a Hosta Church Mouse near the border and something rumbled behind her. After whispering a quick prayer over the plant, she looked toward the cabin. A red SUV was making its way down the driveway. Haven? Wasn't he supposed to be spending time with his son today?

She brushed her hands on her jeans and went to meet him, half-empty wagon in tow. Haven and Reese got out followed by . . . She squinted at the guest. Travis? Luke's brother-in-law? What were they all doing here? She certainly didn't have time to play hostess today.

"Need some help?" Haven called out before walking around the back of the SUV. He took out a cardboard box.

She stood still, her mouth agape. The three walked toward the path, pulling on garden gloves. "You have no idea."

"Luke said you needed help." Travis dug a spade out of the box Haven carried.

"And he sent very handsome angels." Jess hugged each of them.

"Well, I wouldn't go that far." Haven mussed his son's hair. "This kid's got a lot of mischief in him."

"Geez, Dad." Reese ducked away from Haven. "Aunt Callie said you're supposed to order us around, and I'm not supposed to complain, and she said no more tooting talk either."

Jess giggled. "Let me guess, 'tooting talk' were Callie's exact words."

"Well, yeah." Reese kicked at the gravel. "She won't let me say the other word. Mom doesn't mind. Dad doesn't either. He says it all the time."

Haven elbowed his son. "Don't give away our secrets."

"I promise not to say a word." Jess grinned and rubbed her hands together. "I can't think of a better way to spend the day." Now to decide how she was going to delegate. She looked up the path. Giving the guys flowers and saying "Plant them" wouldn't work. Admittedly, she was picky about the design. She tapped a finger on her chin. If she set the plants where she wanted them to go, the guys could take it from there. "Okay, here's what we're going to do . . . "

She laid out her plan, then the four of them spent the afternoon embedding flowers into the dirt, saying a prayer over each. In between planting, they took short breaks for lunches. Callie had even made sandwiches and cut fruit for the crew. With all this help, God must have a plan to bring her parents back together. No way could they fail now.

Finally, after six PM, they tucked the final plants—a Bridal Falls Hosta with heart-shaped leaves and a Cathedral Falls Hosta whose leaves glowed—into the dirt where the path spilled out onto the overlook. They were surrounded by yellow-flowering daylilies and bleeding hearts. Sure they were pretty now, but in a few weeks, after they had time to take root and grow, this area was going to be breathtaking. Next year, once they'd had time to take root, they'd be even more magnificent.

Unfortunately, by the time Callie and Haven had their ceremony, the flowers would be well past blooming stage, but there was beauty in aging too.

Now all she had to do was fill a few containers by the cabin and here at the opening, and the cabin would be ready for her parents' visit. Those could be done after she fed her planting angels and sent them home. Besides, Luke was coming tonight.

Hummingbirds should have danced through her stomach, but instead her gut churned. She appreciated that Luke had been open about his assignment for Harrison, but that still meant he was the enemy.

And that meant their relationship couldn't be the same, especially if . . .

No. She wasn't going there. Tomorrow, her parents would come and they'd be overwhelmed by memories of their romancing days, and they'd drop the crazy idea of divorcing. And then she and Luke wouldn't have to worry about what Harrison wanted to do.

She grilled chicken breasts for her volunteers—only the best for guys who'd given up their day for her—and made the mistake of settling into a cushioned deck chair with her plate. Getting up would be nearly impossible.

She cut into her chicken just as a vehicle crunched down the driveway and parked beside Haven's SUV. Luke! Without thinking, she leapt up, the chicken and fruit splatting onto the deck. Rats! And that chicken was good too.

Apparently, seeing Luke was better. Maybe forgiving him was going to be easier than she thought. She bent to pick up her mess, but Reese volunteered to clean, with a little coaxing from his dad, and Jess ran to greet Luke.

With a quick kiss.

His eyes widened with surprise, but his lips tilted up to the side and he kissed her back until applause from the deck broke them up. She was pretty sure she heard a groan from Reese, too. The poor kid was surrounded by couples crazy in love.

"Now that's an unexpected greeting," Luke whispered, and leaned his forehead against hers.

"Not the greeting I planned for you, either, but I needed to thank you for sending the planting angels up here." She gestured toward the now-completed path "We did it!" She took his hand and dragged him forward, pointing out the varying types of flowers bordering the path.

"It's beautiful, like you." At the clearing, he stole another kiss, and leaned back, his hands firm on her hips. "You are an amazing woman, Jessica Rose."

Her cheeks probably bloomed bright as the geraniums she planned for the container gardens.

But he didn't smile with his compliment, and all the tickly feelings she'd had seconds ago morphed into roiling seas. "What now?"

He nodded to the bench, and they sat beside each other, but she made certain there were several inches between them. He stared out over the lake, his head shaking. "My brother Tim called a few hours ago. I have more bad news."

The seas upsetting her stomach threatened to churn up her throat. Good thing her chicken had ended up on the deck rather than in her stomach.

He squeezed his hands on his thighs and kept his gaze away from her. "Another company is in the running for your land. If Harrison doesn't make an immediate move, Skardell Properties will, and they are no respecter of nature. I have no choice but to make the purchase so this land can be saved."

Chapter Twenty

Why was it every time he saw Jess lately, he had to throw more bad news at her? If only he had the personal funds to buy the land, he'd do it and gift it to Jess. But just because he was a Harrison did not mean that he was overflowing with wealth. His financial advisor had affirmed that on Monday. Someday, maybe, if he ever moved up in the company he could afford it, but for now, he was a peon like everyone else.

He looked over at Jess, still seated on the bench, hugging herself, her mouth set in a stoic line while frigid winds blew off the lake. "I contacted your father, informed him of Harrison's interest, and awareness of Skardell's interest, and asked him to hold off until Monday to make a decision. He promised he would."

"I see." Her chin remained taut. "I guess tomorrow is it. Thank you for letting me know." She got up and hurried down the path.

Luke chased after her and grabbed her arm. "I'll do whatever I can to convince him not to sell."

She shook off his hand and her eyes fired lasers into his. "Fine. Do whatever you need to do, just know that you'll be doing it without me."

"I don't have a choice, Jess."

"People always have a choice."

"Right. Either Harrison buys the land or Skardell does. Either I risk losing my career and my dad's respect, or I risk losing you. How am I supposed to choose?"

"Guess that's your problem." She continued down the path.

Again, he grabbed her arm. "Have I ever told you about Mom?"

Jess groaned and stopped, but said nothing else. Was she willing to listen?

He took her hand and led her back to the bench, her feet shuffling over the gravel pathway, but she took an adjacent chair instead of sitting by him.

Didn't matter. He could tell the story from here too. "Mom and Dad. They met at the candy store."

Jess's head swiveled his way. "I know."

"From what Gran told me, Mom was a free spirit. Bohemian. Hated boundaries and loved adventures. My younger brother takes after her. And Dad?" Luke walked to the edge of the bluff and looked down at the waves crashing against the cliff, slowly beating a new shape into it. Felt like his love life. "Dad was the opposite. Rigid. Hyper-organized. Didn't let feelings or family get in the way. But, for some reason, Mom caught his eye. He was heading up north to check out land for his dad." The grandpa Luke never met because Pops had a heart attack shortly after Lydia was born. From what he'd heard, Dad and Pops were made of the same cloth.

"And he stopped at Gran's store."

Luke nodded. "Mom waited on him, and that was it. Two months later they were engaged. A month after that they were married." Much to Pop's chagrin. "To hear Gran talk about it, they were made for each other, and smoothed each other's raw edges. But Mom never lost the wanderlust."

He heard Jess get up then felt her hand on his shoulder. "They had Lydia after a year. I came eighteen months later, followed by Tim fourteen months after that."

Jess gasped. "I can't imagine taking care of three kids under three."

"Yeah, well, neither could Mom." Luke bent down and picked up a rock and hurled it at the lake. "I remember her being gone more than she was home. And Dad let her go off on her own little adventures with the family credit card. He knew that if he tried to hold her back, she'd resent him. Didn't matter. She still ended up resenting him. And us kids."

"So, you're telling me, candy store romances are doomed to fail?"

"No. That's not at all what I'm saying." He rubbed his whisker-covered face. "Before she died, Dad tried to do it all, so we wouldn't notice her absence. Little league. Hockey. If we were involved, he was there. And sometimes Mom was too."

"I'm sorry, Luke."

He shrugged. "That was normal for us, and I'd been happy with my normal. I had a dad who loved me, who spent time with me, and a mom who brought presents when she returned from her adventures. I had nothing to complain about. But apparently, Mom did."

Even now, nearly twenty years later, that night she'd run off still made his heart ache.

"Hey guys, we're heading out." Haven's voice broke into his reverie.

Luke glued on a smile before turning around.

Travis and Reese stood beside Haven. What had they seen? Heard? Travis knew the story, had helped him through his angry emotions back in college. He might be getting a call later tonight.

Fake smile intact, Luke got up and slapped Haven on the back and fist-bumped Reese. "Thanks, guys, for coming up. The place looks amazing."

"Glad to help," Haven said. "Anything for Jess."

Yeah, Luke would do anything for Jess too.

Did that mean standing up to his dad?

He shook the thought away and slap-hugged Travis, who whispered, "Mom story?"

"Yep."

"We'll chat, and I want you to seriously think about seeing a counselor." Which meant Travis would be waiting for Luke's call tonight, no matter when he got in.

Jess hugged them all, thanked them a hundred more times before they took off, leaving her alone with Luke, who still felt the anger and the guilt from that night his mom had run off for the last time. If he hadn't been such a needy ten-year-old, maybe she would have stayed. And maybe his dad wouldn't have turned into an automaton incapable of feeling.

Jess took his hand and led him to the bench. This time she sat beside him, keeping her hand in his. "What did your mom do?"

"I heard them arguing." His fists balled tighter than a wound-up yo-yo, Luke kicked at the gravel. "And peeked into the dining room. Mom wanted to go off somewhere again. Dad told her it was time she stayed home, took care of her kids. She screamed back that we were nothing but a burden, that she wished she never had us."

Jess squeezed his hand and rested her head against his shoulder.

"Dad told her, fine, go, but don't bother coming back. And don't count on having any more money to spend. And that's when she saw me."

He took several deep breaths before continuing through this part of the story that always managed to rebreak his heart. "I was ten, but I still ran to her, begged her not to go, and her last words to me were, 'You're the reason I'm leaving.' What kind of mom does that? Dad hugged me tighter than he had before and told her to get out. Don't bother coming home again. And she didn't." And somewhere inside him still was that little, scared boy who wanted his mother to love him. Who wanted his dad to hug him like that again.

"Oh, Luke." Jess wrapped him in a hug. "I'm so very sorry. Did she stay in touch?"

He laughed, sarcasm spilling out. "Never had the chance. She took the little two-seater Dad had given her and wrapped it around a tree a few miles away from home. I don't think Dad ever forgave himself—or me—for her running away."

Jess tugged his face toward her. "It wasn't your fault."

"Yeah, well tell that to a broken heart. Dad's heart fractured that night, with Mom removing every last bit of compassion before it was pieced back together." He swiped a hand across his cheek. "I've forgiven Mom way more than seventy times seven, and still today, I need to forgive her again."

"And your dad."

"I don't blame him. He gave her what she wanted, and she rubbed it in his face."

"And now he's doing to you what he couldn't with your mom."

"Say what?"

Jess shifted on the bench, angling more toward him. "He's afraid you're going to leave, like she did." Empathy was written in her moist eyes, the downturn of her full lips.

Luscious lips he desperately wanted—needed—to kiss. With their knees touching just enough to ignite a flame inside him, he drew her to him and pressed his eager lips to her tentative ones, which quickly turned willing.

No one had ever made him feel like this before. More than loved. He was valued. Cherished.

He pulled her closer, kissed her deeper, and drowned out the chiding voice that told Luke he wasn't good enough and that his dad didn't love him.

Oh, he wanted to love her!

And then he'd have another voice whispering "Guilty!" in his ear. With his body compelling him to do otherwise, he backed away. On wobbly legs, he got up off the bench and started pacing the clearing, his head squished like a vise between his two hands. "I'm sorry. I'm sorry. I'm sorry," he kept repeating, fearful of looking back at her to see her contempt. He was a despicable person. Travis was right about counseling. He needed to exorcise this demon, who kept whispering "You're not good enough" and "You're not loved" from his head and heart before he hurt anyone else.

"We didn't do anything." Jess's words were soft, and carried on the cool breeze toward him.

Oh, but he'd wanted to. Still did, if he was honest with himself.

He swallowed the baseball-sized guilt that had lodged in his throat, and looked over his shoulder, back at her. Moonlight snuck between the clouds and glowed off her face. Even dressed in her work clothes, her hands and face still grubby from digging, he'd never seen anyone more beautiful.

"Let me walk you home." He crooked his arm, and she wrapped

delicate hands around his elbow and they traversed the path toward the cabin, stopping at his truck. Instead of kissing her goodnight, he blew a kiss, and bowed. "Until tomorrow." And then he got into his pickup, drove back to the store, and took a long, cold shower.

While drying off, he called Travis and confessed what he dearly wanted to do tonight and why and Travis once again mentioned the counselor. After tomorrow, Luke would make the call, and get his head on straight. Jess deserved that.

Once this land mess was all over, he'd take Jess on that long-awaited princess date, give her Gran's ring, and make Jess promise to keep the engagement short.

All he needed now was a miracle tomorrow that would bring her warring parents back together.

Chapter Twenty-One

Jess lay awake in the loft, her heart still pumping from Luke's kiss. Oh my, he knew how to jumpstart her heart. One minute she was ready to blame him for breaking up her parents, the next they were locking lips so tightly, she thought they'd need a locksmith to pull them apart.

Any other guy would have followed through, and she would have let them. And a part of her still wished for it. But a larger part, the heart that Jesus had washed clean, gave thanks that Luke did treat her like a lady. Well, mostly, anyway.

She pounded the pillow and let out a loud screech. Tucked in this cabin in the middle of the woods, no one else would hear. How could she be so drawn to him, and yet be so angry, or was it mistrustful, with him? Would he choose his dad over her? If he chose her, would the other company vying for the land purchase it instead, and ruin God's masterpiece?

She'd rather Harrison make the purchase, but hopefully, after tomorrow, that wouldn't be an issue. But if seeing the cabin, and walking the garden path, didn't bring her parents back together, Luke would be taking this place away from her. She didn't know if she could ever forgive him for that. Yet, given the same choice, she had no doubt, she'd choose family.

Still . . .

She'd read a Bible passage earlier this week that talked about not being anxious for tomorrow. Now where was it? She pulled her Bible from the bedside table and paged to the bookmark. There it was, in Philippians. *Do not be anxious about anything, but in every situation, by prayer and petition, with thanksgiving, present your requests to God.* That was exactly what she was going to do, and if she stayed awake the entire night making those requests, so be it.

Sleep finally came, and when the sun shone through the windows the next morning, she was somewhat rested, but her anxiety still spilled over.

Today was the day she and so many others had worked so hard for. Today would likely decide the future of her parents' marriage, and she had way too much to do before they arrived this afternoon. That meant skipping church this morning, but worshiping in God's creation would be equally good, wouldn't it? There was so much she had to learn about her faith yet. She definitely felt closer to Him here than back home, or even at the church she attended with Callie, Haven, and Reese.

Where did Luke attend up here? Maybe she should check that out.

Only if today was a success.

She got out of bed and a clap of thunder startled her. No! She looked out the window, and the sunlight that had been streaming through minutes earlier was now clouded over and rain cascaded down the windows. *Not today, God, please.* How would she ever finish filling all the planters?

How would she give Dad the big surprise she had planned for him?

She wagged a finger at the rain. Who was she to let a little rain shower stop her?

She plodded down the stairs and across the living room, then stepped out onto the deck. The roofline extended a few feet beyond the house, keeping much of the rain away. It wouldn't hurt her or the plants to be bedded down in the rain. Probably be healthy for them too.

If the rain didn't wash away the soil. And if the wind didn't pick up and blow down branches again. And if lightning didn't strike . . .

Girl, you are borrowing trouble once again. Those were things she had no control over, but she could control getting those flowers planted.

After downing a mixed-berry smoothie, she donned a rain poncho and went outside to defy the weather. Lightning flashes lit up the clouds as she hurried to the garden shed. She filled the wagon with empty planters. Her favorites were the metal milk pails she'd found in a variety of sizes and bright colors. A little twist on the rustic nature of the cabin. Plus they'd add a splash of color when the flowers weren't blooming, and the colors would pop against the cabin's log siding. All she'd had to do was drill a few drainage holes in the bottom of each, and *voila!* they were ready for plants.

She pulled the wagon up the handicap ramp. Who knew that it would come in handy for something besides a wheelchair? She returned to the shed and hefted a couple of bags of garden soil into the wagon and brought that to the house. Then she made one more trip to the side of the shed where her stash of annuals was kept, and loaded the wagon a third time. With the rain coming down harder now, she tugged the wagon across the gravel driveway to the deck, dragging mud onto the once pristine wood slats. The rain would wash it away, right? One thing she didn't have to worry about.

Now, what to do first? She examined all her different pots and chose the two that would bookend the stairs leading up to the deck. They'd take the longest to fill and were probably the most important for first impressions. She put one large planter inside the wagon to fill it there. Bringing it back down would be so much easier. Another blessing from the ramp.

After filling the bucket two-thirds full of potting soil, she set the plants on top to decide on the arrangement. The tall spike in the center added height and texture. Red geraniums were her mom's favorite, and several circled the spike. For added color and texture, she added vinca vines that spilled over the side of the container and a white trailing Superbell. She briefly stepped back for perspective and, through the rain, approved what she'd created. Satisfied, she removed each flower from their pot and set them into the dirt. She tucked soil around each, leaving no roots exposed, and said a prayer over the container. Finally, she brought the planter down the ramp, hefted it out of the wagon, and placed it beside the deck stairway. After turning it to get the best angle, she stepped back. Not bad, not bad at all. And God was even doing the watering for her, so that was one step she didn't have to worry about.

Now, on to the next planter. One down, and a zillion more to go.

For the other house planter, she mimicked the style of the first and bookended it with the other planter alongside the steps. For the beginning and end of the path, she created similar container gardens in slightly smaller containers.

With the remaining planters, she could be more creative. She used different shades—with generous amounts of red, her mom's favorite color—of petunias and Gerbera daisies, pansies, verbena, salvia, impatiens, and more, and placed each according to which preferred shade, or sun, or a mix of both. Over each completed garden, she said a prayer. Come fall, she'd bury a bunch of tulip bulbs around the cabin and surprise her mom come spring. Also next spring, she'd sprinkle seeds for red poppies where the sun shone brightest, with hopes of creating carpets of red beneath the trees.

Rain still pattered down as she prayed over the final container. Now to distribute them. She filled her wagon again, and trekked down the ramp and aimed for the path. A gust of wind blew off the hood of her poncho, and within seconds her hair was plastered to her head. It made no sense pulling the hood back up. Besides, rain-washed hair had to be healthy, right?

She continued along the path until she reached the clearing. She'd work from the back to the front, spacing the flowers where they would grow the best.

When God planted His first garden in Eden, He must have taken the same care. Imagine what the gardens in Heaven must look like! Someday, she would see it. She would have loved to have seen that very first garden in Eden where life was first breathed, where Adam met his Eve. Where romance began.

Today, God had taken on watering these plants. That was a sign for her parents, wasn't it? That He would water and nurture their relationship and cause it to grow healthy again?

And when they got back together, she could think about a future relationship with Luke.

Luke . . . *Please, God, let me have a future with him.*

That sounded like a very selfish prayer. She pulled the now-empty wagon down the gravel path. Was selfish prayer okay? She had so much to learn.

She rounded a bend in the path and braked. Speaking of Luke, his pickup idled by the cabin.

He was going to see her looking like a drowned rat. Oh joy . . .

Well, if he still liked her after seeing her like this, that meant he was a keeper. That is, if he didn't buy the cabin.

It always came back to that condition.

Should love have conditions? She doubted it, but she also doubted she could get her heart to see past such a betrayal, even if he had no other reasonable choice.

Chin up, she continued down the path, and up the cabin ramp while Luke got out of his truck and ran to meet her.

In the rain. With a smile and a wet kiss. Oh, snickerdoodles, could that man ignite fireworks that even rain couldn't extinguish! Still, she pushed him away. "If you're trying to influence the judge, I'll have you know it won't work."

He gave her a lopsided grin. "Maybe so, my beauty, but it sure is fun trying."

"Help me distribute these planters, and I'll think about it." She bent to pick up a couple of the smaller containers, but his hand on her arm stopped her, and she looked up into suddenly serious eyes.

"Do you mean that? No matter what happens today, will you give us a chance?"

She swallowed hard, staring into those eyes that showed nothing but love for her, and wanted to tell him she'd give him a chance.

But deep in her heart she knew that if he bought the cabin for his dad's company, that would strangle life from their relationship like weeds in a garden, so she looked back down and grabbed a couple of planters and placed them into the wagon.

And he helped her.

Good thing it was raining, so he couldn't tell that uninvited tears leaked from her eyes.

With him working alongside her, it didn't take long to arrange the mini gardens beside the garden path, adding much color to the greens planted there.

With the rain slowing slightly, they walked hand in hand along the path, with her giving a final perusal. She moved some plants around, but for the most part, she was satisfied. They reached the clearing and looked back toward the cabin, and she sighed. It was more than satisfactory.

"It's beautiful." Luke stole her words and kissed her cheek. "You could have a future with landscaping."

"You really think so?" That would be so much more fun than sitting in an office all day long.

"Absolutely." He took her hand and they began a slow walk through the rain, back to the cabin. "Landscaping is a huge part of property development. At least I think it should be. The thing I hate most about city living is the lack of greenery, texture, color."

They climbed up onto the deck, and he opened the door for her.

"One second." She hurried to her planting area and took her final mini garden, a turquoise-colored water-can-turned-planter, and set it in the middle of the patio table. Her final outdoor touch.

"See what I mean?" Luke pointed to the water can. "Proof that you're good. The table was fine without that, but you took it from fine to dazzling."

Standing beneath the cabin overhang, she studied the table while removing her poncho. She might be patting herself on the back, but he was right. The mini garden did add that final touch.

With a smile, and with her muscles protesting from the week of manual labor, she stepped into the cabin.

They both removed their shoes and set them on a mat by the door.

"Have a seat." Luke pointed to the couch.

Even wet, she didn't argue. She lay down, stretching out to the full length of the sofa, and closed her eyes while he got a fire going in the fireplace. Another romantic touch to bring her parents together.

He brought her a mug of white hot cocoa. "It's a concoction Mary thought up. It has lemongrass, lavender, and lime in it. For this fall and winter, we're thinking about adding a hot cocoa bar to the store."

"What a good idea!" If he was thinking about the future of his store, did that mean he was going to go against his father's wishes? With that hope, she took a sip, and her eyes rolled back. Goodness, that was delicious! "Tell Mary, I give it a big thumbs-up."

He grinned. "She'll be happy to hear that." He lifted her legs and sat down then rested her legs on his lap and began massaging her feet.

An unbidden moan escaped her throat. She hadn't realized how sore her feet were until he kneaded them. "Please, don't ever stop."

"It would be my pleasure." He kneaded her heels, her instep, the balls of her feet, her toes. "Back to landscaping, have you ever considered making it a career?"

She'd looked into becoming a Master Gardener, but that was more of a volunteer position. Making a career out of gardening hadn't crossed her mind. "My career was decided for me early on. I was discovered"—she made air quotes—"by a talent scout as a preteen, and I modeled up until earlier this year when my agent and I parted ways. In between gigs, I worked for Superior Suites."

"Well, think about it. If I had any say, I'd hire you on at Harrison to work with all our properties. Making green areas a priority is an aspect of development our company hasn't focused on, but I think it would be very profitable."

"Profit. Is that what matters most?"

"Harrison is a for-profit business, so yeah, profit is important, like it is with my store and your parents' business. But I believe a business should be more than that. Adding green areas would benefit everyone. Beyond the truth that landscaping adds an ever-changing visual aesthetic that man can't create, there's also the science that tells us plants convert carbon dioxide—which cities are overfilled with—into breathable air. I don't think it's any surprise that God created plants to breathe out life for people and animals. You've got the touch—the eye—to enhance our properties, and make them more than an homage to an architect. Think about it?"

She nodded, then sat up abruptly and glanced at the microwave clock. Snickerdoodles, everyone would be here in under two hours, and she looked like the Swamp Thing. "I've got to shower." She leapt off the couch and aimed for the bathroom. She had to do her hair and makeup and nails, on top of prepping food, and most important, her dad's surprise. *Please, God, stop the rain.* The thunder had stopped long ago. Hopefully, the rain would move along with it.

"How can I help?" he hollered after her.

She braked to a stop and whirled around. "Excuse you?"

"Uh . . . " His face scrunched in confusion. "How can I help?"

She giggled. He had no clue what he'd just asked. "Well, I really don't need help in the shower."

His eyes narrowed at first, then his face turned an adorable shade of red. He scratched his head. "I . . . uh . . . Not . . . "

"You are so cute." Any other guy would have played up the shower gaff, but not Luke. She'd never known a guy so sweet, if only he wouldn't . . . Nope, not going to go there right now. Instead, she pointed to the refrigerator. "You may help by cutting up fruit and veggies."

The red slowly faded from his face, and he grinned. "I don't know, helping with the shower sounded a lot more fun."

She feigned an angry face and pointed toward the fridge. "Fruit and veggies. Now."

With one arm behind his back, and the other below his chest, he bowed. "As you wish."

Oh, he was making this hard.

She hustled into the bathroom, but didn't rush through her shower. Today needed to be perfect, and that included her, which meant that every step of her model regimen had to be followed.

She finished her shower and hurried to help with the food, but Luke already had the fruit and veggies cut up and was in the process of arranging them on trays like a professional caterer would. Along with chocolate, undoubtedly from his store.

Even more special was a plastic child cup from *Per Vivere*, one the server had given them when Luke spilled water on Jess. That cup was no longer filled with water, but with a mini lavender-colored rose plant. She picked it up, held it to her nose, and breathed in. Ahh.

"Like it?" Luke quirked a crooked smile.

"It's perfect." She set the plant down and gestured to the spread. "It's all perfect. Obviously, you've done this before."

He shrugged. "Helped out our cook a time or two. Dad's big on parties to help gain business. And with my schmoozer brother, they do well. Now me and Lydia? We'd hide out in the kitchen and help Shirley, our cook."

"Hmmm." She tapped a finger to her lip, trying to maintain a serious expression, but her curving-up lips failed her. "Have you ever considered hosting parties for a living?"

He laughed. "Yeah. Right after candy store owner." He shook his head. "I never would have thought that's what I'd be doing. Turns out I'm not too bad at it." He brought a rose-shaped piece of dark chocolate to her lips, which she gladly accepted.

Mmm, mmm. She licked her lipstick-free lips. "Berries?"

"Yep."

"Another Mary concoction?"

"Nope. Mine."

"Seriously?"

"Would I kid about chocolate?"

She grinned while looking out the window. Was that the sun peeking through the clouds? Please? "Since you have everything in hand down here, I'm going to go get pretty." She turned toward the stairs.

But he caught her by her hips and whispered in her ear. "Darling, you're already beautiful."

She shivered and hurried to the bathroom before they ended up making out again, stealing more time from getting ready. Now tonight, after her parents left, hand-in-hand, and grinning like love-struck teenagers, maybe she'd give Luke a little thank you kiss. Or not-so-little kiss.

Then, maybe, he'd take her on the princess date they'd postponed. *Lord, please?*

There were no guarantees, but why wouldn't He want her parents back together? Or was that out of His control? Another question for Callie or their pastor.

Regardless, her heart told her that her parents getting back together today had to happen. If they didn't reunite, that also meant telling Luke goodbye.

Chapter Twenty-Two

Jess stood in front of the long mirror in the master bedroom and pointed a newly-polished nail at her image. "Girl, you look good." The bold yellow belt around her navy A-line dress emphasized her hourglass shape. And the scoop neck came just low enough to be flirty, but not show anything. She topped off the outfit with earrings and sneakers to match the belt. Luke's eyes were going to bug out when he saw her transformation from Swamp Thing to cover model.

She wasn't going for that, but it certainly couldn't hurt.

Besides, appearances mattered to her parents, and they'd like that she took the time to look her best as she showed off her work.

Soon, she'd find out if all her efforts paid off.

With a half hour to spare before her parents arrived, she sashayed out of the bedroom. No sign of Luke. So she went outside, onto a sun-drenched deck, and found Luke wiping down the furniture, and looking downright sexy doing it.

He glanced up, his face broke out into a wide smile, and he whistled. "Darlin', you clean up mighty nice." He pretended to doff a cap, like a cowboy would.

"You think so?" She twirled around, making her skirt swirl like a dancer's.

"Yes ma'am." He hooked his thumbs into his belt loops and swaggered toward her. "And if you weren't expectin' company, I'd kiss that lipstick right off your lips," he said in an exaggerated Southern drawl.

She giggled and pressed a finger to his chest to keep him at bay. "Where did Sir Luke go to?"

"Darlin', a knight does not feel for his queen what I feel for you, but a cowboy for his girl?"

"How about a prince for his princess?"

"Now we're talking."

He took her hand and led her to one of the newly-dried chairs. He sat and pulled her down on his lap.

"No kissing allowed." She pressed her hand to his lips, which he promptly kissed. "You're incorrigible."

"And you, my princess, are irresistible, but I shall behave as a good knight and will obey."

Why was she disappointed? She rested her head against his and looked out at the floral paradise she'd created around the cabin. No, it wasn't Eden, but for this cozy little cabin in the woods, it came awfully close.

Now, what else needed to be done? The gardens were as ready as they could get. The food was prepared, and Luke had cleaned up the deck. The clouds had given way to blue skies. The day was turning out perfect after all.

Oh, shoot! Dad's surprise! "We have one more job." She got up and hurried toward her car, with Luke following right behind. She pulled out a couple of the larger items and handed them to Luke, then grabbed the lighter things. With the sun shining now, this was going to be perfect!

They carried everything down the path, to the clearing, and past the fire pit where they set up her dad's surprise, the *pièce de résistance* that would be sure to rekindle her parents' romance.

Hand-in-hand, they returned to the deck, and once again, she cozied herself on Luke's lap where she seemed to fit so perfectly. Minutes later, she heard a car on the driveway, and soon Haven's SUV came around the cabin and parked. Nerves zinged through her body. Would he be bringing her parents? Would they arrive together or separate? What if one of them had changed their mind?

She slid off Luke's lap and waited on the deck, her fingers playing a rapid tune on her thighs. Reese was the first out, and he ran around the vehicle to open the back door while Haven hurried to help Callie out. Then Haven reached back inside the vehicle and took out a couple shallow, cellophane-covered boxes, presumably filled with sandwiches. He handed them off to Callie who brought them to the cabin. Jess held her breath while Reese helped her father step out of the SUV. He leaned heavily on his cane. Uh-oh, not a good day for him. And the ground was saturated, which meant his cane would sink into the dirt, and Dad could fall and make everything worse, and . . .

Luke slipped his arm around her waist and whispered in her ear. "Give it to God."

Easy for him to say. This was her parents' future she was fighting for.

Haven stayed beside her dad, and Reese kept hold of her dad's arm as they made their way toward the ramp. Would Dad look at their help and the ramp as an insult? A threat? Or would it make him give up even more? Why hadn't she thought this all through when she was planning this moment?

Her dad paused at the ramp.

And Jess held her breath.

Was he going to take it? Or would he try the stairs to prove he wasn't an invalid? He looked at Reese and nodded. Reese let go of his arm, and her dad caned his way up the ramp. A smile, tiny as a mustard seed, grew with each step until he reached the top and his smile blossomed into a grin.

"Good work, Jessica Rose. Thank you." He stretched out his arm toward her.

And with a relieved sigh, she gave him a hug and a kiss on the cheek, leaving behind red proof of that kiss. "I'm so glad you like it."

"Would you give me the tour?" He crooked his arm and she gladly took it.

"I'll show you the cabin, but the path will have to wait."

His smile disappeared. "She's c...coming?"

"That was part of the deal."

"Hmph."

With that attitude, they'd never get back together. She felt like scolding him, but held her tongue. Encouragement was required here, so instead she led him into the cabin with its new countertops, refinished cabinets, and cozy new living room furniture. If only she had the funds to buy this place, she could easily make it her home.

"Very nice d...dear." He patted her hand. Was he patronizing her?

She tugged him toward the bathroom. "Here's the best part." She slid the pocket door into the wall and let him go in first.

He stopped in the doorway. Was he surprised by what he saw? Mad? Disappointed? Why did she question everything? Finally, he moved inside, and she stepped alongside him. The old bathroom wouldn't have given them room.

"What do you think?" She watched his face, trying to read it. Was that a tear? Did he see the accessible shower as an insult?

He turned to her, cuffed his hands over her arms, and looked down at her. Yes, those were definitely tears in his eyes.

"I didn't mean to hurt you, Daddy."

He blinked and shook his head. "Hurt m...me?"

"That's not . . . ?"

"Oh, no, no, no, my dear." He gestured with both arms to the room. "This is a gift of love," he said with no hint of stutter. "Thank you."

She waved fingers in front of her eyes. No crying was allowed today. "Thank you." It was working. Her dad was remembering how special this place was and that it didn't belong in any other family's hands.

"Y...you are w...welcome." He kissed her forehead, and gestured toward the door.

They walked outside, and it seemed her father's gait was smoother. His physical therapist had told her that attitude would play a huge part in his recovery. From everything she'd seen so far, by the end of the day, he'd be turning cartwheels.

The others on the deck all looked to her, and she gave a discreet thumbs-up. There was a collective sigh as they all realized one hurdle had been passed.

Her father took a seat by the table and hung his cane on the back of the chair.

She rested a hand on his shoulder. "Can I get you something to—"

Another vehicle grumbled down the driveway. Her mom's Oldsmobile. And she wasn't alone. Who . . . ?

The passenger door opened, and mom's sister got out. Jess didn't know if that was a good sign or not. Was Aunt Tib here to deflect attention from her dad?

There Jess went, borrowing trouble again.

Instead of waiting for them to make it to the deck, Jess jogged out to greet them. "Thanks for coming, Mom." She kissed her on the cheek, as much affection as her stoic mother liked. She greeted Aunt Tib, who was Mom's complete opposite, with a hug. "So good to see you."

"You too, dear. Your mother's bragged about your project up here. I can't wait to see what you've done, and meet the young man who's helped you."

Jess's wide-eyed gaze shot to her mom. She'd actually bragged about Jess's work? And talked about Luke, who she hadn't even met? Huh. Too bad Mom didn't share some of that with her own daughter.

Yikes. Stop the complaining, girl!

"I'd love to show you both around." Jess linked arms with her aunt, and they followed her mom up to the house. Mom gave a cursory nod to her husband. Reese stole a hug from his step-Grandma-to-be. Haven got a handshake from her, and Callie a kiss on the cheek.

Then Jess excused herself from her aunt, took Luke's hand, and led him to her mother, praying she'd approve. "Luke, this is my mother, Mackenzie Beaumont."

Luke held out his free hand. "Luke Harrison. I met you a few years back when I worked at my Gran Lavina's store. She brought me up here for family bonfires."

Her mother smiled politely. "Ah, yes, I remember you. Quite the people pleaser you were."

He grinned and squeezed Jess's hand. "Word has it, I haven't changed. Neither have you, Mrs. Beaumont."

She chuckled and patted him on the back. "Always stay the same, young man. You're good for a woman's ego."

Yes, yes he was.

"Now let's see what you've spent all my money on, shall we?" Her mother flared her hand toward the cabin door.

And nerves ignited in Jess's body. Her mom had very particular tastes, and satisfying them was challenging. If her mom liked the changes, would that convince her to not sell? Or would it tell her that more money was to be made from the sale?

There she went, borrowing trouble again.

Still, her stomach twisted as she followed Mom into the cabin, with Aunt Tib close behind.

"Oh my word, you've done a marvelous job, honey dear." Aunt Tib squeezed an arm around Jess's shoulders. "You have the same exquisite taste as your mother, wouldn't you agree, Mackenzie?"

Jess looked to her mother, who nodded. "It certainly has lost much of that backwoods feel."

Was that a compliment or complaint? Ugh!

"The biggest changes are in the bathroom. A wheelchair would fit in there now."

"Let's hope it doesn't get to that point, shall we?" Chin up, Mom walked the short hallway to the bathroom and slid the pocket door into the wall. "Wise decision, dear."

Yay! Jess grinned and her heart did a little jig.

All three women stepped into the once small space, and they still had room to move. Mom motioned to the zero-entry shower opening and the deep bench. "Another smart choice."

What? Two compliments within a minute? That was almost more than her heart could handle, but she did manage to say, "Thank you."

"Now the tiles aren't exactly what I would have chosen, but they work very well in the space."

Though backhanded, Jess would even accept that as a compliment.

Her mother led the women out of the bathroom. "These upgrades will appeal to a broader range of people and will definitely make this building more marketable."

No! Jess felt her heart shatter into a thousand pieces. Her mom had given up. Would today even matter?

"Mackenzie, really?"

Her mom heaved an intentional sigh. "What did I say wrong now?"

Aunt Tib curled hands on her ample hips.

Jess just wanted to slip away.

"I told you to keep an open mind today." Aunt Tib waggled a finger in Mom's face. Only Tib could get away with that. "And that included thinking about keeping this place for your girls, who obviously love it. If you and Ken want to keep being idiots about your marriage, that's up to you, but don't sell off this Beaumont legacy."

Mom shoved away Aunt Tib's finger. "You think I have a choice?" And she glided down the hall with Aunt Tib nagging behind, all the way outside.

Jess stayed in the hallway, wishing she could melt into the floor. Why, why had she put so much effort into this when her mom wasn't willing to give back, even an inch? Why did it matter so much? She sagged against the wall. Most of her friends came from broken homes, why should hers be any different?

But was it wrong to desire an intact family?

Jess pushed away from the wall and forced out the smile she'd groomed in all her years of modeling. The day wasn't over yet, which meant she wasn't about to give up yet either.

With everyone outside, Jess set out lunch on the kitchen island: the trays Luke had pieced together, subs Callie and Haven had brought, and a pitcher of lemonade Luke must have made while she was getting ready.

He was a keeper, for sure. If only he wasn't the enemy.

How could she move past that?

Easy. By staying busy, playing the consummate hostess, and leading her parents on the walk that had to rend open their hearts as it had thirty-some years ago.

Just as it did with Jess and Luke.

She channeled the carefree girl inside her, the one who'd once preened and danced for her paintbrush-in-hand father, and called the family in for lunch.

No surprise, Reese led the way. That kid had more energy than the rest of them put together. He could probably eat four times as much too. He took a couple of subs, one strawberry, one carrot, and began grabbing several pieces of chocolate.

"Whoa, there, kiddo." Haven grabbed his arm. "Think maybe you should take more fruits and veggies and a little less chocolate? Maybe leave some for the rest of us?"

"It was worth a try." Reese grinned and dropped a couple chocolate pieces on his dad's plate then added a few more berries. Apparently, the kid wasn't a big fan of vegetables.

Luke followed her father in. As her dad picked up a plate, Luke reached for it. "Let me help you, sir."

But her dad held it away. "I am f...fully capable of d...doing this m...myself, young m...an."

"As you wish, sir."

This is going to be a fun day. Sarcasm pinched at that carefree girl.

Jess waited until everyone had passed through the line—well, Reese had gone through a second time—before filling her own plate. She carried it outside, and was relieved to hear no arguments. At one end of the rectangular table, Luke, Haven, and her father were in deep conversation about the Minnesota Vikings' chances this fall. At the other end, her mom, Aunt Tib, and Callie were talking wedding plans. Reese had taken off exploring.

Nothing bored Jess more than sports talk, so she joined the women.

Callie beamed at her as she sat down. "I'm so impressed with what you've done with this place, Jess! Our wedding is going to be the most beautiful event ever." No surprise, Callie's eyes were misty. Her sister tended to cry over everything. At least these were happy tears. "I wish we could be married tomorrow."

"Fine by me." Haven interjected from the other end.

"Don't tempt me." Callie teased back.

"Enough of that talk." Mom played her typical killjoy role. "You'll have the rest of your lives to be married and, believe me, it's not all fairytales." Her pinched gaze shot to her husband, who looked down at his plate.

Would the courts blame Jess if she throttled her mom at this moment? She certainly had just cause. Instead, she forced that smile again, though it was becoming more difficult to conjure up with each minute that passed by. She looked at Callie to steer the conversation back to wedding plans. "Have you decided on letting me host a shower yet? A bachelorette party? Please?"

"Absolutely no bachelorette party." Callie shivered.

"We'll keep it clean. And no alcohol. I promise." Jess had been to her share of raunchy parties where mixed drinks flew freely. A few had even had male strippers. When she thought back on the parties, they'd always made her uncomfortable. It was no surprise that so many of those once-happy brides were now bitter divorcees.

"Actually . . . " Callie nodded to their mom. "Etiquette says it's rude to invite guests to a pre-wedding party if they're not invited to the wedding ceremony, so Mom insisted on hosting my birthday party at Élodie's. That way she can throw her fancy party, and you and I can get all fancied up for our guys, and they get to gussy up for us."

"Gussy up?" Jess giggled. "Seriously, Cal? What decade are you from?"

Callie stuck out her tongue, and Jess did it back to her.

"Ladies, really now." This from stick-in-the-mud Mother. "And, yes, I'm looking forward to throwing the party my daughter deserves, even if it isn't a wedding party."

One Callie deserved? Or one their mom felt cheated out of throwing because Callie wanted to keep the wedding simple?

"And I thank you for that, Mom." Callie leaned over and gave their mom a side hug. "Save the date, everyone, for October first."

"I've got a thing that day." Haven made like he was swinging a golf club.

"Yes, you do, mister." Trying to hold in her smile, but failing miserably, Callie fisted both hands on her hips.

Haven winked. "Guess I've been told."

"Get used to it, son," Dad said without an inkling of humor. Her parents were acting like middle school kids in the throes of puberty.

"At that uplifting note . . . " Aunt Tib started gathering the paper plates from the table. "Your compost bin is where?"

"I'll show you." Luke jumped up and gathered the plates from his end.

Aunt Tib followed Luke, but looked back at Jess and pointed at him with a thumbs-up.

"I know," Jess mouthed back. He definitely was a keeper, but one with a super-high wall standing between them.

And there she was worrying again.

She threw off the concern. It was time to show off the rest of the property, and bring her Mom and Dad back together.

She touched Callie's arm. "Would you and Haven mind cleaning up?" She gestured toward the path and the flowers that glistened in the mid-day sun.

Callie nodded and steepled her hands together, letting Jess know she was praying.

"Thank you." Jess pushed back from the table and stood. "Mom, Dad, can we go for a walk?"

"I don't know that your father is up to it." Mom said.

"I can s...speak for myself, Mackenzie, and y...yes, Jessica Rose, I'd be glad to j...join you."

"I'll help Callista with—"

"No, Mom, I want you and Dad." Interrupting her mother was viewed as a capital offense in the Beaumont family, but Jess didn't care. It was time her parents stopped bickering like juveniles. "Do it for me?"

"Fine." Mom got up and headed for the stairs, her stiletto heels clicking. "Really, Mom? Stilettos?" Stubborn woman knew they'd be walking the path today. Good thing the Beaumont women all had the same size foot. "I'll grab you a pair of tennies."

"These will do fine—"

"No, they won't. The ground is saturated, and you'll sink right in and twist an ankle, and then complain for the next two months."

Her mom's lips pursed, but she sat down without another rebuttal. Huh.

Jess hurried up to the loft and dug out a pair of not-yet-worn tennis shoes. Mom would probably find something to complain about them too, but tough noogies for her. She was going to put the shoes on, go for a walk, and even enjoy it. Jess hustled back downstairs and outside and offered the shoes to her mom.

Who took them without a single complaint. Chances were, Aunt Tib had given her a what-for while Jess was gone. Tib was usually the only one who could get away with sassing the haughty Mackenzie Beaumont. Maybe Jess shouldn't think that way of her mother, but the attitude was really starting to grate on her.

Imagine how it had to aggravate her dad after thirty years of marriage. She couldn't blame him for wanting out—

Nope. Didn't matter. The two belonged together, and they knew it too.

Her mom finished putting on the shoes while Jess walked arm-in-arm with her father down the ramp. He was quiet, but that was certainly better than nagging.

They waited at the bottom of the steps for her mom, who came down and started to walk past, but Jess grabbed her hand, then looped her arm, hoping her mom would get the hint.

Oh, she did, with a roll of her eyes and a muttered "Foolishness," but she did link her arm with Jess's.

And they walked slowly and silently across the grass toward the path, not hurrying her father. The silence sizzled, though, with unspoken antagonism.

The gardens would calm that, wouldn't they?

Unbloomed daylilies guarded the beginning of the path. Next spring, they'd bloom a brilliant yellow. And purple irises would grow tall and sprout an intricate flower.

Jess hoped she'd be here to witness it.

The geraniums in the container garden had held well against the rain and greeted Jess and her parents with a smile.

She glanced over at her mom, whose grip had loosened. Her gaze flitted from the path's first steps to the gardens bordering the trail. Was that a smile? She snuck a peek at her dad. No question that he was smiling.

Jess held in a victory dance. Victory wasn't theirs yet, but they'd won this small battle.

"It's absolutely lovely, Jessica Rose." Dad patted her arm. "So easy to w...walk. I can't...all the work you've put in..." His eyes glistened.

"Your father's right, dear."

Dear? Her mother called her dear? And she agreed with her father? Win. Win!

"This is exquisite, Jessica." Her mother stopped to sniff a flower arrangement. "I'm very proud of you."

"W...we're very proud of you." Dad kissed her cheek. "I...I knew you had a g...gift, b...but this...this is beyond w...what I imagined."

"You're father's right." Mom gestured down the wooded path. They could barely see the clearing. "You have a gift that needs to be used, and I had no idea. No idea at all . . . " Was that a tear in her mother's eye? Jess didn't dare look at her, afraid she'd tear up too. Instead she looked to the sky and shouted a silent "Thank you."

"I remember w...walking this path thirty-plus y...years ago with your mother, w...watching her eyes light up like y...yours are doing right now. M...my attempt at planting p...pales to this."

"Oh hush, Kenneth, I really wish you'd stop putting yourself down. Your efforts were beautiful, as was your proposal."

There was a compliment in there, somewhere. Progress, right?

Her dad stopped and let go of Jess's arm. "What happened to us, Mackenzie?"

Her mom let go too, and Jess walked ahead, keeping her ears open, whispering silent prayers.

"I don't know. Attention. Fame. Somehow in becoming Duluth's most celebrated couple, we forgot to celebrate each other. In building up our egos, it broke down our humility and ability to see beyond . . . me."

And then there was silence . . .

But for the gentle loping of waves against the bluff and the laughter of the seagulls above. Jess sat on the bench, eyeing the surprise she and Luke had set up for her dad, while listening for conversation.

Finally, a whisper from her dad. "Have we gone too far?"

And no answer. Only the gentle rustle of feet over the gravel. She looked back and covered her mouth. They were arm in arm. The stern lines had melted from her mother's face into soft sadness, and her father's head was down, carefully guarding each step.

He stopped and stared off toward the lake. "I don't know, Mack—" His eyes grew dark and his jaw rigid, and he jabbed his cane toward the surprise Jess had for him.

Her father rushed forward, faster than Jess had seen him move in months. He grabbed the canvas off the easel and threw it on the ground. He kicked over the easel, splattering paint, then jutted his finger toward her mom. "I t...told you, I'm done. W...we're done. This..." He spread his arms. "This is d...done."

He glared at Jess. "No more de...delays." He caned his way down the path, stumbling, but not falling.

Her mom's pinched face was back, directed toward Jess. "You had to go there, didn't you?" She stabbed a finger toward the now scattered paint supplies. "You've ruined everything."

And with that, her mom tore down the path, stumbling, falling, and scrambling up faster than Jess could get up from the bench.

What happened?

Jess blinked back tears. Everything had been going so well. Dad loved to paint, like she loved working with flowers. She covered her face with her hands, and minutes later, a strong arm warmed her back. "I'm so sorry, Jess," Luke said softly.

Luke. Who was now the enemy. Who, come tomorrow, would yank out the final thread stitching her family together.

"Can't you . . . " She wiped her cheeks, but kept her face averted. "Can't you convince your dad not to buy?"

He inhaled a deep breath. "I wish I could. I'd do anything."

"Well then . . . " She squared her shoulders. "My dad will be looking for a ride home. I suggest you offer to take him."

Luke turned her face toward him.

She refused to smile or frown or show any emotion, like her mom.

"This doesn't have to mean the end of us."

"How can it not?" She stood up and looked down at him. "How would I be able to look at you, knowing you personally took the last remnant of my family's heritage away?"

"I don't have a choice. You know that. We can make it work, Jess." He stood and cupped her face in his hands. "I know we can."

She knew she should pull away, but his touch had her magnetized.

And then he kissed her, lighting sparks she tried to extinguish, but his lips caressing hers with a cloud-soft gentleness awoke a hunger in her for love, and she took the kiss deeper.

He responded, twining his fingers through her hair and down to her shoulders, then he feathered his lips over her jaw line, and down her neck. Oh, the man knew how to kiss!

With a groan, he pulled away, and backed away from her reach, falling bottom first on the bench.

Now she had him where she wanted. She leaned over him, knowing his eyes would be drawn to her loose neckline, and she started unbuttoning his shirt.

He slapped a hand over hers and tried getting up.

She pushed him back down and sat on his lap, wrapping her arms around his neck. "Love me, Luke, please."

"Jess. No." He pulled her arms away from his neck, gently shoved her from his lap, and stood up. "What are you doing?" He swept a hand across his lips that were red from her lipstick, and paced in front of her.

Oh, God, what was she doing? Apparently, the old Jess still had way too much pull on her life. The old Jess would have reacted like this, not the new, clean Jess. She looked up, with fog-covered eyes. *Forgive me?*

And then Luke was in front of her, kneeling, drying her eyes. "Babe, I know you're hurting, but we can make it through this. Together. And do it the right way."

But all she saw was the man who was going to take her dream away. The moment of passion had temporarily chased away that fact, but now it—he was staring her in the face. Love wasn't enough for her parents.

And it wouldn't be enough for her.

"I'm sorry, Luke, but I need you to go."

"But—"

She shook her head, and hugged herself, keeping her gaze averted from his brown, caring eyes.

With a sigh, he stood, then leaned down and placed a kiss on the top of her head. "I love you, Jessica Rose Beaumont, and love perseveres. I will be back." He rubbed a hand across her shoulder. Seconds later, she heard his footsteps fading down the path.

He might come back, but it was going to take her a long time to forgive.

Chapter Twenty-Three

Luke gritted his teeth as he stomped down the path, swearing at his father for putting him in this impossible position, cursing Mr. and Mrs. Beaumont for acting like spoiled children. For wounding Jess so deeply. And there was nothing he could do to fix it.

He'd failed Jess, her family. Himself. And what ate at him most was that he had no choice. If Harrison Property Development was the only interested buyer, he'd leave his dad's company and not look back, but with Skardell's offer, Luke couldn't not act.

Gran once told him *God will give you more than you can handle. The question is, will you give it back to Him?*

Would he?

Could he?

How could he not turn it over? He looked up at the blue skies winking above the waving branches, and all could think to say was, "Help."

He closed his eyes and took several deep breaths, the word *Help* on repeat in his mind, and an idea came to him, lifting some of the weight he'd insisted on carrying alone.

It was time he surrendered his problems to God and moved on.

Starting now, he was done kowtowing to his dad's every wish.

With renewed confidence, he strode to the clearing by the cabin. The deck was empty, and Callie, Haven, and Reese all wore somber faces as they trudged with Mr. Beaumont toward Haven's SUV. That was one task he could help them with.

He jogged over to the family. "I'll take him home."

Haven rested a hand on his son's shoulder and glanced at Luke. "Are you sure?"

"I am." Luke looked to Mr. Beaumont. "Are you okay with that, sir?"

"As l...long as someone g...gets m...me away f...from here."

"Right away." Luke took a step toward his truck then turned toward Callie. "Your sister needs you."

He put a hand on Mr. Beaumont's back and pointed toward his truck. "This way, sir." As he escorted the distraught father, Luke looked back to the others and mouthed. "I've got this." In more ways than one.

He assisted Mr. Beaumont into the pickup then headed south toward Duluth to drop the man off at an apartment where he'd be alone.

Luke's dad had never adjusted to 'alone.'

Jess's dad was alone by choice.

Either way, the drastic life change had to be overwhelming. If Luke could make things easier for Mr. Beaumont, even in the slightest, he would do so.

"I'm glad I have this opportunity to have a word with you, sir." Luke snuck a glance at his passenger, whose focus remained on the door window. Luke had planned to make the request another way, another time, but now he had Mr. Beaumont as a captive audience. "I have a couple of proposals for you." For the next hour, Luke laid out his thoughts and plans.

By the time he dropped Mr. Beaumont off at the assisted living facility, a twinkle was back in the man's eye. Luke hadn't changed Mr. Beaumont's mind about anything, that hadn't been his plan, but he did offer hope. Letting a family man off at an apartment alone was far safer when that man had hope to cling to.

Now, Luke needed to speak with the more difficult—no, not difficult—formidable Beaumont. Mackenzie Beaumont scared the hair off his chest, but if he ever wanted a future with Jess, he'd risk a hairless chest.

"I SENT HIM AWAY," Jess told Callie when she sat on the bench beside her. Callie had the wisdom to say nothing. Instead she wrapped her sister in a hug. That didn't stop the regrets from flooding through. "I haven't changed, Cal."

"What do you mean?"

Jess wiped a hand across her eyes. "Things were going so well with Mom and Dad and then ... " She gestured toward the art supplies strewn across the clearing. "Luke's got to buy this land for his dad, and I was hurting so bad, I tried to seduce him. Right here. With family and Reese feet away. I didn't care. You said with Jesus I'm a new creation, but that was old Jess, trying to bury her pain with sex."

Callie only hugged her tighter.

"When Luke pushed me away, that hurt even more."

"But you're forgetting, Jess, it didn't happen. Being new in Christ doesn't mean you're not going to be tempted, or even give in to temptation, but God has an escape clause. He promises to provide an escape from that temptation, which He did. In the form of a man who obviously really loves you."

Jess wrapped arms around her stomach and groaned. "Those were some of the last words he said to me. He said love perseveres, but I want to give up. Besides, he doesn't love me enough to stand up to his dad. Isn't that what love would do?"

"I don't know. I don't know the circumstances, but I also wouldn't give up yet. No papers have been signed, and Luke took Dad back home."

Jess laughed. "Right, so he can get Dad's signature on a purchase agreement."

"You don't know that."

"All I know is that I'm tired. I've worked my tail off this week, only to be kicked in the rear."

"Then rest. Go back to the cabin, sprawl on the king-sized bed in the master, and take a nap. We'll handle it from here."

"Are you sure?"

"What are big sisters for?"

"Thanks, Super Cal."

"Not you too." Callie swatted Jess's arm, but she laughed. "Now go."

Jess obeyed. She plodded back to the cabin, didn't even look at who was on the deck, and aimed for the master bedroom. All this time, she'd slept up in the loft, saving this room for her parents, who would never use it.

She opened the door and heard sobbing.

"Mom?" Her mom sat on the far side of the bed, hunched over with her head in her hands. Now she was upset about Dad?

"How. Could. You?" Her mom's accusing words came out scratchy and forced.

"How could I what?" Jess sat beside her mom, but didn't hug her. Touch always seemed to aggravate rather sooth her mom.

"Just because I'm poor at exhibiting emotion, does not mean I do not feel."

"I know that." Or did she?

Her mom wiped her eyes and sat up straight. "You blame me, don't you?"

Jess shook her head. "I don't know what you mean."

"You know what ignited the problems? Me trying to get him to paint again, because without that, he feels worthless. I believed painting would bring back the man I fell in love with, but it only reminded him of what he can no longer do. He's lost his job, his hobby, and he doesn't believe he's man enough for me anymore, so he shoved me away. I love that man, have always loved him." A tremble broke her mother's voice. "And my life is worthless without him."

Unwelcome truth slithered up Jess's spine. "So the breakup . . . ?"

Mom dabbed a tissue over her eyes and nodded. "The breakup. Selling our home. The cabin. The divorce. Everything was your father's idea." She pinned Jess with her teary-eyed gaze. "I wanted—still want—to stay together."

Chapter Twenty-Four

Anxiety ate at Luke's gut as he strode toward his office at the Harrison Property Development headquarters, manila file in hand. In five short hours, he'd be confronting his dad. He'd never stood up to his father before, but at the age of thirty, it was about time he manned up.

He loosened the tie squeezing his neck and flexed his toes in the dress shoes pinching his feet. He'd forgotten how restricting business clothes could be. At Harrison, there was no business casual. Harrison upper-level employees were expected to bring their best at all times. Not a bad policy. Actually, at Superior Sweets he had the same expectations, without the confining wardrobe.

Or the antiseptic atmosphere. Walking the newly-remodeled, ultra-modern halls of Harrison almost felt like walking through a monochrome photo. The black, greys, and whites on the walls, ceiling, and carpets were devoid of any life or personality.

Unlike the store.

Or the Beaumont cabin.

He reached his office door and took a breath before heading inside. Just thinking about what he had to do made him sick, but the alternatives were even worse. He stepped inside his windowless office— at least his father had seen fit to give him an office rather than a cubicle. One tiny benefit of being a Harrison. A vice presidency would come with a window view, one of the perks he'd coveted. But no view from Harrison Towers could rival that of his view at Superior Sweets.

He booted up his computer and opened the manila file containing his scattered thoughts and notes and angry scribblings. Now to arrange them in the logical, unemotional manner that his dad expected.

Perspiration beaded down his back as he typed in the final sentence on his first draft of a document that would definitively end his relationship with Jess. He brought up a picture of her on his phone, and a knock sounded on his partially-open door. Tim? He turned his phone over and waved his brother in. No matter what Tim said, Luke wasn't going to change a thing in the document.

"Lydia said you'd like some help." Tim wheeled the guest chair around Luke's desk. "She had family plans, so she sent me."

Thanks, Lydia. That was like sending a shark to a swimming beach.

"Let's see what you've got." Tim turned the monitor toward himself, and Luke backed out of the way. To make nice, he'd listen to his brother, but ignore all his suggestions. Tim would no doubt want to get the property cheaper, have fewer restrictions in the purchase agreement, but Luke refused to hurt the Beaumonts any further.

And Luke wouldn't be talked out of his other plans either. The proposal he'd created for his dad went hand-in-hand with the purchase agreement.

When done reading, Tim reclined in his chair, his fingers drumming on his slacks, then a sly smile spread over his face. "You're really going to propose that to Dad?"

Luke shrugged. "Take it or leave it."

Tim slapped him on the back. "You do have chutzpah after all. I love it. But I have one small suggestion for the purchase agreement."

Why wasn't Luke surprised? No doubt a drastic cut in the dollar figure offered, and fewer restrictions.

But Luke chose to not argue. He'd just ignore whatever Tim suggested. "What would that be?"

Tim laid out his idea, which did surprise Luke. His brother was on his side?

"Hey, don't look at me like I've sprouted horns." Tim turned the monitor back to Luke.

What he'd give to be able to pull off a poker face. Luke dragged his hand across his mouth. "Not horns, but a halo. I hardly recognize you."

"Aren't you the funny guy? I do have a heart you know." Tim wheeled his chair around the desk and stood behind it, his arms propped on the back. "I've been doing a lot of reading. You'd never know Gran didn't have a college education. Wise woman, she was."

Tim had been reading Gran's Bible? "They don't come any wiser."

"Up for dinner tonight? My treat."

"You're opening your wallet? How could I turn that down?"

Tim winked. "Catch ya later." And he swaggered out of the office.

Well, that was strange. Good, but strange. With renewed confidence, Luke made the change Tim suggested. He read over the proposal and agreement a few more times, making certain it had no loopholes. For a final precaution, he zoomed it off to a lawyer friend, who owed him a favor. He got it back with ten minutes to spare.

Every nerve ending in his body zinged as he made his way to the elevator. He tightened his tie, straightened his shirt, made sure his pants weren't tucked into his socks—which had happened once when he had a meeting with his dad—then he rode the elevator to the top floor, the floor he'd longed to have his office on ever since graduating college. The carpets were thicker, the halls wider, the artwork pricier, the prestige greater.

None of that mattered in the grand scheme of life. Or to God. It shouldn't matter to Luke either.

He smiled at his dad's assistant, the one responsible for keeping this company afloat, in Luke's estimation anyway. "Dad ready to see me?"

"He sure is. Never seen the man so excited. He's wanted this for you for a long time."

We'll see about that. "Yeah, me too." He knocked on the mahogany door, but didn't wait for an invitation to step inside the executive suite, Luke's way of taking charge from the beginning.

His dad's smile was wide. That was going to change soon enough.

Luke aimed for the chair opposite his dad's desk, but his dad motioned to the corner of the room, toward the bar. "What'll you have?"

A whiskey would be great to help him work up the courage. Instead he asked for water and said a prayer. His dad poured himself two fingers of bourbon. "Come on boy, lighten up. Celebrate a little. This is a big day for me. For Harrison."

"I'm good." Luke gestured to the brown leather chairs usually reserved for company executives, and his dad didn't argue.

"Let's see what you've got." Dad reached for Luke's file, but Luke held it back.

"There are a few items we need to discuss first." Luke's voice wobbled a bit. He hoped his face didn't belie the confidence he tried showing.

His dad nodded.

"The Beaumonts are aware that Skardell Land Development is also very interested in their property and are prepared to make a generous offer far exceeding what we can offer. After speaking with Kenneth Beaumont, he assured me that given we abide by the stipulations laid out in the enclosed purchase agreement, they will accept Harrison Property Development's much lower offer. If you don't agree, they will work with Skardell."

"Understood. I'm proud of you for using your connections."

Like Luke had any choice.

Trying to mask his scowl, but likely failing, Luke pulled out two copies of the proposal and handed one to his father, whose smile dipped while scanning the document. "This is all in the purchase agreement, too. I want to cover my butt and the Beaumonts'." He turned past the cover. "Closing date will be November first."

"As you'd previously discussed. That's fine."

"Any development done on the property must blend with the landscape and not detract from it. All development will be green and will have handicap accessibility."

"Not a problem. I've been looking into green development for a while now. This will give Harrison the push we need."

Well, that was easy, but it would likely go downhill from here. Luke continued on. "The Beaumont cabin will not be razed, but instead will be a model for any further development."

"Is that wise? The cabin's how many years old?"

"About a century, but it's been updated recently. Has all the modern amenities while still maintaining the rustic appeal. I've emailed pics of the cabin to you."

His dad tapped the paper, probably debating whether he should trust his son or check out the pictures first. "Fine. That's amenable."

Okay then. Luke sat up straighter. This next part would be a tougher sell. "The landscaper is Jessica Beaumont, daughter of the current owner. The Beaumonts will only sell if Jessica is allowed to remain on the property, and if she is hired on as the landscaper for your new development."

"I'm assuming she has a Bachelors or Masters in landscape architecture?"

Luke cleared his throat, and kept his chin high. "No, she doesn't."

His dad shook his head. "Harrison prides itself on hiring the elite. We can't—won't—make that exception."

"Fine." Luke stuffed the proposal into his file and stood. "I'll let Mr. Beaumont know we're not interested."

"Whoa." A grin emerged on his dad's face and he gestured to Luke's chair. "Playing hardball. I like that. Keep yourself seated."

"You agree to hire Jessica Beumont?" That is, if she even wanted the job.

"On the condition that she agrees to further her education."

"With Harrison footing the bill?"

His dad scowled. "You're asking a lot here."

Luke shrugged. "Like you've always asked a lot of me, Lydia, and Tim."

Dad's scowl deepening, he stared off at the wall of windows that overlooked Target Field, his fingers tapping a furious beat on Luke's proposal. "Fine." He growled and turned back to Luke. "But her salary will also reflect her lack of education." Dad named a way-too-low figure.

Luke countered with fifteen grand higher. Dad came back at half that. Exactly where Luke had planned, which was at the top end of what other beginning landscape architects were making. Even with that, the deal Harrison Property Development was getting would put them in the black faster than Luke could say "Go."

But that part of the presentation had gone relatively easy. Now for the bombshell. His stomach churning like a November gale over Lake Superior, he turned to the last page of the proposal.

A frown now permanently etched on his dad's face, he flipped the page over.

Luke watched his Dad's gaze dart over the document.

No surprise, fiery anger lit his dad's eyes. "What's this about?" Dad punched a finger at the paper, making a permanent dent.

"Exactly what it says. You practically stole the Bettis land. You got a great deal on the Beaumont property. You're going to pay through the nose for Superior Sweets."

"That figure's outrageous." Dad downed his bourbon in one gulp.

"The price includes sentimental value, not only for me, but for everyone who travels along the north shoreline. Besides, if I sell the store to you, I'm going to need something to live on."

"What?" His dad's fingers strangled the final page, and his face turned red as Jess's geraniums.

For the first time he could remember, Luke didn't care. He was done trying to please an unpleasable man. The impossible was for God to handle, and Luke was ready and eager to hand it over to Him.

Luke sat up straight and pointed to the papers strangled in his father's hands. "Everything's spelled out there. If you agree to pay my price for Superior Sweets, the store will be yours."

"It's worth half that."

"No negotiation."

"You're being ridiculous."

Luke shrugged. "Take it or leave it."

A vein pulsed on his dad's neck. "Harrison's lawyers will have to check this out."

"Fine. They have until noon tomorrow." Luke stuck his copy of the agreement back into the folder and stood. Normally a negotiation would end with a handshake, but with the steam Luke imagined pouring from his dad's ears, that clearly wasn't going to happen here.

He looked down at the top of his dad's just-balding head and added the final condition, the one that would set Luke free. "Once I get all the proper signatures, you'll receive my official resignation. I'll be done at Harrison Property Development. Forever."

Chapter Twenty-Five

I t was done.

Luke came out of the conference room at Superior Suites, a signed contract by Mr. and Mrs. Beaumont in hand. If it was possible to feel lower than a grub worm, he did. He felt like he'd signed the death certificate for Jess's parents' marriage.

And for his relationship with Jess.

Now to escape the building without running into her. He'd likely turn into a blubbering mess. He reached the elevator and pressed the down button.

At least his dad would be happy. Well, as happy as his dad would ever be. And with the contract only, not with Luke. Two days ago, at the Harrison office, Luke thought his dad was going to have a heart attack right there, wondering how his son could betray him like that.

It wasn't a betrayal. It was Luke finally manning up, as his dad had suggested, and making his own decisions. No matter what he did, his dad wouldn't love him more. That was now clear, so why waste another second of his life chasing after the impossible.

Besides, he had a heavenly Father, who loved him without condition. Luke would much rather follow Him.

He tapped impatient fingers against his thigh. What was taking the elevator so long? Well, no more waiting. He aimed for the stairs instead. Besides, chances were fewer that he'd run into Jess in the stairwell.

He hustled around the corner and "oomph," he slammed into Jess, knocking her down.

"I'm so sorry." Grimacing, he offered his hand to help her up.

She looked at it like he was offering her a glass of water laced with arsenic.

"I won't bite. I promise."

Scrunching her lips, she accepted his help, but her gaze focused on the paperwork in his hand. "Did they sign?"

He nodded. "I'm sorry."

"Enjoy your new corner office." She brushed past him, but he grabbed her hand. "Have dinner with me?"

She snorted. "Seriously? You break my heart then ask me to dinner?"

"This doesn't change how I feel about you."

"Good for you." She took a step around the corner, but this time was stopped by her father, who extended his cane, blocking her way, while he waited at the elevator.

"Hold up there, young lady."

The glare she gave her father wasn't any better than what she'd given Luke. "And why should I listen to you? Both of you are home wreckers."

The man seemed to wilt like flowers too long in the sun. "Yes, you're r...right about m...me, but you have this y...young man all wr...wrong."

She turned away from her father.

But he laid his shaky hand on her shoulder. "I kn...know I haven't exactly earned the t...title of father, but if I understand c...correctly, this Bible y...you and Callie, and now your m...mother, like to read t...talks about honoring your p...parents."

"Fine." With pinched lips, Jess turned around, arms crossed below her chest, completely ignoring Luke.

"I've m...made a lot of mistakes over the y...years, especially in my relationship with your mother and in raising you two g...girls, but I am still your f...father, and if I can offer one n...nugget of advice, it's to listen to this young m...man."

"Please, Jess." Luke honestly didn't have any hopes of getting back together, but he'd never forgive himself if he didn't give it one more try.

She sighed as the elevator doors finally whooshed open. "Fine." She stepped inside and punched a button. "Meet you at Superior Sip'n."

The doors closed before he had a chance to reply.

Luke started for the stairs, but Mr. Beaumont laid a hand on his shoulder. "Go easy, her heart's broken."

Splintered was more like it. "I will, sir."

"And know, that if c...circumstances ever change, Mackenzie and I will w...welcome you as a son-in-law."

"Thank you, sir." On Sunday night, he'd gotten Mr. Beaumont's permission to ask for Jess's hand, and last night he'd received permission from Mrs. Beaumont. Too bad Jess now hated him.

Still, he hurried down the stairs to the bottom floor of the Beaumont building where locally-owned shops flourished. He found the coffee shop, and Jess sitting off in a corner, already sipping on her drink.

He ordered a black coffee and joined Jess, who refused to make eye contact. "I'm sorry, Jess."

She harrumphed and stared down at her whipped-cream-covered drink.

If that was the way she was going to be, he'd have his say, then wish her the best. "I know this won't make you feel any better, but it's in the contract that Harrison will not ruin the integrity of the land. They'll keep it green, and will implement green policies for any developing. They won't touch the cabin or your gardens."

That got her to look up. "Really?"

"It's the least we could do." And there was more, including the job offer for Jess, but until the contract was written by Harrison, he didn't dare mention it.

She covered her mouth, and her eyes looked misty. "Thank you," she said through her fingers. "Is that all?" She gathered her purse from the back of her chair.

"Yes."

She started to stand.

"I mean, no."

She sat back down, her hands clutching her purse.

He reached across the laminated table and laid his hand on hers.

She tried jerking it away, but he grasped it, needing to feel its softness one last time, needing even more to lay out his feelings in a final attempt to piece her heart back together.

"Jess." He whispered her name, and she peered at him through her long, beautiful lashes. "I know I've broken your heart, and right now my name is dirt, but if you ever change your mind, know that this knight is in love with Lady Beaumont, and I'd be willing to start over, from the beginning."

She closed her eyes, and tears glistened on her lashes. Oh, what he'd give to kiss those tears away. Finally, her eyes opened, and her gaze met his. "I wish you the best, Luke."

And with that, she got up and walked away.

Chapter Twenty-Six

N ow what?

Jess combed over her Superior Suites to-do list for the day. The maintenance staff had been kept busy, for sure. Fixing a broken window, cleaning up vomit, unplugging a toilet, and that was just on the first floor. She'd also sent out invoices, paid bills, collected overdue bills, and taken her dad to physical therapy and to counseling. Some days the therapy sessions seemed to make a big difference, and she could see big changes in his abilities and attitude, but most days, he seemed to regress.

And it was all his fault. Not Mom's, but Dad's. She still couldn't wrap her mind around that revelation.

Just like she couldn't wrap her mind around the fact that a mere month ago, she'd walked out on Luke, the man who had stood beside her during her parents' struggles, who had more sweat equity in the cabin land than she had.

Was that because he knew his dad's company would be taking it over?

She couldn't—wouldn't believe that.

In less than a week, she'd see him for the first time since she'd walked away. Callie had forewarned her that Luke would be at her birthday party, since he and Haven had become close friends over the summer. How was she going to act around him? Her invite had said she could bring a plus one, which she ignored.

Would Luke be bringing a plus one?

He had every right, and she'd have no right to be jealous.

But she knew she would be.

She groaned. Enough! She slapped the pen onto the day's to-do list and again asked herself, *Now what?*

Only one year ago she was part of an intact family—messy, but intact. She had a steady modeling career, and a home and a cabin to go to. Shortly after Christmas, she'd finally seen the light Callie had been shining for so long, and had said yes to Jesus. It hadn't been easy, but she'd given up her flirting ways and tried living as the new creation the Bible said she was.

Then life began falling apart. Her modeling career disintegrated. Her parents split up. Sold their home, the cabin. Now she was stuck working here in a job she was good at, but had no passion for. Why didn't they sell this business instead of the cabin? She could have found a different job, become a master gardener, maybe even gone back to school. But no, she was stuck here doing a job the rest of the family had abandoned.

The worst, though, was falling for a man who turned out to be her enemy. Luke was probably sitting in that Minneapolis office tower relishing the window view he'd coveted. If he hadn't already found another woman who encouraged his upwardly-mobile desires, he would soon, and then he'd forget all about his summer fling in Duluth.

But was he really her enemy? Didn't that mean they despised each other? She certainly didn't despise him, but she did hate what he had done.

Maybe someday she'd forgive him, but the hurt was still too raw, and he was the convenient scapegoat.

So . . . *What now, God?*

What did she want do with her life? Her gaze slid to her to-do list. Was marking off items on a checklist all there was for her? She'd thought that becoming a Christian would make life more fulfilling, easier.

Ha!

No more pity party, girl. Time to go do some shopping for the apartment she'd moved into last week, and make the place a home.

She shut off her computer and pushed back in her chair.

Her phone buzzed. What was the receptionist still doing here? Jess glanced at the clock on the wall. Well, technically, the office didn't close for another five minutes, so Jess hit the speaker button. "What's up, Ashley?"

"There's a very good-looking man here to see you."

Her deceptive heart did a shimmy. "Let me guess. Luke."

"Even more handsome than Luke."

Ha, not possible. "Who is it? What does he want?"

Ashley's voice grew faint. "Sir, can you wait?" A sigh came over the phone. "Sorry, Jess, he's on his way back."

Yay. Jess scowled, and got up to tell Mr. Intruder she was done for the day. She opened the door, and a man stood there, his fist ready to knock.

Whoa, Ashley was right. This guy was gorgeous, and by the confident grin on the man's face, he knew it too. He dressed the part as well, looking like he'd just left a magazine shoot.

"Tim Harrison, I presume." She hadn't met Luke's younger brother, but Luke had shared family pics with her. Tim didn't look a lot like Luke with his blond hair shaved on the sides and longish on top, and the barely-there beard that highlighted a strong chin. Reminded her of the worship leader at her church. Luke had told her that women flocked to his brother. She could see why.

"You presume correctly." He gestured to her office. "May I come in?"

"I have one minute." Guess she had changed. A few months ago, she'd have donned her camera-ready smile and told him she had all night. She shivered thinking about the person she had been.

"That's all I need." He strode into her office like he owned the place, then pulled one of the guest chairs up to her desk before sitting. "I have a proposition for you." He laid a file folder on her desk.

She went around the desk, but remained standing as she reached for the folder.

"It's a job offer from Harrison Property Development."

Her hand froze above the folder. "Why would I want to work for Harrison?" She shoved it toward him. It slid off the desk, and papers wafted to the floor.

"Hear me out." Still wearing that grin, he bent over and gathered the papers.

"Did Luke send you?"

"Why would he send me? He doesn't work for Harrison anymore." He straightened the papers and placed them on top of the file.

"What?"

"You didn't know? He resigned right after the paperwork for the Beaumont property was signed."

"But . . . " She sat down in her chair, her unfocused gaze flitting back and forth. "He was supposed to be promoted."

"And he would have been if he hadn't quit." He glided the paperwork across the desk. "Now about the job offer."

She thrust it back again.

He stopped it before it sailed to the floor.

Bummer. "I asked you before, why would I want to work for Harrison?"

"You tell me." He rested his elbows on her desk, drawing close to her, and folded manicured hands. He grinned, which lit up his green eyes. Brother, the man's flirting ways reminded her of her before-Christ days. "Before I came in today, I went up to your family cabin and checked out your work. It looked professional. In order to properly develop this property, Harrison needs a landscape architect who knows the land here, who has an appreciation—a love for it."

"But I'm not an architect."

"No, you're not. Yet. But along with offering you the position, Harrison Property Development is prepared to pay your tuition while you complete a degree in Landscape Design and Planning. If you'd like to go further, we'd also fund your Master's degree program, giving you the official title."

Jess sat speechless. She asks God 'Now what?' and a minute later her dream job is dumped in her lap, along with education? No, this was too convenient. "What's the catch?"

Tim held both hands in the air. "No catch, I promise."

"And salary?"

He opened the file and slid it across the desk. This time, she didn't shove it back. He pointed to an item on the first page. "This is our offer. Plus all the standard benefits like health, dental, optical, life, 401K, etc. And there's one additional perk, I believe you'll greatly appreciate."

Ha. She knew there was a catch. "If it has anything to do with Luke, it's an absolute no."

"Luke? Nah, he's happy with his little store."

Which would also be closing soon. Her heart ached for that too. The area would never be the same without Superior Sweets. "Then what?"

"Whoever we hire needs to live on site. You've got the cabin all fixed up, it'd be a shame to see it go to waste."

She blinked, trying to process what he said. "So, you mean, the cabin would go untouched?"

"That and your path and the private bay below your cabin."

Confirming what Luke had told her prior to her walking out on him.

"And I'd get to live in the cabin?"

"Rent free for you or for whoever accepts the position. Now, the acreage surrounding the cabin and path would be part of the development. Which, with your guidance, we plan to leave as unchanged as possible. Initial plans are for several individual units scattered through the woods, using your cabin as a blueprint. In the clearing, where Superior Sweets now stands, we'll build a lodge, and we will use the latest in green technology for the development."

Her brain swirled with activity, picturing more private cabins nestled among the trees, rather than the big, concrete behemoth she'd anticipated would be built. Could this be an answer to her dream?

"It's all outlined there, if you'd like a minute to read it." He reclined and rested his head in his hands.

Still skeptical, she skimmed through the offer, and it was as he claimed. "I'd like time to think it over." And have her mom and Haven go over it too. It still sounded too good to be true.

He nodded. "Take whatever time you need. The job begins when you sign the contract."

"I'd need to give my notice here. Being it's family owned, I'd like to give at least a month."

"Not a problem." He whipped out his phone and with a stylus, he jotted something. "Done." He got up and offered his hand. "I've overstayed my minute, I'm afraid. Nice to finally meet you, Jess."

She stared at his hand, then up at his face. "Why? Why me when there are any number of people who already have the education, who love nature even more than I do."

"Because you love this place, and I've seen what you can do. You're good, and that skill shouldn't go to waste."

She finally stood and took his hand. "I'll consider it." And pray about it, too.

"That's all I ask. I'll see myself out." He headed out the door, but stopped and turned around. "Oh, and one more thing."

Here comes the catch. She knew it was too good to be true.

"You should also know, this was all part of the purchase agreement Luke put together. My brother's got it bad for you." Tim winked. "Have a nice day." And he whisked down the hall.

Jess dropped into her chair. This was all Luke's idea?

Luke, who no longer worked at Harrison.

How could she possibly work for the company that had brought him so much misery?

But how could she turn down the offer for her dream job, and to live in the cabin?

How could she do any of it without Luke by her side?

Come this Saturday afternoon at Callie's party, she'd probably find out.

Chapter Twenty-Seven

Thanks for stopping by Superior Sweets." Luke waved at the family filing out of the store, each smiling as the bell jingled above, eager to bite into their chocolate-dipped strawberry-yogurt smoothie pops. They were one of Mary Obermiller's best creations yet.

One more month and this building and land would be acquired by Harrison Property Development, and Gran's store would be torn down.

He was already grieving.

He looked around the temporarily empty store. It never stayed customer-free for long, especially this morning with the unusually warm October weather that had shorts-wearing tourists flocking to the area. The marketing help he'd received from Callie, Haven, and . . . and Jess had introduced Superior Sweets to a new generation of people who were conscious of healthy eating. He and Mary had done their best to create tasty and healthy concoctions to sell beside the traditional chocolate.

A small dose of chocolate never hurt anyone.

If only he could keep this place, but then his dad wouldn't have made the offer to Jess.

Had she accepted the position yet? Tim hadn't said. Guess he'd find out this afternoon at Callie's party. He wished some emergency would come up and give him an excuse to stay away. He couldn't stand the thought of seeing Jess again, maybe on the arm of some other dashing knight, but he'd promised Haven he'd be there.

He washed his hands and went into the back room to check on the truffles Mrs. Beaumont had ordered for Callie's party. He eyed the dark-chocolate coated truffles with a red heart swirled on top, and his mouth watered. Amazing! Luke put his arm around his candy maker and hugged her. "You are one gifted woman, Mary." If—when—he opened the new store next spring, Mary was coming with him, and then she'd train the next generation of candy makers.

The building he had his eye on didn't have the views this one had, but it had the same character, and it was in a larger town so that meant more, steady customers, plus a larger employee base to draw from. It even had a small apartment above the store. Purchasing the building would be a win-win for him. He stepped out the back door, onto the small porch overlooking the lake and sighed. Boy, he was going to miss the view.

His phone rang as he watched a tanker cut across the currently calm waters, and he pulled it from his back pocket.

Mr. Beaumont? What would he want?

He tapped 'answer.' "This is Luke."

"Hello son, this is Ken Beaumont."

"How are you, sir?"

"Getting along. S...seems I go two steps f...forward and three b...back."

"Sorry to hear that."

"Th...the important thing is, I keep t...trying. That's what the w...women in my life keep telling me."

"Wise women."

"That they are, b...but listen, son, I didn't call to c...complain. I know you're b...busy with the store, and you'll be at the p...party this afternoon, but would you have a m...minute to stop by the cabin? There's an issue I w...wish to talk over with you."

"Okay . . . " What Mr. Beaumont wanted with him was a mystery, but out of respect, he'd go. "Let me ask my candy maker, see if she can spare me for a moment. I'll call you back." He stepped into the store. Mary had abandoned her truffle decorating, probably to help a customer, so he walked through the back room to the now-packed retail area and found Mary bragging about the new frozen hot chocolate they'd recently begun serving, complete with a red and white striped candy cane. Still made no sense to him. If it's frozen, it's not hot. Mary's response was "pshaw" accompanied by a wave of the hand. What did he know anyway? Mary was the real genius behind the store's success.

He helped Mary with the customers, and when they got a smidgen of a slow-down, he asked about taking a short break.

"Go right ahead. I've manned this store on my own since I was younger than you. I imagine I can still handle it."

"And Zoe will be here shortly, too."

Mary gave him a shove. "Go. I can handle it."

"Yes, ma'am."

He got in his pickup, returned Mr. Beaumont's call, then hurried toward the cabin. What was Jess's dad doing there anyway? Didn't he want to get rid of it because of the memories? Guess Luke would find out soon.

He headed down the driveway, around a bend, and slammed on his brakes. Two vehicles were parked by the cabin: Mr. Beaumont's and a deep-blue Cadillac crossover with a vanity license plate that read HPD 1.

His dad's car?

What was he doing here? Luke hadn't spoken with him since delivering the signed contract. Luke usually wasn't one to carry a grudge, but he'd never had his heart broken before.

Girding that fractured heart, he strode to the cabin and through the front door. His dad and Mr. Beaumont were seated by the dining table, laughing and telling jokes like they'd been best buddies for years. Had he stepped into an alternate reality or what?

He stood there, frozen, trying to reconcile the two men in front of him. Both had played instrumental roles in his breakup with Jess.

"Don't just stand there, Lucas, come join us." His dad pulled out the chair beside him.

Luke took the chair next to Mr. Beaumont. He was done being a toady for his dad, even if it was something small like sitting in a chair other than the one his dad chose for him. "The store's busy, and I only have a few minutes." He set his phone on the table with a timer going.

"Right to the point, like I taught you." His dad folded his hands, closed his eyes, and rested his chin on his hands for a couple of seconds. When he re-opened his eyes, his hands remained clenched together. "I've asked to meet with you and Mr. Beaumont regarding this contract." Dad reached down into his briefcase and slapped the contract on the table. The purchase agreement they'd all signed for the cabin property. His dad's eyes bore into his, making Luke want to sink into the floor.

What did he do wrong now?

"Whose idea was it to include an escape clause in here?" His dad paged through the agreement, and underlined the clause with his finger.

Luke swallowed hard, and forced, "Mine," from his throat. Technically, it had been Tim's idea, but Luke was all for it. A Hail Mary pass that would allow the Beaumonts to break the contract without penalty should they decide to get back together before closing day.

"As I thought." Dad pursed his lips and looked out the kitchen window toward the lake.

"I'll excuse myself." With the help of his cane, Mr. Beaumont got up and went outside, his limp not quite as pronounced today.

"Son." His dad spoke with the voice he hadn't used since before Mom had died, a voice that actually had compassion. "I know I've been hard on you, have been since the day your mother walked out on us. I thought she did it because I'd been too soft, but I'm finally realizing she did it because that's who she was. No matter what I did, she would have rebelled against it. My therapist is helping me see that."

His therapist? Dad had always sworn off counseling.

"Yes, I've been seeing a counselor. And that's thanks to you. When you stood up to me in the office, said you were leaving, just like your mother had left, it did something right here." His dad pounded his fist over his heart. "Your gran implored me to love my kids, and I've finally realized I haven't loved you. Rather, I've gripped you so tight you can't breathe. For that I am very, very sorry."

Joy glossed Luke's eyes and filled his throat, and he glanced up at the ceiling.

"I have no right to ask this, but if you could find it in you to forgive me, and if we could work on restoring our father-son relationship, not the boss-employee relationship, I would be grateful."

For twenty years Luke had longed to hear those words. Did an "I'm sorry" immediately tear down the walls between them? Probably not. When Joshua led the battle on Jericho, it had taken seven days of marching and blowing rams' horns and trumpets before the walls tumbled down. But Luke was more than ready to take that first step. He reached across the table. "I'm willing to work at it."

His dad reached toward Luke, but then pulled his hand back and got up. "My therapist also says a hug goes a long way."

Luke's counselor would definitely agree. Much to Luke's chagrin, Travis had been right about seeing a counselor. He had helped Luke work through many—not all—of his Mom and Dad issues. That could take years. But for the first time since Mom left, Luke was moving forward.

He met his dad at the head of the table, and they embraced for the first time in over twenty years, nearly undamming his tear ducts.

Wiping his nose, his dad went to the front door and called in Mr. Beaumont. Once they were all seated at the table, his dad brought out the purchase agreement again. "We realize that we were both instrumental in breaking apart you two kids."

Luke raised his brow. "I'm thirty."

"And you'll always be my kid."

"And Jessica Rose will always be my little girl." Mr. Beaumont patted his heart. "We hate to see what we've done to the two of you, but we have a plan that might bring you back together."

Okay, now they had his undivided attention.

Luke's smile grew as the dads laid out their proposal, and by the end, he was grinning.

"Are you in?" His dad spread his fingers over the folder in the middle of the table.

"Absolutely." Luke couldn't wait for tonight to come.

JESS MADE HER WAY off the dance floor back to the dessert table. She wouldn't admit it to Luke, but the chocolate truffles he had brought this afternoon were addicting. She bit into her third truffle of the afternoon and flavor exploded on her tongue. If his store weren't closing, he could have added several high-buck clients from this event.

Throughout the afternoon, she hadn't resisted glancing his way. Oh, the man looked scrumptious in his light grey suit with a white button-down shirt and the paisley print tie. She wished, though, that he wouldn't smile so brightly back at her. She'd missed that smile over the past month.

He looked her way again as she finished off that third truffle. She felt like a toddler with her hand caught in the cookie jar. Only this was the candy counter.

He patted the back of the gentleman he was talking to and made his way toward her. If he asked her to dance, would she? Would it be possible for her to say no?

A woodsy cologne drifted her way as Luke also picked up a truffle. The cologne's scent was very subtle, enough to make her stomach turn somersaults.

"Hey." He reached for her, but pulled back his hand before touching.

"Hey."

"You look ... " His gaze scanned her body then met her eyes. "Wow."

She blushed, probably the same shade as her ruby-red dress. Knowing Luke was going to be here, she probably shouldn't have worn the form-hugging dress, but Callie had insisted, no doubt with ulterior motives.

"Thank you. You're not too bad yourself." The man could wear a suit very well indeed.

He grinned. "I try." He bit into the truffle that had begun melting on his hand. "Mmm-mmm, these are amazing."

"Patting yourself on the back?"

"Nope. Mary." He snatched a napkin from the table and wiped his chocolate-covered fingers. "I had nothing to do with these, other than fronting the money to buy the ingredients."

"Tell Mary, they're a hit."

"I will." He stuffed both hands into his front pockets. "How's it going?"

Small talk. That she could handle. "Okay." Did he know about the job offer? Would he ask about that? She was still on the fence about taking the position, though her mom and Haven said it sounded like the real deal, with no strings attached. "And you? How's the store?"

"Very good, actually. We've implemented so many of your and Callie's ideas that we're appealing to an entirely new clientele, while keeping the traditional candies for our longtimers. Gran always said, if you want to keep moving forward, you have to be willing to try something new."

"I miss your gran."

A little of the glow faded from his eyes. "Me too, but she's in such an amazing place, I couldn't wish her back. And speaking of family, Kitty Kat wanted me to tell you something."

"Oh?"

He dug out his wallet, flipped it open, and showed her a picture of Kitty with her mom and dad, unposed, all playing with Lydia's dollhouse and Kitty's unique dolls. "She wanted me to tell you that Mommy now lives at home."

Jess covered her heart with her hand. "That is wonderful news!"

"Thanks to you and your path."

She returned a bittersweet smile. "Well, at least something good came of it."

"More than you realize, Jess." His brown eyes bore into hers.

She looked away, unable to bear his compassion. Instead she

snatched another piece of candy.

Apparently taking the hint, Luke pointed to the nearly empty tray of chocolate truffles in the center of the table. "If you think those are good, can you imagine what heavenly chocolate must taste like? God probably has all his angels on a workout program since Gran arrived."

She laughed.

"I've missed that too." Luke touched her arm.

And she sighed.

"Would you care to dance?"

Fear must have shown in her eyes, because he gave her a sad smile and nodded. "Guess that's the sign for me to go." He took her hand, raised it to his lips, and kissed it. "Good to see you again, milady. I hope to meet again." And he walked away from her, threading between party guests on the dance floor, toward Haven and Callie, who'd spent half the day dancing with each other. Callie had glowed the entire afternoon.

Luke hugged both Callie and Haven before leaving the building, taking another piece of her heart with him.

The Christian thing would be to forgive him.

Her parents had seemed to forgive each other already. Though they hadn't spent much time together this afternoon, they'd been civil with each other. Her dad was having a one-step forward day, which made everyone happy.

And their mom was beaming. Although throwing a fancy party was one of her favorite activities, and she excelled at it.

Today had been no exception. The chicken in creamy white wine sauce served over Minnesota wild rice was to-die for, and the apple rose puff pastries were as tasty as they were elegant. The lemon-blueberry parfaits topped off the meal with wonderful sweetness. All that weight she'd lost this past summer while working on the cabin land would be piling itself back on.

But this was one day of extravagance, not a lifestyle.

And this day, this afternoon, had been a lovely one. She should be thrilled, but after seeing Luke, after watching her parents easily move on from their marriage of thirty years, she could no longer summon joy.

So, like Luke, Jess made her way through the crowd, first to her mom, whom she hugged and complimented on throwing the perfect party. Her mom smiled her pleasure. Then Jess interrupted her dad and some man she didn't know, to say goodbye. Dad stood, using the back of a chair to help him up, and wrapped her in a hug. "I love y...you, my pretty rose. Please don't f...forget that."

"Love you too, Daddy."

She hugged her goodbyes to Callie and Haven, who thanked her for her help today and throughout the summer. In less than a week, the two lovebirds would be saying their vows at the rise of day. Jess prayed constantly for a storm-free morning for next Saturday. Callie didn't care as long as she got to say, "I do."

Jess stepped outside in the unseasonably warm weather, and drove to the cabin that would be in the Beaumont family until the end of the month. She'd only get to spend three more weekends there. Unless she accepted the Harrison job offer.

How could she?

How could she not?

After weeks of praying, she still didn't have a clear answer.

Once at the cabin, she exchanged her heels for tennis shoes, and her sparkly dress for a comfortable white sundress and floppy hat. Though it was still warm outside, she grabbed a shawl too. Once the sun went down, the air would likely cool quickly. Then she aimed for the path, like she had done so many times over the past months, though she'd often walked it with someone else. Usually Luke.

Had renewing this path all been for nothing? Had God not heard her pleas to heal her father? To reconcile her parents?

Soon Callie would be living with Haven, and that would change Jess's relationship with her too.

Without Luke, she'd be alone. Where was God's hope?

She pinched a dying flower from the black-eyed Susan plant and pulled off a yellow petal. "I love him." And another petal. "I love him not." And another. "I love him." She kept plucking until the final petal had fallen to the earth's floor with an "I love him."

And that was true, which made losing him all the more painful.

She knelt beside a mum and pinched off the dead head. She loved how these flowers mimicked the color of leaves at the peak of their fall change. Too soon, the leaves would break away from the trees, and branches would be barren for winter.

But spring always returned, ushering in a kaleidoscope of color and an endless palette of floral scents.

Maybe this was Jess's winter.

She passed more flowers, stopping to deadhead geraniums gasping for their final breath. Maybe the removal would encourage new flowers to grow, even this late in the season. She pinched off the hosta stems that once hosted purple flowers. Next year, the hostas would spread and cover more ground. Same with the daylilies and irises and sedums and coneflowers . . .

She may have bedded these plants into the dirt, but God caused them to grow. Every year, life would return bigger and more colorful as God breathed life into His creation. All she needed to do was pull the weeds.

Maybe that was what hope was really about.

Hope wasn't found in her parents' marriage or in romance or even in this cabin. Her hope was in a God who had taken all these plants from a tiny seed and caused them to grow and bloom into a unique creation.

Just like her.

She reached the clearing and walked to the edge of the cliff. Behind her, the sun was just beginning its descent. This chapter in her life was ending, but that also meant the beginning of a brand-new season. Whatever happened in that season was up to God.

She turned toward the west and lifted her face, letting the sun's warmth course through her. Her shawl slipped to the ground, and she raised her hands in praise of the One who caused the sun to rise and to set each and every day. Which meant tomorrow she'd begin again.

Which also meant she'd call Harrison and accept the position.

Then she'd call Luke and ask if he wanted to start over from the beginning.

LUKE WASN'T SURPRISED TO find Jess's car already at the cabin when he arrived with her dad, though he was surprised Jess had left the party early. He and Mr. Beaumont had wanted to get everything set up in advance, but this was okay. They'd call an audible and make do.

He helped Jess's dad out of the pickup, then grabbed the man's paint supplies and the all-important file folder. Together, they followed the path, rounded the corner, and jerked to a stop. Ahead of them, in the clearing, stood Jess. The setting sun glinted off her face, making her look like an angel.

She'd never looked more beautiful.

Or more at peace.

What had happened between the party and coming here? He had to know, and started forward, but Mr. Beaumont's hand on his arm stopped him. The man put a finger to his lips, and motioned to a spot off the path that would allow plenty of space to set up his paint supplies. Luke helped erect the easel, set the paints and brushes on a tray attached to the frame, and placed the ready-for-paint canvas on the stand. With his hand shaking, Mr. Beaumont squeezed out some paint, dipped his brush, then, after glancing at his daughter, he set brush to canvas.

At first his strokes were short, shaky, but they grew stronger with each swipe, and a vision of Jess began to blossom on the canvas. Hopefully, Mr. Beaumont would finish before darkness settled in.

Luke stepped back, folder in hand, to get a different perspective, and a twig snapped.

Jess's eyes opened wide until they connected with Luke and her father, then they narrowed with confusion. Luke looked to her father, who whispered, "Go."

Nerves tingling, he walked up the path. He brushed her arm, and walked past her to the fire pit. The wood and kindling were ready to be lit.

"What are you doing?" Her gaze flitted from him to her dad.

"You'll see." With the file beneath his armpit, he retrieved her shawl from the ground, wrapped it around her shoulders, then gestured for her to sit while he got a fire going. To Luke's surprise, she remained on the bench, silent, apparently content to enjoy the waning daylight.

That was okay, because he was content to sit here too. He prayed that by the end of this day, the distance between them would be gone.

JESS MOVED OVER, MAKING room for Luke. He sat, but still kept his distance.

What was he doing here? What was that folder on his lap? And Dad? Was that his easel?

She wanted to voice her questions, but the tenor of the evening called for silence. Instead, they watched the fire crackle and burn, sending a burnt wood scent into the air, mixing with Luke's woodsy cologne.

In what seemed too short a time, her father joined them, and Luke gave up his seat for him. The man might frustrate her, but he was still her dad, and he did love her. Jess scooted closer to him and laid her head on his shoulder.

He kissed her forehead. "I w...won't stay long, Jessica Rose, but there's s...something I have to do f...first." He held out his hand toward Luke, who handed him the file.

"What's that?" Her gaze flitted from Luke to her dad.

"You'll see." Dad removed a sheaf of clipped-together papers and laid them upside down on his lap.

She reached for the papers, but her father blocked her hand.

"Not yet." His fingers spread out over his secret, and he looked outward toward the great lake like he was lost in thought. Then he took her hand. "When I had my s...stroke last year, I was fine at first. I was energized and m...m...motivated to get better, and I did. I walked better and talked b...better and my face regained its muscle tone, but the one thing that wouldn't improve was th...this." He held up his right hand, and it trembled violently. "I couldn't p...paint, my one true passion. My br...broadcasting career had only been a distraction. When your m...mother and I went on our anniversary vacation, she s...s...surprised me with an easel set up by a glittering waterfall, and when I tried to p...paint..." His breath caught.

Jess took his trembling hand. "You couldn't."

"Everything else st...started to fail again. I wasn't half the man your m...mother had married, and she d...deserved so much more than me, so I began p...pushing her away. And, God love her, she took all the blame on herself. I wanted her to find a wh...whole man, but that was never who she wanted. She wanted me. And th...thanks to this young man here, who was willing to fight for us and for you, I realized what a cad I've been." He handed the papers to Luke. "Would you do the honors?"

"Gladly." Luke grinned and began tossing the papers one by one into the fire.

"That..." Her dad pointed to the papers, whose edges were now curling and brown with burn. "That is the p...purchase agreement for our cabin."

Jess's hands flew to her face. "You're not selling?"

"Well, yes we are."

"Oh." She deflated as quickly as her excitement had bloomed.

"We s...sold most of the acreage to Harrison. It's too much work for our family, and the taxes have become burdensome, but..."

Gnawing on her lower lip, she peered up at her father, whose little word 'but' gave her hope.

"But we are not s...selling the two acres the cabin and p...path sit on."

"And that also means . . . " Luke pulled a swath of papers from the folder on her dad's lap. "It means Harrison Property Development is still looking for a landscape expert, and they'd really like that to be you."

He handed Jess the papers. "Same salary and benefits outlined in the previous contract, with the exception of the cabin, of course. Same tuition-payment offer."

With foggy eyes, Jess skimmed through the paperwork. It was as Luke claimed. She glanced over at Luke. "What does this mean for your store?"

"It means my store will remain and will become the centerpiece of a new retail development with other similar-styled buildings all independently owned." Luke grinned. "Guess who gets to oversee the project? Make sure it's done right. All because I finally had the guts to speak up to my dad."

Unable to summon her voice, Jess waved her hands in front of her face.

"One m...more thing." Dad pulled another clipping of papers from the folder and showed her the front page.

Divorce agreement? Jess clapped a hand over her mouth. "Does that mean?"

Her dad pushed off the bench, limped to the fire, and dropped the entire bundle onto the blaze.

Joy bubbled up inside her. "You're getting back together."

Dad held his hands out, giving the stop signal, then rejoined her on the bench. He pointed to the fire. "That m...means I intend to court your m...mother again, and really try this t...time to mend our marriage. She's too g...good of a women to give up on."

Then he looked over at Luke. "Son, would you mind?"

"I'd be honored." Luke got up and hustled down the path. Seconds later, he returned with a canvas. He walked around the fire pit—flames illumining his face—and turned the canvas around.

Jess gasped.

Her father had caught her in prayer, with the sunlight reflecting off her face. His strokes were shaky, not smooth like they once had been, but Jess had never seen anything more beautiful.

Her father retook her hand. "Th...thank you, Jessica Rose, for not g...giving up on your mother and me. For some reason, G...God chose to bless us with two amazing daughters who have d...demonstrated what it really means to love." He shook his finger at her. "B...but I am also upset with you for b...breaking up with this young man who not only m...made selling this cabin palatable, but was c...clever enough to write in an escape clause. J...Jessica Rose, if you don't forgive Luke and agree to see him again, I might have to t...take you over my knee and give you a good p...paddling."

Good thing the sun was setting, because Jess was certain her face bloomed a shade of red brighter than the geraniums she'd planted. She looked up at Luke, who still held the painting. "You'll still have me?"

He checked his phone, then looked to her dad. "Your ride is here." Luke came around the fire and helped her dad stand.

Leaning on his cane, her dad gestured to the open seat on the bench. "You take care of your business. I can manage a little walk."

Luke remained standing, the portrait clutched between both hands, his gaze on the pathway. It was obvious that Luke deeply cared for her and her family. How could she have let her parents' poor decisions get in the way of a potential future with him?

She patted the open space beside her. "Have a seat?"

A smile slowly spread across his face. "As you wish." He bowed and sat next to her, yet kept several inches between them. He handed her the still-drying painting.

So that was what joy looked like.

"It's amazing, Jess."

"The best thing he's ever done." He'd completely captured her heart. How had he done that?

"Besides having you for a daughter?"

She laughed.

"I've missed that." Luke touched her arm.

"What?"

"Your laughter. Your smile. Working beside you. You gave me the best summer of my life, and I couldn't make the hard decision for you. I am so sorry."

"Hard? No, it was an impossible decision, and I didn't see that until

I came out here tonight. All along I thought we were creating this garden, this path to bring my parents back together, but God used it to bring me closer to Him. I really am a new creation in His sight."

"Yes, you are. We all are."

"And He brought you alongside to help." She touched his heart. "So, yes, absolutely, I forgive you, if you'll forgive me for turning you away."

"Forgiven and forgotten." He took the painting from her, leaned it against a chair, and inched closer to her.

Masking her smile, she backed away. "Does that mean we can start over?"

He narrowed the gap, leaving barely a leaf's width of space between them. His minty breath and woodsy cologne teased her, and her heart began jogging. He touched her lips with his finger. "May I?"

She took his hand, removing his finger from between them, and briefly touched her lips to his.

He pulled back and gave her a sideways grin. "I take it, that's a yes."

"It's a what-are-you-waiting-for?"

His grin grew. Cradling her head with one hand, he gently pulled her to him, and brushed his lips over hers. Oh the man was a tease! His kiss became more urgent, hungry, and his fingers trailed down her neck, feathering her skin above her low-back dress. His lips pried hers open, and he dove deeper, igniting fireworks in every cell of her being. His heartbeat rushed to the same rapid rhythm as hers. Even the cool breeze now sweeping off the lake couldn't douse the fire in her.

He abruptly pulled away and rested his forehead against hers, his breath coming out in frenzied puffs. "Jess, what you do to me . . . " He brushed a hand through his hair, but his gleaming eyes never left hers. "Remember that date we were going to go on? The one where I wear a tux—"

"And I dress like a princess?" And anticipated a wedding proposal.

"Yeah, that one." He grinned, and he turned on his English accent. "Would you do the honors of joining me on an exquisite evening out next Saturday, following the wedding?"

"I would be delighted, Sir Luke."

Chapter Twenty-Eight

A re you ready?" Jess squeezed Callie's hand as a violinist began playing for KING & COUNTRY's "Priceless."

"Very." Callie smiled, but Jess could tell her sister was nervous, not about marrying Haven, but about being the center of attention. If it had been up to Callie, she would have invited family only for a simple exchanging of vows. As it was, their mom fumed about limiting the guest list to a maximum of thirty, which was the number of chairs that would fit in the clearing.

Even Callie's dress had been the source of consternation for their mom. Callie didn't want a long dress or lots of beading or lace. That wasn't who she was. Callie won on the length, choosing an A-line, cap-sleeve, tea-length dress with an illusion yoke. To stay warm, she topped the dress with a white faux fur stole. Her mom won with intricate, floral lace and beading. Really, they all won, because Callie looked radiant, and would leave Haven speechless.

Someday—hopefully very soon—Jess would be able to gift her mom with the extravagant wedding she'd dreamed of throwing for her daughters. Jess couldn't think of anything more fun than a swanky party thrown especially for her.

And Luke.

Who was sitting somewhere up ahead. Would he propose tonight?

"It's time, ladies." An usher, Haven's AA sponsor and long-time friend, gestured to the path strewn with rose petals.

Jess blew her sister a kiss and whispered, "I'm so happy for you."

She made the walk up the path that, in the end, did have a happy ending. Her parents were courting, and were even going out on a date tonight. Jess and Luke were back together. And now Callie and Haven were having their dream wedding.

She looked ahead, toward the lake. The sun was minutes away from making its grand appearance, but its light already spilled over the lake, coloring the skies and water with brilliant ribbons of red. Jess couldn't think of a more beautiful backdrop for the beginning of a marriage.

She rounded the corner in the path and the guests came into view. Her mom sat in the front row. Haven's dad was on the opposite side. Luke, gorgeous in a navy suit, sat right behind Haven's father.

Haven stood up front, flanked by the pastor and the best man, who happened to be Haven's son, Reese. The kid was actually standing still.

Jess flowed past three rows of seating and stood opposite the men.

The music crescendoed as the violinist repeated the chorus. Callie came around the corner with their father, who'd chosen not to use his cane for the walk. And he was doing very well. No surprise, tears shimmered in Callie's eyes. Jess looked over at Haven, who was blinking away his own tears.

And there was Reese, making faces at the weeping crowd. Jess couldn't help but laugh.

Jess turned as their dad gave Callie a hug and kiss and handed her off to Haven. He took her hand protectively in his. That man certainly adored her sister.

In front of the wedding party, the sun winked above the horizon.

When it came time for the vows, instead of the traditional words, they spoke 1 Corinthians 13 to each other. "I will be patient. I will be kind. I will not envy or boast or be arrogant and rude. I will not insist on my own way. I will not be irritable or resentful. I will not rejoice at wrongdoing, but will rejoice with the truth. I will bear all things, believe all things, hope all things, and endure all things. With Christ at our center, I will love you."

And with the sun rising behind them, they kissed, and the pastor pronounced them husband and wife.

The violinist began playing again as Haven and Callie played usher and personally excused the guests from the rows. Jess caught Luke's eye. He pointed to himself then to her and mouthed "tonight."

Or at least that was what she thought he mouthed.

Regardless, after the post-wedding brunch, after the happy couple zoomed off to wherever Haven had planned, Jess was going to Aunt Tib's to take a quick nap before getting herself spruced up for this evening. If Luke did propose, she needed to be better than her best.

And in the dress she'd purchased earlier in the week, she would be.

JESS STOOD IN FRONT of the full-length mirror at her aunt's home and examined every inch of herself, with her mother looking on from behind. From Jess's hair that had been curled for the evening, to her indigo gown, to her satin pumps with the kitten heel, she'd never felt more like a princess. The beaded spaghetti straps of her gown led to a scoop neck which hinted at her generous bust, but didn't reveal anything. Honestly, it felt more sexy than other evening dresses she'd worn that had shown off her cleavage to the world. It was definitely more sophisticated.

"You look stunning, dear." Mom rested her manicured hands on Jess's bare shoulders. "Luke will not be able to take his eyes off you."

No. No he won't. Maybe it was an arrogant thought, but Jess agreed with her mother. She looked darn good. The form-fitting, embroidered bodice revealed a figure that had been honed over the summer, thanks to hours of working in the garden. Not that she had been out of shape before, but now she was toned in a way she hadn't been in her years of plus-size modeling. The skirt hugged her skin until just above the knees where the mermaid skirt began to flare, then flowed outward, cascading to the floor. She'd never felt more beautiful. Or sexy. Was that a good thing for a Christian woman on a date? Callie had said, "Oh, yeah," but Jess still had her doubts.

"Now it's your turn." Jess stepped aside and let her mom preen in the mirror.

Mom smoothed her hands down her lacy, hint-of-pink sheath that showed off her near-perfect figure, and turned to see her backside in the mirror. Even in her fifties, her mom still had a very shapely backside. "Do you think your father will like it?"

Jess raised her brows. "Mom, *like* isn't the word I'd use. I think Dad will find you irresistibly sexy."

"Jessica, please." Her mother scowled.

"What? Are you going to tell me that once you get married, all the sex appeal is gone?"

"Well . . . " Her mother turned again, scrutinizing herself. "I guess being a little sexy isn't a bad thing. And that goes for you, too."

Jess gave her mom a side hug. "I love that the two of you are romancing each other."

"It's about time."

Yes, yes it was. Their marriage had gone through a prickly time, but beauty was budding again.

Was that what tonight was about? Weathering the prickly times together so beauty is birthed in the end? For both her and her mom?

The doorbell rang, and Aunt Tib yelled out, "I'll get it."

"Do you suppose that's for me or you?" Jess looked at her mom in the mirror.

"Knowing that Kenneth thrives on being late, my guess is that it's your young man."

"Can't argue with that." Jess picked up her clutch and faux-fur shawl, and hurried as fast as her heels and narrow skirt would allow her, to the front door. And was met with a whistle.

From her father.

Who stood in the vestibule, wearing a black suit, and gripping a few red roses in his hand, while leaning on a mahogany walking cane. "My, oh my, you look lovely, dear." His eyes blinking rapidly, he shook his head. "Your young man is going to be speechless."

"Thank you, Daddy. You clean up pretty good yourself."

He tugged at his bowtie and winked. "You expect anything else?" His eyes narrowed. "Maybe I should make you change into jeans and a T-shirt."

"That wouldn't help, sir." Luke came up behind her dad, carrying a single red Gerbera daisy. He looked at her father's bouquet, and with a raised eyebrow, he looked down at his flower. "Guess your father outdid me."

"I saw what you rode up in, son." Her dad nodded toward the outside door. "And you win."

Luke grinned. "I try."

Her dad's eyes widened, and he let loose another whistle. "Ah, there's my lovely bride."

"Kenneth," her mom scolded, but Jess detected a smile in that scold.

"Why don't all you *lovely* people get going, so I can enjoy my book in peace?" Aunt Tib said from her reading chair.

Luke took the shawl from Jess and draped it over her shoulders, then extended his elbow for her. "Shall we go, milady?"

"Yes, we shall." She giggled and entwined her arm with his.

"Adieu, Mr. and Mrs. Beaumont, Aunt Tib." He led Jess out the door.

And she gasped. A white horse-drawn carriage sat next to the curb behind her father's Lexus. And a grey-caped, black-gloved, top-hat-wearing driver stood beside the carriage opening. Her dad was right. Maybe he'd won the flower contest, but Luke definitely won the ride contest.

Arm in arm, she walked with Luke down the short sidewalk to the carriage. The coachman helped Jess step up and in, and Luke slid in beside her. When Luke said he wanted to take her on a princess date, he clearly meant it.

The completely black horses pulled the carriage away from the curb, and Luke leaned over and whispered in her ear. "Did I tell you how stunning you look tonight?"

"You did now."

"Several minutes late, though. I promise to make it up to you throughout the evening." He took her hand, raised it to his lips, and kissed it. "You take my breath away."

The same could be said for Luke in his black tux over a white button-down shirt, and a long black tie. That fit his personality more than a bowtie would have. She leaned in to him, closed her eyes, and breathed in his musky cologne. She didn't know where they were going, but it didn't matter, as long as she was with Luke.

In too short a time, the carriage pulled tight to a curb and drew open Jess's eyes. Leif Erikson Park again? In early-October, peak season for the roses blooming had long passed. Not that that would stop Luke from doing something big. She couldn't wait to see what he had planned.

The coachman helped her step down from the carriage, then Luke offered his arm. He led her across the cobblestone pathway toward the gazebo, which was strangely dark. When they were within a few feet of the gazebo, it lit up.

She gasped.

What was that she'd said earlier about her dad winning the flower contest? He wasn't even close. October might be past rose season in the park, but that hadn't stopped Luke from circling the gazebo and lining the paths surrounding it with vase after vase of roses in a myriad of colors.

He kissed the top of her head. "Sorry we missed flower season. This was the best I could do."

She laid her hand over her pattering heart. His best was beyond her imagination.

He took her other hand and led her inside the gazebo warmed by a patio heater. In the gazebo's center was a white-linen draped circular table and two draped chairs. The table was set with cloth napkins, silverware, already-filled water glasses, and wine goblets. Luke pulled out a chair for her, and she sat. He took the seat opposite her and smiled. "Have I told you how radiant you are tonight?"

She nodded, feeling her cheeks heat to temperatures that could warm the October air.

Luke's gaze flitted to something behind her, and a man dressed entirely in black appeared beside the table. "Wine?" He looked to her.

"Please."

He filled her goblet half full with white wine, did the same with Luke's, and stealthily slipped away as quietly as he'd come.

Luke raised his goblet. "To my glamourous princess."

She clinked her goblet against his. "And to my very handsome knight."

A strain of symphonic music whispered past her on the wind, enough to add ambiance without being intrusive. They were likely playing at the amphitheater not too far away. "Did you plan the music too?"

He just grinned.

The server reappeared with a couple of silver-domed plates and set them in front of her and Luke. He raised both lids, revealing salads that looked more like artwork than food.

They tasted even better than they looked.

The server returned minutes later with plates of halibut covered in a mushroom sauce, which was delectable. Once they were done eating, the server delivered a tall domed tray and raised the cover. Inside was a vase filled with fruits arranged to look like a bouquet of flowers. There were chocolate-dipped strawberries that looked like hearts and pineapple slices shaped like daisies, along with grapes, cantaloupe, and honeydew melon which added color to the bouquet.

"Did Superior Sweets create this?"

"Mary did. We're branching out, and she's loving it."

"It's too pretty to eat." Still, Jess plucked a daisy, bit into it, and flavor danced on her tongue. "You need to double Mary's wages."

He laughed. "I already have."

Then his face turned serious. He removed one of the heart-shaped strawberries and rolled it between two fingers, then held it in his hand in the center of the table. "Jess, when I came north in May, I wasn't a happy man, but you brought life to my heart again, joy to my smile, and I can no longer imagine my life without you in it." The server returned.

He moved the fruit vase to the side and set a different tray in the center of the table.

Jess held her breath as the server raised the lid.

And tears suddenly filled her eyes.

Will You Marry Me? was spelled out with chocolate-shaped rose candies, all except for the dot over the "i" in *will*.

A ring!

Luke picked up the exquisite ring and took her left hand in his. In his sexy English accent, he got down on a knee, took her hand, bowed, and said. "Will you, milady?"

Jess looked upward and silently thanked God for the man kneeling in front of her. Then she looked down at Luke's love-filled eyes, and told him, "Sir Luke, I could think of nothing I would rather do."

THE END

Dear Reader,

Thank you for walking this winding, rutted path with Jess and Luke. Most of us have walked a similar path, but Hope always walks alongside of us.

If you enjoyed this story, I encourage you to pick up the first two books in my Where the Heart Is series, **Risking Love** and **Capturing Beauty**. **Capturing Beauty** follows the romance between Callie and Haven.

Reviews are vital for authors, so I'd greatly appreciate it if you'd share a review on popular book review sites. The review doesn't have to be long or eloquent, just honest.

For the latest information on upcoming releases, contests, recipes, what I'm reading, and more, sign up for my e-newsletter. Opt in at:

http://eepurl.com/MOZZr

You can also stay in touch via my website:

www.BrendaAndersonBooks.com

And via social media:

https://www.facebook.com/BrendaSAndersonAuthor/
https://twitter.com/BrendaSAnders_n
https://www.pinterest.com/brendabanderson/
https://www.goodreads.com/BrendaSAnderson/

I also love hearing from readers as you are the reason we write! You can send a note to:

Brenda@BrendaAndersonBooks.com

Thank you for joining me on this writing journey!

In Him,

Brenda

ACKNOWLEDGEMENTS

I've said it before, but it bears repeating that no book is written as a solitary venture, and it's important to recognize those who've had a hand in bringing this book to print.

First of all, special thanks goes to the many friends who contributed Granisms. I was only able to use a small handful of the wisdom offered, but I loved each and every contribution. Thanks to Tiffany, Sharon, Gay, Chawna, Deb, Linda N, Barbara, Sophia, Susan S, Gayle, Christine, Steph, Denise, Anna, Jill, Betsy, Beth, Dar, Linda R, Julia, Gregg, Jan, Patti, Susan K, Robin, Connie R, Connie S, Ginny, Kathleen, Marlys, Lynn, John, Jane, Yvonne, Kelly Jo, and Sarah!

Special thanks also goes to the real-life Mary Obermiller who came up with the clever name for Luke's candy store, Superior Sweets. I hope you enjoy your namesake!

To my amazing Book Booster team! Thank you for your support and encouragement and for helping create a buzz about my books!

Stacy Monson ~ Thank you for talking me off the ledge so many times with this book. Only with your help, did I eventually type The End! And thank you for your critique of that very first rough draft. The story is much better, thanks to your insight.

Stephanie Prichard ~ As always, your critique really helped shine up an early draft. I'd be completely lost without you!

Gayle Balster ~ You've always been my very brave first reader. Thank you for encouraging me with every step I've taken on this publication road.

Lesley Ann McDaniel ~ Once again, you've helped turn this ugly duckling manuscript into a swan!

George at Think Cap Designs ~ I love how you captured the essence of who my characters are. Your covers are amazing!

To my daughter, Sarah, for nudging me to write about that cute little candy store along Minnesota's North Shore. It took a long time to get Luke's story on the page, but now it's one of my favorites.

To my sons, Bryan and Brandon, who are far better writers than I am! I love watching your journeys!

To my husband, Marvin ~ I know I've said this with each book, but your encouragement, support, and cheerleading make it easy for me to sit at the computer and type out the next words. I couldn't do this without you!

And to the Artist who sculpts and paints earth's gardens with breath-stealing beauty. You are our Hope. Thank you for walking beside me and for helping bring Jess and Luke's story to life.

Take a peek at

Capturing Beauty

A Where the Heart Is Romance #2

He's a nature photographer returning to make amends. She's a camera-shy naturalist seeking privacy. Their love for a boy brings them together, but the camera could drive them apart.

Chapter One

Anxiety curdled in Callie Beaumont's stomach while her heart—and her hopes—twisted in knots. Please, please may this pre-sunrise jaunt to witness God's artistry in action be the soothing balm she needed for today. If she didn't hurry to her prime viewing location, the sun would edge above the horizon and she and her little follow-the-leader buddy would miss its arrival. She tugged her newsboy cap snug on her head and jogged away from the lighthouse at Duluth's Canal Park, young Reece already lengths ahead of her, and prayed the sunrise wouldn't bring a red sky along with it. A red sunrise was breathtaking, but it all-too-often foretold stormy weather.

Her announcement would conjure up its own storm at home. She swallowed back a spike of acid burning up her throat. No! She would not allow worry to steal peace from this morning. This was a time for worship.

She flung out her arms, tossing aside her concerns, and sped toward her best friend's son. Catching up to eight-year-old Reece without either of them getting hurt would be a miracle. That kid could run faster over Lake Superior's rocky shores with his prosthetic foot than Callie could jog with healthy limbs. She reached the end of the lighthouse's pier, and cupped her hands around her mouth. "Hey, slow down there, bud."

Rather than slow, Reece raced down the walkway beside the canal, and toward the lift bridge. What? He was supposed to go to the beach. The doofus was going to make them late! Well, she'd just have to run faster! And next time, she'd be the leader in this game.

With gulls swooping and cawing around her, she ramped up her speed.

And then braked to a stop, grabbing onto the concrete barrier to prevent a face-first collapse. A boat sat silent in the harbor, just beyond the Aerial Lift Bridge. A man lay on the bow, a large camera in his hand. Aimed in her direction.

Goosebumps broke out on her arms, and perspiration prickled down her back. *Get a grip, Callie girl. He's aiming at the lighthouse, not you.* She swiped her hand across her forehead then shook out her arms. No way was she going to let the sight of that photographer make her late to the sunrise.

She inhaled a lungful of air and took off toward Reece, who now aimed for the water. In only two steps, he leapt across the Lakewalk and landed on the pebble-and-boulder-strewn beach. He must be completely oblivious to the fact that this was the same shoreline that took his foot away. At his age, he couldn't care less about the sunrise. Yet. For him this morning was all about besting her, and she loved him for it. But with the dazzling light show birthing around them, God would change Reece's mind.

She shot up a quick prayer of thanks for this opportunity to kidsit her best friend's son overnight, and to show him God's paintbrush in action. If he sat still long enough to enjoy it.

Crossing the Lakewalk took her short legs three steps, then she began navigating the rocky shoreline, following Reece, who did a one-eighty, heading back in the wrong direction. The goofball! Shaking her head, she followed him up the rocky incline. Until the lift bridge snagged her attention. Or rather, the boat beneath grabbed it. Her stomach tossed like waves in a November gale. The man with the camera was still there.

He's not filming you! With trembling fingers, she wiped her forehead. Reece doubled back and scampered past her then began climbing over the sharp-angled boulders. The kid had no fear. He slipped, landing hard on his prosthetic foot, and pain wrinkled his eyes closed.

With a gasp, she ran toward him, but he laughed—he laughed!—and tried again, this time ascending without incident. Oh, to have that level of confidence and stamina. What a day brightener he was. She cupped her hands around her mouth and shouted to him, "Who do you think you are? Michael Johnson?"

He slowed and teetered for a second on a sharp rock, but quickly regained his balance. "Who?" The kid gave her heart more jumpstarts than she used to give her old Chrysler.

She yelled out, "Michael Johnson. Famous Olympic runner, won a boatload of gold medals?"

"Special Olympics?" He actually remained still!

She climbed over rocks and a couple of felled tree trunks before catching up to him, then laid a hand on his shoulder. "I guess he's a few years before your time." Probably about twenty years before Reece's time.

"I'm gonna be in the Olympics." He flexed his skinny, eight-year-old arms.

And she laughed. "Yeah, I bet you will be." She looked toward the horizon then glanced at her watch. About five minutes left before the sun would finally peek over the lake's edge. Plenty of time to do a little agate hunting and reach her spot, but not if she was chasing the wild wanderer. "But for now, this follow-the-leader game is done, and I need to get to my viewing spot. Join me."

She picked her way across the pebbly beach while Reece took the hard way over the boulders. The two of them were no longer alone on the beach either. The shore, illumined in shades of gold by the sun's imminent arrival, was smattered with a handful of other sightseers, many with phones at the ready, others with handheld cameras, and a couple with tripod setups. All aimed away from her and toward the east, thank goodness, but their mere presence still made her shiver. She'd never understand why someone would narrow God's morning hello. What could be seen through a small lens would only capture a miniscule portion of His greeting. She preferred taking in the entire picture.

Seagulls cawed around her, their calls sounding like laughter as if they too were delighted about the dawning day. Whispering waves licked the rocky waterfront and she raised her hands upward in praise. These calm rollers were so different from the storm-powered waves that had hurled boulders onto shore, pounding many into mere pebbles. This beach was a perfect example of God's gentle love and awesome power.

She breathed in the morning's fresh air and relished this gift from God, a gift that made her forget all her worries.

Well, not completely. Holding her breath, she turned around and her gaze drifted toward the lift bridge and beyond. The boat was still there, a mere speck to her from here, but she had no doubt the man was still prone on top. Every cell in her body zapped with electric fear. She shook her hands out, but the tingling clung tighter. With all the cameras on the beach, why that particular shutterbug upset her made no sense. He wasn't even aiming her way, but tension zinged through her fingers.

She knelt and dug through the pebbles, hoping to chase her strain. "Bud, come here. Help me find an agate."

He leapt off a Smart-car-sized boulder, turned a somersault, and stuck the landing. His Duluth Bulldogs baseball cap toppled off, revealing a towhead so different from his mother's auburn. He must have gotten that DNA from his father.

An absentee father.

She flicked on the penlight on her keychain and picked through the stones until she found a quarter-sized rock. Rubbing her thumb over its pitted texture, she examined the rust-red stone. A slight fissure revealed a glossy, tree-like banding. The tell-tale sign that beauty lurked beneath its exterior. It wasn't pretty by any means. Ordinary. At least on the surface. Beneath that plain surface was heart-stopping beauty. Straight from God's hands.

It was always important to look beneath the surface.

"Didja find one?" Reece ran toward her and craned his neck to see what she held in her palm.

"Yep." She rolled the stone around in her hand, and shone her small flashlight on it.

He wrinkled his nose. "It doesn't look like my agates."

"Oh, but it does on the inside. When we're done here, I'll take you back to my place and polish her up. What do you say to that?"

"Cool. Can I do it?"

"You bet you can." A perfect opportunity for him to learn and understand that beauty went far deeper than the surface. She flipped the rock in the air, and he caught it. "Before that we'll have breakfast, play a game or two, then get you back to your mom's."

He huffed and kicked at the ground, scattering pebbles. "Like Mom really wants me now that Bill's around." He took a flat stone and side-armed it into the lake, toward the line of boat-sized rocks a home's-length away. It skipped once and sunk well before it reached the line.

"Listen, bud. She loves you, but she's flying a little high with this new guy, and Bill treats her right." She ruffled his hair. "What do you say you give her a little time to float back down to earth?" At least Bill had better be treating Mandy right.

Yeah, Reece's mom was a bit love struck right now, but her first love was and always would be Reece. He'd realize that again. Probably later today, after Callie dropped him off, and Mandy smothered him with hugs and cooked his favorite meal.

Callie stared off toward the horizon. Smothered with hugs . . . What did that feel like?

Once she dropped Reece off, she'd go home and tell her parents her new plans. Rather than wrap her in hugs, they'd likely chide her foolishness.

Well, tough. She looked around toward Duluth's restored warehouse area and the building where she'd worked since she was a teenager. If her prayers were answered, in a few weeks she'd break free from the stale air of that aging brick building and work permanently amidst God's creation. *Lord, help them understand.*

And help Reece understand that he was ferociously loved by his mom.

He kicked at the pebbled shore. "I wish I could stay with you."

Oh boy. *Lord, what do I say?* She scratched her head, then a smile threatened to show. "Well, you know what happens at night at my house?"

"What?" His eyes grew large as the agate she'd discovered.

She wiggled her fingers in his direction. "The tickle monster comes out!" She tickled his stomach, and he doubled over in giggles.

"You're silly, Aunt Callie."

"That's what they tell me."

She got up and nodded toward her rock. "Coming with me?" She hadn't expected the deep conversation with Reece and time had slipped away. The sun would sneak out any second now.

The goof scampered off.

Heaving a big sigh, she started up the rocky incline toward her special spot. She should make it just in time. She attempted to pull herself up onto her boulder, but her hands lost their grip on the dew-covered stone, and she fell bottom first on rocks still damp from the evening's mist. "Oh, crud on a cracker!" That was going to leave a mark.

"You okay, Aunt Callie?" He hurried back to her, not a hitch in his step.

Grimacing, she stood and wiped the back of her cropped jeans, her bum already tender. "Super great and getting better."

He giggled. "You're too funny."

"Glad I amuse you." Rather than trying to scale the waist-high boulder again, she found a natural stairway of rocks leading to the stone's summit, hoping she'd make it in time. A second later she plopped next to Reece and let her legs hang over the side. "You ready for a breathtaking light show?"

"Yep." He scooted tight against her. "I'm glad Mom and Bill wanted a date last night. You're my best sitter."

She hugged him as she stared off toward the already-bright horizon. God was moments away from announcing the birth of a new day, a fresh beginning with bursts of color unique to this morning.

Now, if her parents would cheer on her news later today, her heart would burst with its own unique colors of joy.

She snuck a glimpse behind herself at the unmoving boat beyond the bridge and its camera-wielding occupant. Slapping down the nerves fighting in her stomach, she prayed again, as she'd prayed for too many years, for peace and a way to banish her irrational fear of photographers.

HAVEN CARLYSLE LAY ON his stomach on the bow of his dad's Hullcraft Nova and aimed his Nikon D7200 toward Duluth's famous lift bridge. Capturing the sunrise from this angle would be the perfect way to begin his first professional assignment.

Just to the left of the bridge rose the lighthouse. A smattering of clouds hid the stars. Precisely the perspective he was shooting for.

With no wind, the boat sat fairly still, but was it still enough? Bracing his camera on a towel by the railing, he switched the shooting mode from full-auto to aperture priority mode and then focused his wide-angle lens. The lighthouse wasn't as clear as he'd hoped it would be. But a longer lens wouldn't allow him to take in the entire bridge.

He checked his watch. Five ten. In just a few minutes the sun would proclaim a new day. Hopefully new beginnings for him too. God wouldn't have led him to Duluth otherwise. Would he?

A wine-red ribbon of light split the horizon from the red-tinted sky, and Haven began clicking the shutter. Purple and yellow hues invaded the red and fought for dominance then exploded into a kaleidoscope of color.

Yes, this was a definite sign from God that today was a day of fresh beginnings. He snapped shots, while slowly raising the exposure, until the sun completely escaped the water's edge and bathed the world with hues only God could dream up.

He kept shooting as the sun arched upward then hung in perfect alignment above the lighthouse, almost creating a cross-like effect. The sun continued to rise above the lake, and the colors of the sky transformed to a brilliant blue. Only then did he lower the camera. He sat back and took in the rest of the sun's ascension, without viewing it through the narrow scope of the lens, and warmth coursed through his body. What amazing artistry! Now, if his camera recorded a smidgen of that beauty, he'd be ecstatic.

He picked up the camera and rifled through the digital images. And bit back a curse. Blurry and too dark. Who was he to think he could capture such an amazing shot? Apparently, some things were meant to be enjoyed in memory only. His gaze went back to the brightening horizon and he smiled. He couldn't ask for a more breathtaking memory.

This wasn't a setback, but rather an opportunity to seek beauty elsewhere.

He packed the camera and supplies into an eight-year-old Snoopy diaper bag that still had a pink bottle of baby lotion showing through the front mesh pocket, and hefted it over his shoulder before crawling back inside the boat.

His dad had fallen asleep in the captain's chair, a Bulldogs cap pulled over his eyes.

"Time to go, Dad." Haven lightly shook his father's shoulder.

"What?" Roland Carlysle startled in his seat and his hat fell to the boat's floor. He shook his head and blinked. "Guess . . . " He cleared the sleep from his throat and ran a hand over his whiskered chin. "Guess I fell asleep there."

"Guess you did." Haven handed him the cap. "I'm done."

"Did you get what you wanted?" His dad stretched his neck from side to side, then rotated his shoulders.

Haven dropped into the passenger seat. "Not this time." He might be foolish believing he could make a career out of this hobby, but God used fools too. Still, it was a good thing his new job at the bank started in a couple of weeks. This photography-hobby-turned-hopeful-career was taking a serious bite out of his cash reserves.

"Next time, then. You're darn good with that camera."

"Thanks," Haven said over the rumble of the motor, and slapped his dad on the back. It was his father's wholehearted support that made this dream seem possible. Precisely what a father-son relationship should be like.

His dad steered the boat toward the docks on the south side of Duluth's Park Point peninsula, a place Haven had called home for the first twenty years of his life.

Until Amanda had coaxed him away.

And then kicked him out.

He'd deserved it.

But that was six years ago, and he wasn't the same man who'd ruined their son's life. He patted the AA Medallion he always kept in his pocket. Sober over six years, just like his dad. That had to mean something to Amanda. Besides, not once had he missed a support payment. He'd even given far more than was required, always accompanied with a letter.

He ran a hand over his whiskered chin. Had she read his letters? Did she realize how much he'd changed? Did his son know how much he loved him, missed him, and ached to hold him?

Not once had he heard back from Amanda, though his checks were always cashed. Maybe a face-to-face would make the difference, and she'd let him come home to be the father he should have been at the start.

Just like his dad was doing.

The Nova sidled up against the dock, and Haven tied her up. He grabbed the diaper bag and pulled out his hand-sized Canon PowerShot, a perfect camera to carry on his daily jogs. His dad stepped onto the dock, and Haven stuffed the camera into a waist pack that already held a bottle of water. He clipped the pack above his hips, hiding it under his T-shirt. "I'm going for a run." He handed his dad the diaper bag. "Would you mind?"

"Not a problem." He flung the bag over his shoulder and Haven winced. That unconventional camera bag hid thousands of dollars' worth of camera equipment and irreplaceable shots.

Lighten up, Haven. The camera equipment was replaceable, relationships weren't.

He'd give anything to restore the relationship with his son.

That started with prayer, and there was no better time for prayer than when out running. He waved to his dad and jogged off the dock while offering up gratitude and praise to the one who created the morning. He followed South Lake Avenue and crossed the lift bridge just beginning to bustle with morning travelers. He sprinted past the marine museum and down the concrete walk to the lighthouse. Blue sky brightened around him, and deep blue water sparkled below. A slice of heaven.

On the shore, a beret-wearing woman clambered over the rocks trying to keep up with a young boy, maybe seven or eight years. Or was the child older? Younger?

Didn't matter. It was beautiful, and that was precisely the unique beauty his editor wanted. He pulled the camera from his waist pack and followed the two—probably mother and son—on the LCD screen, capturing their frolic in still motion. It was obvious the two cared for each other. He prayed daily he'd soon have that kind of relationship.

Keeping his lens focused on the duo, he backed away from the shore. He crawled up the rocks a few yards behind them, sat down, and snapped shots as they flung stones into the lake.

Yep, now that was beautiful.

The woman turned around, giggles shaking her shoulders. Then her gaze met his lens, and she stilled, her mouth draped open, and eyes narrowed. "What do you think you're doing?"

He shut off the camera and lowered it into his lap. "I'm, uh, doing an assignment for a local magazine."

"Well, I don't take kindly to being photographed without my say-so." Scowling, she grabbed the child's hand, and the boy looked up at her bewildered.

"I'm sorry." Haven stepped off the larger rocks and walked toward them. "I didn't mean anything by it. You two made such a beautiful picture of a family having fun, I couldn't resist trying to capture it on film. I promise not to show the pics to my editor."

"Not good enough." She stepped closer and made a stabbing motion toward his camera. "Delete them. Now."

"But—"

"Now!"

He blew out a breath and rifled through his shots, deleting them one at a time. What a waste. These pictures were precisely what his assignment was about: capturing beauty along the North Shore. He got to the last photo and his finger hovered over the delete button but he didn't press it. Keeping one for his memory wouldn't hurt. Besides, it would be an encouragement for him, reminding him that a relationship with his son was worth pursuing regardless of the pitfalls along the way.

"That's it." He shut off the camera, and a tingle of guilt flashed through his brain. But he was the only one who'd see the photo. She'd never know the difference.

Still scowling, the woman tugged on the boy's arm. "Let's go, Reece."

Reece? His gaze snapped in her direction. Did she say Reece? He stared at the boy as the duo ran off. Towheaded and a barely-noticeable limp in the boy's step. Long pants and socks hid the boy's leg. Nah, it couldn't be. Could it? That would be too much of a coincidence.

But wasn't God the architect of coincidence?

He watched them until they disappeared among parked cars. Could it be? Why hadn't he taken a closer look at the boy's face?

And who was that woman? Definitely not Amanda, which meant he was being foolish. His desire to see his son was making him see things where they weren't.

Still . . .

He resisted chasing after them. If that was his son, he'd know for sure tomorrow morning when he met with Amanda for the first time in six years. Maybe soon, he'd be the one on the beach skipping stones.

♡

Capturing Beauty

is available at your favorite book retailer

Coming Home Series

"Anderson thrusts her readers into the gritty underbelly of
family life and she doesn't mince words or shy away from the
difficulties that complicate relationships. The reoccurring themes of
grace and restitution are delivered with heart-wrenching honesty.
These compelling stories celebrate the joys and sorrows of ordinary
living with an extraordinary God."

— **Kav Rees**, BestReads-kav.blogspot.com

If you enjoyed this series from **Brenda S. Anderson**, you may also enjoy the *Chain of Lakes Series* by Award-Winning Author, **Stacy Monson**

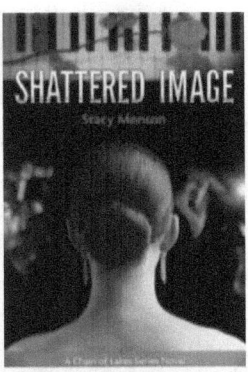

 **Brenda S. Anderson** writes authentic and gritty, life-affirming fiction. She is a member of the American Christian Fiction Writers and is Past-President of the ACFW Minnesota Chapter, MN-NICE. When not reading or writing, she enjoys music, theater, roller coasters, and baseball, and she loves watching movies with her family. She resides in the Minneapolis, Minnesota area with her husband of 30 years, their three children, and one sassy cat. Learn more about Brenda at www.BrendaAndersonBooks.com.